What People Are Saying About

Treasures of Egypt

A unique mythic adventure full of thrilling twists and heart-warming romance!
Cassandra Rose Clarke, author of *Magic of Blood and Sea*

Nefiri's love, determination, and courage will leave you engrossed.
Adora Michaels, author of *Unredeemed*

T0283836

Treasures of Egypt

The Spear & the Scythe

Treasures of Egypt

The Spear & the Scythe

Amr Saleh

**OUR STREET
BOOKS**

London, UK
Washington, DC, USA

CollectiveInk

First published by Our Street Books, 2024
Our Street Books is an imprint of Collective Ink Ltd.,
Unit 11, Shepperton House, 89 Shepperton Road, London, N1 3DF
office@collectiveinkbooks.com
www.collectiveinkbooks.com
www.Ourstreet-Books.com

For distributor details and how to order please visit the 'Ordering' section on our website.

Text copyright: Amr Saleh 2023

ISBN: 978 1 80341 600 7
978 1 80341 611 3 (ebook)
Library of Congress Control Number: 2023941507

A CIP catalogue record for this book is available from the British Library.

Design: Lapiz Digital Services

UK: Printed and bound by CPI Group (UK) Ltd, Croydon, CR0 4YY
Printed in North America by CPI GPS partners

We operate a distinctive and ethical publishing philosophy in all areas of our business, from our global network of authors to production and worldwide distribution.

To my mother,
who taught me to think for myself.

To my father,
who taught me hard work.

MEET
THE
CHARACTERS

It is of utmost importance that we remember our origins lest we lose the light within that will lead us to our destination.
Kupti of Kemi

Introduction

The world has one unchanging constant: Ramesses the Great lives while we die, and our souls pass from Huat to Duat to be guided by Anubis, judged by Maat, guarded by Osiris, and embraced by Isis. I've encountered many gods in my life. Fought the wicked and befriended the noble. I know our deities in all their forms, and Ramesses isn't one. He's very close, though.

I'm aware the chances are slim that you will read our story. It had originally been my intention to document our adventures once our king joined his ancestors in the Field of Reeds. But, since I'll soon be reunited with my dear beloved in the afterlife and our pharaoh is determined to outlive his subjects, I will share with you a story your generation will never find in its history books.

If, by a miracle, one of the few copies that escape Ramesses' grip lands in your hands, wherever you may live in this vast world we inhabit, I ask you to keep an open mind and imagine the worlds only a handful of living humans have ever seen, where I've traveled between the realms of the living and the dead, in search of the treasures of Egypt.

—Nefiri Minu, the Treasure Hunter

Chapter 1

Comrades in Crime
Egypt, 1274 BC

The Egyptian sun scorched the town of Avaris, burning the sand on the path as we hurried to get my little brother's medicine. His small hand shook in my grip whenever he glanced at the hostile Hyksos who inhabited the city. Their bloodthirsty stares followed us through the lines of Egyptian soldiers guarding the main road to Set's temple.

Our brave warriors tapped their spears on the ground to greet us on our way to the temple. They crossed their weapons before the unpleasant sight of the dirty Hyksos. My brother looked up at me, his eyes full of pride when the soldiers announced my arrival.

"Lady Nefiri Minu, grand vizier's apprentice, warden of Avaris, and future grand vizier of the Egyptian Empire."

They forgot to add: *poorest government official because of a stupid cap on the earnings of an apprentice.*

Oh, knowledge was the ultimate payment, my master said. A bright future full of wealth awaited me, explained the scribes in the royal palace. I was only sixteen and should be patient, advised my aunt. Yeah, right. Maybe *they* should walk in my too-small sandals all day.

We reached the temple of the god of destruction and were immediately greeted by its majesty. The bronze gates of this colossal building exuded the grandeur of the deity. Purple and black writings decorated its red walls, symbolizing the colors of the scarlet desert, Set's kingdom in Duat—the realm of the gods and the dead. My brother and I stepped closer, following the aroma of irises that escaped the temple's entrance and mixed with the stench of nearby garbage mounds.

"Look, Hote," I said to my brother, trying—and probably failing—to sound optimistic. "At least you get to visit Set's temple for the first time."

"Wh-why are we here?" Hote asked. "I want to go home." He tugged on my white dress and tried to pull me back toward the canal.

"I have some work to do." That technically wasn't a lie, right? No, it most definitely wasn't. My main job was to keep my brother safe; that was precisely what I was doing now. If I didn't get his medicine from my supplier in the temple, Hote would die, and if that happened, why in the gods' holy names would I ever leave my bed again? My only predicament: my supplier was an untouchable Hyksos. Worse, he was a thief. So much for me being the lady of law and tradition.

"But why did you take me to work this time?" Hote asked.

"Aunt Meriti is busy today, so you're stuck with me. Also, every Egyptian must visit Set's temple at least once. You're eight. You're old enough."

"I don't want to visit his creepy temple. I want Aunt Meriti!"

The passing priests shot Hote a disgusted glance. Despite being members of the clergy and under its protection, they were still untouchable Hyksos—remnants of their fallen tyrannical ancestors—and it was quite bold of them to direct such a vile expression at an Egyptian child, especially in my presence. I had been too lenient with them lately, hadn't I? Punishment was in order. A reminder of the Hyksos' natural place in society. But later. Yes, no need to show Hote my... other side.

"I won't leave you alone at home," I said, "and it's too late to argue now, don't you think?"

"No," Hote said, tears streaming down his reddened cheeks. "I want to leave Avaris. The Hyksos are creepy, and Set is a scary god."

"We won't be long."

"I don't care! I want Aunt Meriti!" Hote tensed and pulled his arm away from me, desperate to avoid entering the temple.

Hote's distress was understandable, but we needed his medicine, and time was short. I tugged him forward. "Please, I'm not telling you to hug a crocodile. Could you *just* please come inside so we can…" I pulled him too hard, and he stumbled, falling to the ground with a thud.

"Oh, gods!" I knelt and inspected him for injuries. "I'm so sorry! Are you hurt? Do you feel dizzy or nauseous?"

"I'm fine." He rubbed his eyes, grinding his bony hands against his skinny face.

I swallowed the lump in my throat, unable to ignore the scratches on his knees. Gods, what a fine sister I was. My work in Avaris was making me too harsh.

No, this was just a minor accident. Was it? Of course. I… I could still control myself. The job hadn't changed me. Had it? No!

I helped Hote stand, brushed the dust off his white kilt, and gently cupped his hollow cheek with my hand.

"I'm sorry for being so harsh," I said. "We'll buy whatever you want on our way home."

Hote's dark eyes widened. "Really?"

"If my dear Hote wishes for it, he shall have it."

I had been saving up for some new sandals to replace the ones killing my feet, but I could wait a little longer if it would make Hote happy. Another reason to invest in my brother's medicine, other than keeping him alive, was that I needed him to grow up and get stronger. He would probably need to carry me around, since my feet would fall off at this rate before I could save enough money for the sandals. Lady Nefiri Minu, Paser's Cobra, carried through Avaris by her younger brother because she was too poor to buy new footwear. Gods, the irony.

"Can you buy me an apple cake with honey and dates?" Hote asked.

I rolled my eyes. Though the overpriced healers had forbidden Hote sugar because of his honey urine disease, desperate times did call for desperate measures. "Fine, as long as you promise to behave and—"

"Thank you!" He hugged me. "I love you, Nef!"

Oh, well, what could I do? Eating apple cake once wouldn't kill him, and it was better than him not getting his medicine.

"Is everything all right, Lady Nefiri?" Commander Ahmose's deep voice called.

I looked up at the commander of the Medjay—the Egyptian force I controlled, which was responsible for policing the town of Avaris. He was a short, bald man wearing a simple white kilt and a decorative linen collar that extended over his shoulders and cascaded over his chest. He was a brave and loyal man like his namesake, Warrior-Pharaoh Ahmose, who had freed my people from the Hyksos' tyranny. Just like Hote, Commander Ahmose was one of the few people who still liked me after I became warden of Avaris. Ironically, he would also be the one to drag me to the dungeons if my illegal dealings with the Hyksos thief were ever revealed.

"Everything is all right, Commander Ahmose." I allowed him the honor of helping me stand.

"I wasn't informed of your visit to Avaris today, Lady Nefiri," Commander Ahmose said.

"It's a surprise inspection, commander," I said. "I don't want the Hyksos working inside the temple to feel special just because the clergy protects them. Also, I wanted to show my brother…"

I lowered my gaze to Hote, whose eyes were glued to a line of chained Hyksos being dragged toward the desert.

"What…" Hote tightened his shaking grip on my hand. "What are they doing to them?"

Commander Ahmose glanced at the passing Hyksos in their chains. "Right. This is your first time in Avaris." He eyed Hote, causing him to hide behind my leg. My brother was quite short for his age because of his illness. "That, my boy, is your sister's fine work."

No, no, no! I didn't want Hote to know about my work. I didn't want him to see me in Avaris at all. Gods, thanks for nothing, Aunt Meriti! Hote was still too young to understand what my work meant. He couldn't possibly comprehend the true, vile nature hidden deep inside each and every Hyksos. He might think I was being a heartless monster for the sake of it. I wasn't.

"Why are those Hyksos being dragged away?" I asked Commander Ahmose. Maybe if I played dumb, Hote would forget my involvement in Avaris's security.

"We caught an Egyptian traitor today, my lady. Those are the Hyksos who helped him," Commander Ahmose said. My heart froze. "The traitor was in love with a Hyksos woman. I took the liberty of sending the man to the capital's Egyptian side so the grand vizier can deal with him. Was my decision to your satisfaction, Lady Nefiri?"

"As you know, commander, Egyptians fall under my master's jurisdiction, and the punishments for treason are well known."

Oh, those punishments visited my nightmares each night. I dreamed that my secret dealings with the Hyksos thief had been discovered. Commander Ahmose dragged me to the desert, stripped me naked, strapped me to a boulder, and left me to die under the burning sun while I cried that I had broken the law to save my brother.

Commander Ahmose lowered his eyes toward Hote, whose gaze was still glued to the Medjay as they beat the chained Hyksos.

"Ah, don't frown, my boy," he said. "Three hundred years ago, *you* would have been the one chained, and the Hyksos would've been the ones beating you."

"You did this?" Hote looked at me, ignoring the commander, and pointed at the beaten Hyksos.

"Well..." I swallowed. "It was more of a team effort. A system, really."

"Nonsense!" Commander Ahmose laughed. "Our lady is being modest. We call her Paser's Cobra because if any Hyksos fall into her grip, they don't escape their grim fate no matter what they do. She puts an unbreakable spiked leash around the necks of those untouchables."

Hote hugged my leg and buried half his face in my white dress.

"Commander." I glared at the man. "Would you—"

"Oh, my boy," Commander Ahmose continued. The man's nationalistic pride was reaching its peak. Great! "You should see those lowlifes when they beg her for mercy. But Lady Nefiri, like her master, will have none of it. She knows the Hyksos are all guilty, rotten to their core, and depending on their crimes, she throws them in the dungeons, or feeds them to the lions, or—"

"Let Hote keep his innocence, commander," I said in a stern tone that shook the commander of the Medjay out of his babbling state.

Commander Ahmose cleared his throat. "Of course, Lady Nefiri. Of course." He eyed Hote. "I'll teach you everything about your sister's work once you join the Medjay."

"I don't want to join the Medjay," Hote said.

"You will grow up and join the army, then?" The commander scoffed. "We, Medjay, do the real work, and you boys want to become soldiers."

"I…" Hote released my dress and looked at the temple's scarlet stairs beneath his feet. "I won't grow up."

Commander Ahmose hesitated. His face softened. I pushed Hote's head against my waist. He must've heard what the healer had told me yesterday. That Hote didn't have much time left.

Lies! He *would* grow old. He would eat all the food the healers didn't allow him to eat. I would heal him, become grand vizier, and feed him apple cake with honey and dates every single day. He wouldn't die. It was my responsibility to prove the healers wrong, and the key to fulfilling my promise of keeping Hote alive lay with my contacts inside the temple.

I took Hote's hand. "Keep up the good work, commander."

"Will do, Lady Nefiri. Will do." Commander Ahmose bowed his head.

Hote and I passed through the temple gates. The temple was guarded exclusively by the army, which meant there were no Medjay here to tell my brother about my work. Thank the gods!

Inside the temple's main hall, Hyksos priests and clerks bustled around, going about their business under the watchful eyes of eight Egyptian soldiers who monitored their every move.

Giant murals depicted Set's story. The god of destruction had a rich lore connected to him. He failed to kill his brother, Osiris. Then his nephew, Horus, thwarted his attempts at usurping Egypt's throne. My master, Grand Vizier Paser, taught me that the shared streak of wickedness and failure explained the Hyksos' fascination with Set and why his cult had fallen under their control.

I sat Hote on a bench near the entrance and knelt before him. I fished an apple out of the brown leather bag strapped across my chest and gave it to my brother.

"I want to go home," Hote said, rotating the apple in his tiny hands. "Please."

"I have to talk to someone, and by the time you finish your apple I'll be done, and we'll go home."

Hote didn't answer. Didn't even glance at the magnificent murals that decorated the temple's interior.

I put my hand under his chin and raised his absent gaze. "I promise I won't be long."

"Will you throw me in the dungeons?" Hote asked, his face growing pale.

My heart skipped a beat. "Wh-what?"

"If I become bad like the Hyksos, will you let the lions eat me too?"

"Oh, no, no!" I hugged him, pressing his head against my breast. "How could you think that I, of all people, could ever hurt you?"

"But you hurt the Hyksos."

"I don't hurt them." That, technically, wasn't a lie. My Medjay were the ones who did the actual harming.

"But the Medjay said—"

"The Medjay was messing with you." I rubbed my tears before looking my brother in his tired eyes. "Do you truly believe I would hurt you?"

He shook his head.

"And you know I will do anything to protect you, right?"

He nodded.

"Then don't give me this talk about me hurting you or about you not growing up."

"But I heard the healer say—"

"Hey, you trust your big sister, right?"

He nodded.

"Then trust this promise. You *will* become an old man one day." I poked his nose. "So old, in fact, that you won't have enough teeth to eat your favorite cake."

Finally, my little brother chuckled. "Like Aunt Meriti."

I nodded, smiling. "Now, eat your apple while I finish my work." I stood and straightened my dress. "Look at the murals and try to decipher their meanings. I will quiz you on our way home."

He nodded and began munching on the apple, eyes scanning the temple's interior walls. I had been teaching him to read, since no teacher would accept him, making the stupid excuse that they couldn't waste time and resources on a kid who wouldn't survive until next winter. Stupid teachers. Hote didn't need them. He didn't need anybody but me. I was going to teach him. I was going to heal him regardless of what everybody said.

I made my way across the hall toward Setu, the clerk, the childhood friend of the thief who supplied me with Hote's medicine. I took a deep breath to keep my tears from emerging. I couldn't cry here. This wasn't a place to show weakness. Here, I was Lady Nefiri Minu, the grand vizier's sole apprentice. I had to remain powerful and in control; otherwise, I'd lose my job and, by extension, my access to my brother's medicine. I would gladly feed everyone in the town of Avaris—no, the entire capital city of Peramessu—to the lions myself if it meant my brother's survival. I couldn't lose my apprenticeship. I couldn't let my brother die. I couldn't.

The priests and clerks—all Hyksos and under the clergy's protection—glanced at me as I crossed the main hall toward Setu. Egyptians stuck out whenever they entered the town of Avaris. On average, we were tanned compared to the Hyksos, whose lighter complexion and colorful clothes separated them from us. Those differences were a handy detail for catching any untouchable who dared cross to the capital's Egyptian side.

I approached Setu's desk beside the rear gates and coughed to gain his attention, but he was too focused on a scroll. I stepped forward and stole a peek at the scroll's contents. A long list of names and ages of orphaned Hyksos children whom the high priest of Set would send to live on the Egyptian side of Peramessu, so they didn't die on the streets of Avaris.

Something didn't make sense, though. Some names were either written twice with different ages or rewritten in different variations, which could only mean that... oh gods!

"Are you manipulating official records?" I slammed my hands on Setu's desk. The clerk jumped back and fell to the ground.

"N-Nefiri! I... I didn't hear you coming."

"The registration scrolls! You're manipulating them, aren't you?"

"I... I can explain. It's not wh-what it looks..."

The color left Setu's face when a shadow extended behind me onto the trembling Hyksos. I turned my head toward the Egyptian soldier whose bronze spear was tilted at Setu, ready to strike.

"Is the Hyksos bothering you, Lady Nefiri?" the soldier asked.

Tears appeared in Setu's brown eyes. Why couldn't those Hyksos just follow the law? As the grand vizier's sole apprentice, I should punish him for his crime. But I couldn't. I needed the idiot and his thief of a friend for my brother's medicine, and they knew it. They received payment and protection from me in exchange for the medicine.

"Stand down," I ordered the soldier.

Was my order a massive betrayal of my core beliefs of never letting a Hyksos go unpunished? Of course. Was I committing treason by rescuing a Hyksos who I'd caught forging official records? Not if nobody caught me.

"Are you sure?" the soldier asked.

I shot him an annoyed glance. "Leave. Don't interrupt my work again, or you'll hear from the grand vizier."

The soldier tapped his spear on the ground and returned to his post, his head bowed. Ah, the irony. So much authority, yet I couldn't afford new footwear.

I sighed and snatched an inked feather from Setu's desk.

"Th-thank you," Setu said, returning to his feet. "I survived the soldier on account of what you did."

"You're an idiot." I marked the scroll for apparent signs of manipulation. Gods, it was such obvious forgery. It was as if he wanted to get caught.

"Nevertheless, you protected me from—"

"The temple must register every underaged orphan in Avaris," I said before he could say something that might get us both killed. Protected him? A Hyksos? Of course not. I... he was just more useful to me alive. I didn't protect Setu because I cared about him—he could drop dead for all I cared—I was simply keeping my part of the deal to get Hote's medicine.

"Never repeat such ridiculous mistakes, clerk!" I announced so everyone in the temple would hear me scold him. "Fix this mess. I'll check on you tomorrow and won't be so kind if I find any mistakes." I tossed the feather onto the desk.

I straightened my back and raised my chin. Image was everything. As long as my master's spies saw me doing my regular job, none would suspect I was breaking the law.

"Now," I said, "I wish to inquire about the whereabouts of Khaf—"

"Oh, Nef!" Khafset's singsong voice rang out inside the temple, turning the rest of my very well-thought-out and articulate sentence into gibberish.

Those present, Egyptians and Hyksos, shifted their focus toward me when the thief dared call me Nef in public—a short name reserved only for those closest to me.

"Oh, Nefi, Nef, Nef!" Khafset emerged from the library's door, and his honey-colored eyes stared into my soul. He possessed the most gorgeous eyes. Too bad. They were wasted on a thief.

The vulgar Hyksos laughed inside Set's holy temple as he approached me, hiding behind the protection the sacred site granted him. He allowed himself to lay his hand on my exposed shoulder, dragging us closer together. The man needed but a minute to break every rule of decency. Even the smell of his breath was scandalous. It had a faint hint of wine, declaring him to be the degenerate he was. Who drank wine so early? Worse, who would dare intoxicate themselves inside a holy temple? Gods, the thief was the definition of a lowlife.

The soldiers tensed but, following my recent order, didn't leave their positions. It was safer for them to wait for my call instead of acting alone.

Setu was easy to control, as most Hyksos were, but Khafset, oh the thief, was a different beast, too smart and proud to bend with brute force. Even if I despised him with the passion of a thousand Egyptian suns, I had to fake a smile for Hote's sake. The soldiers relaxed. Probably after they registered my fake smile.

"Buddy." Khafset raised Setu's fallen chair and gently guided him to sit. "A clerk should demand respect."

"A *Hyksos* clerk shouldn't," I reminded him.

"Look who's talking." Khafset squatted behind Setu's desk, resting his arms on its surface. "The Egyptian traitor," he whispered and, in a typical lowlife fashion, winked at me.

My heart froze, but I stood my ground. I raised my chin to regain control over the situation. "Mind your manners, Hyksos. Your behavior is most uncouth."

Khafset's and Setu's eyes widened, smiles emerging on their faces.

"My behavior is what now?" Khafset asked, soft chuckles interrupting his words.

I swallowed, trying to keep my prideful stance. "Un-uncouth."

The clerk and the thief bit their lips, trapping their laughter in their chests. Khafset's head fell forward onto Setu's desk, which absorbed the chuckles the lowlife couldn't hide any longer. At least the idiot was smart enough to hide his laughter and not draw the soldiers' attention.

I glared at Setu, who was better at controlling his annoying self, but he didn't stop laughing at me. Now that his powerful thief of a friend was present, Setu wasn't afraid of me anymore.

Gods, why were these two the only people in the world with access to Hote's medicine?

"Could you stop," I hissed. "You'll draw attention."

Khafset's head rose, revealing his smile, red face, and teary eyes. "Of course." He chuckled and slapped Setu's shoulder. "Stop. That's such... uncouth behavior."

The idiots paused, looking at each other, and then chuckled again. Khafset lowered his gaze toward the desk as he fumbled with Setu's work. His eyes froze over the scroll I'd corrected, and his smile vanished. His face looked like it had never experienced the joy of laughter. He signaled Setu to stop chuckling, and the clerk obeyed.

"What happened here?" Khafset asked, skimming the corrected scroll.

"She did this," Setu said.

Khafset eyed me, his honey-colored irises glowing with a startling intensity. "You did this?"

"Well," I said, "good to know you can control—"

"Answer my question," he said, and I fought the urge to step back from his harsh tone. "Answer it, or our deal is off."

I glanced at Hote, my heart pounding in my chest. Since when did Khafset dare speak like this? Even he understood the limits of how much teasing he could do in public. What was it about those scrolls that had gotten him so angry? They were just records of orphans. It wasn't like I was sending *him* away.

"Of course, I did this." I met his defiant eyes. "It's my job."

Khafset's face turned crimson.

"But," I said, my voice lower than intended, "I am willing to view Setu's actions as mere oversight and not attempted... wait, were you involved in this?"

"Oh, please," Khafset said. "I'm a law-abiding citizen."

"You're a thief," I whispered, my voice stern.

"Very well. I'm a law-abiding thief." The lowlife winked, the crimson hue fading from his face.

I rolled my eyes but kept quiet. No need to lose my temper or beat Khafset to death with the torture device that was my small sandal. "I'm busy, Khafset. Do you have my item?"

"Of course, Your Highness." Khafset snatched the scroll and tapped Setu's shoulder. "Don't worry about the scroll. I got this." He walked toward the temple's rear gate, signaling me to follow.

I glared at the clerk who had allowed a thief to steal an official document. After Khafset's nonsense, it would be weeks before I could regain control over Setu.

"You can send the soldiers after him if you want." Setu grinned. "But we both know you won't. You know, on account of you not being able to afford to restrict Khaf's medicine-supplying movements."

I tightened my fist, digging my nails deep into my flesh. Could I punch a clerk? Probably. But I would have to explain my reasons to Master Paser, and he might deduce my treason.

"Hote!" I shouted.

My brother ran across the hall and grabbed my hand. I waited for a moment, counting my increased heartbeats, so nobody would suspect I was following the thief.

We walked out of the temple and rushed to catch up with the lowlife, whose steps covered twice the ground that poor little Hote could hope to match.

"Hurry," Khafset said.

"Slow down!" I said.

"What was that?" Khafset increased his pace.

We took a left turn around the temple and walked alongside the abandoned slums that bordered the building's west side. The cursed thief was leading us away from the soldiers and the Medjay!

"She said slow…" Hote stopped. He bent over, leaning on his knees, and coughed until he vomited.

I hugged him until his coughing stopped, then wiped his mouth with a cloth I had stashed in the leather bag strapped across my chest. This was too much. My brother was dying, and I could only watch.

Khafset's shadow extended on the golden sand beneath my worn sandals. My gaze rose past his bare chest, red from the sun.

"What's he doing here?" Khafset asked.

Hote hid behind me and hugged my leg. I understood my brother's fear. At sixteen, Khafset was my age, but he was a head taller than me, which, combined with his muscular body, lent his presence an imposing weight.

"As far as you're concerned, Hyksos, he isn't here." I covered Hote with my arm and met Khafset's defiant eyes.

He pointed the scroll at Hote. "Your brother should *never* come—"

"Khaf!" two squeaky voices shouted, followed by two little girls who ran toward us from the direction of the slums.

"Oh, for Baal's sake!" Khafset threw his hands in the air.

Baal? What was that? Had the idiot forgotten how to speak Egyptian?

The girls arrived, and their big brown eyes stared at Khafset as if, dare I say, they were delighted to see him.

"Go home, girls," Khafset said.

"What?" the taller girl said.

"Yeah, what?" the more petite girl echoed. "Khaf, you're the one who—"

Khafset hummed, and the girls smiled at each other.

Khaf? Why were those girls so familiar with the thief that they used his short name?

He shifted his attention to Hote, and his frown turned into an amused smirk. "Girls, why don't you play with this Egyptian boy?"

The girls ran behind Khafset and held his black kilt. Unlike other Hyksos, Khafset never wore colorful clothes. Gods, even among his people the thief was a rebel.

"No!" the taller girl said. "You told us the Egyptians are dangerous."

"Yeah!" the smaller girl said. "They're scary."

"Now, girls, be nice. Go play with little Hote."

"I'm not little!" Hote said, and the girls giggled behind Khafset's legs.

"And he's not playing with anyone here!" I told the tall idiot.

"Don't worry. We don't eat Egyptians. Not in daylight." He laughed at his stupid joke.

The girls snapped their jaws teasingly, and Hote tightened his grip around my leg. Khafset had a point, though. Hote shouldn't hear my conversation with the thief.

I knelt before Hote, granting my aching feet a brief pause. "Go and play with the girls."

"I don't want to!"

"Are you scared, Egyptian?" The taller girl laughed.

"No!"

I met Hote's gaze. "Play with them. I'll talk with Khafset for a minute, and then we'll get your apple cake."

"With honey and dates?"

"Yes." I poked his nose, smiling, then rose. "Hote has agreed to play with the Hyksos girls."

"Oh, how generous, Your Highness." Khafset nudged the giggling girls toward us. "Bennu and Iti have agreed to play with the Egyptian boy."

The girls took Hote's hands and guided him toward the palm trees between the temple and the slums.

"Please be gentle with him!" The plea escaped me, and a smile overtook Khafset's smug face.

"What?" I asked.

"Nothing. I just love it when your gentler side escapes you, Nef."

"You shouldn't call me Nef. We aren't friends, and I'm the grand vizier's sole—"

"Paser's lackey. Yeah, I heard you the first thousand times." He waved dismissively and sat on a wooden bench before the temple wall, where a giant mural depicted Set and his wife Nephthys sitting on their thrones.

Khafset stretched his hand underneath the bench and brought out a clay bottle. He drank, leaking a red liquid onto his chin. Wine. Of course. He couldn't spend a moment away from the cursed poison.

"You shouldn't drink so early," I said. "At least not while I'm here."

Khafset shrugged and wiped his chin. "Priests drink all the time."

"Priests? What does a thief have to do with priesthood?"

"Oh, didn't I tell you?" He laughed. "Why do you think we've been meeting in the temple these last two months instead of our old spot in the wheat field? I'm going to become a priest."

"What?" My mouth dropped.

"Sethos, the high priest of Set, may his belly grow while ours shrink, has accepted me as a student for priesthood."

Oh, the gods curse us! The clerk was falsifying official records, and the thief would become a priest. What a disgrace. What a... nope. The clergy was *not* my problem. I had more pressing matters.

I sighed and scanned my surroundings for passing soldiers or lurking spies. Gods, I hated Khafset for forcing this exposed meeting place on me.

Reassured that we were alone, I took a sack out of my bag. "I have your payment."

In a heartbeat, Khafset snatched the sack with a thief's speed and precision before I could realize what was happening, then returned to his bench.

Khafset fished a coin out and smiled at its shining golden metal. "Ah, the handsome face of Pharaoh Ramesses the Great. May he reign as long as he deserves." He counted the remaining coins and then smiled at me. "Ten golden coins as agreed. Thank you for stealing this from your master."

I shushed him, my heart racing. What was wrong with this madman?

"Can I have the medicine now?" I asked.

"Of course, you can..." He trailed off when the children's laughter reached us. Hote stood alone and watched the girls as they climbed a palm to throw him the dates he loved.

The girls were strong and healthy. Hote could've been mistaken for a poor Hyksos beside those girls, who looked like Egyptian nobility.

I turned to Khafset. "Where are the girls' parents?"

"Why do you care?" Khafset held to his smile. Gods, his arrogance was impenetrable.

"They are orphans, aren't they? That's why you need the coins. You're taking care of these girls."

"You have no proof."

"Hyksos children are never so healthy and clean. Especially..." My eyes widened when a realization hit me. "You and Setu were manipulating the records to hide those two!"

Khafset sighed. "And why does Paser's Cobra care?"

Paser's Cobra. The name my Medjay and the Hyksos of Avaris had given me. A symbol of my strength and might. However,

20

Khafset used it to humiliate me even further. I once overheard him brag to Setu about how he had tamed Paser's Cobra.

"You must report the girls to the Egyptian authorities for relocation," I said.

"Kidnapping, you mean."

"We'll offer them honest work and shelter. Better than dying on the streets."

"Honest work and shelter?" Khafset scoffed. "You mean humiliation and death."

"Lies. You'll eventually get caught, and the girls will be counted as your accomplices."

"And what about you and Hote?"

I folded my hands over my turning stomach. "Wh-what about us?"

"Aren't you accomplices, Nefiri? Aren't you orphans as well? Didn't your mother die during childbirth? Shouldn't you both experience this wonderful life of honest work and shelter?"

"It's not the same. We aren't Hyk—"

"Aren't you begging for Paser's approval, fearing he'll abandon you like your father did when he discovered Hote's illness?"

Had I really shared all of that with him? When? Oh, curse this thief. Even my deepest secrets weren't safe from his sticky fingers. Each time we met, he must've tricked me into sharing a tiny detail about myself until he knew everything about me. Curse him!

"Can you just *please* give me Hote's medicine?"

He paused.

"Khafset?"

"I need another payment."

"I have absolutely nothing to offer you. The little I have left is for the cake my brother wants."

Khafset paused again, his honey eyes scanning me. "I want you to give me an order."

I arched my eyebrow. "What?"

Khafset unrolled the scroll. "Order me to destroy this scroll because it would've sent innocent children into slavery. A shameful and disgusting action, befitting an Egyptian official."

"Not slavery. Safety. The grand vizier assured me—"

"Say it, Egyptian!"

I clutched my arm and scanned my surroundings. Could I say it? They were just words. I didn't have to mean them. But the spies. Master Paser saw and heard everything. No, I couldn't say those words. They could be our death.

"Well?" Khafset said.

"I—can't."

Khafset scoffed. He took a cat-sized bottle from under his bench and left it on the sand. "Out. Take the medicine and your brother and leave me. Starting next month, find someone else to get you his medicine. I'm done with you."

"No. No. Please!" I sat beside Khafset beneath Nephthys' feet. "What would I do next month? My brother will die! Would you let a child die? Look at him, Khafset. Look how sweet and innocent he is."

"You're the one who wanted to send children into slavery."

"Not... I won't do it. I swear. You can keep the girls. But I can't say the words you wanted. Ask for anything else. Except this. Do you want me to beg? I'll do it, but don't deny me Hote's medicine. He needs it. I don't know where else to go. Please!"

Khafset glanced at my swollen feet, his harsh expression softening. "Don't cry. And never beg." He wiped my tears. "Hey, come on. You know I wasn't being serious. I'm sorry. It's been a stressful day. I shouldn't have taken it out on you. It's just the image of your damned soldiers taking the girls away from..." He drew a deep breath and picked up the bottle. "For your adorable little brother."

I tried to claim the bottle, but Khafset retracted his hand.

"First, promise to forget the girls," he said.

"I swear by Ra and the Holy Ennead."

"And call me Khaf."

Yet another eternal humiliation. But if he was going to call me Nef anyway, I might as well call him Khaf.

"Fine," I said.

"Fine, what?"

"Fine... Khaf."

His honey eyes sparkled. "I love that. Khaf and Nef, best friends and comrades in crime." He handed me the bottle.

I stashed it in my bag. Gods, such misery for just one bottle. Hote glanced in my direction. I sent him a comforting smile, sniffing. He shouldn't sense my weakness. He had many reasons for pain, but at least he felt safe, knowing his strong sister loved and protected him.

"Isn't this beautiful?" Khaf asked, looking at the kids playing. "Egyptian and Hyksos children having fun together. They don't even care which side of the canal they came from. When do you Egyptians start injecting the poison inside your children's heads?"

I stood, mostly to escape the wine infesting his breath, but also not bothering to dignify his comment with a response. "We're leaving now. See you next month."

"Wait." Khaf caught my hand.

"What?" I jerked my hand free from his grip.

"I have a proposition for you. Would you prefer the seeds of your brother's medicine?"

My heart skipped a beat. Gods, the nightmare would end. Oh, I would crush the lowlife and his friend for all the humiliation they had inflicted on me! I could throw them in the dungeons. No, lions! No, what was more painful than lions? Oh, the sheer horror I would unleash on those two!

"Your proposition intrigues me," I said, trying to contain my excitement.

"How far are you willing to go?"

"As far up as Ra's solar barque!" I drew a deep breath and raised my nose to regain my composure. "I mean, within reason, of course. What do you expect of me, exactly?"

He shrugged. "Nothing significant. You don't even have to steal."

I gave Khaf my first sincere smile. "Well, speak."

"Open a window for me tonight."

"Excuse me?" I jumped away from the scandalous lowlife. "Under no circumstances will I open my window for you. Enough is enough! I demand respect, you—"

"Ah, don't compliment yourself! I'd rather kiss a cow!"

That... strangely felt like a slap on the face. Not because the Hyksos wasn't showing interest in me. By the gods, no! But why a cow, specifically? I was too thin, my lips too narrow, and my hips were... wait, did he mean my nose? He did make fun of my "big nose" when we first met two years ago. Oh, curse that lowlife and the cow he'd rather kiss!

Khaf took a deep breath. "I need you to open a window to the room in Ra's temple where the priests keep Set's spear."

I retreated, ready to storm out of Avaris with my brother. "Forget it! I'll never help you steal a divine weapon."

"The grand heist." Khaf grinned.

"Excuse me?"

"It's called the grand heist."

"Call it what you want. I won't be part of it."

"Consider the task for a moment. You'll just be an Egyptian visiting Ra's temple. Approach the spear in the temple's highest tower and open a window to enjoy tonight's blood moon. A window you'll forget to close, clumsy as you are. I'll take it from there."

"Are you listening to yourself? How will you even cross to the capital's Egyptian side?"

"Tonight is Queen Mother Tuya's birthday, and the few soldiers who aren't marching to battle with Ramesses will guard her feast. As to how I'll cross the canal..." He held a golden coin. "Even Egyptian soldiers have their price." Khaf rose from his bench. "Help me steal Set's spear, and you'll never see me again."

As dreadful as it sounded, it was a dream deal. "One last task?"

"One last task." Khaf slammed a coin into my palm. "Buy yourself some new sandals. Consider it an apology for my behavior today."

I stared at my feet. My sandals' tight straps had trapped the blood in my swollen toes, shooting painful waves up my legs. New sandals sounded nice. I walked all day to uphold the law in the pharaoh's name. I spent my days worrying about my brother's health. Didn't I deserve something nice for a change?

No! I broke the law to save Hote and not for personal gain. The thief would not steal what remained of my integrity. I would help him steal the spear in exchange for the seeds, but I wouldn't accept the coins.

I tightened my grip on the coin. "Hey, Khaf."

"Yes, Nef?"

"Despite what you're trying to prove, I'm not a thief." I threw the coin in his smug face. "Hote! Time to go home!"

Chapter 2

Honor among Thieves

On the capital's Egyptian side, torches lit the golden pathway that linked the royal palace to the three primary temples of Ra, Heka, and Astarte. The flames flickered on either side of the path, vanquishing the darkness of the night and bestowing upon the white sandstone road its renowned golden tint. Despite having walked this route numerous times, I never failed to experience a sense of awe at the sight of the colossal temples, each the size of a small neighborhood. The golden path itself was a symbol—a radiant bond between the divine and the palace, the gods and the pharaoh.

The blood moon rose behind Ra's temple. It glared at me, warning me to abandon Khaf's malicious plan to steal Set's spear. But the spear was my only method of claiming the seeds of Hote's medicine. I could finally grow the ingredients and gain freedom from the Hyksos thief.

I ascended the ridiculous number of stairs that led to the temple's golden gates while thanking the gods that Aunt Meriti had bought me new sandals that morning. Oh, my dear aunt. She always knew exactly what I needed—eventually. As it turned out, the reason Hote couldn't stay with our old caretaker this morning was because she had left to buy me new clothes.

My new dress and sandals, which I had never seen in the market, combined with Aunt Meriti's motherly warmth that radiated from the white fabric, gave me some comfort in my otherwise miserable life.

Before the gates, a tall ceremonial statue awaited my arrival. A figure of a huge muscular man, with a lion's head, holding a butcher's knife. This was Shemzu, the god of blood. The deity who protected us on the nights of a blood moon and fought the evil spirits with his army of soldier hyenas. He was also the punisher of the wicked who touched what didn't belong to them. Yep, his statue was a pleasant sight just before I helped a Hyksos steal a divine weapon.

Something wasn't right, though. I hadn't spotted a single soldier guarding the golden path. Were they guarding the queen mother's feast? There was a shortage in security forces since most soldiers had followed the pharaoh to battle in Kadesh. Maybe... nope. Not my problem. I just had to worry about Khaf's heist. Security on the Egyptian side was my master's task anyway, and I was already stretched thin.

Before I entered the temple, as was the custom, I untied the white ribbon that held my hair, and its black strands cascaded over the golden shawl around my neck. I loved my hair. Aunt Meriti once told me it was as divine as Queen Nefertari's. I hated everything else about myself, though. I was considered short, since our queen—who set the beauty standards—was said to be as tall as most men. Unlike most women my age, I was too bony, and my lips were too thin. Khaf had also mentioned that my nose was too big. He said it the day we first met two years ago. Probably the reason he compared me to a cow today. That uncultured, uncivilized, foul-mouthed Hyksos trash.

I took a deep breath to clear my head. No need for more self-loathing at the moment. I had a lifetime ahead of me for that.

I stepped inside the high temple's main hall—which had a panoramic view of the night sky—and froze at the sight of an old lady sitting on a bench by the rear balcony of the empty building. A woman who outshone the blood moon with nothing but her presence. Her aura breathed life into the countless murals on the temple walls that depicted Ra as he sailed the heavens on his solar barque and fought the evil serpent of chaos.

I'd heard of only one person who possessed such a peaceful yet crushing presence: Queen Mother Tuya.

My heart contracted in my chest. I collapsed to my knees and hit the temple's golden granite floor. No, by the gods! Why her? Why here and now? I shouldn't have agreed to Khaf's plan. What good were the medicine seeds if my brother and I were thrown in the dungeons for treason?

No, I just had to calm down. I was just visiting Ra's temple... in the middle of the night.

"Queen Mother." I lowered my gaze. "I apologize for disturbing Your Majesty's peace."

She didn't answer. I stole a glance at Tuya's face. Her gentle features were easy on the eyes, like any grandmother walking the kids to the market, her ridiculously expensive green dress and silver jewelry notwithstanding. But those dark brown eyes of hers. Oh, they spoke volumes. They revealed wisdom only attained through a life a commoner like me couldn't comprehend.

"Why were you avoiding my gaze?" Tuya asked.

"I... I've never spoken to people from the royal family." My heart skipped a beat. "I don't mean you are people, of course! I mean, you *are* people. You aren't animals—"

The queen mother arched her graying black eyebrows.

My body jittered from the catastrophe I had just uttered. "Please, Your Majesty, could you allow me to shut up?"

The queen mother laughed. Not the merchants' loud glee nor Khaf's vulgar roar. No, her controlled, melodic laugh filled the celestial hall of Ra's temple with grace and majesty.

"So you speak and get yourself into trouble, then stay silent and regroup in your head. Same as your father."

My stupid instincts overcame me, and my mouth dropped. "You knew my father?!"

"Come, child." Tuya patted the empty spot beside her. "Sit."

I crawled toward the queen mother while thanking the gods that Aunt Meriti had gifted me the new white dress that fell above my knees, granting me great mobility. Come to think of it, my new clothes were perfect for a heist. A heist that had failed before it began.

"Oh, by the gods," Tuya said, rubbing her temples. "Stand up and walk like a normal person."

I jumped to my feet and rushed to sit beside her.

Tuya captured my left hand between her palms, holding to her gentle smile. "Oh, child. Fierce yet weak. Smart yet naive. It's as if Maat has merged Bastet and Sekhmet on her scale for you to appear."

Maat, Bastet, and Sekhmet? What connection did I have to the goddesses of justice, protection, and war? I should've asked, but another question overtook my thoughts.

My father. Not that I cared for the despicable man who left me to care for Hote when I was just eight. But I needed to know what linked that vicious snake to the queen mother.

"My father. You knew him, Your Majesty?"

"I did. Sutmheb was my late husband's private messenger, after all. Unfortunate how ambition claims even the best of us." Tuya trapped me in her intense gaze. "Do you wish to know more about Sutmheb?"

Yeah, right. I sure was dying to know more about that traitor of a father.

I shook my head. "I'm thankful for the offer, Your Majesty, but my father has been dead to me since his treason against my family."

Tuya sighed. "Paser told me you were smart. I'm still waiting for proof." She released my hand, leaving a golden scarab in my grip. "Keep this near your heart, child. For good luck."

I inspected the hieroglyphs on the scarab. I could read the symbols, but the words were gibberish. Great! This night was drifting from frightening to insane.

"Don't sell it before you figure out its meaning." Tuya poked my nose the way Aunt Meriti did with Hote. "It doesn't have any value. Unlike the golden coins you have been stealing these last two years."

My heart stopped.

"I... I..." It was a trap! That explained why everything was so quiet. Why the celebration hall was silent, and the soldiers who guarded the golden path were absent. It was an ambush!

I dropped to my knees and touched my head to the cold floor at her feet. "I am so sorry, Your Majesty. May Ra witness my words. I had every intention of repaying the coins' worth."

"Ten golden coins. Each month for the past two years, I counted the treasury and spotted ten missing golden coins. Every month, I replaced the coins behind Paser's back. You always took ten. Never nine, and never eleven. That is an impressive amount you have stolen from us."

"I swear, I stole for my—"

"Your excuses do not concern me, child."

"Then I'll settle my debt. I'll abandon my apprenticeship and work as your maid if you command it so. And... and if you wish to punish me, I beg you to pardon my little brother. He's ill and didn't know about my crime."

"I don't inflict pain on children," she said. "And you could work ten lifetimes as my maid, and you would not come close to settling your debt." She laid her hand on my cheek, steadying my trembling head, and her smile warmed my freezing heart. "Your debt is forgiven, child."

"What?" My mouth dropped. "Why? I deserve punishment, not forgiveness."

"You shall receive your punishment, but not for your past theft."

Past theft? How would I be punished for a future... oh gods, the queen mother knew about Khaf's grand heist!

"Nefiri, isn't it?"

"Y-yes, Your Majesty. Nefiri Minu."

Tuya closed her eyes and repeated my name in her melodic voice. "What a delightful name. Nefiri Minu. 'Beauty endures.' How true." She gazed at the moon's red light leaking onto the ceiling of the celestial hall like dancing flames. "How sad."

"I don't understand, Your—"

"I guess I'm done here for now." Tuya stood. "I have a feast to attend. Our nobles wish to drink and dance until sunrise and need old me as an excuse." She walked toward the temple gate.

"Why?!" I had to know the truth. Why did she forgive me?

"Fierce, yet weak. Smart, yet naive." She shook her head, exiting the temple. "So, so naive."

Chills vibrated my spine. A single name thundered in my mind: Khafset of Avaris. The queen mother must've learned of Khaf's scheme. Why else would she warn me about my punishment for future theft? Her visit was a last warning to avoid the spear. I was Master Paser's student, and he had been the queen mother's friend since childhood. She must've warned me to leave so I wouldn't bring him shame. Yes. Why else would she care about me and forgive my debt?

Should I leave? Khaf wouldn't be able to enter the temple if I didn't open the window. Would he? No, he would find a way to execute the heist without me. The missing soldiers must've been stationed in the tower to guard the spear and await our arrival. They would catch Khaf, and he might snitch on me out of spite.

But I could use the soldiers in the tower to my advantage. They could function as witnesses, and I could frame my actions as a scheme to catch the thief in the act. Yes, an intricate plan executed by the grand vizier's sole apprentice. Master Paser might even reward my heroism and force Khaf to give me the medical seeds.

I raised the golden collar I wore that extended like a shawl over my shoulders and placed the scarab above my heart. Then I lowered the shawl, covering the scarab's bulge over my breast.

I ran through the hall of the temple, capturing the torches' scarlet flames in the winds of my sprint toward the tallest tower. Tuya was wrong. I was fierce and not weak. Smart and not naive.

The empty corridors surrounded my path up the spiraling tower stairs. The serpent of chaos slithered in the painting on the wall, guiding me toward Set's spear. I reached the door at the tower's peak and drew a deep breath, preparing myself for the theatrics I needed to perform for the soldiers who guarded the spear.

"Help!" I slammed the wooden door wide open. "Oh, help! A Hyksos is..."

The drab chamber was unoccupied. I couldn't even register any mosquitoes that the candle flames should've drawn inside. The sole noteworthy detail in this empty room was the spear that lay unguarded on a tall red pedestal.

Why weren't there any soldiers here? Should I just leave? Khaf wouldn't be able to enter the temple if I left the window closed. But he might find another way. He might snitch and ruin my life if he got caught in my absence. It was better for me to catch him in the act and control the narrative.

I opened the window and leaned over its frame. The road behind the temple was empty. A wide grin claimed my face. So, the proud thief of Avaris was a coward after—

A hook whipped upward outside the window. I flinched, escaping the hook's sharp edge as it latched onto the window frame. The rope stiffened and swung left and right until a brown mop of hair ascended, followed by Khaf's honey eyes.

"Aren't you a pleasant sight." Khaf smiled. "You should tag along on more—"

"Leave! There's nothing for you here!"

"Having cold feet before the fun part, are we?" He jumped inside the chamber. "You realize you could've just left the window closed."

"You would've found a way, thief. You always find a way."

Khaf chuckled. "I'm flattered, but no. I couldn't have gotten past the soldiers and the Medjay. This heist will succeed because of you." He gave me a sarcastic bow. "Our esteemed Cobra."

"Don't put this on me," I said. "You would've found a way inside regardless of my help."

Khaf arched his eyebrow, grinning. "And why did I ask for your help if I didn't need it?"

I opened my mouth and closed it. That was an excellent point, actually. Curse him! Of course, he wouldn't have entered the temple without my help. Why did I keep treating him like an unstoppable force? He was just a man, a mere mortal.

"Your faith flatters me, Egyptian." Khaf winked, then turned to the spear about fifteen paces from him. "Ah, look at it. Isn't it just—"

"The queen mother spoke to me tonight."

He turned to me. "Look at you climbing up the social ladder. First Paser and now Tuya."

"No, you idiot, you don't understand."

He glanced at the spear, his smile fading. "I understand you're still here."

"Tuya knows about the golden coins."

Khaf's face turned pale, his eyes narrowing. "Did you snitch?"

"N-no! Tuya knew and covered for me. It was a warning. A power move. The royal family will kill us both if you take that spear."

"Ah. So you came to save me? Good to know there is still honor among thieves."

"I am not a thief!" I was a victim. Khaf practically held my brother hostage. But no more. I clenched my teeth and glared at the real thief in the room. "I'm here to stop you, Hyksos."

"I see." Khaf frowned and walked toward the spear. "You always disappoint, Egyptian. And here I assumed you had dressed up for the heist. The new dress and sandals look divine on you. I felt bad for the cow joke, but considering the upgrade, I might need to compare you to a few more animals."

Fierce and not weak. Smart and not naive. I kept repeating the opposite of Tuya's words, but my legs remained frozen. "Stop, or I'll force you!"

He glanced over his shoulder. "How, Egyptian?"

"I will grab Set's spear and fight you with it if I must!"

He laughed and continued his march across the room. "Only the spear's chosen one can touch it. Set became the Baal of the Hyksos after you Egyptians betrayed him for Horus and his parents."

Baal? There was that word again. What, in Ra's hidden name, was Baal?

Khaf stopped, an arm's length separating him from the spear. "And our Baal's spear will only allow those worthy among his people to touch it and live. I assure you..."

He stretched his palms out—against the air. "Well, this is new." He cursed and banged the air; each of his strikes was countered as if there was an invisible wall separating him from the spear.

"No. No. No!" Khaf drew his dagger from underneath the brown belt that fixed his black leather kilt around his waist.

"I will get that spear!" He hammered his dagger against the invisible wall.

He was distracted! This was my chance. I ran toward Khaf and pushed him to the ground. He punched my ribs during his fall. I stumbled back and fell beside the spear's pedestal.

"Damn it!" he said, rising to his knees. "Sorry, didn't mean to hit…" He froze, his gaze shifting between the spear and me kneeling beside it. "How, in Baal's name, did you cross the barrier?"

Khaf and I glared at each other from opposite sides of the invisible wall. Our gazes shifted to the spear. I leaped toward it. Khaf's lightning-fast reflexes pushed him to his feet. He launched himself forward, hit the invisible wall, and fell back, cursing.

I reached for the spear.

"No, don't touch it!" Khaf shouted.

I seized the divine weapon and aimed it at the thief. He stepped back, his eyes widening.

"No!" He collapsed to his knees. "Why? I told you not to touch it!"

"You will not steal Set's spear, Hyksos."

"Gods, what have you done?" Khaf laid his hands on his shaking head. "You've doomed yourself, you stupid, stupid girl!" He jumped to his feet and spun around. "There must be a way to fix this. You can't be the Chosen." He sheathed his dagger and rushed toward the window.

"Wait!"

Khaf froze. There was something wrong with him. A strange sparkle in his eyes. Why did he seem worried? He was a Hyksos. He should've threatened me—tried to kill me even. This lack of savagery was a strange deviation from my master's teachings. Was the man still drunk? Yes, of course. That would explain his strange behavior.

"Bring me the seeds, or I'll tell Master Paser everything and urge him to snatch Hote's medicine from your dead hands."

"Oh, Nef. You have no idea how much trouble you've brought upon yourself." Khaf grabbed the rope that hung from the window.

"Khaf, wait!"

"Don't worry. You'll see me sooner than you expect." Khaf jumped out the window, catching hold of the rope. It shook and stiffened as he descended to the street.

"Yeah, you'd better run!" I shifted my weight onto Set's spear to support my shaking knees.

Why wasn't he angry? He sounded, dare I say it, concerned.

No! I had defeated him, and I had every right to enjoy my victory. He would not steal this from me! Finally, after two years of constant humiliation, I stood tall while the proud thief of Avaris ran like a coward.

I laid the spear on its pedestal, but my right hand refused to release its gold-scarlet metal. My gaze couldn't stray from this magnificent weapon, and before I knew it, I lost myself in the spear's divine elegance.

I traced my index finger over the spear's golden shaft until I reached the black tip. The divine blade sliced a tiny gash in my thumb and released a sparkling scarlet trail of blood onto its exotic metal.

A scarlet glow pulsed from the spear. It thrust me across the room with crushing velocity. I collided with the wall and crumpled to the floor.

I rubbed my head, moaning from the pain. I opened my eyes, and my vision refocused, revealing the scarlet vapor that leaked from the radiating spear.

Come to me, my chosen! A harsh voice growled in my head. I tried to stand, summoning all my power and courage to escape, but a crushing presence weighed on my back.

Bring me my spear!

I jumped. Dozens of tiny scarlet hands launched forth from the glowing mist that covered the floor. The hands pulled me down, pinning me on my stomach, facing the radiating divine weapon.

"Get out of my head!" I tried to squeeze the agonizing ringing out of my skull. "Let me go!" I struggled to free myself from the claws of those tiny hands.

COME, MY CHOSEN!

The scarlet mist enveloped me like a death shroud, filling my nostrils with a metallic tang. Tiny hands crawled over my skin and burrowed underneath my flesh. The spear's eerie glow exploded with an otherworldly radiance, blinding my senses with its divine might. My world tilted and spun as my vision wavered and flickered, leaving me vulnerable on the floor. From the edges of my consciousness, darkness crept in, smothering my thoughts with a cold, suffocating grip until my mind drifted into a realm of darkness.

Chapter 3

The Age of the Sha

Hisses. Gods, hundreds, no thousands of hissing noises consumed my mind as I crouched in a dark void, holding myself tightly. Dozens of tiny warm hands crawled all over me. One hand, sharp as a dagger, pierced my chest, seized my heart, and twisted my soul.

Reality pulsed around me. The hands and hisses faded. Colors returned to my world with the smell of oil burning in the blazing torches. As I regained focus, the entrance to Ra's temple appeared.

What happened? How had I returned to the celestial hall? Why did I faint? I'd felt a crushing presence as if... a divine spirit had visited me! It must've been Ra. He must've embraced me for defeating a Hyksos in his temple. I was simply too weak to withstand Ra's magnificent aura and collapsed. He must've brought me to the entrance of his temple so I could return home unharmed.

Ra gave me his divine approval because I'd redeemed myself tonight instead of assisting Khaf with his sinful scheme.

I stood and straightened my white dress. Time to pick up Hote from Aunt Meriti's and get a very well-deserved rest.

I exited the building. Troops populated the golden path from Ra's temple to the royal palace. My knees went weak from the disheartening sight.

Had they captured Khafset? Did the lowlife snitch?

No, I had to remain calm. That was the guards' normal position. They had stood there in two perfect lines every day since I was born. This was ordinary. Yes, there was no cause for alarm. There must've been a strategic reason for the soldiers' disappearance and reappearance.

I trotted along the golden path between the stiff soldiers, the desert's chilling wind freezing my arms.

No eye contact. Remain calm. Everything was going to be…

"Nefiri!"

Goosebumps rippled across my flesh at the last voice I wished to hear. I hugged myself and turned to see the confused round face of the grand vizier.

"Master!"

The grand vizier studied me with narrowed eyes, adjusting the expensive leopard skin around his shoulders. That was his default facial expression. My teacher's suspicion knew no bounds. He might've considered his black wig a potential traitor for slipping off his bald head.

"A little late for sneaking into Ra's temple, don't you think?" Master Paser asked.

"Sneak? I was visiting on the evening of the blood moon." That, technically, wasn't a lie.

"In the middle of the night?"

"That's a—Nubian tradition. Learned it from my mother."

He narrowed his eyes. "Perhaps you should not take such public pride in your Nubian side, future grand vizier of the *Egyptian* Empire."

I bowed my head, nodding. Harsh but fair. Government officials looked down on me for my mother's Nubian origin. Despite the Egyptians' contempt for their Nubian subjects, my mother's people were *not* like the Hyksos. They were never tyrants. They'd just… had a lapse of judgment when they allied with the Hyksos to free themselves from Egyptian rule.

Not that I cared about the unlawful Nubian struggle. I was Egyptian—a proud, loyal servant of His Majesty and The Two Lands.

"I apologize, master. It was a foolish mistake to indulge my Nubian side."

"Tell me about Avaris."

I raised my head, my cheeks going numb. "Avaris?"

"My spies spotted you and your brother across the canal."

"I was working. Aunt Meriti was busy today, so I took Hote. It was an opportunity to pray for his health."

He raised an eyebrow. "You sought the god of destruction for healing? An unorthodox behavior, don't you think, my apprentice?"

Should I give him a piece of the truth to satisfy his suspicion? No, my master enjoyed nothing more than a good, hearty debate.

I collected my thoughts, straightened my back, folded my hands over my stomach, and raised my chin. "Is this an interrogation?"

"A conversation."

"And am I conversing with my master or the grand vizier?"

"Both."

I held my stoic face. "My brother's illness has progressed, and I'm desperate. Furthermore, Hote must learn that our brave Medjay will protect him from the wicked Hyksos if he wishes to visit *our* god."

"And have you spoken to those—wicked Hyksos?"

"Possibly. Those lowlifes require a firm hand sometimes."

"Did those lowlifes include a brown-haired boy? The one you met in seclusion behind Set's temple. Did your brother play with two Hyksos girls?"

"I was inquiring about the children's parents." That, too, wasn't false. As a matter of fact, I hadn't spoken a single lie. I had to stay collected. Nothing I'd done was particularly out of the ordinary. "Forgive me, master, but is it unlawful for a government official to investigate suspicious behavior in Avaris?"

"Not at all. However, my spies recounted a different story. According to them, you shared a tender moment with the untouchable behind the temple."

"Master?" I fought the instinct to retreat when he stepped closer to me. "The untouchable is a novice clerk. He... I was warning him that his new position doesn't change—"

"They reported you crying while the boy comforted you." Blood drained from my cheeks, and he squinted his eyes. "And now I catch you sneaking around in the shadows of the night in glamorous clothes. Have you heard about the Egyptian we caught today? The one who had an affair with a Hyksos? Should I worry, my apprentice?"

"Master!" I faked a gasp. No, he hadn't caught me yet. I could still turn this around. "Aunt Meriti gave me those clothes because I outgrew my old ones. I retreated behind Set's temple to grieve for my brother, but the untouchable pursued me and attempted to exploit my vulnerable state. I rebuffed his inappropriate advances." I squinted my eyes to release as many tears as possible. "Oh, my dear master. Despite my struggles, I've never asked for help, and I've always enforced the law in the pharaoh's name. Is this how you repay my unwavering loyalty? You question my honor and integrity?" I covered my face and shook my head. "Oh, my dear master."

I glimpsed his relaxing expression through my fingers, and a veiled smile emerged behind my palms. Yep, crying never failed. But gods, I was stupid. How had I been so reckless? Of course, the grand vizier's most cynical spies swarmed Set's temple. As always, it was Khaf's fault. *He* changed our usual meeting place from the hidden fields of wheat.

Master Paser lowered my hands and wiped my tears. "My heart aches for your struggles, my dear apprentice." He took off his ring. "Take this."

"Master?"

He presented his shiny golden ring. "Pay for a healer from Heka's temple. They can minimize the pain of Hote's incurable illness."

"Oh no, master. I can't accept this."

I had already robbed him blind. Gods, I wished my need for Hote's medicine didn't force me to commit such thievery.

"You cannot learn if your mind stays preoccupied with your private troubles." Master Paser took my hand and slid the ring onto my thumb. "Use the ring's remaining value to buy food for yourself and Hote." He smiled at me like I assumed a father would do with his daughter.

My eyes welled up with tears at his compassion. This time, my tears were genuine. How was he so kind and virtuous? My master devoted his life to serving Egypt. How could the cursed Hyksos ever accuse him of cruelty? Those ungrateful lowlifes should look into their ancestors' history of oppression and brutality before they spoke ill of our great grand vizier.

"Thank you, master. You're too kind."

He squeezed my hand and released me. "The bond between teacher and student is holy, Nefiri, blessed by the gods."

Why couldn't he be wicked and abusive? At least my crimes would've been justified. At least he would've deserved it. But he had to be perfect, didn't he? If I ever got caught, my master's disappointment would be unbearable. His spies were on to me. I had to act fast and rectify the situation. Tomorrow, I would assemble the Medjay, capture Khaf, and force him to surrender the seeds of my brother's...

A scarlet beam rose from Ra's temple to the sky.

The soldiers broke formation and gazed at the heaven.

Master Paser turned. "What in Ra's hidden name?"

"Master, what is—"

The beam widened. An explosion erupted, obliterating the entire upper half of Ra's temple. Huge chunks of the temple's blocks rained down on the closest soldiers, crushing them. Stone slabs—the size of grown men—tumbled in our direction. I froze as a massive boulder flew toward me.

"Nefiri!" Master Paser slammed his shoulder against mine, pushing me away from him. The boulder missed me and crashed into the ground. Dust exploded from the impact.

"Ma—" I coughed. "Master!"

"I'm fine!"

"Inay!" a woman's voice boomed from the celebration hall. A figure emerged on the rooftop, surrounded by a magnificent white aura. Was... was that... oh gods, that was the queen mother!

Four glowing rings descended and encircled the temple, forming a shimmering dome.

"Oja!" Tuya's voice rang out in the chaos. A burst of light flared from the nearby celebration hall. The dome vibrated at her command and shifted to protect the soldiers from the debris raining upon them.

A scarlet sphere rose from the temple's ruins, encircled by a whirlwind of stone. A burst of lightning illuminated the sky, and the resulting thunder shook the ground beneath my feet, stirring the sand along the golden path.

The cataclysmic event shook the heavens and shattered the world with its sheer enormity, unleashing a force that left me reeling. I clutched my ears and screamed.

"Traitorous parasites of Egypt!" a deep voice consumed the heavens. Its force shook every organ in my chest and turned the surrounding soldiers hysterical. "The end of the falcon's age is nigh, and the sha's age is upon you."

Sha? Wasn't that the mythical dog-like creature? The one connected to... wait, I knew that voice. I'd heard it when... when I... oh gods, when I touched the spear! That was our shackled god. Set!

"Spectate! See the beginning of your demise," Set said.

The sky blazed with a scarlet light, consuming the blood moon and casting an eerie glow over the land. An image materialized in the heavens, revealing our soldiers being mercilessly slaughtered by the Hittites in Kadesh. The image shifted, focusing on our pharaoh, who stood alone amid the chaos, drenched in blood and wounded. With nothing but a shattered sword, the Lord of The Two Lands fought valiantly against the overwhelming enemy forces. A Hittite soldier raced on a black stallion through the madness. He charged straight toward our king and decapitated him with a single stroke of his ax. The enemy horses trampled over Ramesses' head, crushing it under their hooves. The battlefield echoed with the cries of our defeated army.

"Ramesses!" Master Paser screamed.

"We will lose the battle of Kadesh!" I covered my mouth.

"Rectify your injustice." The image in the sky refocused on the pharaoh's deformed, headless body, surrounded by his slaughtered soldiers. "Cleanse yourselves of your sins and save your pharaoh and nation. Find the one who touched the spear and awoke me. Send the Chosen to my prison so they may free me, Set, your Baal and the rightful god-pharaoh of your ungrateful lands."

The scarlet light retracted into the sphere that contained Set's spear. "The end of Horus's age is nigh, and Set's age is upon you."

I laid my trembling hands on my head.

It wasn't a dream. I'd touched the spear. Ra didn't visit me. I'd unleashed the god of destruction and doomed the pharaoh and Egypt with him.

Set chose me!

"Nefiri!" Master Paser knelt before me and shook my motionless body. "Speak to me, girl! Are you hurt?"

I shook my head.

He turned to the collapsed temple, his body shaking, and laid his hands on his bald head. Oh, my master had lost his wig. How sad.

What? Who cared about a stupid wig?

Master Paser stood still. His head rose, and his trembling body calmed. In a heartbeat, my master regained his composure and exuded confidence to lead his people, while I cried on the ground like a spoiled child. Oh, what a fine apprentice and future grand vizier I was.

"Men!" he called to the soldiers crying on the ground. The sheer power of his voice snapped them out of their hysterical state. "On your feet!" He turned, his arms crossed, and glared at me. He wasn't my sympathetic teacher anymore. Right now, he was Grand Vizier Paser—the second most powerful man in Egypt. "Speak. What do you know?"

"I... why would I know about this?"

"You were in Set's temple, weren't you? You sought the god of destruction for healing."

"Thousands visit the temple each year."

Master Paser studied me. "Come with me."

"Where?"

The soldiers rose behind the grand vizier. "We'll search for the spear's chosen and shove Set's weapon in his traitorous skull."

My master walked toward Ra's destroyed temple, his soldiers marching behind him.

Chapter 4

Lady of Grace

The crimson moon cast its violent light on Ra's home. The once-glorious temple lay in ruins, hidden in a thick veil of dust that drizzled like droplets of blood. It shrouded the collapsed celestial hall in an eerie reminder of Ra's wrathful spirit that vowed to search for the sinful mortal who had caused the destruction of its holy sanctuary. In other words, me! Great!

A Medjay force—led by Commander Ahmose—arrived from Avaris to offer their support while the army secured the perimeter.

"Found something!" Commander Ahmose called. His men flipped over a giant plate, revealing the spear. The commander knelt beside the divine weapon and reached out to grab it.

Master Paser turned. His eyes widened as the Medjay commander's fingers stretched toward the spear. "No, don't—"

Scarlet bolts sparked around Set's spear. Commander Ahmose screamed. He jerked his hand, but his fist remained clenched around the weapon. Blood oozed out of his ears, nose, eyes, and mouth.

"Grand Viz..." Commander Ahmose's jaw detached from his dissolving face. His decaying eyes shifted toward me. He collapsed, his body disintegrating into dust. Its ashes rained down on the floor of the destroyed temple, covering the cursed spear. A spear I had activated with my stupidity when I touched it. I'd caused the death of a high Egyptian official, hadn't I? Commander Ahmose had a family. Gods, I'd orphaned Egyptian children because of my dealings with a Hyksos!

"Gods, have mercy!" Master Paser dusted the fallen commander's ashes off his white kilt. "Nobody approaches the spear."

The Medjay hastily retreated.

"Why did Ahmose look at you?" Master Paser asked me, his voice stern.

"I don't—"

He laid his hand on my shoulder and gave it a gentle press. "What are you hiding?"

"Master, I'd never—"

"Nefiri, talk to me while I can still protect—"

"Paser!" A woman's voice exploded inside the temple's unstable halls. The echoes of her mighty voice were followed by... by... oh gods! A roar!

A tall woman strode into the collapsed celestial hall, a majestic lion by her side. Intricate silver patterns decorated her white gown, which flowed gracefully behind her like a river of light. The gems on her golden falcon crown sparkled like the stars, catching the flickering torchlight and casting a dazzling aura around her head.

Behind her marched a contingent of eight soldiers, each armed with a wooden shield and a bronze spear. Adorned in bright yellow kilts, they were known as the Thunderbolts— the fierce and newly formed royal guards, feared by all as the army's deadliest and most ruthless unit.

"Your Majesty." My knees weakened, and I disguised my collapse as kneeling before the Lady of The Two Lands.

The queen passed by me as if I didn't exist, but her lion stood beside me because, apparently, there was no other free spot in Egypt.

I tried to retreat from the lion, but I didn't have the nerve to move.

The Thunderbolts encircled us. They wouldn't care who they had to kill to keep the queen safe, including the Medjay and the grand vizier himself.

"Queen Nefertari." Master Paser bowed. "I have this under control. There is no reason for—"

Nefertari raised her hand, interrupting my fierce master's words with her mere gesture.

"You have this under control, you say?" Nefertari said. "Ra's temple has been destroyed. Set spoke to us and promised my husband's death and the demise of his kingdom." She closed her left hand in a fist, shaking her expensive silver bracelets. "And the sky has turned scarlet!" Her voice reverberated through the trembling temple, shaking its unstable foundation. The Thunderbolts' spears tapped the ground in unison, unleashing a deafening echo in the halls. Beside me, the lion roared with a force that shook my heart within its cage. One of my Medjay collapsed unconscious at the feet of this royal manifestation of might.

Nefertari took a deep breath and walked to her lion. I turned my head away from her and toward the trembling Medjay.

The queen knelt beside the lion and patted his head. "Easy, Slayer. Don't anger yourself, my dear. Not yet."

Her gaze met mine, and a sudden tightening in my chest left me breathless. I understood why Ramesses called the queen of the Nile *the one for whom the sun shines*. What better reason did the golden Egyptian sun need for its daily return than to steal another glimpse of Queen Nefertari's face? Her eyes were pools of infinite blackness, deep and endless as the night sky. Her nose was perfectly chiseled, a mark of her noble heritage, and her strong jawline exuded an air of power and authority. A river of ebony silk flowed from her head and cascaded down her slender frame, shimmering in the light like a thousand tiny stars.

Aunt Meriti had lied. My hair wasn't as divine as the queen's. Nothing about me was comparable to Her Majesty. I was a bug gazing up at a gazelle.

"And who are you?" Nefertari asked.

"I... I..." My heart nearly broke my ribs.

"This is Nefiri, Your Majesty," Master Paser said.

"How does her name answer my question?"

"She is my apprentice."

The queen nodded and turned to my master. Despite the lion standing beside me, I couldn't help but gaze in awe at the woman I'd idolized my entire life.

Our queen was the most intelligent woman in Egypt, evident by the seven languages she spoke and her ability to read and write—a unique set of skills that prompted Pharaoh Ramesses to appoint her as his highest diplomat.

Our pharaoh declared his love for her with pride, calling her "sweet of love" and "lady of grace." He fought tradition to honor his wife by building her statues as tall as his own because he demanded that the world see her as he did—as a woman of unparalleled intelligence and grace, deserving of the highest praise and recognition.

"Nefiri!" Master Paser shouted.

"Y-yes, master."

"Stop daydreaming!"

"It's the middle of the—"

He glared at me, tapping his fingers on his crossed arms. "What did the queen ask you?"

My mouth dropped. The queen had spoken to me, and I hadn't responded! What was wrong with me?

"You didn't pay attention, did you?" he asked, his face crimson.

"I… I have a lion flashing his teeth at me!"

"Slayer," Nefertari said. "Come to me, my dear."

Slayer sat beside her like a small cat. Of course, a couple such as Nefertari and Ramesses had a pet lion. What else were they supposed to have? A chicken?

I stood and dusted my white dress in a faint attempt to regain a shred of my composure. "I'm sorry, Your Majesty. Please forgive me, but could you repeat the question?"

Nefertari crossed her arms and studied me. "Nefiri, wasn't it?"

"Yes, Your Majesty."

"Paser told me you might have information that could lead us to Set's chosen."

Gods, why hadn't I told him everything when I had the chance?

"Nefiri," Nefertari said.

"Yes, Your Majesty."

"When the Lady of The Two Lands issues a demand, your ultimate goal, your sole purpose in life, is to fulfill it." Slayer rose, and the Thunderbolts tilted their spears toward me. "I demanded an answer, and my patience is wearing thin."

I must direct their attention away from me. "There is a Hyksos thief called Khafset. A clerk in Set's temple named Setu informed me two years ago that Khafset had a secret Hyksos cure for my little brother. During our last meeting, the thief mentioned he wished to steal the spear."

Master Paser's eyes widened. Yep, now he knew what a great apprentice I was.

Nefertari shot my master a withering stare. Gods, if looks could kill! "Her traitorous act of trading with an untouchable aside, did she report the thief's plans to you or the Medjay?"

Master Paser hesitated, his eyes scanning me as I fought to stay on my feet.

"Yes." His voice was calm, as if his lie was the ultimate truth that nobody, not even the queen, could deny.

I resisted the temptation to embrace myself and weep. Master Paser, the embodiment of the law, had lied to the queen on my behalf! He remained steadfast, undeterred by the queen's challenging gaze or the menacing presence of her beast and guards. Right now, no one stood taller in my eyes than my dear master. The only man to protect me, and for that, I held him above all else.

"Nefiri informed me of a Hyksos thief she is trying to capture," he continued in his steady voice while the queen's face turned red. "I gave her full authority." He glanced at me. "However, I must admit, her decision to hide the thief's scheme was a catastrophic lack of sound judgment."

"I... I didn't take the thief's ambition seriously. I didn't wish to distract you or the Medjay with minor details. The untouchable likes to talk big, and he—"

Nefertari raised her hand. "You are in no position to give us your insight."

"Some details are missing." Master Paser eyed me. "Your story makes little sense. The spear needed contact with the Chosen. How did your untouchable pass by the guards?"

"Maybe he had inside help," Nefertari said.

Master Paser nodded, pressing his lips together. "But who is that traitor? A soldier?"

A single step separated him from the truth. A mere thought separated my teacher from discovering the crimes of his traitorous student.

Three Thunderbolts entered what used to be the celestial hall through what used to be the main gate. They dragged a beaten man with them. Despite his bruised face, his curly brown hair and defiant honey eyes screamed his identity. Khafset! Gods, they'd caught him.

"Your Majesty," a Thunderbolt said. He held Khaf's dagger in his hand. "We have captured this untouchable lurking near the temple."

Master Paser's eyes darted toward me. "Your Hyksos, by any chance?"

Khaf was gagged. He couldn't contradict my claims. The Thunderbolts would execute him without hesitation. They simply needed an order. Being a Hyksos justified his death, didn't it? Such were my master's teachings. But... but... oh gods, according to his teachings, as a traitor, Hote and I should be executed for my treason.

On second thoughts, Khaf didn't deserve to die. Yes. Despicable as he was, he had done nothing that justified his death. He hadn't even touched the spear.

I caught my master's intense gaze. He raised a hidden finger beside his leg, and I held my tongue. Why did Master Paser wish for me to remain silent?

"It was this untouchable's fault!" Master Paser announced. "He brought destruction upon our peaceful lands like his ancestors before him. Sure, my apprentice failed to stop him. But so did great pharaohs of ages past who died in their struggle against the untouchables. We shouldn't throw around pointless accusations and forget the real enemy." He glared at Khaf and raised his fist. "Medjay, cut his—"

"Don't kill him yet," Nefertari said, her tone unimpressed by my master's speech. "I wish to hear the thief's plea."

Master Paser and I exchanged glances while a Thunderbolt cut the cloth around Khaf's mouth. Curses, she was too smart!

The Hyksos was free now, ready to spew his venom.

"Ah, finally!" Khaf gasped for air, chuckling. "Now, if you'd be so kind, return the dagger you've stolen from me."

The Thunderbolt who held Khaf's dagger banged him on the head. Khaf crumpled in a heap. He twisted on the floor like a snake and laughed. "I—heard Commander Ahmose's screams. Where is..." His gaze fell on the spear, covered with the commander's ashes. "Oh!" A twisted grin overtook Khaf's face. "May Ammit rip his soul apart before he spends eternity in the Lake of Fire."

"Don't you dare disrespect Commander Ahmose!" I said. "He was a great man!"

"He was an animal!" Khaf said.

"Enough nonsense," Nefertari said. "Your last words, Hyksos."

"Last words? Then what? Will you kill me? How's killing me supposed to keep Set in his prison?"

"The spear should deactivate if we kill its chosen," Master Paser said.

So, my master knew I was involved but didn't deduce that I was the Chosen. Did I overestimate his abilities or underestimate his trust in me?

"The spear should deactivate?" Khaf chuckled. "That's a theory. A flawed one, but you tried your best." He sat on his knees and stretched before the queen and grand vizier. Was the idiot giving them more reasons to kill... wait, did the Thunderbolt say Khaf was lurking near the temple? Why would he willingly stay near... oh gods! He'd warned me we would meet sooner than I thought. Khaf had gotten caught on purpose! Whatever was happening here was part of his plan!

"You should only blame yourselves, Egyptians. You are the ones who changed the spear's location."

"The high priests of Ra, Astarte, and Heka chose the spear's location," Nefertari said. "You want us to believe you know better?"

"You didn't mention the high priest of Set," Khaf said.

"Give a Hyksos the fanciest of clothes and titles, and he will remain an untouchable who should live, die, and rot in Avaris," Nefertari said.

53

"True, that particular Hyksos isn't the best of us." Khaf grimaced.

Why did he despise the high priest of Set? The man helped us save Hyksos orphans by sending them to us. True, he received a fine payment, but it was only fair considering his hard work. Khaf could've learned a thing or two from his Hyksos high priest.

"Nevertheless," Khaf said, "your three golden high priests left the spear above the wrong gateway."

"Gateway?" Nefertari's eyes shifted to Master Paser.

"We know of anomalies beneath the four temples of Peramessu, but we never fully understood them."

"How are these gateways related to Set's spear?" Nefertari asked.

Khaf's head fell. "Ah, for Baal's sake. Why do you think my people chose this place to build Avaris?"

Nefertari crossed her arms, demonstrating an inhuman level of emotional control. "Enlighten us, thief."

"The gateways under the four temples lead to the Land-Between-Realms. A reality that allows living mortals to move between Huat and Duat."

Huat and Duat! Was there really a way to travel between the mortal and divine realms?

"Is this true?" Nefertari asked Master Paser.

"Perhaps. Before his death, Pharaoh Seti moved the spear to Ra's temple at the urging of a source known only to him. Of course, this was a massive project since no one could touch the spear. Heka's priests used their magic to move the entire chamber that contained it."

"What a waste of good magic." Khaf smiled. "The gateway under Set's temple offers the shortest path to his throne, while the one beneath us in Ra's temple, or what's left of it, offers the shortest way to Set's prison."

Master Paser scoffed. "The untouchable fancies himself a knowledgeable thief."

"I studied in Set's temple and learned everything there is to know about the god of destruction and Horus's test. I'm well prepared to save Egypt."

"Do you want us to believe Egypt's fate concerns you, Hyksos?" Master Paser asked.

"Egypt is a shitty home, but it's still our home, whether or not you admit it." He smiled and winked at me. "A fair price couldn't hurt, though. You know, for high morale and such."

I scoffed. Gods, I wanted to pick up the spear and stab this smug thief.

"What is your advice, Paser?" Nefertari asked.

"I suppose—"

"His advice should be to send the Chosen to steal the other half of Set's weapon from his prison in Duat," Khaf interrupted. "This should cut Set's connection to our world."

"I will never entrust Egypt's future to an untouchable," the queen said before my master could order the cursed lowlife never to interrupt him again!

Khaf's smug smile shifted toward me. "Good thing I'm not the Chosen, then."

My flushing face turned numb. Every set of eyes stared at me. Gods, everyone. The queen, my master, Khaf, the Medjay, the Thunderbolts, and even Slayer. I crawled until my back hit the wall, raining dust on my head.

"Nefiri, did you touch the spear?" Master Paser asked.

I breathed through my clenched teeth. My heart pounded in my chest. My master's wide eyes stared at me. His head shook as if denying the truth.

"My brother didn't know! Punish me, but please don't—"

"Thunderbolts!" the queen said. "Arrest the traitor."

"No! I only wanted to save—"

The Thunderbolts pointed their spears at me, and the words evaporated in my throat. The armed men formed an arc that trapped me against the wall. Khaf's manic laughter merged with my cries, and Master Paser turned the other way.

A blinding scarlet flash consumed the celestial hall. An object hit my hand, and I involuntarily clutched its metallic surface. A man's scream erupted from Khaf's direction. The scarlet light faded. I sat with Set's spear in my hand. The Medjay cowered on the floor before me. The Thunderbolts rushed to encircle the queen. Khaf stood in the corner holding his dagger with his victim lying unconscious beside his feet.

"By the gods! Nefiri!" Master Paser said.

Khaf laughed. "Did you think the spear would let you harm her?"

"Master Paser, help!" I shook my hand to release the spear, but my fist refused to relax. "I swear by Ra's hidden name; I didn't mean for any of this to happen. Khafset told me to open the window in exchange for the seeds of my brother's medicine. But I stopped the thief. I wielded the spear only to fight him, then left. That's when you found me. I swear that's what happened. I swear!"

"Why didn't the soldiers stop them?" Nefertari asked.

"There were no soldiers," I cried. "Not a single one."

"Impossible," Master Paser said.

"Nefiri and the soldiers were in different places," Khaf said. "When you build a structure over a gateway, it exists in the Land-Between-Realms. Take notes before you unlearn this." Khaf smiled when Master Paser's face twitched. "The spear pulled its chosen to the Land-Between-Realms. Why it pulled me as well is beyond my understanding."

"Good." Nefertari turned to Khaf. "Since you are not the Chosen, Slayer can rip you apart."

"I don't fear death." Khaf pointed his dagger at his neck.

"Do it then," Nefertari said. "Cut your throat, and I will hang your corpse in Avaris for its untouchables to witness how your flesh rots and your bones decay. That's how you will be remembered. A revolting pile of decaying rot."

Khaf tightened his grip on the dagger, squeaking the brown leather around its hilt.

"Maybe—we should entice the thief instead of antagonizing him," Master Paser said. "Same goes for Nefiri."

I raised my gaze toward my master. Was he defending me again? I was a traitor. Why did he keep breaking his teachings to protect me?

"What?" Nefertari glared at the grand vizier. "These two must be punished, not rewarded."

"And if that's your wish, it shall be fulfilled, Your Majesty. But you asked for my advice earlier. Set's spear was going to find its chosen, following Horus's will. It's his ultimate test for us; therefore, we must send the Chosen to fend off Set's influence. These two are our only chance to prove our worth to Horus and save the pharaoh." Master Paser bowed. "I have given my advice and, with it, fulfilled my duty as the grand vizier. The decision is yours, Your Majesty."

Oh, my dear master. He was too good to me while I had always been less than what he deserved.

Nefertari took a deep breath. "Of course, I accept your advice, Paser." She turned to Khaf. "How much gold will satisfy you, thief?"

Great strategy. Khaf loved gold. He was a thief to the bone. A model Hyksos. The queen must've figured him out at first glance. Khaf would do anything for enough gold.

"Equal rights," Khaf said.

My mouth dropped. What?

"Excuse me?" Nefertari asked.

"I want the Hyksos of Avaris to have equal rights to the Egyptians. I want them to be treated as legitimate inhabitants of this land. Give us the right to work, trade, and join the army."

"Never! Last time we opened our arms to you parasites, you enslaved us in our own lands."

"I don't care what happened centuries ago! I care about those alive today. Children who may grow old instead of being sent to die in shackles. My childhood friend who wishes to become a respectable priest. I want those rights for them and every poor soul in Avaris." Khaf drew a deep breath and pressed the dagger against his neck, leaking his blood onto its blade. "You need a Hyksos guide between the realms, and everyone in Avaris would rather die than help you. I know how to reach Set's prison. If you don't agree to my demands, I'll kill myself. Soon after, Ramesses will die, and the Hittites will invade Egypt."

What? The Hyksos wasn't pursuing personal gains? That couldn't be! He must be lying. That wasn't what my master taught me.

"Your Majesty," Master Paser said, "I believe only the pharaoh can make such a promise."

The queen paced slowly back and forth before her Thunderbolts. Slayer's eyes monitored our movements.

That was how a proper politician behaved. No matter what happened, she remained calm and maintained her authority and composure. While it only took a wink from Khaf to anger me. I was never going to be like the queen or my master, was I? I wasn't the grand vizier's sole apprentice. I was his only mistake.

Nefertari gazed at the blood moon through the celestial hall's collapsed ceiling. "Without this deal, we will not have a pharaoh. It is my duty to protect Egypt in Ramesses' absence. This is my burden as the Lady of The Two Lands."

Master Paser bowed. "As Her Majesty commands."

"I will grant you your wish, Hyksos." The queen tapped her crossed arms, eyeing Khaf. "But I swear by the gods, you filthy untouchable, if you play any games or fail in your mission, I *will* burn Avaris to the ground."

Khaf's body shook. "What?"

The queen ignored him and turned to me. "As for you, traitor. Steal the other half of Set's spear, and you will be pardoned for your treason and receive the seeds you required from the thief. You will report the outcome of your mission; then, I want you and your brother out of Egypt." Nefertari's arms fell beside her, and her chin rose. "These are the orders of the Lady of The Two Lands and your payments for defeating Set."

"Defeating Set?" I covered my mouth with my free hand.

The queen walked toward me, Slayer beside her. She towered over me, and I hugged Set's spear by instinct.

"The only reason you and your Hyksos are alive is that you are the only two able to enter Set's prison to cut his connection to Huat."

"I will die, Your Majesty!"

"Probably. But look at it this way. Take your chances with Set and you may survive, or stay with me in the royal palace."

"I just want to go home."

"No, traitor. That's not how this works. You're the same as the untouchables of Avaris now, and for that will be treated like them. Think of your little brother. If you stay, I will burn down your house with him inside, and you can listen to his dying screams. Then I will keep you in the royal palace until a messenger arrives to inform me of my husband's death. And girl, if you think Set is terrifying, trust me, you shall witness true horror when I execute my revenge on my husband's killer. So what will it be, traitor—Set, or me?"

Burn Hote? No, please! I did all this for my little Hote!

I swallowed. "S-Set, Your Majesty."

"Smart girl." The queen glanced at Master Paser. "Prepare the traitor and the thief for their journey to Set's prison." She glared at me. "Should you fail, and by some miracle of the gods survive Set, I expect you to surrender yourself. And if you try to escape, remember…" A prideful smile overtook the queen's serene face. "I have your brother."

Chapter 5

A Place We Call Home

Cockroaches crawled on the walls of the narrow corridor, racing Khaf and me as we followed Master Paser toward the gateway in the dungeon beneath Ra's temple. I fumbled with the ring my master had given me, wishing this was a nightmare. I'd tried to return the ring to my teacher. He shot me an annoyed glance and left me standing alone. As a matter of fact, my master hadn't spoken to me since our audience with Nefertari. He'd instructed the guards to give us leather bags packed with supplies; then, we followed him underneath the collapsed temple to the gateway. Strangely, my master didn't take his guards with him. Did he fear his own guards because he'd protected a traitor? Gods, was my master in danger because of me?

No, I was overreacting. He wasn't some random grand vizier. He was the great Paser, the war veteran and future high priest of Ra—the lifelong friend of Queen Tuya and Pharaoh Seti. The uncle who taught Queen Nefertari and Pharaoh Ramesses everything they knew. My master wasn't in danger. He'd transcended that possibility long ago.

"Hey, Nef," Khaf whispered. "Hey, Nefi, Nef—"

"Don't speak to her," Master Paser said. Darkness surrounded the golden hue his torch cast around his body. "Don't look at her. Don't touch her. Not in my presence."

"Fine, O grand vizier." Khaf bowed. Curse him. The Hyksos was smart enough to know Master Paser couldn't kill him.

"Master, could you please—"

"There are no words. Not a single syllable to describe my disappointment in you."

"I just wanted to save my brother's—"

"There is no cure for honey urine. A sad reality you refused to accept, and now you have brought the gods' wrath upon us."

"But Khaf did—"

"Khaf?" Master Paser scoffed. "Just how close are you to that untouchable?"

"My name is Khafset," he said. "And Nef and I are best friends."

"We most definitely are *not!*"

Khaf arched his eyebrow. "Are we—more than best friends?"

"More?!" I screamed. "We are less! Way less! We are *nothing*! You hear me?! Nothing!"

"And what cure did your Khaf offer?" Master Paser asked, his calm voice overpowering my screams and Khaf's chuckles.

I took a deep breath to regain my composure. Oh, curse the irritating untouchable! "He gave me poppy juice, master."

"I see," Master Paser said. "A cure that could lessen Hote's pain *and* eventually kill him."

"What?" I glared at Khaf.

"That's not true! Your brother has been getting better, hasn't he?"

I nodded but lowered my gaze when Master Paser looked at me.

"Do not be so foolish as to blindly trust that untouchable."

"My name is—"

"Khafset." His intense glance slowed Khaf's pace. "I heard you. Now keep quiet." He returned his gaze to the dark corridor.

Khaf crossed his arms, his face turning red.

"Hote's condition has worsened, Nefiri," Master Paser continued in his calm voice. "Yet you insist on believing otherwise. You could have come to terms with Hote's fate and made his remaining moments memorable before his soul departs to the afterlife. Instead, you obsessed over the impossible, driven by your hubris and desire to prove others wrong. Though motivated by your love for Hote, your actions have led you on a path of destruction. You indulged in your own passions, and now, look at what you have wrought. Every moment you spend in Duat is time you could have enjoyed with Hote."

I clenched my teeth. I didn't indulge my hubris and passion! Every action I took was out of love for my brother! I longed to scream those words but knew better than to provoke my master further.

"The great Paser has gone mad, they said," he continued. "His decision to appoint a fatherless half-Nubian girl as his apprentice and successor over the noble Egyptian boys was ill-judged, a sign that age had caught up with him. Despite their malicious gossip, I stood by you with unwavering pride. And now, the queen accuses me of trusting a traitor."

"You should move to Avaris," Khaf said. "My people aren't so judgmental."

We reached the wooden door at the end of the dark corridor, and Master Paser turned to Khaf. "I know you are having your fun, thief. But I will not indulge it."

Khaf grinned. "I *am* having fun. I can't deny it." His defiant honey eyes stared at my master. "We both know I'm too important to kill, and for all the power you have, O great Paser, you stand powerless before me."

"Slither inside the room, snake." Master Paser nodded toward the door.

"I want my dagger back." Khaf pointed at my master's belt, where he'd hidden the dagger beneath his leopard skin. "It belongs to me."

"You will get it before you leave. Now out of my sight."

Khaf hummed, his hand rising above his head. I followed his movement, unsure of what he was planning. Suddenly, Khaf brought his hands together with a sharp clap, the sound echoing through the dark corridor. Without a word, I traced the reverberation of his action deeper into the darkness, my heart pounding with anticipation.

"What was that?" I asked. "Have you gone mad?"

Khaf glanced at me. He winked and slipped through the half-opened door.

"What just happened?" I asked.

Master Paser slammed the door shut. His focus shifted toward me, his face dark and eyes dead.

I lowered my gaze to the cracked floor and clutched my left arm. "Master, please. What will happen to my little—"

He raised his hand, and words stuck in my throat. "You failed me. Failed your gods, your pharaoh, your brother, your country, and its people."

I bowed my head, clutching my dress.

"Yet I failed you too, my apprentice."

My gaze rose. "Master?"

"So young, yet you carry a weight that could break the backs of those twice your age." He shook his head. "I taught you mathematics and politics, yet I failed to teach you the intricacies of life and those who live it. You failed as my apprentice, but I, too, failed as your master."

"No. You have been nothing but kind to me. If it hadn't been for my brother's—"

Master Paser shook his head. That was my signal to keep quiet. "Too many excuses, Nefiri. The wise do not pursue a path of destruction, leaving a trail of excuses behind them." He cradled my shaking hands. "You are strong and smart, yet you are not wise."

"I'm neither strong nor smart. I have proven today what a failure I am."

"You are a survivor, Nefiri—a young woman who never ceases to amaze despite the odds being stacked against her. You resemble Isis in that regard. Same as you, our goddess fought against the odds to protect those she loved."

"You think too much of me, my master."

"And you too little of yourself, my apprentice." His gentle, fatherly smile returned. "Hote will be safe. After much negotiation, I convinced the queen to allow him to stay in my house. I will see to it that the servants fill my private pool for Hote, as exercise could improve his condition. I will instruct the cooks to take his special diet into consideration. Every measure will be taken to ensure his—"

I hugged him, buried my face in his chest, and my tears soaked his leopard skin. "You are the greatest, kindest, most chivalrous man to have ever graced The Two Lands with his presence, my dear, *dear* master."

He eased me out of the hug and smiled, wiping my tears. "Now, you have no excuse. Your mind should be clear of distractions. Use that smart head of yours to succeed in your mission."

"I—won't succeed. I can't survive Set."

"You will. Bring the scythe to Egypt and save the pharaoh. Achieve this, and I will convince the king to annul your exile. Do it, and I will turn you from a traitor into a hero." He held my hand, bringing his ring into my sight. "May this ring be the part of me that accompanies you on your journey. May it remind you to have faith in your grand vizier as he has faith in you."

I bowed my head. "I'm forever thankful, my dear master."

He gently squeezed my hand and opened the door to the small, empty room. My eyes widened at a baffling sight: Queen Mother Tuya stood before Khaf, holding his dagger while the thief directed her.

He had regained his dagger! When? How?

"And that's the scorpion stance," Khaf said.

"Incredible!" Tuya said.

"Get away from her, you parasite!" Master Paser shouted, and Khaf jumped back.

"Ah, relax, dear Paser. The boy was showing me how to wield his dagger." Tuya regarded the weapon's blade. "Such great craftsmanship. The Hyksos are indeed talented blacksmiths. My deepest respect to the blacksmith, child."

Khaf's face twitched before a smile overtook his lips. "Thank you."

"Did you know?" Tuya pointed Khaf's dagger at Master Paser. "There exist twelve techniques for wielding a dagger?"

"No," Master Paser said in an exhausted tone.

"Neither did I, and yet here we are, two gray Egyptians who have learned something new from the young Hyksos."

Master Paser's eyes darted toward Khaf. "When did you steal the dagger?"

"When I raised my arms and clapped, making you and Nef follow the echo." Khaf brushed back his long brown hair, smiling. "And technically, *you* stole the dagger from *me*."

I clenched my teeth. "You dare call my—"

"So you bested Paser," Tuya laughed, tracing her finger over the dagger's blade. "You should have seen the grand vizier when he was your age. Nobody bested that old man back then. Not even my late husband." She slapped the dagger against Khaf's chest.

"Step back from the queen mother and sheath your dagger, Hyksos!" Master Paser said.

"Oh, my dear friend, I'm old but not fragile. I can defend myself just fine."

She could. I'd seen her standing on top of the celebration hall when Ra's temple exploded. She wielded incredible magic. Real magic! Without her, many more would've died. The rumors must be true. She *was* the human incarnation of Isis. How else had she stopped Set's attack?

"Your queen mother is… fascinating," Khaf said.

"What?" Tuya asked. "You, too, think I'm Isis?"

"Oh, Isis wishes."

I arched my eyebrow while the thief laughed with the queen mother. What in Ra's hidden name was happening?

"Same as your apprentice, the boy has a unique charm," Tuya said to Master Paser. "Speaking of which…" She looked at me. "Approach me, child."

I walked toward her, my head bowed. "Y-Your Majesty."

"Child." Tuya cupped my cheeks and raised my head. "*Always* keep the golden link next to your heart."

Golden link? Did she mean the golden scarab she had given me? Yes, that must be it. Was it?

"I'm not sure I understand, Your Majesty."

"Most people don't." Tuya smiled. "But you will. Soon enough. Consider it another step toward your father." She took my hand and linked it to Khaf's. She placed us before the widest wall of the rectangular room and grabbed our shoulders. "Egypt was a kinder home when an Egyptian and a Hyksos last worked together. I hope, for our sakes, you will always remember that the light awaits you when your legs are at their weakest. Never forget you both were made from Egypt's black mud, and its Nile flows in your veins, and you will return to them in the end regardless of what you choose to call yourselves."

She released our shoulders. "Abis Duru!"

The air chilled. Black mist leaked from the gaps between the wall's yellow-painted bricks and swallowed its surface. The mist thickened, forming a black barrier before us.

"Go through the gateway's black mist, travelers. May its darkness lead you to the light." Tuya nudged us toward the gateway. "Save this place we call home."

"Hyksos!" Master Paser called from behind us.

We turned.

"What now?" Khaf asked.

"Return to Huat without my apprentice, and I swear by the Holy Ennead, I *will* hunt you to the ends of the lands."

Khaf tightened his grip on my hand. "Grand vizier. I will clash with the gods to bring her home unharmed if I must."

My shocked gaze stuck to the Hyksos. Did... did he... oh gods, he'd said something respectable!

"Nefiri," Master Paser said, tears flowing from his eyes. "Come back to me, girl."

I held my master's fate in my hands. If I didn't cut Set's connection to Huat, he would die in the battle of Kadesh. "You too, my dear master. Return victorious from Kadesh."

I turned to the gateway's black mist, my hand holding tightly to Khaf's. I found comfort in his warm grip, even if I couldn't explain why.

"Ready?" Khaf asked in a new soft tone I didn't know he could produce.

I nodded, staring into his honey eyes. Another lie. How could anyone be ready for this insane task? But it was too late now. Khaf and I walked into the gateway's black mist.

Chapter 6

Land-Between-Realms

The yellow-hued sky of the Land-Between-Realms stretched above the endless desert. Two vibrant green suns entwined in a mesmerizing dance, swirling and merging like yolks on the sand. I knelt before the empty mirror image of Ra's temple, taking in the fantastical scenery. The desert's vast expanse stretched before me, its endless dunes and swirling sands inhabited by the ghostly silhouettes of distant human-shaped shadows wandering aimlessly.

"This is it," Khaf said. "The Land-Between-Realms. Our first step toward Set." He entangled the fingers of our held hands.

I jerked my hand away from the thief. "Never touch me again!"

Khaf smiled. "What's this new fierce side I'm seeing?"

"Get used to it." I tied my loose hair into a bun with my white ribbon, then raised my chin, mimicking Nefertari's prideful pose. "I'm fierce and not weak. Smart and not naive."

Khaf laughed and walked away.

"Hey, don't leave me alone!" I ran after him. Khaf halted, and I bumped into his bare muscular back.

So much for me being smart. I had fallen for the oldest trick in the book.

Khaf turned. "You have to answer this question since you are neither fierce nor smart..."

"That's not true!"

"Do you think I'm strong?"

Reluctantly, I nodded. Curse him. He'd defeated an unstoppable Thunderbolt to regain his dagger.

"You're strong but not smart," I said. "Your heist failed."

"Step one of my grand heist succeeded." He pointed at the empty, windless desert. "I'm precisely where I wanted to be. I needed access to the gateway, and Nefertari gracefully obliged. I'm marching toward Duat by an Egyptian royal decree. True, I never thought you'd accompany me." He slung his arm around me. "But rejoice, my dear Egyptian friend, for you'll be part of the greatest heist in human history."

I pushed him away and grabbed Set's spear from behind my back. I freed the weapon from its white cloth and pointed it at Khaf. "Don't you dare lay a finger on me again!"

Khaf pulled his dagger from underneath his brown belt. It hadn't taken him long to show his true face.

"Your stance is wrong," he said.

My hand fell beside me. "What?"

"We'll face many obstacles, and you must use the spear correctly." He placed one foot behind the other, forming a straight line with his toes. "Copy my stance."

I sighed and humored him. To be fair, this was useful information.

"Good. Now straighten your back."

I complied.

"This is the viper's stance. You aim with your left hand and thrust with the right. This stance is for close combat and requires agility instead of strength. It should suit your physical build."

"Why are you teaching me this?"

"Don't interrupt. Now thrust the spear." Khaf shifted his stance and positioned the dagger before his face. "Do it. Attack me."

"I might hurt you."

Khaf grinned. "Didn't you ever dream of sticking a knife in my eye?"

"Always!" That was a lie. Unfortunately, the Hyksos had gorgeous eyes—his irises were like the finest honey contained in the fanciest glass.

"Consider this your chance," Khaf said.

"I need you alive to guide me to Set's prison."

"Don't need both eyes for that."

"I said no!"

"So you'll fail as my apprentice as well?"

Oh, surely the untouchable had *not* just compared himself to my dear...

"Lowlife!" I tightened my grip, and the spear's blade glowed scarlet.

"That's it! Attack me!"

I thrust the spear toward Khaf, but he deflected it with his dagger. Brilliant scarlet and golden flashes sparked from our blades, and the force pushed me backward. I stumbled and fell on my back.

I shook my head, trying to regain my senses while Khaf's silhouette paced frantically.

My vision refocused. Black lines formed on his body, drawing indecipherable hieroglyphs across his chest.

"What's happening to you?" I asked.

"I don't know!"

"What game are you playing?"

"I'm as surprised as you." Khaf sounded... hesitant? He studied the gibberish on his chest. "Hieroglyphs' original purpose was to record spells." He hummed. "It's worth a try, I suppose."

"What's worth a—"

Khaf tightened his grip on the dagger, and the hieroglyphs on his chest glowed gold. He stamped his foot, creating a massive wind that instantly propelled him fifty paces away from me.

My mouth dropped. How? He was fast, but not that fast! Nobody was.

Another explosion erupted in the distance, and Khaf reappeared before me, leaving a trail of raging sand behind him.

"That was *amazing!*" Khaf wasn't even panting. "It felt... *so* natural. Like I knew exactly what to do. As if I was awake, like *truly* awake, for the first time in—"

I hugged the spear and crawled away. "You *are* a sorcerer!"

"Oh, I wish," Khaf said. "Maybe it's a side effect of leaving Huat or..." He lowered his gaze toward his weapon. "My dagger? But how?"

"Did you steal the dagger from the temple?"

He shook his head. "My father gave it to me."

"So *he* stole it."

Khaf's smile disappeared. "My father forged it in his smithy. I was there. There's nothing special about this dagger except it being his gift to me."

"So, how do you explain your powers?"

Khaf hummed, then his eyes widened. "Tuya! *She* asked to hold my dagger. She cast the spell!"

Had Tuya granted the Hyksos magical powers? Was the woman stupid? No. She set up the spell to activate in the Land-Between-Realms, where nobody could know that she had assisted a Hyksos.

A shadow extended over me. My gaze rose to Khaf, who gave me a strange stare.

"Stop staring." I stood and dusted off my white dress, ignoring his stares.

"Why aren't you married yet?" he asked.

My gaze darted toward him. Where, in Ra's hidden name, had that come from? "I could ask you the same question, Hyksos. You're sixteen. Why aren't *you* married?"

He grinned. "So, you're keeping track of my age."

My cheeks burned, but I stood my ground. "You're embarrassed by the question, so you're trying to change the subject."

"I'm not."

"It's all right. I know why you're embarrassed."

"I'm not…" Khaf took a deep breath. "Why do you believe that?"

I had him. Gods, I had a clear shot at his intolerable ego.

"Of course. What woman would marry you? Even Hyksos women must have standards. That's why you wanted to become a priest. You gave up."

"I never wanted to become a priest." Khaf laughed, waving dismissively. "It was just an excuse to access the temple's library in preparation for the grand heist. If I wanted to get married tomorrow, Hyksos women would line up for my consideration. I came close to getting married once, actually. Gods, I dodged an arrow with that one."

"If you never sought priesthood, being unmarried means you are lying to yourself and me." I chuckled at his absurdity. "If I'm wrong, please tell me why the man who claims to drive women insane is still single."

"Maybe I have my eyes on someone." Khaf shrugged. "But *you're* Paser's sole apprentice. You're a catch, even if you're poor and fatherless."

Curse that thief! His ego was impenetrable.

I gazed toward the two half-merged green suns and held my left arm. Prolonging this conversation was pointless. I had to give him something.

"There's no guarantee of finishing my apprenticeship. Whomever I marry might end up with poor fatherless Nefiri, who failed in her career and couldn't care for her ill brother." I drew a deep breath. "Basically, where my life is at right now."

"Do you need those titles or a father to have value?" He flipped open the brown leather bag strapped across his upper body and fished out three small sacks. "You're smart and charming! Shouldn't that be enough?"

"Charming?" I swallowed. This was the exact opposite of comparing me to a cow. "What do you mean?"

"You're stupid." Khaf sighed and walked away.

"Excuse me?"

"For all your wits, Nefiri, you're an idiot sometimes."

I didn't answer. What was wrong with him? He flirted with me, only to insult me a moment later.

"Why so silent suddenly?" Khaf scooped some sand into his sacks.

"Why are we waiting before Ra's temple?" I asked, tapping my feet on the ground. "You're babbling on instead of explaining our journey to Set's prison."

"Well, after two years of constant insults, I'm finally getting to know the real you. Take my question about your marriage. It revealed plenty about you, even if the question didn't interest me."

"It didn't? Then why ask?"

"Why so disappointed?" He smirked. "Did you expect a proposal?"

Disappointed? Gods, no! I was irritated. "I wouldn't marry you if you were the last man in the world."

"Well, we are in the Land-Between-Realms, so I *am* the last man in the world."

"Lucky me," I scoffed.

"You're also the last woman in the world." Khaf stashed the sand-filled sacks in his leather bag. "Which isn't bad. You're quite pretty."

I drew a deep breath. Oh, how far the grand vizier's sole apprentice had fallen. The first man to call me pretty wasn't a prince or a nobleman. No. It was Khafset, the untouchable.

Khaf sighed. "I was complimenting you, Nefiri."

"That's your way of making fun of me."

"Not at all. You, Nefiri Minu, are indeed pretty. You don't have any competition in the Land-Between-Realms, so you win by default. Huat is a different story, though."

"Yes, the line of starstruck women who want to marry Khaf, the thief."

"What? No, no, you shouldn't compete with those women. I was referring to the cow."

I tightened my hand on Set's spear, glaring at the disgusting lowlife.

Khaf's infuriating, smug smile emerged. "Remember the cow?"

"I do. The one you kiss, you cow-loving untouchable."

"Oh, struck a nerve, have I?"

"You still haven't answered my question. So if you're done behaving as the lowlife you are, I'd like my answer now."

"Which one? You asked many questions."

"Answer them all!"

"Very well. Your reaction to the marriage question revealed that you desire companionship and love, despite thinking nobody would want to marry you. A criminally wrong assumption, by the way." He glanced at the merging suns. "Am I right so far?"

I fought the urge to nod. I failed. Curse him!

"As to what we seek in the Land-Between-Realms..." He pointed at the spear. "Draw an hourglass on the sand."

I humored the thief and drew two opposing triangles connected at their tips.

Khaf sat beside the drawing. "Imagine the hourglass's upper and lower triangles as Huat and Duat. In this analogy, the Land-Between-Realms would be the narrow neck. That's where we are."

I leaned on the spear and studied the drawing. "How will we reach the upper section?"

"We wait for the hourglass to flip."

My heart bumped against my chest, vibrating my ears. "Wh-what?"

"We wait for the world to turn upside down." Khaf glanced at the two merging green suns in the yellow sky. "They are almost united. Plant your spear in the sand, but keep its blade pointed upward."

"Why should I—"

"No time. Do it!" Khaf grabbed my hands and used them to plant the spear in the sand. He held me tight by my waist and pushed us together toward the weapon.

"What do you think you're doing?" I jerked to free myself from him.

"Let go, and we die."

I froze.

"Hold tight. Don't worry; I've got you."

"Why do you have to hold my waist?"

"I can't touch the spear, can I?"

Reluctantly, I endured Khaf's tight grip. The melting suns fused, and a green flash consumed the sky. A piercing screech swept the Land-Between-Realms, churning its waving sand into a frenzy.

My hair rose as if I was dangling from my feet. A force launched us toward the yellow sky. Khaf jerked, flipping us both. That's when the reality of our ascent to the heaven hit me. We weren't flying. Gods, we were falling! This wasn't a sky. It was another desert above our heads.

The hourglass had flipped.

"Hold tight, Nef!"

"What's happening?" I screamed.

Scarlet energy engulfed the spear and spiraled around us, decreasing the speed of our descent. The spear hit the sand, and we fell beside it.

The desert was filled with countless statues of human-shaped hyenas holding curved swords. About fifty paces from us sat a giant lion-headed man on his haunches. He slumbered before a massive misty gate, holding a butcher's knife twice my size. His breathing vibrated the sand beneath my chin.

I knelt, only for my heart to freeze when the surrounding statues shook.

"Stop. Moving," Khaf said, still lying on his stomach. "Or you'll wake him."

"What is he?" I asked.

"Shemzu, the god of blood. Osiris's executioner, slaughterer of souls, protector of the death-gate, and, most importantly, our first obstacle."

Chapter 7

Osiris's Executioner

The death-gate's black mist raged behind the slumbering god of blood. His golden fur rustled in the wind, reflecting a flickering light on the desolate landscape of skeletons around him. Leaning on his human-sized butcher knife, blood dripped from his long fangs, staining the surrounding graveyard red.

There was no chance I was getting anywhere near Shemzu. Even if I dared to approach him, which I didn't, my body remained paralyzed.

"The hyenas' statues aren't shaking anymore." Khaf was still lying on his stomach. "I think they register movement."

Large movements, perhaps. Speaking was technically a movement.

"Hey, Nef. Talk to me."

I swallowed but couldn't speak. This had to be a dream—a grim nightmare.

"I'm scared, too," Khaf said. "There's no shame in—"

"I hate you. *You* brought me here."

"Technically, Nefertari sent—"

"You're the reason I touched that cursed spear. Why couldn't you have just sold me the medical seeds?"

Khaf didn't respond. Of course, he didn't. What could he say?

"I promised to protect you," Khaf said. "You *will* return home unharmed."

"I'm not going anywhere."

"Are you staying here forever?"

"That's the plan, yes. Why move and die while I can stay still and live?"

"You'll move, eventually. A sneeze, a muscle spasm, or you'll fall asleep, and the hyenas will break free."

Curse him; he was right.

"Let's run as fast as we can to the death-gate," Khaf said.

"No!" I glared at him. The hyenas didn't react. So sound and eye movements didn't trigger them. "Hyenas are faster than humans."

"Damn it!"

"Just—give me a moment to think."

Thirty-six statues stood along the seventy paces that separated us from Shemzu. How would we get past them? Khaf got us here, so he might have useful information I could use to save us. Maybe just this once, if I wanted to reunite with my brother, I could swallow my pride and ask the Hyksos for his knowledge.

"Explain how we got here," I said.

"What do you mean?"

"You awaited the suns' merger and spoke as if knowing a particular path to access the death-gate."

"A scroll in Set's temple mentioned duality. I noticed the two suns fusing and assumed the spear could pull us toward the death-gate when they merged."

That was... brilliant! Did a Hyksos outsmart me? His logic made perfect sense. Shemzu was the god of blood and wine. Slaughterer of the wicked and protector of the virtuous. The god represented duality.

Wait, that didn't explain all of Khaf's behavior. "Why did you hold me?"

"I wanted to keep you safe. If you die, I can kiss my accord with your queen goodbye."

"Nefertari doesn't care about me. The spear should choose you out of necessity if I die. So why care for my safety?"

He paused, his eyes scanning the statues. "What a surprisingly good question."

Was it stupid to ask? Maybe. However, if *I* recognized that my death could benefit Khaf, *he* sure thought of it. I had to understand his schemes to protect myself from his wicked tendencies.

"I'm still waiting for an answer, Khafset."

"Setu." Khaf's gaze held mine. "The stupid clerk loves you. I'm protecting you because I care about *him*. Your death would break his heart."

A Hyksos. In love with me? Setu? The man trembled each time he saw me. I'd always assumed it was out of fear. Did he really…

No! Focus on Osiris's executioner.

"We were mirroring each other's position when we landed," I said. "The hyenas didn't react when we achieved our version of duality. Do you see the hyena standing to your right?"

Khaf's gaze wandered over to him. "Yes."

"When I give you a signal, we both move our heads in its direction."

"What signal?"

"I don't know. Something that doesn't need major movement."

Khaf grinned. "Wink at me."

"Excuse me?"

"It's a minor movement."

"I could just speak."

"Visual cues are faster and more reliable."

"There's no way I'll wink at you, Hyksos!"

"Do it for your country. Yes, wink at me for Egypt."

I glared at the lowlife, weighing my options. What was more painful? The shame of winking at him or agonizing death by Shemzu's hyenas?

"Fine," I hissed.

Khaf's smug smile reached its full width. "Nice."

I took a deep breath, cursing the lowlife, then winked.

"What was that?!" Khaf asked.

"I winked."

"Is that how you wink? Gods, I thought you were having a stroke."

I couldn't tell whether he was joking, which made him more irritating than usual.

"Fine. I won't wink."

"There, there. Don't frown. I'll wink at you."

I released the air trapped in my lungs.

"But try not to faint," he said.

Gods, I wanted to shove Set's spear down his throat.

The smiling Hyksos winked. We turned our heads toward the hyena on Khaf's right side. Our eyes remained locked to keep our sync. We returned our heads to their original position.

The hyenas did not react.

"It worked!" Khaf said. "Paser didn't oversell you. You really *are* smart!"

I fought the urge to return his smile. Yeah, I, too, could figure stuff out on my own. "If I jump to my feet, could you mirror my movement?"

"Yes."

Of course. Asking a thief if he could run and jump was like asking a bird if it could fly. "I will count to three, and we will reach for Set's spear together." I glanced at the spear lying between us. "The moment we touch it, we jump and turn its blade toward the ground. We'll break our sync for a moment since I have to touch the spear first, and you'll have to lay your hands on top of mine. But we should be fine if we don't linger."

"Understood."

"One. Two. Three."

I grabbed the spear. Khaf's quick reflexes kicked in. He caught my hands, avoiding the weapon's curse. I jumped, and Khaf swiftly rose from his stomach. We turned the spear in midair. Unlike Khaf, who landed steadily as a palm tree, I stumbled. Khaf tightened his rugged grip on my hand, preventing me from falling back. He leaned back to mirror my stance and pushed our hands down to anchor the spear in the sand.

Shemzu's petrified soldiers surrounded us as we held tight to each other, leaning away from the spear. They didn't move much. Thank the gods!

"You... you got me?" I asked.

"Always."

Khaf pulled us toward the spear. I gasped for air while his honey eyes gazed into my soul. Curse him and those eyes!

"Hey, Khaf."

"Yes, Nef?"

"Why are you staring at me?"

"You know. Duality and such."

"You're disgusting."

"I try."

There was no use teaching proper manners to an untouchable. "Just walk sideways toward the gate."

"Like crabs?!"

"What are crabs?"

Khaf chuckled. "Never mind."

We walked toward the death-gate, Khaf's warm hands on top of mine. How many crimes had his hands committed? How many lives had they ruined besides mine?

Khaf fell silent, his eyes scanning the desert. I had his undivided attention a moment ago, but now it was as if I didn't exist.

"Something wrong?" I asked.

"Did you hear that?"

"Hear what?"

"I've been hearing something in the distance since we arrived in the Land-Between-Realms."

"You're imagining things. It happens when people are stressed."

"Oh, I'm not stressed at all. I think this is all lovely."

"No sane person, Egyptian or Hyksos, could think this is lovely."

"Don't undersell our situation. We're wandering together through the Land-Between-Realms. Soon we'll pass through the death-gate and enter Duat. I have a literal god beside me, Set's spear in my hands, and your lovely face before me."

"Something is very wrong with you, Khafset."

"I'm crazy, aren't I? Maybe that's why I called the grand vizier's apprentice pretty. I meant it, you know."

"Lucky me. A thief finds me pretty."

"Thieves are very good at identifying beauty."

I filtered out Khaf's idle chatter and focused on my movements, ignoring my increasing heartbeats. Lovely, pretty, and beautiful? Me? Lies! No man could call any woman pretty after witnessing Queen Nefertari—terrifying as she was. Compared to her, I was... no, focus!

One step to the right.

Pause.

Another step.

Pause.

Another step and... Crack!

My heart stopped. Khaf's breathing intensified. I tightened my grip on Set's spear. On the sand beside me lay the hyena's statue I had just bumped into in my stupidity.

Khaf pressed my hands. "Stay still. Maybe the hyena won't—"

The statue shook. Cracks slithered along its rough surface, releasing the creature's chilling growls. The rocky layer around the creature broke, and from its debris, Shemzu's monstrous soldier rose on its hind limbs. It growled, dripping saliva from its snout onto its brown fur as its red eyes glared at us.

Khaf shoved his bag against my chest. "Hold on to this."

"What are you—"

The monster roared at Khaf. It jumped high into the sky, centering itself between the colliding suns. I craned my head toward the dark silhouette. Khaf pushed me. The hyena landed where we stood and struck the sand with its black sword.

Khaf grabbed his dagger and tightened his grip on its hilt. The hieroglyphs on his chest flashed. He bolted in circles around the hyena, raising the sand and creating a cylindrical wall around the creature. The Hyksos jumped, his blade pointed at the monster's head. He landed on the hyena and delivered a deadly blow to its skull.

The remaining statues shook, groans escaping from the numerous cracks forming on their surface.

"Run!" Khaf raced toward the death-gate's black mist.

I ran after him, still holding his bag and the spear. The first free hyenas chased us. Judging by their vicious giggles, they were approaching at a speed we had no chance of outpacing.

"Use the dagger's magic and leave me! You don't have to die with—"

"I'm not going anywhere without you!"

The monsters encircled us. Khaf and I turned, our backs stuck to each other as we searched for an escape. There was none. The hyenas roared, shaking my world with their resonating voices. They charged to deliver their lethal blows like a deadly storm. My knees lost their remaining nerves, and I stumbled. Khaf's bag fell. I hit the ground with Set's spear, preventing my collapse, piercing the bag with its blade.

This was it. My death. Killed by Shemzu's hyenas in the Land-Between-Realms before the death-gate. Not an awful way to die, really. It was too glorious for me.

A breeze of scarlet smoke evaporated from the spear's tip. The hyenas froze, one of their curved swords an inch away from my face. Khaf froze, too, his dagger ready to stab the hyena's neck to save me.

Behind Shemzu, a mirage freed itself from the death-gate's mist. A black-furred man with a mythical sha's head. His long red braids floated with the black mist. Set!

The god of destruction's phantom faded and reformed behind me. He lowered his snout beside my ears and whispered an incomprehensible phrase.

"Ga'ab Neyat?" I mimicked Set's words.

Scarlet energy spiraled down the spear's metal. Set's magic leaked into the sand and slithered in a circular pattern, feeding a semi-transparent scarlet dome around Khaf and me.

Set whispered another phrase in my ears.

"Shama'at Morot!"

A massive pulse launched from the spear. The sand exploded, creating a swirling vortex around the protective dome. A scarlet inferno erupted from the ocean of fine golden grains. Shemzu's hyenas burned in Set's flames of destruction. Their fur evaporated, and their bodies, down to their bones, melted into nothingness.

Set's phantom lowered its clawed hand onto my shoulder. *Come to me, my chosen.* His words echoed in my head. *Bring me my spear.*

I collapsed with Set's destructive flames and protective dome.

Khaf unfroze and slashed the air where the dead hyena's neck was supposed to be. "What the..." He spun and studied the empty desert where only he, I, and Shemzu remained.

"Where did the hyenas go?" Khaf asked. "Nef, are you all right?"

"I used his magic!" I cried. "Oh, gods, forgive me. I tapped into Set's cursed magic."

"*You* destroyed the hyenas?!"

I ignored him, consumed by a strange obsession with my sin. Was it a sin? Of course! Why though? I didn't care!

"That's Baal's power working through you!" Khaf's mouth dropped. "How powerful is Set himself, then?" His confused face studied me. "Are you—"

A roar shook the desert. Khaf lost his footing and fell beside me. Fifty paces from us, across the ocean of raging sand, before the death-gate's violent black mist, Shemzu, the god of blood, rose from his slumber.

"Mortals!" Shemzu freed his butcher's knife from the sand. "Undead souls outside Huat!" He stretched out his arm toward me, trapping me in the accusing stare of his red eyes. His gaze sparked a raging guilt through the fiber of my being.

You sinned! Countless voices screamed in my head, pulling me toward the only being capable of offering me salvation. I walked toward Shemzu, holding Set's spear and Khaf's bag.

"What are you doing?" Khaf reached for my arm. Shemzu waved his hand. An invisible force pushed Khaf behind me.

I ignored Khaf's curses and marched toward the god of blood.

"O great Shemzu. I, Nefiri, the sinner of Peramessu, ask for your divine punishment."

"Nefiri, you idiot, come back! He's controlling you!"

Lies! Shemzu wasn't controlling me. I willingly desired nothing more than to be torn apart by the slaughterer of souls.

Blood leaked from the graveyard of skeletons beneath Shemzu's feet. It oozed above his head, forming a liquid crimson sphere.

Yes. Approach your god, mortal. The voices screamed in my head. *You know what you've done. You've endangered your brother. Disappointed your master. Betrayed your country. Fancied the descendant of those who enslaved your people. Accept your punishment, sinner.*

Yes, that was the truth I hid from everyone. The great sin I wished to deny. In my moments of weakness, I did fancy the untouchable.

"I accept my punishment, O great Shemzu." I rushed toward Osiris's executioner. "Show me no mercy, for I deserve none. O great Shemzu, please—"

Idiot! Set said. His empowering presence overtook me. My grip tightened on his spear, and his phantom reemerged around my body like armor. Set forced my hand to stab the sand with the spear's blade.

"Ga'ab Neyat!" Set forced me to say.

Shemzu roared. He launched six arrows of blood from the crimson sphere above his head. They collided with the scarlet dome's protective surface and resolved into nothingness. Set's spell was pure power. His Destruction magic was superior to Shemzu's Blood magic.

"Nef!" Khaf screamed behind me. He stood at the end of a trail of raging sand at least forty paces from where I'd left him. Blood covered his injured arm and dripped from his hands onto the sand.

The fog covering my mind faded. Where... What had just... Khaf! Gods, he was bleeding!

I ran toward the Hyksos, shattering the surrounding dome.

Khaf's face grew pale. "Watch out!" The hieroglyphs on his chest pulsed. He bolted forward and grabbed me in his sprint.

We came to an agonizing halt that shifted my organs. Shemzu rose from where I had stood a heartbeat ago. He would've killed me! Did... did Khaf... oh gods, he saved my life!

"You can run, mortals, but you cannot outrun me forever, for I, Shemzu, am the executioner of Osiris, and you shall not enter Duat alive."

"He's right." Khaf pointed his dagger at the god of blood. "Shemzu! I, Khafset of Avaris, challenge you to battle!"

"What are you doing, idiot?"

"Shemzu is a warrior god. He can't resist my challenge."

"That's not the point!"

The slaughterer of souls pointed his butcher's knife at Khaf. "And I, Shemzu, the god of blood, accept your challenge."

"Told you." Khaf winked. "Run to the death-gate the moment you see an opening." He walked toward the god. "Trust me, Egyptian."

"Khafset, stop!"

He ignored me.

This insane Hyksos was challenging a literal god! Was he stupid or brave? A thief or a hero? I didn't know. But one thing was as clear as the colliding green suns. He was a madman.

Khaf stood before the slaughterer of souls. "Let it be known in Huat and Duat that I, Khafset of Avaris, fought the great Shemzu to the death!"

The writings on Khaf's chest pulsed. He charged, his body ablaze with a brilliant golden light. The sand rose in great billowing clouds as Khaf clashed head-on with Shemzu. Their blades met in a deafening clash, sparking a wave of crackling energy. The thief and the god raced across the vast desert, the sand surging behind them in a frenzy. Their steps shook the ground, unleashing a storm of crimson and golden flashes that exploded from the clash of Khaf's enchanted dagger and Shemzu's Blood magic.

Now was my chance. I ran toward the death-gate, the sand beneath my feet rippling from Shemzu's roars.

You should be ashamed! Set said.

I collapsed from his overwhelming presence and dropped his spear and Khaf's bag.

"Get out of my head!"

Shame! The Hyksos fights a god while you run like a coward!

"I'm too weak to fight a cat, let alone the lion god!"

We'll see.

Scarlet energy consumed Set's spear, and his power pulsed inside me. My skin burned, and the cursed hisses returned to consume my thoughts. Set's power exploded inside me, granting me that amazing feeling that there wasn't a thing in the world I couldn't destroy. I grabbed his spear and rose.

Yes! Rise, my chosen. Remind those fools of how powerful Set, the Baal of storms, truly is.

I turned toward the raging battle, Set's phantom forming around my body. Guided by Set, I pointed the spear toward the god of blood.

"Shemzu!" My amplified voice shook the Land-Between-Realms.

The god punched Khaf, thrusting the Hyksos toward an explosive crash into the sand.

"Look at me, Shemzu!" Set's growling voice echoed mine. "I am Nefiri Minu of Peramessu!" Set's deep voice overtook mine. "I will defeat you, Shemzu!"

Blood leaked from the crimson sphere above Shemzu's head. It painted his golden fur and black knife red. "I will destroy you and your chosen, Set!" He shot a stream of blood from his butcher's knife toward me.

I took Khaf's viper stance and pointed the spear at the crimson river of death that raged toward me.

"Shama'at Morot!"

A scarlet beam launched from the spear. The magical energies of the gods of destruction and blood collided, vibrating the ocean of sand beneath my feet. The beams annihilated each other in a brilliant red explosion that consumed the desert with its glow and pushed me onto my back.

I coughed, trying to pull myself up again to sit. What happened? What took over me? Why didn't I just run through the death-gate?

Shemzu lay motionless on his back. A soft moan caught my attention. Khaf rose to his feet, rubbing his chest. Gods, he was still alive! How? He'd fallen to his death!

I grabbed Set's weapon and Khaf's bag. I took a step toward Khaf. Shemzu growled.

I froze. "S-Set! Where are you? I... I still need your help."

He didn't answer. I couldn't feel his presence.

"Damned mortal!" Shemzu's back rose.

As all hope left me, a neigh captured my attention. A blue mare bolted across the desert, uninterested in the livid god of blood.

What... The noise Khaf had been hearing! No wonder he couldn't describe it! Gods, the horse's speed alone was indescribable!

The mare came to a halt, shifting the countless silver grains that sparkled underneath her blue skin. Her golden eyes stared at me. She neighed and snaked her head toward her brilliant red saddle.

Shemzu rose. I jumped on the mare's back, held tight to her reins, and... froze.

Should I save Khaf? But I might die. Hote needed me. I had to survive for his sake. But Khaf had fought a god to save me. I couldn't just abandon him, could I? Gods, what should I do? I needed...

The horse turned without my command and galloped in Khaf's direction. No, she didn't gallop. There must've been another word for her speed. She was faster than an arrow.

Khaf jumped onto the horse in front of me. He swung her reins, and we bolted toward the death-gate.

"Filthy mortals!" Shemzu said, the sky above us turning crimson. Blood leaked from the sand and turned the desert into a crimson swamp. Arrows of blood filled the sky, obscuring the colliding suns, all directed at us.

I pointed the spear's tip at the sky. "Ga'ab Neyat!" A scarlet shield formed above us, protecting us from Shemzu's magic as we entered Duat through the death-gate's black mist.

Chapter 8

The Field of Reeds

The glowing emerald grass gently tickled my back, easing my sore muscles. A celestial blue stream shimmered in the sparkling dark sky and illuminated the towering reeds. The tall plants swayed in the gentle breeze, their golden hue dancing in harmony with the shadows to the magical melodies of the harp that played out whenever the wind brushed through the ethereal flowers.

"The Field of Reeds," Khaf said. "We made it!"

"We really *are* in Duat!" I turned to Khaf, leaving a glowing green print where my back had pressed against the grass.

Khaf's honey eyes shifted toward me, his face dark. Why did he look so gloomy? Had he noticed my hesitation to save him?

"You were going to abandon me, weren't you?" he asked.

Yep, he'd noticed. "Of course not!"

This, technically, wasn't a lie. I didn't abandon him. He... I was still assessing the situation and weighing the viable... well, it wasn't my fault the horse decided for me! I still could've saved him.

"I saw you looking at the death-gate," Khaf said.

"The spear stopped working, and a good politician never jumps into an unknown—"

Khaf gave me a dismissive wave. He stood, triggering another wave of soft tunes from the vibrating reeds.

Why didn't he let me finish? Khaf, annoying as he was, had always given me a chance to explain myself. *Then* he would dismiss my logic. What was different now?

"Are you mad at me?" I asked.

"Mad? I'm thankful. Each time I forget, you remind me you're just another Egyptian."

Khaf walked toward the horse. He traced the shifting silver particles underneath her blue skin, then murmured something in a strange language.

I stood, brushed the leaves off my white dress, then approached Khaf and the horse, leaving a trail of glowing footprints behind me. No need to dwell on his sudden cold attitude. He was Khaf, the thief. Any moment now, he would crack an unfunny joke.

"What's that language?" I asked.

"The Canaanite language."

"Didn't know you spoke another language." I tried to suppress my growing annoyance that he wouldn't look at me.

"Your soldiers cut out Hyksos' tongues for speaking it."

That was a lie. I'd never punished a Hyksos for not speaking Egyptian. Those lowlifes gave me plenty of other reasons. Everything from disobedience to murder. They always denied my Medjay's allegations, of course, but my master had taught me better.

"What did you say to the horse?" I asked.

"I was thanking the goddess for her gift."

"Goddess?"

"Astarte. I've read about her horse at Set's temple. How typical. She gifted the horse to an Egyptian instead of a Hyksos."

"She's an Egyptian goddess. Pharaoh Ahmose returned her cult to Egypt after conquering Avaris and defeating—"

"Do you wish to anger me even more?" he asked in a chilling, low tone.

"No." That was the truth. "I'm sorry." That was a lie. "Does she have a name?"

"Ishtar."

I patted the horse's neck. "We are grateful for your help, Ishtar." I smiled at Khaf. "Her name is quite—"

"We need to rest." He walked away.

Oh, the nerve! Here I was ready to speak to him, and he simply left. He didn't even ask if I was hurt. True, I wasn't, but he didn't know that, and he knew... a lot!

"Hey, Khaf."

"What?" He sat on the glowing grass that gathered itself to form a cushion.

"How did you survive Shemzu's punch? And why isn't your arm bleeding anymore?"

"Tuya's enchantment helped." He opened his bag and took out a folded blanket, three sacks, and a scroll. "And I'm a tough guy."

"No human is that tough!"

He filled the sacks with glowing grass and parts of the reeds. "Your damned soldiers toughened me up early in life."

"You wouldn't have survived our soldiers if they were as evil as you claim."

"Evil? They are *vile*. I might be a thief, but at least *I* don't murder innocents and accuse the ones I spare of false crimes so *you* can punish them."

I clenched my teeth but didn't dignify his ridiculous allegations with a response. None were punished for a false crime under my watch. None!

"How did you discover the path to Set's prison?" I returned to the original line of questioning. "And why do you keep collecting stuff in those sacks?"

"The sacks are none of your business!" He took a deep breath and gazed toward the blue stream in the dark heaven.

"And I told you, I prepared for the grand heist during my fake apprenticeship in Set's temple."

"Yeah, but in two months? That's complicated theological knowledge. You couldn't have—"

"Oh, for Baal's sake!" His finger pierced through the tear I had punctured in his bag. "How did you stab my bag?!"

"It was an accident! I stumbled and planted the spear into the ground to stop myself from falling. The bag was in the way."

"Nothing is ever your fault!" He fished in the bag for some dark bread and a clay water bottle. "It's always something evil that forces good, pure Nefiri to act against her flawless nature." He drank his water, then pointed the clay bottle at me. "Never your fault. Ever! Always someone else's."

"Fine, I get it! Sorry for stabbing a hole in your precious bag that doesn't even belong to you!"

Khaf slammed the bottle down on the soft grass. He unrolled the scroll and fell silent.

I rolled my eyes. No. I wouldn't indulge his vulgar behavior. I sat at a spot near him and put my blanket around my shoulders, then ate my bread and drank my water. I didn't need him for safety, of course. We just didn't know what lurked in the dark Field of Reeds and needed to watch each other's backs. Yes, my decision to remain near him was based entirely on mutual benefit.

The infuriating Hyksos kept his attention on his reading while I ate the last chunk of bread. I wouldn't talk to the thief. The first word would never be mine. I deserved respect.

What made that scroll so fascinating, anyway? I sat before the man, ready to speak, but he chose to read instead of conversing with me. Gods, such an infuriating, vulgar, uncivilized…

"What are you reading?" Curse my curiosity!

"Our route." Khaf didn't look at me.

At least he was talking to me again. Yes, no reason to stop now.

"To Set's prison?" I asked.

"What do you think?"

I rolled my eyes. "And where is that? I think it's about time you share—"

"It's in Abydos."

"What's that?" He didn't answer, and I sighed. "Why are you mad at me, Khafset?"

His eyes darted toward me.

"Didn't you tell me to escape when I saw an opening?" I asked. "Well, I saw one."

Khaf tossed the scroll aside and stared at me with narrowed eyes. "Was that before or after you fought Shemzu?"

I, too, could narrow my eyes, so I did and pushed my face closer to him. I saw an ostrich do that once, and she looked terrifying. "You would have done the same."

Khaf moved his face closer to mine. "I didn't, though."

"Fine." I was an ostrich. Yes, a big, scary ostrich. I squinted my eyes even more and pushed my head forward.

Our noses touched.

"Would you have hesitated to save me if I were an Egyptian?"

"Of course, I would have—"

"Liar!" Khaf pulled away, and I almost gasped when he took his warm breath with him. "You would've saved me without hesitation. That's what they teach you, isn't it? The untouchables of Avaris are a worthless lot. Look me in the eyes and tell me I'm wrong!"

I lowered my head to avoid his accusing gaze. Would I have saved an Egyptian? I was afraid to die and leave Hote alone. But I was the grand vizier's apprentice. My duty was to sacrifice myself for the people of Egypt. Which side would've won? My love or my sense of duty. Oh, it always came down to that, didn't it?

"Honestly... I don't know."

Khaf scoffed. He lay on his side and pulled his blanket over him.

I wiped my cheek, gathering the dampness on my finger. Was that a tear? Had I shed a tear for a Hyksos? No, that wasn't possible. Was it? What I had done was awful, wasn't it? Khaf had fought a god to save me while I fled. Set spoke the truth. I should be ashamed of myself.

"Hey, Khaf."

He didn't answer. Why should he? I'd told him his life was worthless.

"Khaf, you're annoying, infuriating, and sometimes scary."

"Stop talking!" Khaf jumped to his knees, his honey eyes glaring at me. "I know you hate—"

"You and Setu are also the closest thing I've ever had to real friends. It might be difficult to believe, but I did look out for you in my own way."

"Yeah, that *is* hard to believe."

"I ordered the soldiers at Set's temple not to harass Setu, and I moved the Medjay away from the neighborhoods where you were stealing. My master punished me countless times for my 'poor judgment.' He wasn't wrong. I broke the law and compromised my integrity to get Hote's medicine. I'm not perfect. But I am also not the heartless monster you think I am."

Khaf opened his mouth. He hesitated, shifting his blanket around his shoulders. "I... didn't know that."

"As the grand vizier's apprentice, I had to be strict and ruthless. Hote's life and our family's future depended on it. However, I tried to show mercy whenever I could, but—"

"Egypt doesn't allow us to be merciful; otherwise, it will crush us."

I nodded. "We aren't in Egypt anymore. Whatever danger awaits us in Duat doesn't care about our peoples'... disagreements. We should be able to trust each other if we want to return home." I gathered my strength and gazed into his honey eyes. "I will not apologize for abandoning you because I didn't. But, I'm sorry, I hesitated to save you when I could. Next time, I *will* save you."

Khaf smiled, and now, following the realization that I might've never seen his smile again, I found it to be somewhat comforting and even, dare I say, pleasant.

He began rolling back to his sleeping spot. "Good night, Nefiri."

"Wait." I stretched out my arm toward him, glancing at his scroll. "Tell me about Abydos before you sleep?"

"No. I'm tired and not in the mood."

"*Please.* I can't sleep otherwise."

Khaf sighed. He crossed his legs and shifted toward me. "The desolated city of Abydos is cursed. Isis moved it to Duat to become Set's prison."

"Why?"

"During the ancient war of the gods, Set killed Osiris and claimed Egypt's throne. He cut his brother into fourteen pieces and scattered his remains across The Two Lands. Isis gathered her husband's parts but couldn't find his heart. She disguised herself as a mortal and asked the people of Abydos for her husband's organ, but the city's inhabitants couldn't give her the heart. Their king had eaten it."

"What?!"

"If you eat a god's heart, you gain their power. But the poor king didn't have the chance to enjoy his godhood. His family devoured him in his sleep, and during the same night, the people of Abydos stormed the palace and ate them. Isis revived her husband, but Osiris couldn't return to Huat without his heart. He remained here in the Field of Reeds."

My stomach turned, and I fought the urge to vomit.

"Something wrong?" Khaf asked.

"When I fought Shemzu, I sensed Set's presence. When he left me, emptiness consumed me."

"You felt Set?"

I nodded, disgusted by the memory of the wonderful feeling his magic had given me.

"Interesting."

"Do you know why that happened?"

"No, but it explains how Ishtar was able to track us."

I sighed. "The only god to help is the god of destruction. The most wicked among our deities."

"Set is a good god."

"I really don't understand why you, Hyksos, love him so much."

"Before the war of the gods, Ra skipped Set and chose Osiris as his heir. Following his wife's betrayal, Set left Egypt and moved to Canaan. My ancestors called him Baal, or Lord, in their tongue. They worshiped him as their god of storms. The faith of mortals is a god's primary source of power, and my people's love for him made our Baal mighty enough to defeat Osiris."

"Why didn't your Baal stay in Canaan, then?"

"Set wished to claim Egypt's throne and unify Egypt and Canaan under his rule."

"Well, good thing Horus defeated him. We Egyptians are doing very well on our own, thank you very much."

Khaf gave a dismissive wave. "There is no use talking to you Egyptians."

"I'm just saying, take Set or Baal and return to Canaan. Don't you miss your ancestral land?"

"Egypt *is* my ancestral land."

I chuckled at the absurdity. "No, Khaf. Egypt is our land, not yours."

"Really?" Khaf's smug smile emerged. "And why is that?"

"Well, for one thing, I was born in Egypt."

"So was I."

"My parents too."

"So were mine and those of every Hyksos born in the past five hundred years." Khaf smiled at a glowing blue scarab crawling on his black kilt. "My father loved to wander the streets of Avaris. Like any Egyptian, he loved fishing and coloring the eggs during the spring festival."

"Well, it's not your land! Never again! Egypt belongs to the Egyptians!"

"We *are* Egyptians."

"You most definitely are not! We welcomed your ancestors in Egypt, and how did they repay our kindness? You usurped the throne and enslaved us in our lands. If Pharaoh Ahmose hadn't freed us, you would've been the one calling me an untouchable."

"Sounds interesting. How would you feel about being called an untouchable?"

I opened my mouth and closed it. Twice. Me? An untouchable?

Khaf pulled his blanket over his shoulders. "Sleep, Nef. We have a long day tomorrow." He winked, then lay on his side.

I did the same, but I couldn't sleep.

I'd always thought the Hyksos of our time deserved their suffering for the deeds of their malicious ancestors. There had been generations of Egyptians who suffered under Hyksos rule. What if the Hyksos ruled again? Wouldn't they say the same about us Egyptians? Absolutely!

My master spoke the truth. He always did. The Hyksos of Avaris were our greatest threat.

Chapter 9

Memories of Loss

"We've been walking for hours, and I still don't know where we're heading." I tried to speak over the tunes of the swaying reeds.

Khaf continued his jog ahead of Ishtar and me. He had been testing me about the gods ever since we began our hike. Probably to enjoy my lack of theological knowledge. The previous night, I had discovered that the thief was the religious type when I overheard him praying. A devout thief. Perfect! Why not, at this point?

"Khafset!"

He pointed at the glowing blue stream in the black sky. "Do you know what that is?"

"Assume my answer is always no."

"That's the divine Nile. It flows from the Field of Reeds to the scarlet desert, where the Abydos-gate is located. We need to sail the divine Nile, and for that, we need Ra's solar barque."

"You want to hitch a ride with Ra!" My mouth dropped. "You're insane!"

Khaf stretched his arms out on either side, brushing harp melodies out of the glowing reeds. "I got us into the Field of Reeds. Alive! Of course I'm insane."

Ra's barque? The king of the gods himself! Maybe asking Khaf to walk beside me wasn't a bad idea. The Field of Reeds could be dangerous and, well, I didn't want to walk alone!

"Hey, Khaf. No need to run. You can... walk beside me."

Khaf grinned. "Do you want me beside you?"

"I didn't say that! I just want you to stop running!"

He sighed and turned away from me. "I'm walking, Nef."

Curse that stubborn man! "Well, you walk like a thief!"

"I walk like a survivor. Had to keep light feet while on the Egyptian side of Peramessu."

I rolled my eyes. "Couldn't you just get a job?"

"As a Hyksos?" He slowed to walk beside Ishtar and me. Finally! "Ignorance truly is bliss."

"Many Hyksos work in Avaris. Take your father and Setu, for example."

"Your stolen coins paid for Setu's expensive education, and my father, despite being the best blacksmith in Avaris, couldn't feed us because of your greedy kings and their taxes."

"At least your father didn't abandon you like mine did. I struggled to feed Hote. Didn't become a thief, though."

"Yeah, you definitely didn't steal those coins from Paser."

"*You* forced me to steal them. I wished you could've asked for another payment."

"Well... there were other forms of payment, but I thought the grand vizier's sole apprentice was above them."

I scoffed at the lowlife. "You're a disgusting man."

"And you are a hopeless woman. Why can't you admit you're a brilliant thief? You're not Paser's apprentice anymore. You're finally free from all that nonsense. Why do you have to fake cruelty to satisfy a system that accuses you of treason?"

I took a deep breath, then focused on the glowing reeds and the blue lotus's watery smell to calm my irritated nerves. Was I a traitor? Maybe. But my master promised amnesty once I'd saved the pharaoh. I shouldn't lose faith. I shouldn't.

"Hey, Nef. Talk to me."

"Your mother."

"Excuse me?"

"You never mention the woman who raised the delightful pile of Hyksos annoyance walking beside me."

"She died during childbirth."

"Oh! I'm sorry."

"Spare me your fake condolences."

"They aren't fake, all right? My mother died during childbirth as well. But at least *you* had a loving father."

"Yeah."

"Maybe you should return your father's love and help him in his smithy."

"I will return to the smithy after the grand heist."

My mouth dropped. "Really?"

"Yes."

"Amazing! Good for you." I tapped his arm and whistled. "No more Khaf the thief, only Khaf, the blacksmith. It's the end of an era."

"It sure will be." The sudden gaze of his honey eyes startled me. "What about your father?"

"What about him?"

"You barely mention him."

"Because he doesn't deserve it." I tightened my grip on Ishtar's reins. Gods, blood boiled in my veins each time someone mentioned that man.

"Was he that cruel?"

"Dad was the sweetest man. He brought me amazing gifts from across Egypt. That is until Mom died, and he discovered Hote's illness. He became obsessed with reading and stopped traveling. Seven years ago, he left and never returned. Thank Taweret, Aunt Meriti moved in after Mom's death; otherwise, Hote and I would've died."

"So your father left after Seti's death?"

"He was King Seti's messenger. He couldn't just leave an employer like him." I blew out the fragrance-filled air from my lungs. "I don't want to speak of him."

"Your dad can't be that evil. He paid for your education, didn't he?"

"Probably to marry me off to some nobleman. Joke's on him. I was the best in my class. When he left, and I couldn't pay for school, my teacher introduced me to Master Paser, and my master sponsored my education and took me in as his apprentice when I came of age."

"So that's why you love Paser so much."

"I owe everything to him. My master was a kinder father than Sutmheb ever was."

Khaf froze in his tracks. I stopped with Ishtar and turned to him.

"Sutmheb? Is that your father's name? 'Set is in jubilation'!"

"So what? Pharaoh Seti was named after Set. Even you are named after the god of destruction, Khaf*set*. He is still a supreme god of the Ennead."

"I'm Hyksos, and Seti was a redhead. It makes sense we're named after Set. But your father is neither." Khaf's smile turned vicious, and I stepped back. "I struggled to answer your questions yesterday about Duat and the spear, while you had the perfect answer."

My heart pounded in my chest. "My father's name doesn't answer the questions I had. You know, the ones you still have to answer. And if you don't mind, I'd prefer it if you stopped talking about my father."

"How didn't you piece it together?" He walked toward me, his honey eyes glowing with intensity. "Your father's name *is* the answer to your questions."

"What?" I retreated, and he caught me.

"Sutmheb's disappearance. Meriti's refusal to mention him. Tuya pushing you toward your dad. Not to mention that your father's name means 'Set is in jubilation.'" He held my arms and shook me. "And Set's spear chose *you*, of all people!"

"Stop your nonsense, Hyksos!" I jerked away.

"Oh, Nef. Oh, Nefi, Nef, Nef. Everything makes sense now. Of course, the spear wouldn't just choose anybody. Something must be inherently special about the Chosen. Set must have a spawn." Khaf's smile widened, revealing his teeth. "You aren't a nobody. You're Set's daughter. A demigoddess."

Was my father a god? No, that couldn't be! Could it?

"No, it makes no sense. How could Dad be Set if he's shackled in Abydos?"

"Maybe a mortal acted as his vessel. A priest, perhaps. That would explain the name." Khaf's eyes widened. "Oh, I hope the vessel was a priest!"

"Wh-why?"

"Set's priests come from a single group of people." Khaf grinned and leaned on Ishtar's back. "Now, what do you enjoy calling those people?"

"Oh gods, no!" I jumped away from him.

"You could be half Hyksos!" Khaf's manic laughter erupted.

"No, no." I paced between the reeds, increasing the intensity of their melodies. "Lies! Nonsense! Sutmheb was the king's messenger. He was no Hyksos."

"How would anybody know?"

"Appearance."

"Oh, please. Ramesses has red hair. His skin is lighter than any Hyksos, and he's the king of Egypt. Looks aren't an indication, especially in the north. You'd be surprised how many North Egyptians have Hyksos ancestry. Why do you think we're trapped in Avaris? If we spread out across Egypt, we'll be impossible to recognize."

I shook my head, pacing before Khaf and Ishtar. No. No. No! I wasn't a demigoddess. I barely stood a chance against

Shemzu, even with Set's aid. Even Khaf was stronger than me. He didn't hesitate to trade blows with Osiris's executioner while I froze. But my dad was fair-skinned, and he was named after Set. He also ran away for no reason. I sure wasn't a demigoddess, but Sutmheb was... he might... oh gods, my dad could've been a runaway Hyksos masquerading as an Egyptian!

"Nef, are you all right?" Khaf caught me, bringing my pacing to a halt.

"Each time you open your cursed mouth, I—"

"Khafset." A hoarse man's voice called from behind me.

Khaf's eyes widened, his face turning pale. I turned. A trembling brown-haired man stood among the radiating reeds. He seemed familiar. Too familiar.

Khaf stepped back. "Dad?"

"Dad? What's your dad doing here?"

Khaf ran to his father and helped the old man sit on the grass. "This... this can't be."

"I'm freezing, son. I've built a camp. With a fire. Let's go there. Where it's warm."

"A camp?" Khaf asked. "What camp?"

"Come with me, son."

Khaf jumped away from his father. "Come with you where exactly?"

"Nef." A boyish voice called behind me, sending chills down my spine.

I turned toward the last voice I wanted to hear in the Field of Reeds. My brother stood there, shivering among the reeds and hugging himself with his little hands.

"Hote!" I ran to him. "How did you get here?"

"I... I don't know. I was shaking. Aunt Meriti hugged me until I fell asleep. She looked different. Big, Nef. Huge!" He hugged me, digging his face against my breast. "Nef, I'm scared. I want to go home. Let's go home."

"Yes. I will take you home. Whatever you want." If Hote wished for something, he should have it. Anything for my sweet little brother. Anything for his happiness.

"Nef!" Khaf called. "Nefiri!"

Khaf stood alone, holding his dagger. Blood dripped from his weapon onto his father, who lay on the ground.

"What happened to your dad?" I turned and hid Hote behind me. "Khafset, what did you do?"

He pointed his dagger at Hote. "Get away from that thing."

"Watch your mouth, Hyksos. He's my—"

"Get away from him! And look the other way."

"Nef, I'm scared." Hote tugged down on my dress. "The Hyksos scares me."

I grabbed Set's spear from behind my back and pointed it at the Hyksos. "Stay away from my brother!"

Khaf walked past Ishtar, whose glowing golden eyes shifted between us.

"Nef, I'm scared!" Hote pushed his face against my leg.

"Don't be scared." I patted his head. "I'll keep you safe. Your big sister will always protect you."

I planted Set's spear in the glowing emerald grass. The hieroglyphs on Khaf's chest flashed.

"Ga'ab Neyat!"

A semi-transparent scarlet dome formed around Hote and me, pushing against the reeds. The plants dissolved, and their soft melodies turned into a shriek.

Khaf bolted through the reeds, pushing their lights and melodies into a frenzy. He bumped into the protective dome's glassy surface. "Drop the shield, you idiot!"

"Stay away from my brother!" I hugged Hote with my free hand, keeping the spear planted in the now barren ground. "You're scaring him."

"Let's leave this place, Nef." Hote pulled my leg. "I know a way out."

"Yes, we must leave."

"This isn't your brother, you idiot; it's a Majuwd." Khaf walked back to his father's body. He returned, holding a bald black cat the size of a toddler. He shook the dead cat, flapping its leathery wings. "They are the shape-shifting guardians of the underworld. They know we don't belong in Osiris's kingdom. So break your damned dome before that thing you're protecting eats your soul."

"Nef, I'm freezing." Hote's pleading, innocent eyes stared up at me. "Take me home. Please. I want Aunt Meriti."

Tears fell down my cheeks. This wasn't a Majuwd. It couldn't be. It was Hote. Sweet little Hote for whom I sacrificed everything. This couldn't be a Majuwd because... my little Hote hadn't... No!

I gritted my teeth and glared at the Hyksos. "You're lying! The Majuwd can only depict the dead. Even *I* know that. Hote isn't dead." I smiled at my brother to comfort him. "He's alive and well. I'm holding him right now."

"My father died when I was seven, Nef! That's why the Majuwd—"

"Liar! You're trying to manipulate me as you always do!"

Khaf bit his lip and glanced at the divine Nile above us. "Idiot!" He raised his dagger and struck the shield but couldn't crack it. "Oh, you're such a naive little—" Khaf's eyes widened, and color left his face. "Watch out, Nef!"

A kick from behind brought me crashing to my knees. A tiny hand grabbed my hair and pulled me down onto my back. Hote jumped on me and pinned me to the ground. I struggled to free myself, but he was too powerful.

"Mortals in Duat." Hote spoke in a scratchy voice. "Undead souls. Hearts that weren't weighed against Maat's feather. You will come with me, human. Osiris awaits you at the scales."

Hote opened his mouth, revealing a set of fanged teeth resembling a cat's. A yellow glow tainted by a faint red hue rose from my chest into Hote's body, and drowsiness slithered through me.

Khaf's muffled callings and the banging of his dagger against the dome echoed in my fading mind. The darkness consumed me, ever grimmer with each passing moment.

Was this it? Death in a place where I didn't belong? A failed sister. A disappointing apprentice. A traitorous Egyptian.

My head fell to the side. A faint noise hissed in my ears. The spear glittered at the center of my shrinking sight. Master Paser's golden ring glistened in the darkness. Oh, my dear teacher. I needed your guidance now more than ever.

May this ring be the part of me that accompanies you on your journey. His words flowed in my numb mind. *May it be a reminder to have faith in your grand vizier as he has faith in you.*

My master always spoke the truth.

My fingers twitched.

I wasn't wise.

I pushed my numb arm toward the spear.

But I was a survivor.

I opened my palm. The spear drifted through the air into my grip. Set's energy soared from his weapon into my veins. I jerked my arm with my remaining energy and thrust it with all my might into my brother's neck.

Hote screamed. He retreated, clutching his wound.

I stood with the spear's help. "Hote... would *never* harm me! He was the kindest little boy in the world."

The Majuwd flashed its fangs at me. "Damned mortal!"

The impostor charged. I flipped Set's spear, thrust it into the Majuwd's heart, and swung it away.

The Majuwd collapsed on its back, its twisted face shifting back to Hote's innocent expression. Its chest rose and fell, accompanied by painful coughs.

I stepped toward it.

"Stay where you are!" Khaf called.

As the protective dome collapsed, I fell with it and cried. "I stabbed my brother!"

"That wasn't your brother." Khaf picked the Majuwd off the ground, and it turned into its cat form in his arms. "And the other wasn't my father." He tossed the Majuwd away and sat beside me.

Unable to find any way to release my sorrow, I hugged Khaf and cried. "Hote is dead. Why? I did everything to save him. Why did my little brother die?"

Khaf held my head close to his chest.

"I did everything for him. I committed countless crimes just to see him grow and be happy. Why did he die after everything?"

"Sometimes, we can't—help those..." Khaf's voice broke, and his tears fell on my shoulder. "I'm sorry."

Ishtar neighed. She jumped in circles, prompting Khaf to reach for his weapon.

"Nef, I know you're devastated, but I need you to pick up that spear and be ready."

I didn't react. It didn't matter anymore. Whatever was coming to kill me could gladly have its way.

"Nefiri, something is coming!"

Black mist rose between the reeds, covering their glow and leaving the divine Nile in the heaven as our remaining light source.

"You have killed two of my Majuwds, mortals!" A deep voice echoed through the tall black reeds.

Black vapor rose beside Ishtar. It thickened like dark paint, forming a man with a black canine head who stood twice Khaf's height. With each step, the man walked toward Ishtar, shaking the golden decoration around his dark blue kilt.

"Anubis!" Khaf reached for my hand, and his warm grip turned cold. "Damn it, we're doomed!"

The god of the dead patted Astarte's horse. "Welcome, my guest." His black eyes glanced at us. "Approach me, mortals." He tapped his silver scepter on the ground. Black mist engulfed us and pulled us toward Anubis.

"Great Anubis." Khaf swallowed. "We... we're just passing. I swear, we only—"

"I... Has..." I bit my lip to stop myself from crying.

Anubis's eyes shifted to me.

"Have you seen my brother? M-my real brother. Hote M-Minu. Did he—"

"I saw him," Anubis said. "He stood before Maat's scale and was judged either to be devoured by the demon Ammit or live eternally in the Field of Reeds."

"What was his..." My tears returned. I sobbed, unable to finish my question.

"What was his judgment?" Khaf asked. "In which direction did the scale tip? Was his heart heavier, or Maat's feather?"

"The divine laws forbid me to say."

He passed. I knew in my heart. The feather was heavier. He was forever happy and healthy in the Field of Reeds. My little brother had the kindest heart. Lighter than a feather.

Khaf patted my shoulder, then returned his focus to Anubis. "Will you take us to Maat's scale, great Anubis?"

Anubis ignored him and looked at me. "Your Ka is unsettling?"

My heart froze at the sight of Anubis's chilling gaze.

"Ka, great Anubis?" Khaf asked.

"Yes. Her Ka. The soul. It is tainted by Frenzy."

I opened my mouth to answer, but I couldn't speak. Thousands of questions soared across my mind, but I could only sob over my dead brother. Oh, my little Hote. It was still too soon for him. I wasn't even by his side when he passed to the afterlife. Even during his last moments, I'd failed him.

"I'm waiting for an answer," Anubis said. "What is wrong with her? How are you both here?"

Khaf gave my shoulder a gentle press and refocused on Anubis. "Nefiri has been chosen by Set's spear, great Anubis."

"I see. So Horus's plan is finally in motion." Anubis sighed. "I still despise him for allowing Frenzy to touch the mortal world. It makes me... anxious. But fine. So be it. It is his burden to bear. What is your next destination, mortals?"

"Ra's solar barque, great Anubis," Khaf said. "We must find the barque-gate."

Anubis shook his head. "The barque-gate isn't here. First, you must pass through the heaven-gate." He stretched out his arm toward me, and I cringed.

"Don't fear," Anubis said. "I want you and the spear out of Osiris's kingdom. My father might be less tolerant of my brother's radical plans."

Black mist spiraled over Anubis's clawed hand, creating a necklace with a black crystal amulet shaped like a cross with a loop at the top. This was an Ankh, the holy key of life!

"The Ankh shall grant you access to my Soul magic. It will help you control my black mist and unlock the gates."

I took the amulet and bowed my head. I tried to thank him, but no words could escape my throat.

"We're thankful for your gift, great Anubis," Khaf said.

"Say 'Abis Duru,' and the heaven-gate shall present itself to you." The tall god of the dead looked down at us. "Don't show me your faces again before your deaths." He tapped his scepter to the ground, and his body dissolved into a black mist.

"Abis Duru?" Khaf asked. "Wasn't that what Tuya said when she opened the gate for us? Why did she word a spell if she was Isis, and how did she gain access to Anubis's magic? Gods, what is that woman?" Khaf focused on me and laid his hand on my shoulder. "Are you all right?"

"No." I jerked away.

112

A frigid chill soared from the amulet into my body at the mere thought of tapping into Anubis's Soul magic, as if I had jumped into the Nile's freezing waters before sunrise.

"A... Abi..." I bit my lip and took a deep breath. "Abis Duru."

The Ankh vibrated around my neck. A black mist rose from the ground and formed the heaven-gate before me.

I grabbed Ishtar's reins and walked through the heaven-gate's black mist to leave this miserable place. I would never return to the Field of Reeds. I'd failed my master and now my brother. I had no chance of passing Maat's scale. I didn't belong here, neither alive nor dead.

Chapter 10

Cruelty Left Behind

We emerged through the heaven-gate's mist. The raging wind lifted our feet. We clung to Ishtar's saddle, steadying ourselves, and walked beside the horse along a limestone path surrounded by an azure void. We reached a brown wall, its surface decorated with hieroglyphs, and leaned against it for shelter.

"What is this place?!" I shouted, hoping Khaf could hear me despite the gale.

"I don't know!" Khaf nudged my shoulder and nodded left. "Look!"

The ceiling spiraled around a massive structure. A passageway carved into the massive structure's surface, with one wall absent, afforded us a clear view of the external environment.

A white cotton-shaped object flew past us in the azure void.

"That... wasn't a cloud, was it?" I asked.

"I know where we are!" Khaf said. "We're on the heaven pyramid!"

Pyramid? I studied the spiraling path around the structure that widened as its route ascended.

"Similar illustrations in Set's temple spoke of it," Khaf said. "It hangs from the heaven of Duat and points opposite the pyramids in Egypt."

"Whatever. Just show me the way."

Khaf stretched his arm toward me, and I cringed.

"How are you holding up?" Khaf asked. "Is there anything I—"

"I'm fine. I'm just not in the mood for talking."

"You're right. I'm sorry. But if you want to talk—"

"I said I'm fine, Khafset! Just tell me where we should go. Up or down?"

"We should rest. Give you some time to deal with Hote's—"

I glared at him, and he shut his stupid mouth. I didn't want to deal with anything. I crossed my arms and dug my nails into my skin, my teeth pressing against each other.

"It's not good to keep sadness inside," Khaf said. "Trust me. Let it out. The sooner you do, the sooner you'll deal with Hote being gone."

"Shut up!" I screamed, and Khaf flinched.

Gone! Hote was... I didn't even tell him I... couldn't be by his side when...

This had all been for nothing!

After all my theft, lies, and treason, I failed my brother. Gods, I wished I could hurl this heaven pyramid down onto the gods' heads. Maybe then they could share my pain. Maybe then they would regret not answering my prayers.

"Nef," Khaf laid his hand on my shoulder.

"Don't touch me!"

Khaf jumped back, jerking his hand away. "Gods, you're burning! You sure you're all—"

"Up or down?" I glared at him.

He swallowed, rubbing his hands. He pointed toward the top of the heaven pyramid.

"Good." I climbed on Ishtar's back. "Hop on."

"It's fine." He grabbed the horse's reins. "Have some time by yourself. I'll lead."

***

My world resembled a dream. There was no sun in the azure heaven to give a sense of time. Hours could've passed, or days. Not that I cared anymore.

I fumbled with the golden ring Master Paser had given me for Hote's healer. Yet another loved one I'd failed.

How did my life fall apart so quickly? All I wanted was to shut myself in my room and cry. Even that was beyond my reach.

I had been a fool. Since my father's betrayal, I had one goal: keep my brother alive. I did everything. I betrayed my master's trust by stealing for Khaf. I doomed Egypt by helping Khaf steal Set's spear. I committed every crime to get Hote's medicine from Khaf.

All my mistakes, all my misery, had one thing in common: Khafset, the Hyksos thief of Avaris.

"He would've died," I said. "Had I refused to steal the coins or the spear, you wouldn't have given me Hote's medicine, and he would've died."

"No."

"Which despicable action are you denying?"

"All of it. You assume I'm heartless. A bunch of lowlifes, aren't we? Khafset, the untouchable, would definitely let a child die."

"You want me to believe you were bluffing, you manipulative lowlife?"

His head twitched toward me. "Despite your insults, I do care about you and Hote."

"Stop saying that! Enough lies! Why would you care if my brother died? You want my people to suffer. You said so almost every time we met these last two years."

Khaf stopped and took three sacks from his brown leather bag strapped to Ishtar's saddle.

"Oh, you're ignoring me now?"

"What do you expect me to say?" He collected three small rocks off the ground and stashed them in his sacks.

I gritted my teeth. "You just have to steal something, don't you?!"

Khaf ignored me again and stashed the sacks in his bag. He grabbed Ishtar's reins and continued our march up the path.

"Khafset!"

"I'm collecting gifts for Setu and the girls."

"What girls?"

"Iti and Bennu. They played with Hote near Set's temple."

I scoffed. "Yes, the girls for whom you threatened to deny me Hote's medicine."

"The girls you almost enslaved, yes. You were right. They *are* orphans."

"Yeah, I figured. Knowing you, I'm sure you kidnapped them or are holding them hostage to gain — "

"Your soldiers killed their parents like they did with my father."

"Oh."

He nodded. "I couldn't allow the girls to become thieves or, even worse, end up in the Tavern of Avaris, so I adopted them as my sisters. It's not easy to see your parent get murdered. It — does something to a child. I would know."

My heart turned cold in my chest. I knew what it felt like to lose one's own parents. To feel alone in the world, trying to protect a sibling who had nobody else. Yes, it did something to a child. It did something to me.

"Khaf, how did — your father die?"

He hesitated for a moment. "My dad forged my dagger for my seventh birthday. A gift from him and my dead mother. It was the spring festival. A beautiful day. Or — so I thought. The innocence of a child, you know. Thinking back, it was a nightmarish day that ended with your soldiers breaking into our smithy. They stole everything for the army. Every last piece of metal. When I screamed at their captain, he punched me so hard that the memory still hurts. My dad's pleas to spare me were enough defiance for your soldiers to beat him."

That was the reason Khaf defied Nefertari and Master Paser to reclaim that dagger. Why he thanked Tuya, who complimented his father for his talents.

"I attacked the soldiers with my new weapon, but their captain caught me and snatched the dagger. He was merciful, though, and didn't kill me."

Despite his chuckle, my heart sank from the pain in his voice.

"I don't remember much about the captain but never forgot what he told me. 'You're in dire need of a history lesson, boy. Let me teach you about the fate of the Hyksos when they cross the Egyptians.' Then he took my dagger... and..."

Was he crying? No, Khaf didn't cry. He was the proud thief of Avaris. The strongest man I knew. My rival never cried, yet here he was, sobbing over his father's memory.

Khaf wiped his face. "They stabbed my dad in the heart with the dagger he forged for my birthday! *Your* soldiers did this. Not my ancestors, not a so-called untouchable. They were thieves and murderers dressed as soldiers protected by *your* king. *Your* soldiers killed *my* father!"

Mine? No. I'd never ordered my Medjay to commit such actions. Strict as I was, I would have never orphaned a child. But Khaf's father died before my time. Those were Grand Vizier Paser's soldiers. Those were Pharaoh Seti's orders.

But there must've been an explanation for my master's orders. Some strategic goal or purpose. Whatever cost the Hyksos had to pay was just, because they had to pay for their ancestors' crimes. Right? Yes! My master said... he taught me... he... he... seven? Khaf was Hote's age. My brother barely understood why we hated the Hyksos, and yet Khaf witnessed his father's murder at an age when he wouldn't have understood why we hated him. Gods, did we hate the Hyksos of the past so much that we turned into them? Had we become tyrants?

"Khaf, I—"

Khaf turned. The sight of his tears pushed my words down my throat. "I hate the Egyptians who orphaned me. The ones who worked Setu's parents to death and murdered the girls' parents. So you damn well should believe me when I say you're important to me despite being an Egyptian!"

I wiped my tears, jumped off Ishtar's back, and held Khaf's shaking hands. "I promise you; I never ordered anything so brutal. Nothing justifies these crimes."

"Did you really think you were stricter than Paser? Did you believe your beloved master was a savior? He was gentle to you, perhaps. But cruel as you were to us, he was a monster."

I lowered my gaze. "No wonder you hate me."

"You're the one who hates *me*."

"I... don't hate you. You annoy me, sure, but I don't hate you." I released his hands and turned to Ishtar. "What did hating the Hyksos get me? I lost my brother, whose last cheerful memory was playing with your sisters in Avaris. The system I served with undying loyalty calls me a traitor for wanting to save my brother. I caused pain to rescue my family. But not you. You seek justice and equality instead of revenge." I chuckled, and my cold heart sank deeper with my chest's vibration. "The irony. I believed the Hyksos were an immoral bunch. That's what my master taught me, after all. But here you are, a man whose goals I can't help but respect. An untouchable who's better than me, the great Egyptian." I glanced at him. He stood, frozen, his mouth open and eyes wide. "Without my brother, I only have our mission to drive me forward. If we survive, I have nothing left back in Egypt."

"But Paser promised you—"

I shook my head. "What good is being his apprentice if I don't have Hote? Even if I returned to him, I'd end up disappointing him again. That's what I am—a disappointment to everyone I love."

"You're being too harsh on yourself," Khaf said.

"I wanted to believe that I didn't need anyone to like me as long as I had Hote. But he's gone, and now I'll only be remembered as a monster."

"Hey, come on. You're not—"

"I'd like a fresh start. Become friends, maybe. If I'm to die on our mission, I hope for someone who doesn't hate me to hold my hand." I gathered my strength and gazed into his honey eyes. "I promise I'll try to be more open to what you're trying to teach me about your people. As a start, I won't insult you for being a Hyksos again."

Khaf caught my hands and gave them a gentle squeeze. "You won't die. I promise." He led me to Ishtar and helped me climb on her back.

"You know," I said, "you can be quite gentle sometimes."

"Oh, I know. I wasn't joking about Hyksos women lining up to marry me."

And just like that, despite my misery, Khaf made me smile.

***

"Should I be worried about you?" I asked when Khaf stopped our march and began sniffing like a hunting dog.

"You smell that?" He stood before the horse.

"I smell the pyramid's wet bricks."

"Not that. Someone is baking bread!"

My stomach growled. "We've been riding for hours. You're imagining things because we're starving."

"I'm not imagining it. I have very sharp senses. Someone *is* baking bread."

"Well, your sharp senses have failed you. Who would live here, let alone bake bread?"

"I don't know. Maat is having breakfast, maybe."

I smiled at the image of the goddess of justice munching on a loaf of bread.

"We should investigate." Khaf handed me Ishtar's reins and jumped on the horse behind me.

"What are you doing?"

"Tell Ishtar to go up the path."

I fumbled with Ishtar's reins, but she refused to obey. Despite Khaf's lessons, I still couldn't control the horse.

"For Baal's sake, we've been practicing this for hours. Here, I'll show you again." He held the reins by placing his hands over mine, and commanded Ishtar.

I swallowed, ignoring the warm wave soaring across my body at his touch. Why did he always find excuses to touch me? Did he enjoy being close to me? No. I was overthinking this. He was just the flirtatious type. I simply needed to set some boundaries. It was only fair. He had taught me so much, and I should return the favor by teaching him how to behave around women who didn't fill him with wine and treat him like a king to get his money. Not that faking liking Khaf's looks was a difficult task. The man's eyes alone were a work of art. If anything, those women should give him *their...*

"You don't have to hold me each time I ride Ishtar." I blushed. What was I just thinking?

"Ah, don't compliment yourself, Egyptian. Touching you brings me no pleasure. I don't understand what Setu sees in you."

"Yeah, right. That's why you keep finding excuses to touch me."

"Was I giving you wrong signals?"

"Yes!" I stared at his hands on top of mine. "Very wrong signals!"

"You're right. I'm sorry. Truth is, each time I touch you, I have to fight the urge to puke."

I frowned. Did he really mean that? He called me pretty in the Land-Between-Realms. But he also compared me to a cow back home, and now, he admitted to finding me so repulsive that he would puke at my touch. That was the truth, wasn't it? Calling me pretty was just his playful attitude. He did find me ugly.

"Hey, Khaf."

"Yes, Nef?"

"Let go of my hands."

"Oh. Yes, sure." He released me.

We rode up the path in silence. Why should I care about his opinion anyway? It wasn't like he was the god of beauty. Oh, his eyes were so gorgeous. Nonsense. Someone else, somewhere in the world, must have similar eyes.

"Hey, Nef."

"*What?!*" He flinched at my response. Why was I so irritated?

"You know I was joking, right?" Khaf asked.

"Of course." I shrugged. "Very funny."

"I do think you're very—"

"Can you change the subject?"

"Oh, sure." He paused. "I might've figured out something about your heritage."

"I know. Set could be my father, and I might be half Hyksos if he used one of his priests as a vessel. It's all just speculation, so no need to dwell on it."

"Yeah, but Anubis said your soul is tainted by Frenzy. I read about Frenzy before but didn't understand what it meant. I think Set's Destruction magic is simply an offshoot of Frenzy. A subcategory. If it's part of you, this is a strong indication that my theory might be correct. You truly might be his daughter."

What? No! This... this was just speculation, right? But Anubis called it a taint. Good things weren't described with such a negative word. Gods, what was hiding inside my soul? Didn't I have enough reasons for misery already?

"Your mother was Nubian, right?" Khaf asked.

"Yes. If you want to get technical, I'm only half Egyptian."

Now he would definitely point out the hypocrisy of how I mistreated his people while the king I served also mistreated my mother's people.

"If your mother was Nubian," Khaf said, "and if you're Set's daughter and his vessel was a Hyksos, then, in theory, that means you..."

My heart stopped. No!

"You're not Egyptian!" He laughed.

No, gods, please! I wasn't Egyptian. Of course, I was. The Hyksos were Egyptians now, right? But... I insisted they could never be Egyptians. So, by my own logic, I wasn't Egyptian. According to my beliefs, Hote and I were untouchables of Avaris. My sweet little brother should've experienced the life I tried to inflict on Khaf's sisters!

I pulled Ishtar to a halt.

"Why did you stop?" Khaf asked.

"Hold my hands again."

"What?"

"Please!" My scream startled him, and he grabbed my hand.

"Nef, I was joking. Of course you're—"

"I'm sorry!"

"What?"

"I'm so sorry for ever saying your people weren't Egyptians." I dug my nails deep into his thumbs, pulling his warm hands toward my stomach. "I'm sorry I tried to kidnap your sisters and sell them into slavery."

"Relax. I appreciate the apology, but you're far too uptight to be a Hyksos. 'Oh, I will report you to Master Paser, Hyksos. Respect the law, thief.' For Baal's sake, only an Egyptian can be so annoying."

"I'm a horrible person. I'm... so..."

"Please don't cry. It was a stupid joke. I'm sorry."

"Your jokes are becoming too hurtful," I said, holding back my tears. "Respect that I'm currently mourning my brother."

"You're right. I'm sorry. I shouldn't tease right now."

"Why tease me at all?!"

"Well... back home, teasing you was the only way I got you to speak to me as Nef and not as Paser's apprentice."

He was right. I tried to keep our conversations formal. How could I, Lady Nefiri Minu, the warden of Avaris and future grand vizier, have a normal chat with an untouchable?

"You aren't a horrible person." Khaf pushed his head beside my ear. "Frustrating at times, sure. But I'm enjoying my time with you, Egyptian."

"I—am enjoying my time with you as well." I turned my head, and our noses touched. "Thank you, Hyksos."

"For what?"

"My brother's medicine. You gave me more time with Hote, and for that, I'll always be thankful."

He smiled and then glanced at our hands. "Should I release your hands?"

My cheeks burned, and I flinched away. "Maybe... leave them. They're warm, and I'm freezing."

"Oh! Wait a moment." Khaf released me. He fetched a blanket from his bag and put it around my shoulders.

He then gave me his hands, and a long pause followed. I should've thanked him for the blanket, but the tenderness of his hands as they gripped mine and the warmth of his breath against the back of my neck, mixed with his smell that spread from his blanket, clouded my mind. Gods, he wasn't an evil Hyksos thief, was he? He might've been... noble?

We turned around the spiraling path, and Ishtar came to a halt. A settlement emerged inside a cavity cut deep into the pyramid. No, not a settlement. An entire city! Crystal palaces stood throughout the city, reflecting the rainbow's colors. The ibises sang, flying over the trees that decorated the gardens. People were talking, singing, and eating on the streets.

"How is there a city here?" I asked.

Khaf jumped off Ishtar's back and walked toward the city with his hands on his head.

"Did you read about this place in Set's temple?"

"I thought it was a legend."

"What is this place?"

He turned, revealing a grin like Hote's when mischief overtook his thoughts. "It's Byblos of the heaven pyramid!"

Chapter 11

Byblos of the Heaven Pyramid

F lowery vines rose from the pyramid's ground, forming colorful arches before the bustling settlement—an ever-rising city built upon the pyramid's steps. Colorful palaces were visible across the horizon, their crystal walls emitting a faint glow, shifting between rainbow colors.

Ibises flew over the city, gliding between tall palm trees along the path connecting the numerous gardens between the scattered palaces. Men and women bustled along the busy streets.

"How is this place possible?" I asked, wrapping my blanket around me as the chilling breeze blew. "All dead mortals should be in the underworld."

Khaf's eyes followed the flying ibises.

"We shouldn't stay here for long."

"Why? What is this place?"

"I told you. It's Byblos of the heaven pyramid."

"Yes, but... Khafset!" I snapped my fingers before his face. "Tell me what Byblos is."

"During the war of the gods, Set trapped Osiris in a sarcophagus and threw it into the Nile. The sarcophagus landed near a small settlement called Byblos in eastern Canaan. A tree as high as the clouds grew from Osiris's corpse. Byblos boomed around the tree, becoming a prosperous Phoenician city."

"Wait, didn't Set cut Osiris into pieces and scatter his body throughout Egypt?"

"That was his second attempt at killing his brother—after Isis found her husband's remains." He grabbed the blanket's edges, wrapped it around me, and pulled it over my head like a cloak, his eyes following the flying birds. "Isis told the city's king her story, and to her surprise, and Set's, the people of Byblos cut the tree down and sacrificed their riches to reunite Isis with Osiris."

I lowered the blanket off my head. "My master never told me this—"

"Leave it." Khaf removed my hands. "Those ibises work for Thoth, the god of wisdom. He's Maat's husband, and we most definitely don't want him telling his wife that Set's chosen is entering her city. It's one thing for Anubis to suspect that you've been touched by Frenzy, but Maat is a different story. She's a primordial goddess. A being on a whole other level, even among the gods."

"Oh!" I wrapped the blanket tighter and turned my back on the city's flowery gate. "But I did nothing wrong. We're just trying to reach Set's prison to save Egypt. I don't even understand what 'tainted by Frenzy' means."

"It sounds bad," Khaf said. "Maat is the judge. She upholds the laws of the world. Kind of like you in Avaris but on a cosmic scale and... well, more just and less tyrannical."

I lowered my gaze, wishing the ground would swallow me. He had every right to call out my...

"I'm sorry," Khaf said, and my head rose. He was the one apologizing! "I shouldn't have said that. It was a cheap shot. I know you're beginning to regret your past actions." Khaf smiled and leaned on Ishtar's red saddle. "Maat is a great goddess, though. She was so impressed by the people of Byblos that she moved them and their city to Duat to live an eternal life in her care. These are the people of Byblos who helped reunite Isis with Osiris ages ago."

"But some are wearing Egyptian clothes. White kilts and all!"

"Do you know the purpose of the heaven pyramid?"

I shook my head.

"It guides the dead pharaohs with their families and servants to Duat."

My eyes widened. "Wait, you don't mean—"

"Some of those Egyptians are former pharaohs."

My mouth dropped. Gods! I could converse with any pharaoh Maat deemed worthy of her care!

Khaf sported his smug half-smile that indicated his excitement, but his eyes were narrowed, which usually meant he was deep in thought. Two expressions his face never displayed simultaneously.

"Something wrong?" I asked.

"Ahmose is here. Maat must've chosen him as a worthy king for defeating the Hyksos and conquering Avaris." Khaf walked away from Ishtar, caressing the brown hilt of his sheathed dagger. "The Egyptians never learned of his brutality. My ancestors deserved punishment, sure, but that monster tried to kill every Hyksos; man, woman, and child."

This was my life now—a traitor's life. I could meet the great Ahmose, yet he would urge Maat to punish me if he found out who I was.

Khaf's absent gaze focused on me. "Nef, are you all right?"

Was that pity in his eyes? I'd put my guard down around him since Hote's death, hadn't I? I must pull myself together— enough weakness. If I was good at anything, it was putting on a strong front no matter how much I hurt.

I pulled every muscle in my face to form a smile. "Never been better."

Khaf's eyebrow rose. "Your face looks weird."

"Ah, just hungry."

"So am I." Khaf inspected the city through its entrance. "Tell you what, wait here. I'll find us supplies and gather information about the barque-gate's location."

"Are you going to steal in Maat's city?"

He smirked. "There's no Paser here. So please, spare me your—"

"I want to join you."

"What?" The Hyksos almost gasped.

"Teach me how to become a thief. I'm a fast learner. You said so yourself."

"Nef, you—"

"Let me enjoy myself for once in my miserable life! I'm done being the uptight Egyptian!"

Khaf stepped back, his eyes wide. "What would Paser think of his star pupil?"

"He isn't here, is he? What did following the law get me, anyway?" I paced back and forth before him and Ishtar, hiding my face from the birds beyond the city's gate. "The law sure didn't save Hote's life. But the proud thief still has his family while I have nothing. You're happy while I'm miserable!"

"I'm not..." Khaf caught my shaking shoulders, bringing me to a halt. "Nef—"

I gazed into his honey eyes. "I tried to be an upright citizen, and look what it got me. Let me try your way of life. Didn't you urge me to admit that I'm a talented thief? Well, I'm admitting it."

"Nef, you're really romanticizing a thief's life."

"No, I'm not!"

"You're just trying to cope with Hote's death. It's normal. When my father died—"

"You were seven!" I pushed his hands off my shoulders. "I am a grown woman!"

Khaf opened his mouth, then closed it. He stared at the cavity's ceiling and took a deep breath. "Fine. First lesson. Stop screaming in the place you're going to rob." His eyes landed behind me, and a smile emerged on his face. "I'll teach you, my Egyptian." He spun me around and directed my gaze toward a small wooden hut outside the city. "That's your first target. Fit for an amateur thief."

"Wait? Am I going to steal alone?"

"Indeed." He laid his chin on my shoulder. "You rob the hut while I take care of the city."

"Why can't I just come with you?"

"You'll slow me down, and I'll blend in easier with the people of Byblos."

"And I'll blend in with the Egyptians."

"Stealing in Maat's city is dangerous."

"Yeah, unlike everything else we've faced—"

"Did you talk back to Paser so often during his lessons?"

I tightened my fist under the blanket, blood rushing to my cheeks. Again he had compared himself to my wise master. But I couldn't afford to call out his hubris. Regardless of my feelings, Khaf was now my new teacher. If he truly thought I shouldn't accompany him into the city, then he must have a good reason that only an experienced thief could understand.

"How do I rob someone's home?" I asked.

"You're a smart girl. Figure it out. Consider it a rite of passage. Do this right, and I will teach you how to become a professional thief."

"Should I... can you at least give me a tip?"

"Don't get caught this time."

I embraced myself underneath the blanket. "Fine. But please don't do anything stupid. You have that look on your face."

"Oh, Nef." He retreated toward the city, and his smug smile reached its full glow. "Oh, Nefi, Nef, Nef." He threw his hands in the air. "How boring would your life be if I stopped doing stupid things?" He winked and entered the city.

I grabbed Ishtar's reins and walked away from the gate. Khaf would either find the barque-gate and supplies, or get us killed. Extremes were the norm for this thief.

I left Ishtar beside the fence in front of the hut. Inside the garden, I walked along the paved way to the porch, where I found a table bearing a bronze cup, a bottle, and two apples.

What should I do now? Did Khaf plan his heists in advance or follow his instincts? Knowing him, a bit of both, probably.

I sat on the chair to plan, and lost myself in the hut's charm and the delicacy of its well-groomed garden. Azure and white lotuses, lilies, and sunflowers decorated the green grass. The soft wind brushed against a tall tree in the garden, scattering its pink leaves on the water of a spring near the fence. The hut reminded me of Egypt in a way. It was plain and deserted, yet its elegance hid in its fascinating details.

I turned to the apples and clay bottle on the wooden table beside me. My stomach growled, and pain radiated from my dry throat.

My primal instincts overtook me, and my hands snatched the apple. I took a bite, releasing the apple's sweet juice in my dry mouth, and gobbled the rest until nothing was left except its core. Gods, such refreshing sweetness. Was it my excruciating hunger, or was it really that delicious? It didn't matter. With my hunger and thirst somewhat under control, I could plan how to break into...

A white object flew before my eyes, nearly yanking the blanket off my head, and landed on the table with a thud.

I turned my trembling head toward the table. My neck muscles tensed. Finally, the creature came into sight: a white ibis with a black head, gray beak, and ashen legs. It stared at me, then shrieked.

I bounced away from the bird, heart racing.

"Thief!" a woman called.

I spun, the blanket falling, revealing Set's weapon. I reached for the spear and froze as the woman pointed a knife at me.

"I'll cut you before you touch that weapon," she said. Her dark brown eyes signaled her serious intent.

I froze, unable to think or move, the apple's sweet taste turning sour.

The woman walked toward the chair and stood beside the ibis. Her face was round, her nose small, and her eyes wide. Her skin had a unique brown tone that shifted with the light. Typical royal features. But her patched white dress and lack of makeup and jewelry declared her an Egyptian servant. A royal bastard, perhaps?

"A thief in Maat's city," she said, shaking her head. "You were stealing under the watchful gaze of the goddess of justice. What is wrong with you?"

"I... I... I'm not a—"

"Silence!"

The ibis called. It flew out of the cavity toward the azure void surrounding the heaven pyramid.

"No, please don't!" I called. This had been the third time Khaf had sent me on a mission. My streak of failure was still unbroken.

"You should worry about *me*, thief." She sat on the chair. "Once I'm done with you, there won't be anything left for Maat to judge." She pointed at the grass beneath my feet, and my body collapsed. Gods, not even Nefertari forced me to reach that level of submission!

"Stealing is a sin despised by the gods," she said. "Stealing in Maat's city is an abomination!" She regarded me from her chair. "Voice your excuses, thief."

"I was hungry and thirsty. I thought I could borrow food and water from you."

"Without asking? That's theft, girl." She slammed her knife on the table, planting its blade in the wood.

I held my arm and nodded. "I am very sor—"

"Which pharaoh do you serve? I will have a word with him."

"I... I serve Pharaoh Ramesses the Second."

"I've never heard of Ramesses." She stroked her chin as if she had a beard. "How could his servant be in Byblos if Maat didn't invite him?"

"Oh, no, he isn't dead!"

The woman leaned forward. "Are you alive?"

I nodded.

She studied me with narrowed eyes. "Are you the pharaoh's treasure hunter?"

"Treasure hunter?"

"Is this your first mission?"

I nodded. Technically, it was my first mission of this kind.

"So, you're still being tested. Some pharaohs don't like to disclose the job until the treasure hunter's return." The woman smiled. "Treasure hunters' identities are kept secret. They are thieves who travel across Huat and Duat to steal divine items for the pharaoh. Only the king and those whom he trusts know their identity."

Oh, she was so mistaken. I was a treacherous thief, not a glorified one.

"Tell me about your mission. You treasure hunters have the most magical of tales. Consider it your payment for the apple you stole." She pulled her knife from the table and pointed it at me. "And each time you impress me, you shall receive a slice from the second apple." She struck the fruit with her knife and pulled it to her other hand.

"It's a long story."

"I have an eternity's worth of time." She crossed her legs and straightened her back. "So, entertain me, thief."

"I—"

"Choose your words wisely," she said, carving out the first apple slice. "Lying in Byblos would also anger Maat."

My mouth watered when the apple's juice leaked onto its red surface. "Set's spear has chosen me. Queen Nefertari sent me to Set's prison to cut his connection to Huat and save Egypt from his influence."

"Set?" She whistled. "Such a brave adventurer."

"I'm neither of those things."

She threw an apple slice my way. I caught it and savored each bite.

"You know," she said, "I'm glad my deeds during my life paved the path for women to be entrusted with such monumental tasks."

She threw me another slice. I caught it midair and tossed it into my mouth. Her deeds? What did she mean? If she only knew the spear chose me because I might be Set's daughter.

Another slice fell on the dirt before me. I didn't react this time. Had I fallen this low? I'd always used my brother's illness as an excuse to steal. What was my excuse now? Hunger and thirst? I'd punished criminals who shouted the same pleas, begging me to show mercy. And here I was, a pathetic thief full of laughable excuses.

"What?" the woman asked. "Should I throw you another bite? Or has the food finally become too unclean for your taste?"

"I... I..." My head fell. "I think I'm full. Thank you."

Thunder erupted outside the cavity. Dark azure clouds raged in the void surrounding the heaven pyramid.

"Is this normal?" I asked.

She shook her head, glancing toward the azure void. "How many companions do you have?"

"One."

"Only one? He must be something special."

"He's something for sure," I mumbled.

"What's his name? And yours, for that matter."

"I'm Nefiri Minu, and his name is Khafset."

"Doesn't he have a second name?" She took a bite from the apple.

I licked my dry lips. "I only know him as Khafset of Avaris."

"Avaris? Is he a Hyksos?"

"Yes." So she had lived after the Hyksos built Avaris. Gods, did I snitch on Khaf by mistake?

She choked on her food, laughing. She grabbed the clay bottle and drank. "Oh, gods!" She coughed between her chuckles. I'd never seen a woman do that. Frankly, her behavior and gestures often drifted toward the masculine side.

"Oh, dear Ahmose," she said. "I so wish to see his face when he finds out the queen of Egypt sent a Hyksos to save her kingdom."

"Is… is Pharaoh Ahmose here?"

"Yes." She waved her hand. "Pray Ahmose doesn't find your…" She arched her eyebrow. "Is Khafset your husband or lover?"

"Neither!" Her expression hardened, and I cringed. "He's just… A companion. Yes, Khaf is just my companion. Nothing more and nothing less."

"Khaf?" She giggled, this time in quite a feminine way, in a steady rhythm, with her hand covering her mouth.

I raised my chin to regain a shred of my dignity. She'd had enough fun. "I'm sorry, but if I may ask, which pharaoh do *you* serve?"

The woman's laughter stopped, and her face turned red.

"I'm sorry." I cowered.

Her chin rose. "You are in the presence of Pharaoh Hatshepsut Maat-Ka-Re. The foremost of noble women and the Lady of The Two Lands."

I rolled my eyes. There had never been any female pharaohs. Hatshepsut raised her eyebrow. "You don't seem impressed."

I shrugged. "Why should I be?"

"Ah, I see." Hatshepsut smiled. "You may know me as Hatshepsu. I presented myself as a man to secure my rule."

She studied my face, and I gave her a skeptical look. Gods, she'd given me such a hard time for being a thief, but she was a blunt liar.

"You don't know me, do you?" Hatshepsut asked.

"Nope. Never heard of you."

"So you're uneducated."

"I'm highly educated! I am Grand Vizier Paser's apprentice. I know of every pharaoh who ruled Egypt." Gods, my heart danced with the pride that filled those words.

"You're a thief." Hatshepsut spat the truth in my face.

"My life is complicated."

Hatshepsut scratched her nose with her knife. "If you're educated as you claim, you must have seen my buildings. Hasn't your grand vizier sent you to Thebes to study the grand mortuary temple? It's a work of art. The biggest in the city. Carved into a mighty mountain."

"I studied it. The Djeser-Djeseru. The Holy of Holies. Built by Grand Architect Senenmut."

"Ah, Senenmut." Hatshepsut's face brightened. "Yes, I commissioned Senenmut to build the Djeser-Djeseru."

Enough lies!

"I didn't see your name," I insisted. "I only read the name of Pharaoh Thutmose the Third as its builder."

"What?" She stood, her voice so loud it might've cracked the heaven pyramid. "I ordered its construction!" She screamed. "It's mine! *My* grand achievement!"

I crawled away, my bravado fading like Hatshepsut's sense of self-control. "I'm sorry, but I only found Thutmose's name."

Hatshepsut fell on her chair, breathing heavily.

"That little... ah! He stole my work!" She caught her head, fingers in her hair. "That temple was Senenmut's gift to me. A symbol of our love and the prosperity of my reign."

Gods, I was trembling. The woman was out of control, and she had a knife! Should I run? Where? Maat already knew about me, and I had to wait for Khafset's return. What was taking that idiot so long?

"You still think I'm lying, don't you?" Hatshepsut asked.

I didn't answer. After countless hours of diplomacy lessons, here I sat, unable to figure out the correct answer to a simple question.

"I'm in Maat's city," Hatshepsut said. "Why would the goddess of justice invite me if I was a liar? The people here are either royalty, servants, or the original inhabitants of Byblos. I don't have anyone to serve, and I sure don't look like the Phoenicians. What role do you think is left for me to fill? How would I know of the treasure hunters if I didn't have my own?"

I covered my mouth. "Gods, you aren't lying, are you? You *were* a pharaoh!"

Stealing an apple or some coins was something, but stealing a person's lifework was indescribable. Hatshepsut. I must have read that name somewhere—some footnote in some scroll.

"Wait!" A memory nagged at me. "Queen Hatshepsut. Daughter of Thutmose the First, wife of the Second, and stepmother of the Third."

"Daughter. Wife. Mother." Hatshepsut frowned. "Is that my legacy?"

"Well, if it's any consolation, Thutmose the Third was a great pharaoh. He founded the Egyptian Empire. You raised a strong man."

"A man who was good at waging war. How original." She threw her knife on the table. "He couldn't outdo me, so he erased me from memory. What a pity." She rubbed her temples, sighing. "At least Egypt remained strong during his reign, and my subjects enjoyed a prosperous life after my death. There is comfort in that."

"Well, Set did promise he would destroy Egypt and kill its pharaoh, so—"

"Girl, you just want to ruin my day, don't you?"

"But Khaf and I will stop him." I sat on my knees, straightened my back, and smiled. "I promise."

"An Egyptian and a Hyksos working together to save Egypt." Hatshepsut crossed her arms, and her smile returned. "There is hope in that, I guess."

How, by all the gods, did she regain her composure so quickly? It would take me weeks, no, years, to get over a devastating revelation like the one I'd dropped on her.

"You have earned yourself some juice, girl." She grabbed the bottle and poured the drink into the bronze cup. She presented it to me.

"Thank you." I took the beverage. The drink's strong familiar scent wafted into my nose. Its greenish-red color looked... familiar. "Is this poppy juice?"

Hatshepsut laughed. "No, this is sugar cane juice mixed with apple nectar. A Hyksos idea. But Ahmose outlawed the Hyksos drink, of course."

My gaze remained fixed on the drink's sparkling reddish-green surface. My tears dripped into the cup, and my heart froze. The thief of Avaris had scammed me. Hote never received a cure. My life fell apart for nothing!

"Are you all right, girl?"

"No!" The cup fell from my shaking hands. "Khaf sold this to me for ten golden coins a bottle as medicine for my brother."

"You could buy an entire field with that amount." She laid a hand on my shoulder and gave me a gentle pat. "Poppy juice is yellow, girl. I'm afraid your companion was stealing from you." She placed her hand under my chin and raised my gaze toward her stern face. "May this be a lesson, grand vizier's apprentice." She rubbed my tears with her thumb. "Every thief eventually gets outsmarted by another."

I had begun to believe Khafset was a good man. I even doubted everything I knew about the Hyksos. But yet again, I had fallen for his schemes! Yet again, he had dragged me down to his level!

I grabbed the cup and shook it in front of Hatshepsut. "This is proof that Khafset is just another lowlife like all the untouchables of Avaris."

"This is the wrong attitude that naturally led you to the wrong conclusions. Don't the Egyptians steal? Didn't I catch you red-handed? Hypocrisy is a bad trait, girl."

"So is betrayal! If it's not a matter of origin, then it must be one of gender. Same as my father, whoever and wherever he is."

Hatshepsut gave a slight nod. "Some men are good, though. Senenmut was good. Name me a good man you have in your life."

I didn't even have to think. "Master Paser. The grand vizier. My dear teacher."

Hatshepsut smiled. "Don't let hatred and pettiness consume you, girl. It's so easy to pass judgment, yet effort and insight are required to pass the just—"

An armed man entered the garden. An original citizen of Byblos, judging by his strange colorful dress-like attire.

"Your Majesty." The man bowed. "The Ennead has called a meeting."

My eyes widened. The nine high gods were in Byblos!

"Why?" Hatshepsut asked.

"The guards captured a drunken man in the tavern. He is going to stand trial before the Ennead for judgment."

"Who dared commit a crime in Maat's city?" Hatshepsut glanced at me and tilted her head. "A crime that might offend the Ennead."

"I don't know, Your Majesty. But in his drunken state, he kept telling the women there that he is the proud thief of Avaris."

Hatshepsut glanced at me. "Your companion?"

I nodded. Failure, stupidity, wine, and women. Yeah, that was Khafset.

"Very well." Hatshepsut stood. "Rise, Nefiri. Let's see what crime the Ennead thinks your companion has committed."

Chapter 12

Maat's Justice

A luminous yellow glass bridge extended from the pyramid's interior walls to a floating island, where a magnificent temple stood tall. The temple's glass walls rose from solid ground, emanating a soft blue glow illuminating the heaven pyramid's heart.

I walked over the glass bridge alongside Hatshepsut and Ishtar, our steps creating pulsating footprints behind us. Former pharaohs surrounded us, each borne upon golden thrones carried by their attendants, as they made their way toward Maat's crystalline temple where Khaf's trial would take place.

"Didn't you say you were a pharaoh?" I asked Hatshepsut, my feet aching from the long walk.

"I did, and I was."

"Then where are your servants? Why do you look so miserable?"

"Miserable?" She shot me an annoyed glance. "Someone really needs to put a leash on that tongue of yours."

"I'm sorry. It just would've been nice for someone to carry me to the temple."

"How would *me* having servants lead to *you* getting carried?"

I opened my mouth and closed it. I couldn't argue with that.

She chuckled. Or maybe scoffed? Probably both. Master Paser showed a similar reaction quite often.

But I really needed to know why she wasn't treated like the other pharaohs. "Why don't you have servants?"

"Knowing what Thutmose did, I'm sure he didn't give me a royal burial. He probably threw my mummy to the jackals."

"Oh. You must hate him for it."

"I don't hate him. I'm annoyed, sure, but one should never pass judgment before hearing the entire story."

"But he betrayed you! What explanation could he have?"

"I don't know. That's why I need to hear it before I pass judgment." She smiled at me—more in a compassionate way than her usual high and mighty expression. "People's actions and the stories behind them are always complex. Only a hypocrite would pick and choose parts of the story in the name of justice."

I didn't respond. This was almost naive. Thutmose had betrayed her. That much was as evident as the sun. His actions weren't complex. But still, she wanted to hear his story. To give him yet another chance to hurt her. Yeah, no wonder she lost to Thutmose.

"What's going on in that head of yours?" Hatshepsut asked.

"Why are the nine high gods gathering to judge Khaf?"

Hatshepsut chuckled.

"What?" I asked.

"I find it amusing how you emphasize your hatred toward the boy and yet keep calling him Khaf."

My face turned warm. "*He* forced me to call him that!"

"And yet you continue to use the name. Are you sure you only see him as a companion?"

"After discovering his lies, I see him as less than a companion."

"If you say so."

"He sees himself as a hero who never does anything wrong— unlike us cruel Egyptians. Now look at him. Even if the medicine wasn't fake, you're witnessing his annoying nature firsthand. Why, in Ra's hidden name, did the idiot get drunk?"

"Does he drink a lot?"

"Oh, all the time!" I threw my hands in the air. "He always stinks of either wine or beer."

"And you never asked yourself why he drinks? Why he sought refuge in a tavern, an objectively stupid hiding place, instead of returning to you? Do you know the full story before you pass judgment?"

"It's just the way he is. He's the Tavern of Avaris's biggest customer."

"Senenmut had a similar phase."

"Oh, I would never compare Khaf, the thief, to Senenmut, the brilliant architect."

"When I found that brilliant architect you worship, he was a commoner who possessed nothing but the clothes he wore and a dream. They are more similar than you think. The architect drank for the house he couldn't build, while the thief drinks for the gem he can't steal."

"I don't understand."

She smiled. "Give it time. To answer your original question... The Ennead of Byblos isn't the Ennead you know. They are nine former pharaohs."

"Do you know who they are?"

Hatshepsut shook her head. "This is the first time they have called a meeting since my arrival."

"Is Ahmose part of the Ennead?"

"Probably. His mother is the high priestess of Maat."

"So Khaf is doomed."

"Oh, definitely."

Ishtar grew restless, and I patted her to avoid Hatshepsut's piercing glance.

"How does his fate make you feel?" she asked.

"He deserves to face justice for his crimes."

"Your words are harsh, but your blushing face betrays you."

"My face is red because I'm furious! He is the reason doom is looming over Egypt. He used my brother's illness against me. All for his so-called grand heist. Gods, to think I begged him to make a thief out of me. I never learn, do I?"

"Ah, judgments. Easy to make and hard to justify."

"What do you mean?"

"It's your lesson to learn, not mine to teach."

We arrived at the bridge's terminus, where the former rulers left their servants before entering the temple's hallowed gates. We joined the assembly of pharaohs in the grandiose main hall. Standing beside Ishtar and Hatshepsut, I took in the sight of the nine mesmerizing crystal thrones, spiraling elegantly from a smooth, arc-shaped platform crafted from shimmering glass.

A bald priest entered the hall. He cleared his throat, shifting the leopard skin on his shoulders, and the crowd fell silent. "Silence in Her Holiness's presence. The voice of Maat, the subduer of rebels and guardian of The Two Lands. High Priestess Ahhotep."

The attendants bowed in reverence as Ahmose's regal mother made her entrance. Her sandals resonated softly against the crystalline floor with each graceful, poised step, creating a rhythmic, mesmerizing echo. Adorning her neck was a magnificent golden medallion, an emblem reserved solely for esteemed Egyptian generals. Even amid the shimmering rays permeating the translucent white walls, the former queen's commanding presence and her exquisite emerald robe drew every gaze, making her the undisputed focal point of the chamber. She stood before us, her back facing the nine high thrones, and the intense amber eyes of her majestic golden-eagle crown pierced into my soul.

This priestess was Queen Ahhotep! *The* Ahhotep! The only woman to have commanded the Egyptian army. She fought the

Hyksos herself when her husband and son died in battle, until Pharaoh Ahmose came of age and conquered Avaris.

Ahhotep tapped her silver cane on the floor, shifting the golden scales on its top. "Rejoice, for here they come. Snefru, the beautiful, Khufu the builder, Sobekneferu the golden, Seqenenra the brave, Kamose the martyr, Ahmose the liberator, Thutmose the warrior, and Horemheb the believer. The Ennead of Byblos."

Azure mist swirled in front of eight of the nine thrones, manifesting the pharaohs within its luminescence. My heart raced, almost shattering my ribs, as I beheld the most magnificent pharaohs to have ever ruled Egypt—legendary men who had always seemed like mythical figures from ancient tales.

Except a woman stood among the kings. Sobekneferu. Gods, between Hatshepsut and Sobekneferu, how many women ruled as pharaohs that my master had hidden from me?

"Thutmose is part of the Ennead!" Hatshepsut covered her mouth. "Why him and not me? Why, Maat?"

I tried to find some words that might soothe her. How could I comfort a woman who had suffered such injustice from a traitorous man? Oh, I could relate to her so much right now. I, too, suffered injustice from a treacherous snake of a man! Two men if I counted my father.

The pharaohs took their seats, leaving the middle throne empty.

"I thought nine pharaohs were in the Ennead," I whispered. "Where is the ninth?"

"Good question."

"Bring in the savage," Priestess Ahhotep said.

The temple gates opened, and two guards dragged the shackled Hyksos into the hall's inner circle. They pushed Khaf, and the weight of his chains pulled him to the floor.

Why was he like this? Each time I left him alone, he returned to me beaten and in bonds. The more important question was why, in Hathor's name, did my heart contract in my chest when my gaze fell on the beaten, proud thief of Avaris?

"My dagger!" Khaf said in a hoarse voice. "It belongs to me, you—"

"Silence!" Ahhotep said, and a guard punched Khaf in the head, smashing his face to the ground.

My legs twitched toward him, only for Ishtar to bite my shawl and Hatshepsut to grab my hand.

"Don't be stupid, girl!"

"Call his crimes, Priestess Ahhotep," said Pharaoh Khufu— the builder of the great pyramid.

"Yes, we shall not grant him more time than he's worth," Pharaoh Horemheb said—the king who returned the old gods after the death of the heretic pharaoh Akhenaten.

"As the Ennead of the Byblos wishes," Ahhotep said. "This man committed the crime of—"

The temple's silver gates opened, and silence captured the hall. A king entered the room, the Pschent crown he wore containing two headdresses: the red Deshret crown of Lower Egypt and the white Hedjet crown of Upper Egypt—the symbol of The Two Lands.

The Ennead of Byblos rose as the pharaoh reached Ahhotep. Who was he? What man could bring the members of the Ennead of Byblos to their feet?

"What?" the pharaoh asked the priestess. "Won't you announce my presence?"

"Of... Of course, Your Majesty." She turned to the standing Ennead. "Kneel before him, for he has graced us with his presence! The first conqueror. Horus's first incarnation. The first Nesu-Bity. The unifier of The Two Lands and founder of Egypt. Pharaoh Narmer, king of the Ennead."

Everyone in the hall, including the priestess and the Ennead, knelt before Narmer while I stared at him like an idiot.

"What are you doing? Kneel!" Hatshepsut dragged me toward the floor.

Narmer reached the middle throne, and our eyes locked. "You." He pointed at me, trapping the air in my chest. "Approach the Canaanite."

"Go," Hatshepsut said, and Ishtar nudged me toward Khaf.

I walked under the gaze of our nation's founder until I reached Khaf. The traitor turned his head upward and smiled.

"Hey, Nef." Khaf grinned, rising to his knees like the snake he was. "Hey, Nefi, Nef, Nef."

"What did you do, you idiot?" I whispered, taking advantage of the distance between us and the Ennead.

"Something stupid." His breath sent the stench of stale wine up my nostrils. "Too stupid. I messed up."

"Rise," Narmer said.

The crowd rose to their feet, and the pharaohs of the Ennead returned to their thrones.

"Call his crimes, Priestess Ahhotep," Narmer said.

"In our tavern, the criminal bragged drunkenly about being a Hyksos," Ahhotep said.

"This doesn't constitute a crime," Pharaoh Snefru, the beautiful, said. The king who built the ancient Egypt upon which my modern Egypt stood.

"To you, maybe it doesn't," Pharaoh Ahmose finally spoke. "You died long before witnessing the sheer savagery of those untouchables. Give my mother a chance to finish announcing his crimes."

Snefru signaled the priestess to continue.

"The untouchable tried and almost succeeded in assassinating Pharaoh Ahmose in his palace."

The crowd gasped.

"You did what?!" I snapped.

Khaf shrugged, and an infuriating smile appeared on his face. "Couldn't resist the temptation."

"May I remind the residents of Byblos and educate the newcomers," Ahhotep said. "If you die in Duat by a divine blade, such as the untouchable's enchanted dagger, your soul will be destroyed. No resurrection or hope for salvation."

"Is that crime to your satisfaction, Snefru?" Ahmose asked. Snefru nodded.

"How did the savage enter Duat, let alone Byblos?" Seqenenra asked—the father of Ahmose and Kamose and the king who started the liberation war against the Hyksos rulers.

"And how did he find Ahmose's palace?" Pharaoh Sobekneferu asked. The pharaoh who... Ahhotep called her the golden and... well, I didn't know anything about her, really. But as Isis was my witness, I would devour every scroll in The Two Lands to find out everything about her and Hatshepsut.

"Not just that." Ahmose's gaze fell on me. "Why is a living Egyptian journeying across Duat with a damned Hyksos?"

"That's easy, brother," Pharaoh Kamose grinned. The king who died in the Egyptian–Hyksos war. "She's a traitor."

The pharaohs of the Ennead nodded in agreement.

"I can answer your questions," Narmer said. "What's your name, girl?"

My chest vibrated, and my mouth refused to open. My name? Gods, my name! What was my name?

"Nef, speak," Khaf whispered.

"Her name is Nefiri!" Hatshepsut called from the crowd, and those standing beside her and Ishtar jumped away.

Thutmose's eyes locked with his aunt's.

"Nefiri." Hatshepsut's defiant gaze glared at her stepson. "And she is *not* a traitor."

"You are part of this?" Thutmose rose from his throne. "An annoyance in death as you were in life!"

"This is coming from you," Hatshepsut said. "I know of your despicable—"

"Silence!" Priestess Ahhotep slammed her cane on the ground. "Another show of disrespect to the Ennead will lead to your exile from Byblos. Pharaoh or otherwise, the rules apply —"

"You are too loud," Narmer said in a tired tone, his forehead resting on his palm. "You are all shouting in my presence, and I still haven't heard the girl's voice." He glanced at Thutmose. "Sit."

"You must exile Hatshepsut for her —"

"Your private quarrels don't concern me." Narmer shifted his uninterested gaze to Thutmose, who refused to sit. "Are you disobeying the king of the Ennead?"

Thutmose fell to his throne, shaking his head.

"Good," Narmer said. "Very good." He returned his gaze to me. "Nefiri, now, wasn't it?"

I nodded.

"Words." Narmer sighed. "Answer me with words. Let me judge your voice. Is it deep or high? Outgoing or reserved? Loving or hateful? I ask twice and never thrice. What is your name?"

"N-Nef... Nefiri, Your Majesty."

"Interesting," Narmer said. "Very interesting. Your voice is tough to judge." He pointed at me with his free hand, keeping his other palm on his forehead. "Now unveil the weapon strapped behind your back."

My eyes widened. Not Set's spear!

Narmer glanced at the guard who held Khaf's dagger. "Satisfy my curiosity. Unwrap her weapon."

"No!" I said. "Please. I'll do it. Don't let anyone touch it. I beg you!"

Narmer nodded.

I grabbed the spear behind my back and laid it on the ground. I removed the white cloth around it, revealing the divine weapon. Gasps fluttered through the crowd. The spear's vibrant scarlet energy seeped into the crystal floor's translucent white core, reminiscent of hues blending in an artist's palette.

"She's Set's servant!" Kamose said.

"And a traitor who colludes with the Hyksos against Egypt!" Ahmose said.

"An enemy of the empire I built!" Thutmose said.

"Yet she defied Narmer's orders to prevent anyone from touching the spear," Sobekneferu said.

"She protected the soldier from destruction," Khufu said.

"Indeed," Narmer said. "Fascinating. Highly fascinating."

"She is probably still a traitor, though," Pharaoh Horemheb said.

"Perhaps." Narmer smiled at me. "What is your defense?"

"Your Majesty," I addressed Pharaoh Horemheb, "I serve as the apprentice of Grand Vizier Paser, whom you knew as an army officer. You must've witnessed his loyalty to Egypt. Would a man like him break tradition and appoint a woman as his successor if he had the slightest suspicion that she might be a traitor?"

"That would contradict Paser's alleged sound judgment," Narmer said, his face alight with amusement. "But if, as the spear suggests, you serve Set, Paser would not have been able to discern the truth. Set's guidance would have shielded you, veiled you, for who could deceive the most cunning of tricksters?"

"I don't serve Set," I said. "Khafset and I are on a royal mission to stop Set from escaping his prison in Abydos. We want to steal his scythe to cut his connection to Egypt and protect our king and his men, who are fighting a fierce battle in enemy territory. I'm not a traitor, Your Majesties, and neither is Khafset, unbelievable as it may be. Egypt hasn't always been kind to us, but we remain our pharaoh's loyal servants."

"Your pharaoh," Khaf said, smiling.

I glared at the Hyksos as a frightening realization hit me. Khafset, the proud thief of Avaris, the cunning trickster, might not be as smart as I thought. He was simply a lucky idiot with a death wish. Perfect!

"Did the guard hit you too hard on your head?" I asked. "Control yourself, or they might kill you."

"Ahmose *will* kill me, regardless of my behavior." He looked at Ahmose. "But if you are to grant a dead man a last wish, O great Ahmose, I wish for Nefiri to receive my dagger. I'd rather see my father's gift in her hands than sullied by your blood-soaked claws!"

Ahmose rose from his throne. "Kill him!"

The guards tapped their spears on the ground. They flipped their weapons, pointing their tips at Khaf.

"No," Narmer said, and the guards stopped. "Sit, Ahmose."

The warrior-pharaoh scoffed but obeyed.

Narmer's amused gaze shifted to Khaf. "You seem certain we won't kill her, Canaanite. Why?"

"Nefiri is the only one capable of reaching Set and saving Egypt. If you kill her, you will commit the crime you falsely accuse Nefiri of. You'll betray Egypt."

Priestess Ahhotep tapped her cane on the ground. "Watch your filthy—"

"You have eased my judgment, Canaanite." Narmer straightened his back. "Members of the Ennead, who among you agrees to the Canaanite's execution?"

The eight pharaohs beside Narmer raised their hands.

"Good," Narmer said. "Very good." He focused on me. "And the girl? Who agrees to her execution for the crime of treason?"

Six members beside Narmer raised their hands. Only Khufu and Sobekneferu refused to agree to my execution.

"Give her a chance to prove her loyalty to Egypt!" Hatshepsut called from the crowd.

Thutmose rested his forehead on his hand and shook his head. "She just can't help but make a scene."

"What do you propose, Pharaoh Hatshepsut?" Narmer asked.

"Let her execute the Hyksos," Hatshepsut said.

"What?" I shouted.

"Yes!" Khaf said. "I agree."

"You agree?! I don't agree! Not one bit!"

"She knows the way to Abydos." Khaf ignored me, keeping his eyes on Narmer.

"She doesn't need the Hyksos anymore," Hatshepsut said. "His life is worthless compared to Nefiri's and her mission."

"It most definitely is not!" I shouted.

"Her life is much more valuable," Khaf said. "Let her strike my heart with Set's spear. That weapon will destroy my soul."

"What's wrong with you two?" I demanded.

"Fascinating," Narmer leaned back on his throne. "Highly fascinating." He studied me. "Very well. Kill the Canaanite, and you may continue your journey to Abydos."

"No, no. I won't kill him. I can't."

"Don't you hate him?" Hatshepsut asked. "You said he deserves justice? You can execute that justice with your own hands in Maat's temple inside her heaven pyramid."

"Yes, I said that, but—"

"Nef," Khaf called, his voice gentle.

I turned to Khaf, and my heart skipped a beat when he smiled.

"Please don't give Ahmose the satisfaction of killing me. I'd rather it be you."

"I won't kill you!"

"They will kill us both if you don't!"

"No, no, no. I can't kill you. I can't—"

"Imagine a life without the Canaanite?" Narmer's words flowed into my ears. His voice seemed so thick I could almost touch it. "What would this life be like? Peaceful maybe? Even prosperous, perhaps? How many times did he cross you for his own benefit? Would he hesitate to kill you if it was him standing in your place?"

I swayed where I stood, entranced by Narmer's voice.

"Nef, are you all right?"

Didn't he use your ill brother? Sweet little Hote. Narmer's voice echoed in my head, but his lips weren't moving. *Isn't Hote worth picking up that spear and executing Maat's justice on the Canaanite?*

Narmer's voice captivated my every thought, pushing me into pure rage.

"My brother's medicine." I glared at Khaf. The thief who used my brother's illness against me. He ruined my life. He *should* pay for his crimes.

"What about Hote's medicine?" Khafset asked.

"Was it real?"

"Of course it—"

"Were you forcing me to steal a fake medicine? Did Hote suffer while I could have been searching for a real cure? Did my brother die for your grand heist, Khafset?"

"Yes!" Narmer said. "Hold tight to that rage!"

"Nef, I—"

"Did you give my brother a fake medicine, yes or no?"

Khafset's defiant eyes stared into mine. "Yes."

I opened my palm, Set's scarlet magic flickered around my fingers, and the spear rose to my grip. "You lowlife Hyksos bastard!"

"Yes!" Narmer jumped to his feet. "Execute Maat's justice in her temple! Strike him down with all your rage!"

"Nef, I tried to find a real cure for Hote but failed. You did everything for your sibling, as did I. Setu, Iti, and Bennu needed those coins. I'm not sorry for what I did, but I'm sorry I did it to you."

"I don't care. You killed my innocent little brother."

The scarlet energy spiraled around Set's spear. The guards pointed their weapons at us. An object glistened in the hands of the guard who had brought Khaf before the court of Egyptian kings.

Khaf's dagger.

I froze; the full story of that tragic blade came crashing back into my mind. I met the thief's anticipating honey eyes, and for the first time, I saw him. The person. The human. The full story of Khafset of Avaris with all of its complexities.

Khaf, the scared little boy, no older than sweet Hote, watched as our soldiers murdered his father with that dagger.

By order of our pharaoh.

Khaf, the rebellious young man, took two little girls in to protect them from the world. My world. Where I almost enslaved them.

By order of my pharaoh.

Khaf, the shackled thief, awaited his death to save Egypt, which had hurt him and everyone he loved. He surrendered himself so I could kill him.

By order of the first pharaoh.

No. No. The Hyksos was still influencing me. His father's story might've been fake. This... must be some twisted plan of his. He was still in control. We were all definitely doing precisely what he expected from us. This was all a lie, so he could... could... what was wrong with his goals? He didn't lie for gold or riches as I once believed. He lied to save his people.

Same as my lies, for my brother's sake. Same as my crimes, my schemes, my betrayal. Gods, I was just like him, wasn't I? Two lowlifes living on different sides of Peramessu. Two thieves who'd do anything to protect their people.

I fell to my knees, and the scarlet glow around Set's spear disappeared.

"What are you doing?" Narmer asked.

"He deserves a painful death for his crimes. But I'm guilty of the same crimes. Remove the labels we received at birth, and you will have two liars. Thieves and traitors who endangered their lands to satisfy their goals. Khafset and I deserve the same fate. *That* is Maat's justice."

Khaf's hands trembled, shaking the chains attached to his shackled wrists. "Nef, I—"

I turned to him. "I chose to commit all my crimes, including stealing from Master Paser. It was also my choice to let Shemzu kill you. I used my position to threaten your sisters just to spite you. I told the soldiers not to harass Setu because I wanted to bully him myself to feel better about my sad life. I chose to believe the lie that the orphans of Avaris were being sent to a better place instead of being enslaved, not because of my career but because I didn't want Master Paser to abandon me like my father. I didn't want him to think I wasn't worth keeping. But it's too late for us to seek redemption. This is Maat's temple. This isn't a place of forgiveness. This is a place of justice."

"Nef, I—"

"Good!" Azure energy spiraled around Narmer, covering his entire body in its glow.

"Very good!" a woman said from inside the glow.

The light faded, revealing an azure-winged woman. She stood tall in Narmer's place between the pharaohs. Her black hair, decorated with a feather, fell down her slender body, cascading over her white dress.

I swallowed. "Is... is that..."

Everyone in the hall, including the Ennead, knelt before the tall woman.

"The goddess Maat!" Khaf said.

"A fine judgment." Maat walked toward us, vibrating the golden braids decorating her hair. "A just judgment." She turned to the crowd and stretched her glowing azure wings. "Nefiri of Peramessu has judged to bind her fate to that of

Khafset of Avaris. A judgment I accept. One that proves them worthy to continue their journey to Abydos. They have fallen as criminals and shall either perish together or rise beyond any human before them. Such is the judgment of your goddess. Such is her justice."

Maat waved her hand, and Khaf's chains dissolved into an azure mist. She presented me with a black necklace with a half-silver, half-gold pendant—a pair of scales. "Wear this. It will give you access to my Air magic to reach Ra's solar barque."

I bowed my head, my heart pounding in my chest. I tried to thank her, but words couldn't leave my throat in her presence.

Maat laid her hand on my cheek and rubbed away the tears of my confrontation with Khaf. "You did well, child." She hung the necklace around my neck and settled it so the scale pendant dangled underneath Anubis's key-shaped Ankh. "So did you, Canaanite." She glanced at Khaf and snapped her fingers. Khaf's dagger flew from the guard's hand to his. The hieroglyphs reappeared on his chest the moment he touched his weapon. "You might be worth keeping after all."

"Worth..." Khaf swallowed. "What do—"

"Pharaoh Hatshepsut, approach me." Maat's imposing voice rang against the crystalline wall of her temple. I stepped back, and Khaf, who was in the process of standing, fell backward onto the ground.

The former pharaoh's chin rose. She walked with Ishtar toward the goddess, but, despite her steady steps, the tense muscles in her face betrayed her fear.

"Great Maat." Hatshepsut bowed before the goddess of justice.

Maat glanced at Ishtar before focusing on Hatshepsut. "You have shown great judgment today, child. Choosing to guide the wielder of Set's spear despite her flaws. Showing mercy for her situation. Trying to teach her despite her stubbornness. Suggesting she execute the Hyksos despite the compassion you feel for him. You prioritized Egypt's fate, and for that, your goddess is most pleased with you."

"She feels compassion for me?" Khaf's mouth dropped. "Ahmose's granddaughter?"

Maat smiled, keeping her eyes on Hatshepsut. "Horus made a fine judgment in delaying your ascension to the Ennead. It was important you met the spear's chosen first."

I held Hatshepsut's hand when she couldn't stop them from shaking. "Does that mean—"

"Yes," Maat said. "Narmer has accepted the greatest honor I can grant a mortal. He is now part of my essence. This means a throne on my court awaits you. It's time you took your rightful throne as a pharaoh of the Ennead."

I smiled at Hatshepsut. Gods, finally, some justice!

"I am, great..." She cleared her throat, her voice breaking with each word. "I am thankful for the honor, great Maat."

Maat turned to me and Khaf, who was now back on his feet. "You should be on your way. The barque-gate is at the hall's center. Use Anubis's magic to open it. While riding the horse, say 'Thihier Hawa.' My magic will give her the ability to fly. Beyond the gate's mist, fly to the divine Nile and await the barque's arrival."

Maat turned to the Ennead of Byblos. "From now on, Pharaoh Khufu will become the new king of the Ennead of Byblos, for Pharaoh Hatshepsut has taken Pharaoh Narmer's place after his last ascension."

The goddess of justice traced her hand on Hatshepsut's neck, revealing the number nine on her skin. "You have my blessings, Pharaoh Hatshepsut of the Ennead."

Maat turned back to us, laid her hand on Khaf's cheek, and gazed into his honey eyes. "There is hope." She smiled. "This one gives me hope in both of you. I see Astarte's grace in those eyes of his." She released Khaf, and an azure glow spiraled around her. "Farewell, travelers." The glow broke into tiny specks of glowing dust, and the goddess disappeared.

Khaf and I shared a glance while the members of the Ennead took their new positions, with Khufu sitting in the middle.

Hatshepsut took my hands and smiled. "Take good care of yourself, girl. And of that insane boy beside you. The gods know you need each other."

"I will take care of myself."

"And I will take care of her," Khaf said.

I rolled my eyes.

Hatshepsut leaned closer to me. "Remember the comparison between the boy and Senenmut. Remember to always search for the full story before you pass judgment."

I nodded, trying to ignore Khaf's wine-infested smell. She was right. She was trying to teach me a lot despite the unfortunate circumstances of our introduction. She didn't judge me for trying to steal from her. Gods, I could've learned so much from her, but I chose not to listen.

"Thank you for everything," I said.

"No, no. Thank *you*." She pressed my hands. "Promise me something."

"Anything."

"Write about your adventures. Both of you. Your pharaoh will try to steal your accomplishments. Document everything and hide it. Maybe a future generation in a kinder age will appreciate you. Promise me you will do it."

"I will write about you so the Egyptians won't forget who you were. Maybe they will for a while. It may take hundreds or thousands of years, but the truth will be revealed. One day your descendants will admire you for the magnificent woman you were. That I promise you." I bowed before her. "My Pharaoh."

Hatshepsut laid her hand on my cheek and smiled. "Farewell, Nefiri, the treasure hunter." She glanced at the Hyksos. "And her Khaf."

She walked to her new throne and stood between Thutmose and Sobekneferu.

"You may go on your way, travelers," said Khufu, the new king of the Ennead.

We climbed on Ishtar's back.

"Abis Duru," I said.

Anubis's amulet vibrated, and black mist rose at the hall's center, forming the barque-gate.

"Thihier Hawa." I worded the second spell. Maat's necklace filled me with the goddess's Air magic and a weightless feeling. Golden wings sprang out of Ishtar's body. She neighed and rose, almost throwing us off her back.

"Easy, Ishtar. Easy." Khaf patted her on the side until she relaxed.

I swung Ishtar's reins, and she walked toward the barque-gate's black smoke.

"Wait." Ahmose stood, and Ishtar stopped. "Even though I don't agree with the result of the trial or forgive the Hyksos for his attempted assassination, I will accept Maat's judgment that you aren't a traitor, and for that, I will give you a piece of advice."

Khaf's breaths increased, blasting his hot wine-infested breath on the back of my neck.

"Don't trust the Hyksos sharing that horse with you," Ahmose said. "He will act innocent. He will play the victim's role. Don't believe those illusions. The moment you outlive your usefulness, he will stab you in the back. It's in his blood, and he can't help it. This is my advice. My warning to you to heed, if you are as innocent as Maat claims you are."

I glanced over my shoulder and met Khaf's honey eyes.

"I can get off Ishtar's back if you don't want me with you," Khaf said. "But spare me that condescending Egyptian look of yours."

"No." I ordered Ishtar to enter the barque-gate's black mist. "We need to talk, Hyksos."

Chapter 13

Greatest of Warriors

Strings of light emitted a dim blue glow in the surrounding black void. The divine Nile flowed beneath Ishtar's hooves, illuminating the darkness. The river's glowing sand-like particles collided and emitted a soft swooshing noise.

There had been no signs of life in this part of Duat. It felt almost like a dream that wasn't yet complete. A realm not yet awakened. In other words, the perfect place to catch my breath before Ra's solar barque arrived.

Khaf and I sat on Ishtar's back, awaiting the mythical vessel. I held my head, trying—and failing—to calm the raging headache in my skull. Was traveling through the black mist bad for health? My head had been about to explode ever since we passed through the barque-gate.

"Are you all right?" Khaf reminded me of his irritating existence, his voice followed by a faint echo.

"I'm fine."

"Your head keeps twitching. Are you sure—"

"I said I'm fine, Khafset!"

My headache wasn't going to get any better if he kept talking.

"Hey, Nef."

Gods, he just would not shut up! "What do you want?"

He laid his hand on my shoulder.

"Don't touch me!"

Khaf retracted his hand as if he'd touched a beehive. "I'm—sorry. I... are you sure you're all right? Your shoulder was quite... warm, I guess?"

"Oh, I'm fantastic."

"You don't sound so—"

"I'm not done!"

"Sorry. Didn't realize there was more."

"Oh, there is more. A lot more! What were you thinking, trying to destroy Pharaoh Ahmose and jeopardizing our mission?"

"I admit, I let my personal feelings toward Ahmose get the best—"

"And not just that!"

Khaf sighed.

"Instead of returning to me so we could escape, you seek out a tavern, get drunk, and try to impress the women there with your crimes."

"To be fair, they were very impressed."

"Well, good for them!" My voice echoed in the dark void.

Khaf's laughter erupted.

"You think laughing in the face of danger makes you look strong?" I said, and his laughter stopped. "It doesn't. Never did. It makes you seem arrogant, foolish, and, to be frank, pathetic."

"No need to insult me," he said, his playful tone fading into a serious one. "What I did was stupid. My hatred toward Ahmose blinded me, distracting me from our mission. I admitted my mistake and was ready to die for it."

A thin stream of glowing yellow particles leaked into the river's blue flow. The barque must be near.

"Everything you say is a lie," I said.

"That's not true."

"You promised you cared about Hote and me, but you never did."

"I didn't lie."

"Liar! I confronted you with your fake medicine before the Ennead of Byblos and the goddess of justice, and you said you would do it again."

"And you call me a liar." Khaf scoffed. "I couldn't have been more honest. Nef, your coins kept Iti and Bennu warm and fed. They paid for Setu's education. I would've been cruel and selfish if I'd refused the coins just because I grew fond of an Egyptian."

"Grew fond of an Egyptian?" I fought the urge to turn around. "What do you mean?"

"Ah, don't compliment yourself—"

"No! Enough with your vague responses! Answer the question. What did you mean?"

Khaf sighed. "I grew to appreciate you."

"Yeah, right. That's why you decided to harm my family."

"Your people harm us all the time!"

"Why do you punish *me* for my people's actions?"

"Said every Hyksos. Also, don't act innocent, O Lady Nefiri Minu, warden of Avaris."

"I ignored my master's teachings and allowed you to break the law."

"Yeah, right. You definitely didn't do it for Hote's—"

"I could've had you and everyone you love thrown in a dungeon." I gathered my courage and turned to challenge Khaf's glaring gaze. "I could've tortured the medicine's recipe out of you."

Khaf's face reddened. "No amount of torture could've broken me."

"True. I would've targeted Setu. Then the girls. I might've sold them to the most despicable noblemen I knew. Oh, I could've broken you, Hyksos. I *chose* otherwise. I stole, lied, and betrayed despite having an easier method. I kept you and your loved ones safe. But you kept pushing and pushing until you took everything. And what do I have now? Nothing. Not even my brother."

Khaf's face relaxed, its red hue fading. He opened his mouth but didn't speak.

I turned and inspected the divine Nile's stream that now shimmered yellow and blue.

"I... am sorry." Khaf's words hit me like lightning. "I've always seen you as two people—Lady Nefiri Minu, the grand vizier's apprentice, and Nef, the woman I tried not to harm. That... might've been a mistake."

"You manipulated a worried sister who wanted to find a cure for her ill brother. You hate my people for our cruelty, but you became just as cruel the moment you had the power."

"Don't ever compare me to your people!" Khaf's voice rang out inside the void, shaking me. "I am *not* a tyrant. My actions were for a good cause."

Good cause? Yeah, I'd heard those words before.

"We must keep the Hyksos of Avaris beneath our feet," I said. "If we empower them, they will destroy our lands, just as their ancestors did. This might be cruel, but it's for a good cause."

Khaf clutched my shoulder and twisted me to face him. "What did you say, Egyptian?"

"That was my master's answer when I asked him why we're so cruel to your people. He, too, said our actions were justified because they were for a good cause." I jerked my shoulder, and Khaf released me, his face turning paler. "You spoke the truth in the Field of Reeds, Khafset. You're an Egyptian. The moment you had power, you caused harm, and I was your first victim."

I turned, keeping Khaf dumbfounded behind me, and shifted my focus to the golden divine Nile that still had a fading blue sliver.

"Nef, I—"

"I don't wish to speak to you right now."

"Do..." He paused, his usually confident voice hesitant. "Do you hate me?"

Oh, I should've loathed him. But our relationship had outgrown easily defined emotions such as love or hate. The evil thief was now the Hyksos, whom our soldiers had orphaned. Khaf, with whom I loved to talk. An orphan who protected his adopted family. The man who called me Nef and fought the gods to save me. Khaf wasn't perfect. He wasn't a hero fighting for justice and equality. He was too emotional and not even all that smart. Khafset of Avaris was a deeply flawed person whose only redeeming quality was his love for his family.

He was my Hyksos counterpart.

"The river is yellow." Khaf's hands shifted toward my waist. He hesitated and reached for Ishtar's red saddle. "Hold tight. The barque is about to arrive."

Ishtar walked upstream. First, in small steps, then picked up speed. She spread her wings, floated into the dark void above the divine Nile, and bolted in the barque's direction.

A boat—as wide as the divine Nile—appeared in the distance. It sent shockwaves through the river, pushing its glowing particles into stronger and more intense waves. Brilliant yellow energy consumed the surrounding darkness, turning the black void sun-gold.

Ishtar dove in a straight line toward the approaching barque.

"Brace for impact!" Khaf said.

Ishtar's hooves collided with the barque's wooden floor. We flew off her saddle and rolled until we crashed into a set of stairs at the barque's center that led to a cabin.

"Nef!" Khaf's muffled voice called, his hand tapping my cheek. "Nefiri!"

"Ishtar!" I said. "Is she hurt?"

"She's fine. What about you? Are *you* hurt?"

I sat on the floor, the world rotating around me, and hisses whispered in my ears. My vision refocused on Khaf's face, and the hisses faded into Khaf's deep voice. His expression was calm, but his eyes, those honey-colored irises, betrayed his buried truth—a scared little boy lurking inside a proud man. Why did I see all these new details all of a sudden?

"I'm fine." I pushed his hand away.

Khaf lowered his gaze toward a small cut on my left arm. "You're bleeding!"

"It's not a big deal."

"Of course it's a big deal!" He reached for the bag strapped across his chest and fished out a jar containing a green paste. "Don't worry. I've prepared just the medicine for..."

He looked at my injured arm, and his eyes widened. I lowered my gaze. My wound wasn't bleeding anymore!

"What?!" Khaf said. "How?!"

"It must be the spear. It's... changing me. I've felt strange since I touched it, but I started noticing it more after we passed through the barque-gate."

"Nef..." He swallowed, folding his hands over the medical jar. "The spear shouldn't have this effect on you."

"Well." I shrugged. "You said I'm a demigoddess, didn't you? Some durability must come with that."

"I—guess." He released the air trapped in his lungs, his eyes switching between me and the spear. "Nevertheless, let me apply the paste just in case." He smiled. "We don't know if demigods are immune to infections."

He grasped for my hand and hesitated. I rolled my eyes and gave him my wrist.

"How would a thief know about wound infections?" I asked.

"You still underestimate me, Egyptian." Khaf smeared the paste on my wound. "Give it time." He sat beside me and leaned against the stairs.

"Even I don't know anything about medicine, and I've received a tutorage that would put Setu's overpriced education to shame."

Khaf shrugged. "Picked up a few recipes while searching for..." He cleared his throat, his gaze escaping me.

My eyes widened. "While searching for a real cure for Hote. Gods, you weren't lying, were you?"

"I tried to save him. I promise you I did everything..."

Khaf broke off, his eyes flickering over the barque's dark recesses. He jumped to his feet and spun around, holding out his dagger.

"What's wrong?" I asked.

"We aren't alone!"

"How do you keep hearing things I can't?"

"Shh. Grab the spear."

I held the spear and turned in circles, my back stuck to Khaf's.

Footsteps echoed in the shadows, accompanied by a faint growl. The barque's wood screeched, and whispers scattered around us.

"Do you smell this, sister?" a melodic, almost hypnotic woman's voice said.

"I do," a harsher woman answered. "I smell blood."

"Mortal blood." The first woman giggled.

"Souls in Duat that haven't tasted death!" A roar vibrated the barque's floor.

The writings on Khaf's chest glowed. He grabbed my waist and dashed toward Ishtar at the barque's front. An explosion erupted where we had stood a heartbeat ago.

Shards of wood sliced the air. I planted the spear on the wooden deck. "Ga'ab Neyat!"

Set's protective dome formed around us. The shards hit the dome's scarlet surface and faded into dust.

"What was that?!" I asked.

The smoke cloud from the explosion vanished, revealing a woman with a lioness's head.

"Not bad, mortal." She walked in our direction, ribbons of smoke gliding through her black fur. Her golden armor clacked when it rubbed against the two swords behind her back.

Her yellow eyes stared at Khaf. She drew her swords and pointed them at him. "Did you visit my father's barque to challenge me?"

"Oh, no, no." Khaf gave a nervous laugh. Good for him for just being nervous. I, for one, was about to faint.

Khaf's grip shook around my waist. "I would never dream of challenging the goddess of war to battle." He stood behind me but didn't sheath his dagger. "I acknowledge my inferiority to you, great Sekhmet."

"S-Sekhmet!" I swallowed.

"Isn't he cute?" A woman walked from the shadows with feline elegance. Her appearance resembled Sekhmet's except for her slender body, cat head, and white dress. This had to be Bastet, the goddess of protection, and her warrior sister's opposite.

"They are foul," Sekhmet said.

"Oh, no, sister," Bastet said. "They look like cute little scarabs crawling on our father's solar barque."

"Little scarabs who aren't where they belong!" Sekhmet's body tensed. "Little scarabs whom I will squash." She charged, roaring.

Sekhmet collided with the dome's glass-like surface and banged it with her swords. Cracks slithered up its surface with each blow.

"Damn you!" Sekhmet said. "You and that spear!" The first portion of the dome's protective layer fell into specks of glowing scarlet dust. "Come out and fight me!"

"Doesn't the girl look marvelous with her tiny human hands?" Bastet giggled. "An adorable creature wielding a god's weapon."

"I will cut off those hands and throw them to Apep when he arrives," Sekhmet said. "Maybe that will satisfy him this round."

"She can help you fight Apep!" Khaf said.

"What?" Sekhmet stopped.

"Yeah, what!" I glared over my shoulder at the Hyksos.

"Set used to fight the serpent of chaos, and Nefiri wields his weapon. She's even using his magic right now!"

"But that fragile little thing will break the moment she faces Apep." Bastet walked toward Sekhmet and guided her reluctant sister away from the dome.

"Fragile? Who? Nefiri Minu!" Khaf laughed. "She's Egypt's greatest warrior."

"She is?" Sekhmet regarded me from top to bottom.

"Of course! Ballads were written about her battles."

"They were?" Bastet clapped her hands before her breasts.

"Indeed, great Bastet, indeed. She's even the pharaoh's champion."

"I am?" I said out of the corner of my mouth.

He tapped my back with his elbow, still holding tight to his dagger.

"Yes, I am," I announced.

"Oh, I remember!" Bastet smiled and lowered Sekhmet's hands. "She's the one taking Horus's test. That's why she wields our brother's spear."

"I guess the spear would choose a warrior." Sekhmet scratched her snout with her golden sword. "But look at her, sister. No, I'm not convinced. Your pharaoh prayed to me while marching to battle. Why would he fight without his champion?"

I swallowed. "Erm... well... because..."

"Because she is so powerful, it would have been a hollow victory!" Khaf said. "Our mighty pharaoh wanted the battle of Kadesh to stay fair. Thirsty for a fight, Nefiri challenged Set by grabbing his spear, and of course, it chose her. In her infinite wisdom, our queen sent her husband's champion to clash with the god of destruction."

Mighty pharaoh? Wise queen? Gods, he was such a blunt liar. He'd contradict his core beliefs just to achieve his goals. But... to be fair, his methods were effective.

The cat goddess smiled at us and laid her head on her sister's broad shoulder.

"Can't your mighty warrior speak for herself?" Sekhmet asked. "Did my sister eat her tongue?"

"I'm a warrior. I fight. I have Khafset to take care of boring matters like speaking." I glanced at Khaf, and a strange warmth filled my chest when he gave me a slight nod, his lips pressed together in a smile.

"Is he your husband?" Bastet asked, and my heart froze at the audacity.

Khaf gave a disgusting laugh behind me. He sure was having fun. Well, two could play this game.

"Khafset is my servant."

Bastet frowned. "He is?"

"I am?!" Khaf barked behind me.

"Yes. He carries my stuff and praises my victories. He's Hyksos, so we can't really expect much more from him."

"Why his hostile reaction then?" Sekhmet scanned us. "If he's used to being called a servant?"

"He suffers from a severe inferiority complex." I sighed, shaking my head. "But don't worry, great Sekhmet, I can get him in line." I grinned at Khaf. "Aren't you my servant?"

Khaf bit his lip. "Yes, I—am."

"And why are you my servant, Khafset of Avaris?"

Khaf gritted his teeth. "Because I'm just a Hyksos."

I had him! Gods, I finally got some justice. I had Khaf right under my thumb; he was at my mercy. So why did my smile fade? Why did it feel so wrong? Where was the joy I expected? I turned my gaze to the goddesses to avoid Khaf's scowl.

"Oh, come on, sister," Bastet said. "Believe the Egyptian and her Hyksos servant."

"Why should I?" Sekhmet said. "Their very presence on this barque defies most divine laws! Aren't mortals supposed to stay away from Frenzy? Because if not, then why are we fighting Apep in the first place?"

Bastet hummed, her clawed cat finger under her chin. "Perhaps they are immune to it?" She clapped her hands. "Yes! Horus would never allow the spear to choose a mortal who might be overtaken by Frenzy. Look at the girl. She has been holding the spear for Atem knows how long, and her brain still has not exploded."

Exploded! My brain! Gods, no wonder I'd been feeling weird.

"True." Sekhmet eyed me. "I guess it *is* a testament to her strength." She sighed and lowered her weapons. "Fine. They can distract Apep. Better than nothing."

"Would you consider breaking the shield," Khaf said, "Cobra?"

Goosebumps crawled on my skin at that word. Sekhmet gave a slight nod, probably assuming it was a servant's way of showing respect to his warrior master. But I knew what he meant. Paser's vicious cobra that everyone feared. The monster Khaf claimed to have tamed. He was reminding me that I was Master Paser's servant while he had always been a free man. Oh, even with a thousand daggers pointed at him, the thief could always twist his target's heart.

I broke the shield but kept my gaze away from him. I didn't have it in me to look into his honey eyes.

Khaf sheathed his dagger and bowed before the goddesses. "We are thankful for your mercy."

"Come, mortals," Bastet said. "We must explain the battle to you before Apep arrives."

"If the goddesses would be so kind," Khaf said, "could I have a word alone with the warrior?"

"What?" Sekhmet growled. "This is Ra's solar barque, not your war council, you little—"

"But of course." Bastet held Sekhmet's arms. "We'll await you in the cabin." Bastet dragged her growling sister. They entered the cabin at the barque's center, leaving me alone with... with... oh gods! Alone with Khaf.

"You sure had your fun, didn't you?" Khaf asked.

I shook my head. "That wasn't fun. It felt horrible."

Khaf raised an eyebrow. "Aren't you going to give me a monologue about how I deserved it?"

"Yes!" I pointed my finger at him. "Exactly. That should've been my reaction. Why didn't I do that? Why do I feel so terrible?" I glanced to the side to avoid his eyes. Not because they were angry. Curse him; his expression was sympathetic. "I promised never to insult you for being a Hyksos. Our fight doesn't excuse me for breaking my promise. I'm sorry."

Khaf held my chin and guided my gaze toward his smile.

"Khaf," I said, trembling in his grip.

"Yes, Nef."

"Why are you staring at me?"

"You look pretty when you overthink." His voice was different. Smug as always, sure. But it felt... genuine? Like I was hearing his authentic voice for the first time. As if the real Khaf was finally revealing himself to me.

"Please—stop."

"What? It's the truth." He chuckled. "And you're free to step back if you wish."

My heart pounded, and a strange sensation gathered in my belly. I pushed him away and turned. Curse him and those eyes of his!

"Mortals!" Sekhmet roared. "Cabin! Now!"

"Aren't they so adorable you want to rip them apart?" Bastet's giggles escaped the cabin.

"I *want* to rip them apart. The only thing stopping me is Horus's test and the distraction they will provide against Apep."

"Hey." Khaf stood behind me, his warm breath brushing my neck. "I'm sorry. I didn't mean to upset you." Again. There it was—his strange genuine tone.

How was I even able to function anymore? I was standing on Ra's solar barque, surrounded by Khaf, Astarte's horse, and two goddesses, not to mention the serpent of chaos looming in the distance. And apparently, my brain might explode!

I drew a deep breath to regain my composure and turned to face Khaf. If I was good at something, it was keeping myself together even when I was about to shatter into a million pieces. "What was that about my brain exploding?"

"Ah, don't worry. They're overreacting."

"I don't think they are."

"Yes, they—"

"Khaf, I'm not well. I've been feeling warm since we passed through the barque-gate and... and I keep hearing strange hissing noises in my ears. What's happening to me, Khafset?"

"I—don't know."

"Then who would?!" I snapped, and he flinched.

"I... look, I don't know what's happening, but I know the spear can't do anything to you. That Frenzy thing they're all afraid of is just gods being gods. They overreact. They can only see the big picture, which tends to leave them a little blind."

"Are you sure?" I asked.

Khaf stepped toward me, smiling. "I'm sure about one thing. I promised to bring you home safely and *will* keep my promise."

"Mortals!" Sekhmet shouted from inside the cabin. "Apep is about to arrive!"

"I'm not fighting the serpent of chaos, am I?" I asked.

"You're not," Khaf said. "I'll get you out of this."

"Then do it!"

"What is taking so long?" Sekhmet barged out of the cabin, dragging her sister, who was trying—and failing—to keep her in place.

A smile formed on Khaf's face, and the goddesses' footsteps halted behind me. Good to know Khaf's arrogance startled even the gods.

"Great goddesses," Khaf said, "we have come to the most disheartening realization. Our champion has reminded me she cannot waste her energy against Apep before fighting Set. I do apologize for making empty promises on behalf of our warrior. A stupid mistake by an ignorant servant. We would be eternally grateful if you could point us to the demon-gate so we can continue our journey to Abydos."

"Leave?" Sekhmet laughed. "Apep will arrive at any moment."

"Any moment?" I raised my head toward Khaf. The goddesses were going to witness how Egypt's greatest warrior was about to faint.

"Oh yes, any moment," Bastet said joyfully. "Oh, sister." She clapped her hands. "The warrior and her servant could be our new Set and Nephthys."

Khaf nodded, but his bare chest, inches from my face, was tense. I was stressed, too. So much, in fact, I nearly hugged Khaf. Would it be so bad to hug him? It might relieve my stress. This situation was so awful, and the Hyksos was my only source of comfort. I frowned at the thought. What was wrong with me today?

"Khaf, look at me."

He lowered his gaze, and his honey eyes stared into mine.

"I won't fight Apep."

Khaf swallowed. "Maybe—"

"There is no maybe. I can't under any circumstances clash with the serpent of chaos."

"Everything all right back there?" Sekhmet asked.

I caught his arms—and increased the pressure of my grip when the width of his arm muscles caught me by surprise. What human could pack so many muscles into such a lean body? Gods, it was as if... no, focus!

"Fix—this," I hissed.

Khaf sighed, and his fake smile returned. "Great Sekhmet." He walked toward the goddesses until he stood between them and me. "And, of course, great Bastet."

"Get to the point!" Sekhmet said.

"He is simply adorable when he tries," Bastet said.

"I apologize." Khaf bowed. "Our warrior and champion would love nothing more than to clash with the serpent of chaos. I mean, look at her. Look how bloodthirsty and hungry for battle she is."

He pointed at me and then frowned when I tried to flex my arm muscles. I had none.

"You shouldn't draw our attention to her physique," Sekhmet said.

"I'm afraid it doesn't help your argument, child," Bastet said.

"She doesn't look like much," Khaf said. "If anything, she looks like a lost child searching for her mother. But don't let that masterful illusion trick you, O mighty goddesses, for behind that fragile and, I admit, underwhelming physique lurks a bloodthirsty beast."

How did he do it? How did he lie so easily? A new sense of wonder overtook me—a strange appreciation of how he didn't surrender.

"That fierce woman over there," Khaf continued, "never lost a battle in her life." He smiled at me, trapping the air in my chest with his intense gaze. "No matter the odds, Nefiri never met a challenge she couldn't overcome."

"What is your point, mortal?" Sekhmet asked.

Khaf walked toward me. "My point is, she would love nothing more than to clash with Apep in the hope of finally meeting her match. But a glorious battle against Set awaits her in Abydos." He stood behind me and laid his hands on my shoulders, shrinking me in his grip. "For that reason, she must pass through the demon-gate even if it means passing on the glorious opportunity to fight Apep." He sighed. "A warrior's duty, I'm afraid."

"What a shame." Sekhmet smiled, revealing her fangs. "You missed the demon-gate."

"We did?" I asked.

"Yes," Bastet said. "The barque passes through twelve gates in Duat each day. The demon-gate is somewhere between the first and the second. We are now heading toward the last gate, where Apep will intercept us before we enter Huat. If you survive him, you can seek the demon-gate once we reenter Duat."

"In other words," Sekhmet said, "you are twenty-three gates too late."

I shook, either because of my impending death or Khaf's trembling grip on my shoulders.

A gentle smile overtook Bastet's compassionate cat face. "Follow us, mortals. We have something to show you before Apep arrives." Bastet took her sister's hand and walked into the cabin.

"The barque passes through twenty-four gates," Khaf said to himself. "I didn't know there were gates in Huat. How fascinating."

"Now, mortals!" Sekhmet shouted from inside the cabin.

Khaf sighed. "Come before Sekhmet kills us." He took my hand and guided me to the cabin.

We entered, and I was immediately overwhelmed by the numerous objects that filled the room. Gorgeous bronze mirrors, shelves adorned with countless scrolls, chests overflowing with coins and jewelry, armor made of exotic metals, foods I couldn't name, and wine racks.

Normally, all of that would have caught my attention. I would have run to the scrolls and gobbled up the knowledge and secrets from their pages while fighting the temptation to touch the coins and jewelry. Everything in this cabin would've been a source of absolute fascination for me, had it not been for the throne inside the cabin and the being slumbering on it—a man with a hawk's head, wearing a red kilt. Gray feathers covered his dwindling body and vibrated with his soft breaths.

"Is that..." I couldn't finish the question and covered my mouth.

"It can't be him," Khaf said in an equally shocked voice.

"It is him," Bastet said, her tone somber. "Our father. The great Ra. I wanted you to see him before the battle."

"What happened to him?" I asked.

"Set and Nephthys happened to him," Sekhmet growled, patting Ra's clawed hand. "Ever since they defied our father and left the solar barque, Ra has been fighting Apep alone. When Bastet and I were old enough to join the fight, our father went into the deep slumber you are witnessing. Ra's battles against the serpent of chaos had consumed him. Burned even the sun god himself." She turned to us. "Look at him, humans. See how a true god sacrifices himself for his mortals. That's the difference between him and Set. Ra never surrendered or allowed temptation to overcome him. He fought Apep alone each day to protect humanity and guard the rising of the sun. And look where it got him."

Bastet held Sekhmet's hand.

"He was the first warrior," Sekhmet said. "Compared to him, we all pale."

"What happens if Apep wins?" I asked.

"Then he will devour the solar barque and gain the ability to enter Huat," Sekhmet said.

"Oh, the sheer horror of that fate!" Bastet said. "Frenzy would consume Huat. The world would plunge into darkness. Demons from the ages before the gods would rise. The dead would return, blurring the lines between the realms, and a new age of chaos would be ushered in."

I glared at Khaf. "And I'm supposed to fight—"

My heart stopped. My skin burned as if flames were eating my flesh. Dozens, no hundreds, no thousands of hissing voices consumed my thoughts. My knees weakened. I lost my balance, and Khaf caught me.

"Nef, are you all right?" Khaf growled. "Gods, you're burning!"

"The spear!" Bastet pointed at Set's weapon behind my back.

I caught a glimpse of myself in the smooth bronze surface of one of the mirrors. The spear's blade was pulsating with a scarlet light.

A maroon glow exploded in the dark void. Its rays slithered into Ra's cabin and dissolved like salt in water. The barque shook, scattering the surrounding coins and artifacts. A loud hiss consumed the barque, forcing even the goddesses to cover their ears.

"He is here!" Bastet said. "Apep has arrived!"

"Battle stations!" Sekhmet said, and the goddesses ran out of the cabin.

"That's it," I said, holding tight to Khaf. "We have finally met an obstacle that will kill us."

"D-don't…" The hand of the proud thief of Avaris trembled on my waist. "Don't fight him."

"What?! But you said—"

"I've changed my mind." Khaf's honey eyes met mine. "I… I don't know if I could protect you against Apep. Please, hide."

"I've been protecting myself my entire life, Khafset." I gathered my strength to stand without his help. "After our fight against Shemzu, I promised you I wouldn't run away and leave you to die."

"I relieve you of that promise," Khaf said. "Please, you… well, I don't want you to die, all right?!"

I stepped back, my hand over my chest. This was strangely blunt by his standards.

"Khaf, I won't run. So you can either let me fight unprepared, or skip the nonsense and share your plans with me. A brilliant lie, or information you learned in Set's temple. Anything."

He tried—and for the first time failed—to form his smug smile with his trembling lips. "You think my lies are brilliant, Egyptian?"

"Khafset, focus! I know you're as terrified as me, so drop the act. Do you have a trick to save me from Apep?"

Khaf glanced at the slumbering Ra and, following a long pause, shook his head.

"Gods!" I laid my hands on my head. "Apep is going to devour me."

The barque shook, and I leaned on the object beside me, only for my heart to stop when I caught my reflection in a mirror. I was leaning on the king of the gods!

"Mortals!" Sekhmet shouted, and I flinched away from Ra.

"Just discussing strategy!" Khaf called. He grabbed my arms and dragged me closer to him, sending yet another unfamiliar shiver down my spine.

Too much. This was all too much. Fear paralyzed my body while Khaf clouded my mind.

"Nef, listen to me."

"I will die. Oh gods, I will die the most gruesome death possible!"

"No, you won't. I promised, remember? I won't let you fight Apep alone."

"Alone! A thousand people like us don't stand a chance against Apep."

"There are no people like us. Look where we are." He gently traced his hands over my arms. A movement that enraged another storm of emotions inside me.

I pulled free and turned away to collect myself. My heart was beating too fast; my body was raging hot; the world around me was too slow. Apep's hisses were getting louder each moment. Was this what people experienced when facing certain death? These new sensations couldn't be related to Khaf. They couldn't!

"I might have a plan," Khaf said.

"You do?" I spun around and punched his rock-hard chest; pain soared in my knuckles. "Why did you hide it?!"

"I... didn't wish to use it yet."

I gave him a suspicious look.

Khaf's face turned serious. "We're going to ask Set for help."

"Are you mad?!"

"Set is our only hope." He pointed to the hole in his leather bag. "Remember what you did?"

"Are you really going to complain about that when Apep is nearly here?"

Khaf sighed. "Remember what happened after you ruined my shiny new leather bag?"

I rolled my eyes while recalling the events of Shemzu's encounter. I stumbled and pierced his bag with the spear. Then I... My eyes widened. "I felt Set."

He nodded.

"Khaf... What's in that bag?"

He fished out two silver scarabs, one of which had a burn mark. Both looked like Tuya's golden scarab that I hid over my heart.

"What are those?" I asked.

"Set's scarabs. They are gifts from the gods to allow us humans to communicate with them in, let's say, different capacities."

"What?"

"The silver scarabs create a mental bridge between a mortal and a god, like the one you had with Set when he helped you defeat Shemzu. It only needs to be pierced by a divine item to activate. Like when you struck it with Set's spear. You do that again, and let's hope Set can help you against Apep."

So silver was for making a mental connection between a god and a human? What was the golden scarab's function?

"Mortals!" Sekhmet roared. "I won't call again!"

"Take it." Khaf pushed the scarab into my hand. "Keep it hidden from the goddesses, and remember, don't think of Set as the god of destruction; simply think of him as your potential father."

That was the problem. I hated asking my father for help more than accepting Set's aid. But what choice did I have? I hid the scarab under my dress over my right breast.

Khaf coughed, reminding me of his presence. He turned and looked outside the cabin.

Had... had I just shown him my breast? On second thoughts, agonizing death by the serpent of chaos wasn't so bad anymore.

"Are..." Khaf cleared his throat. "Are you done?"

"Y-yes."

Khaf turned, revealing his red face. Why was Khafset, of all people, blushing? He bragged about sleeping with all these women in the Tavern of Avaris and never... oh! He blushed because it was me. So... not as ugly as a cow after all?

"Let's go before Sekhmet kills us," Khaf said.

We walked to the barque's front position where the goddess waited beside Ishtar.

"One more glorious battle!" Sekhmet shouted at the raging black clouds in the stormy maroon void. "One more day of your delusions." She slashed her black and golden swords together, releasing their energies. "Not today, Apep!"

Chapter 14

The Serpent of Chaos

A maroon storm encapsulated Ra's solar barque, trapping its golden rays in a prison of madness. My head ached. The divine Nile raged. Silver clouds collided. Hisses thundered, their magnitude vibrating every bone in my body. If I could rub two mountains together as one might do with stones, their sound would've mimicked Apep's.

Despite the madness, the chaos, and the sheer horror, Apep remained hidden.

I sat on Ishtar's back, my grip tight around Set's spear, my body tense. I had no time to focus on the pain in my head, the hisses in my ears, or the heat crawling on my skin. Only one person claimed my attention in this realm filled with gods and monsters.

Khaf.

How would he survive Apep with nothing but a dagger? Why did his fate consume my thoughts? We both knew we might die before reaching Abydos. There was no explanation for the weight crushing my chest each time I imagined Khaf being devoured by the serpent of chaos.

"Where is he?" Sekhmet shouted.

"Apep's never done this before," Bastet said. "He always attacks the moment we enter his storm."

Sekhmet grabbed Bastet's arm. "Stay by our father's side and protect him."

Bastet nodded and ran to Ra's cabin.

A silver bolt struck above the barque, its force shaking and twisting the ship's wood.

"Steady, mortals. Don't let Apep's mind games trick you."

A glowing maroon mist rose from underneath the barque and covered its floor. The dust vibrated and shifted beneath Khaf's feet as if... as if reacting to... oh gods, the dust slithered!

"He's under the barque!" I shouted over Apep's loud hisses.

Khaf gritted his teeth, the hieroglyphs on his chest glowing.

"Damn you, Apep," Sekhmet said. "Why are you acting strange?"

Apep's gray tail launched from the barque's rear. It towered over us like a mountain. Its scales glistened, shifting a maroon pulse to the blade at his tail's end. He plunged it toward us. The air shrieked from his attack.

Sekhmet launched herself at the falling tail, Khaf bolting by her side. The ship shook, and Khaf lost his footing, causing him to collide with the goddess of war. The force of their collision sent both the goddess and the idiot crashing to the floor.

"You braindead fool of a servant!" Sekhmet shouted.

"I'm sor—" His wide eyes met the falling tail.

Refusing to be useless anymore, I snapped myself out of my frozen state and pointed Set's spear toward the descending tail. "Shama'at Morot!" A scarlet beam launched from my divine weapon and hit its target. The monster's looming tail faltered.

"Set!" Apep hissed from beneath the barque. He retracted his tail.

"Not bad!" Khaf said.

"It's not over yet, mortal," Sekhmet said, rising from her fall, her hand rubbing the spot on her head where Khaf had hit her in his stupidity. "It's just the beginning."

I met Sekhmet's dizzy eyes. How did a simple accidental knock from Khaf affect the goddess so much? She seemed unable to focus since her failed attack. No. She couldn't have failed. Her attack would probably have been successful if it wasn't for Khaf's weak legs.

The serpent's tail launched from the barque's side and twirled around its structure, trapping the gigantic ship in its grip. I pointed the spear at Apep's body.

"Shama'at—"

"Watch out!" Khaf shouted behind me.

Following Khaf's pointed finger, Sekhmet turned, and her eyes widened. I turned to the barque's front. Apep's serpent face rose from the divine Nile, dwarfing the solar barque. His forked tongue slithered through his fangs, and even his teeth were taller than me!

"Great Sekhmet!" Khaf said. "What should we do now?"

"We should… We should…"

Apep's red eyes stared at Sekhmet, and the goddess fell silent. She seemed to be struggling to move her gaze away from Apep's glaring eyes, but her head kept returning to its original position. After much struggle, her hands fell beside her, and her body swayed in unison with the serpent.

"Great Sekhmet?" I commanded Ishtar to approach her.

"Stay where you are!" Khaf retreated from Sekhmet, and Ishtar stopped. "Apep has hypnotized her!"

Apep's hisses exploded around us as if the storm was an extension of him. "Bring me that spear!"

The goddess of war roared. She jumped toward me. I screamed. Khaf's hieroglyphs flashed. He intersected Sekhmet's attack, launching the goddess toward the left side of the barque.

The maroon mist rose from the ground and parted, marking the goddess's path.

"Run!" Khaf said.

Sekhmet freed herself from the damaged wood in the side of the ship. She dashed toward Khaf, capturing the maroon mist in the winds of her sprint. Khaf's chest glowed. He struck the ground, ready to bolt, pushing the mist into a frenzy. The goddess caught Khaf's neck and punched his chest, thrusting him toward the barque's right side.

I tapped Ishtar with my feet. She galloped toward the barque's rear. Sekhmet ran beside Ishtar, matching her insane speed, turning the grounded maroon mist into a raging storm. The goddess delivered a mighty blow to Ishtar's side. The horse collapsed, launching me off her back. I rolled across the barque's wooden deck until I hit the stairs leading to Ra's cabin.

The glowing mist crawled over my skin. It covered me and pulsed, shifting from maroon to rose. A spark ignited inside me and snapped me out of my dizziness. Gods, it felt as if someone had kicked me in the chest. I fought the disorientation, headache, and hisses whispering in my ringing ears and stood with the spear's help. Despite the blood obscuring my vision, one thing was as clear as the sun. The goddess of war was walking toward me, her golden eyes filled with violence.

"Kill the Chosen!" Apep hissed. "Bring me that spear!"

"Ga..." I spat out blood and planted the spear in the wooden floor. "Ga'ab Neyat!"

Set's protective dome formed around me, shielding me, Bastet, and the slumbering Ra in the cabin.

Sekhmet reached the dome. She banged on its scarlet semitransparent surface with her swords. The glass-like surface of the shield cracked. I laid my hand over my heart, and the bulge caught my attention. Set's silver scarab! He could help me. He was still my god, after all.

I gritted my teeth and glared at the goddess. No. If Set could fight Sekhmet through me, then I was capable of defeating her myself. I would never surrender myself to the god of destruction, especially if he was my father.

"Do it!" I screamed at the hypnotized goddess. Was I afraid? Of course not. I was terrified. However, death in battle against the war goddess wasn't a bad way to die. Oh, the glory I could claim if I managed to deliver a single blow to the mighty war goddess! One success in the colossal failure that had been my life.

Sekhmet landed her shattering strike on the shield. I took Khaf's viper stance, and the spear's blade glowed scarlet. The mist rose, trying to reach the divine weapon. I thrust the spear at the goddess's shoulder.

The war goddess deflected the blow with her swords. She ducked under the spear and rose on its right side. Her hand descended toward me, her black sword pointed at my heart.

Bastet jumped from the cabin and fell on Sekhmet. The sisters rolled until Bastet landed on top and pinned her sister to the floor.

"Snap out of it, sister!" Bastet said. "Don't let Apep control you. We need you."

The hypnotized goddess roared at her sister and tried to bite her.

Apep's tail rose over the two goddesses.

"Oh no, you don't!" I pointed the increasingly heavy spear at Apep's tail. "Shama'at Morot!"

The scarlet beam hit his tail. The serpent roared but didn't retract it. The beam was too weak. *I* was too weak. Why was I losing energy so fast all of a sudden?

Apep hissed, his red eyes glaring at me. I'd gotten his attention at least.

"Begone, vessel!" Apep launched his tail toward me.

I braced myself for his fatal strike.

Time stopped.

Khaf emerged. He grabbed me by my waist and bolted away. My hand trembled. The spear fell from my grip, and the mist rushed to swallow it. Despite Khaf's velocity, Apep's swiping tail hit him in the side. We crumpled to the floor, Khaf's weight pressing me against the wooden deck.

Apep attacked, and Khaf shielded me from the strike. The serpent's tail hit again, and a crack tore through Khaf's body. Khaf hugged me tighter. How, in Sekhmet's name, was he surviving Apep's attacks?

Khaf's bloodshot eyes focused on me, his tears raining on my face. He gritted his teeth and glanced over his shoulder at the serpent. "You will *not* harm her! You can devour the entire world, but you won't have her, Apep!"

"Khaf!"

Apep hit him again. Khaf screamed but didn't let go.

"Khaf, run! He only wants me."

"N-no. I told many lies, but my promise wasn't one of them. You *will* return home!"

I couldn't find a word to describe the Hyksos. The gods trembled before Apep while Khaf defied him to protect me.

"Insects!" Apep launched his tail toward us.

We braced for the hit. It never came. Instead, Apep's tail struck a green barrier that mirrored Bastet's glow.

"Run, humans!" the goddess of protection shouted. "I can't contain my sister and protect you at the same time."

"Help me reach the spear," I told Khaf. "I'll accept Set's help."

"T-too… late." Khaf's voice! Gods, as if a corpse was speaking! "Take Ishtar. Leave. Go home. Escape with… Setu and the girls. Please. I love you. Love you all."

"If we don't reach Set and steal his scythe, Egypt will be destroyed. Your people won't get their freedom."

"I—failed." Khaf gritted his teeth, and the hieroglyphs' golden glow leaked from his chest, covering his body. His skin cracked, and blood escaped from his wounds.

Gods, he was calling more magic. He still wanted to fight! He wouldn't survive. His body was too weak.

I hugged Khaf. "Please don't leave!"

"Sorry." We bolted from our spot to the barque's rear, barely missing Apep's tail. Khaf broke free from my grip and dashed across the ship, reappearing in front of the serpent's face.

"Khaf!"

"What are you doing, human?" Bastet shouted, struggling against her sister. "Get away from him!"

The proud thief of Avaris marched toward the serpent of chaos, holding nothing but his dagger. Khaf grabbed his head. His golden glow intensified. His skin cracked. Then he screamed. No, he roared.

Apep launched his tail toward Khaf.

Khaf's magic exploded. The Hyksos shone like a raging sun. He jumped on Apep's tail and bolted up it, leaving behind a spiraling trail of the serpent's blood that dissolved in Khaf's golden rays.

Apep roared and pushed him off his tail with the sheer power of his voice. He raised his tail and slammed Khaf onto the deck of the barque. Khaf bounced from the power of the impact and let out a pained gasp. Apep's tail slithered over the barque's surface. He captured Khaf and raised him in front of his face.

"I will crush every bone in your body, Canaanite!" Apep tightened his grip around Khaf's body. The Hyksos gave an excruciating scream that twisted my soul. "I will squeeze your insides out of your skin like paste."

Ishtar cried at me, signaling to her saddle with her head. I couldn't look away from the screaming Hyksos. Should I honor his last wish? Should I return to Huat? A world without the proud thief of Avaris. The Hyksos who brought me to Duat.

Because of him, I spoke to gods and ancient pharaohs. He was the reason I met Hatshepsut. I couldn't have dreamt of witnessing all this without Khaf in my life. The thief who compared me to a cow, just to call me pretty. The man who protected me, only to admire me as the smartest and strongest woman in Egypt.

It was all him.

Khafset of Avaris.

My comrade in crime.

I ignored the voice hissing in my head, urging me to escape. I ran toward the spear. I wouldn't abandon Khaf. Never again. I didn't want him to die. Not because we deserved the same fate or because I'd promised never to abandon him again. Gods, curse him.

I loved the idiot!

The mist covering the barque pulsed underneath my feet, sending a glowing rose wave that swallowed Apep's maroon hue.

Once in the spear's range, I stretched out my arm. Scarlet energy sparked at my fingertips, and the weapon flew into my grip. I grabbed the silver scarab from under my dress, then laid it over the spear's tip, a finger separating their metals.

"Apep! Do you want the spear? Take it yourself!"

The serpent of chaos dropped Khaf, and his black irises shifted toward me.

"Run, mortal!" Bastet shouted.

Apep extended his neck toward me until I stood between his glowing red eyes. He opened his mouth, revealing his fangs. His rotten breath stung my nostrils, and I almost vomited.

"The Chosen," he hissed, his eyes scanning the now rose-colored mist. "A new child of Frenzy. A creature of passion."

The shadow of Apep's tail slithered behind me.

A few more moments.

I would show him true frenzy. Oh, I would show him the most passionate madness he had ever witnessed.

"Give me the spear willingly, and you can be my chosen," Apep hissed. "Join me, and I'll teach you about your dormant powers."

One more moment. A couple of heartbeats until his tail was right behind me. I counted the seconds and ignored him. I wasn't going to listen to any more promises. Oh, I'd been promised wealth, power, and glory. What did it make out of me? I tortured innocents—sent defenseless children to a life of humiliation. No. I didn't wish for power. I only wished for one thing: to reunite Khaf's family with their brother. They would *not* lose their brother like I did!

"Follow me, and we'll free the realms from the gods' tyranny," Apep hissed. "Together, we can end the unnatural world they have created and usher in a new age of chaos. A pure world the way nature willed it before the gods' corruption."

Oh, lucky me. He was a self-righteous monster with a dream. Perfect!

"Be my link to Huat, and I shall reveal the secret that Horus hid about your father. Obey me, and I will resurrect Hote."

My face twitched at his last promise. Could he really... No! My brother was dead. He was happy and healthy in the Field of Reeds. He was at peace with our mother. I did everything in my power to save him, and now I had the same duty toward Khaf and his family.

I grinned. "It's a very tempting offer."

"Be my chosen. Be my agent of chaos, or Frenzy will consume your Ka. I will teach you how to control it, wield it, how to become a goddess."

I hummed, not paying the empty promises any attention. Let that Frenzy thing eat my entire Ka if it wished. I didn't care. It wasn't like I ever had a pure soul anyway.

Apep's tail was right behind me, ready to pierce my heart. Yep, he was a snake, all right.

"An amazing offer." I retracted my finger from the scarab. "Too bad I'm already chosen."

I connected the spear's blade with the silver scarab. A scarlet wave pulsed from the scarab and froze reality as Apep thrust his tail toward my heart.

"Set! I could *really* use your help if you ever wish to see your spear again!"

Do you accept my help? Set's deep voice threw me off balance. *Do you willingly accept the aid of the god of destruction? Do you accept me as your Baal?*

"I do." I had lied for less. "Now, help me defeat Apep."

Very well, my chosen. Very well... my liar.

Set's power exploded inside me. It pulsed through my body, granting me the beautiful sensation of might I'd had against Shemzu.

I stood between the frozen gods. Set's scarlet magic leaked from me and cracked the deck and sides of Ra's barque. I breathed in, basking in the divine energy. Set's phantom formed around me like armor, granting me yet another layer of might.

The mist arose from the ground, pulsating between its scarlet, maroon, and rose hues, and spiraled around my arm, feeding the scarlet glow of Set's spear. They seemed to merge, proving Khaf's prior assumption correct. Both Destruction and Chaos magic were aspects of Frenzy. This had one simple implication. If I could tap into Set's magic, I could do the same with Apep's magic and turn it against him.

I smiled at the serpent of chaos and said the eternal words Ra had declared since the dawn of creation, "Not today, Apep." I pointed the spear at his vibrating black irises."Shama'at Morot!"

A magnificent triple-colored beam—rose, scarlet, and maroon—launched from the spear's blade. It collided with Apep, unfreezing reality. The serpent's head plunged backward from the blast. I spun toward Apep's retreating tail.

Set whispered a new spell in my ear. "Sa'ot Senem!" A long scarlet blade extended from the spear's tip. I swung the spear and slashed Apep's tail.

Apep screamed, his severed tail falling behind me as I ran toward his head. I whistled, and Ishtar joined my sprint. Set's energy shifted to my knees. I jumped and landed on Ishtar's back.

"Thihier Hawa!"

Ishtar's wings sprang from her sides, forming a rose-misty arch around us. Her hooves lifted from the barque toward Apep's head. I floated before Apep's face, surrounded by the colliding maroon and scarlet storms. Blue particles floated from Ishtar's wings around me like dandelion fluff.

"Set!" Apep hissed.

"No, I'm not Set." I pointed my spear at him. "I'm Nefiri Minu, the thief of Peramessu." The scarlet energy of destruction spiraled around the spear. "Shama'at Morot!"

A scarlet beam, vast as the divine Nile, launched from the spear's blade. The beam blasted Apep's face, and a massive explosion erupted, engulfing me in a gray cloud.

"Ga'ab Neyat!" The protective sphere formed around Ishtar and me, sheltering us from the smoke.

Beautiful silence surrounded me. No screams. No hisses. No storms. Just calmness.

I did it. Apep lost! I achieved what Ra and Set had achieved since the dawn of time. No mortal should be capable of that, but I did it. That was the secret Horus hid about my father—the reveal that Apep used to seduce me. Khaf was right. I was Set's daughter. I was a demigoddess. I wielded the power of the gods and turned it against them.

"Set, are you really—"

Set's phantom evaporated in a misty scarlet stream, removing my connection to him.

Soon. It wouldn't be long before our reunion in Abydos.

I patted Ishtar's neck. "Let's—"

Thunder erupted in the cloud that surrounded me and Ishtar. Roars emerged, vibrating my bones. The smoke spiraled, revealing the rapidly healing scars on Apep's face.

"No!" I screamed. "I… I defeated you! I won!"

"Parasite!" Apep banged the protective dome with his head, shattering it and launching Ishtar and me toward the barque. We crashed into the deck. I tumbled off Ishtar's back and rolled until I hit the side of the barque.

Apep glared at me. "You shall witness true…" His gaze shifted beyond the barque.

A giant collection of black mist appeared in the distance. The gate to Huat! We were almost back in the mortal realm.

"Fine!" Apep's regrowing tail twirled around the barque until its entire structure was in his grip. "I don't require the spear or an agent of chaos anymore. Ra has finally lost." He opened his mouth, and little by little, the barque began its descent inside the serpent of chaos.

Curse him. The serpent could now devour the barque without resistance.

I stretched out my arm toward the maroon mist to draw some of Apep's magic. It turned rose at my touch. Apep lowered his gaze toward me. He hissed, shaking the world. I covered my ears and screamed. The mist retreated and abandoned ship.

Bastet screamed, staring at Apep. She could only witness our defeat, unable to give up her struggle against the hypnotized Sekhmet.

Then she did something unfathomable. A divine act that was the pure definition of horror. A scene no mortal should ever witness.

The goddess began to pray.

"O Atem! O He who created Himself! O Lord of the gods and all that exists! O perfect one! Protect me, for I have taken refuge in you. I am your daughter. I am one of you. Repulse your foe so we may be safe. Awaken your son, the king, the star, so that we may be secure from the wicked one. O Atem..."

Bastet kept praying, her divine tears raining on the face of her roaring sister. But the goddess was about to learn the lesson any mortal could've taught her. The one I'd learned while I cried for my ill brother. Prayers were seldom answered.

"Nef!"

My gaze darted toward... Khaf? "What the..."

He crawled toward me. How was he moving? How was he even alive? Gods, the sheer determination of that man!

"Oh, thank the gods, you're still alive." Khaf helped me lean against the side of the barque and sat beside me.

How was he able to speak? How much must he have endured to have become so durable? No. This wasn't normal. His wounds weren't bleeding anymore. Was this the effect of Tuya's enchantment?

Khaf's honey eyes gazed into mine, and, as he always did in our darkest moments, he smiled.

I hugged him, ignoring my bewilderment and his moan of pain. "We're the worst. We released Apep."

"Yeah." He laid his hand on my head, leaning it against his bare chest. "You looked very fierce over there, though."

Apep hissed, the solar barque fully inside his mouth. I shivered and dug my face deeper into Khaf's chest. There must be something I could still do to stop Apep.

I searched for Set but couldn't sense his presence. My gaze shifted to Bastet, but she was still struggling against her sister, her prayers getting louder with each word. Ra's cabin was quiet, its mighty god oblivious to the world's impending doom.

We lost, didn't we? It was over. The age of chaos was upon us.

"Hey, Nef."

"Y-yes, Khaf?"

"Do you still hate me?"

"This... this is hardly the time, Khaf."

"The world is going to end. There is nothing we can do anymore. This is exactly the time. Now or never. We can't leave our questions unasked, hoping for a better chance tomorrow because... well, there is no tomorrow. So... do you still hate me?"

I used to hate him with the passion of a thousand Egyptian suns. But my feelings when Apep almost killed him weren't hatred. They were something else. Something foreign. A strange sensation I had never experienced in my life, comparable to pure frustration. The image of my world without Khaf emptied my heart as if something essential was missing. As if, dare I say, all the joy and comfort had been sucked from my life.

"Is it such a hard question to answer?" Khaf asked.

"No." I tightened my hug, digging my nails deeper into his back. "I don't hate you."

"Are you just saying that to protect my feelings?"

"Your feelings?" I scoffed. "Don't compliment yourself, Hyksos."

Khaf chuckled. "Oh, Nef, you've come a long way."

"Told you I'm a fast learner."

He tightened his hug, warming my body in his embrace. "I still stand by what I said. You shouldn't bother comparing yourself to the women of Avaris."

I broke our hug and glared at his infuriating smug smile. Was the world about to end? Yep. Were we about to die? Sure. Was our death the most important event? Absolutely not! Nothing could stop Apep, so this was my final chance to give the thief of Avaris a piece of my mind.

"You can't help yourself, can you, Khafset? Each time I warm up to you, you say something stupid."

Khaf arched his bloodied eyebrow. "Warm up to me?"

My mouth dropped. Heat consumed my face. Curses, what did I just say! "No, no, I... I didn't mean to—"

Khaf laid a finger on my lips. "You are above and beyond any woman in Egypt."

He brought my face closer to his. It was slow. Too slow. Probably only slowed in my head because the serpent of chaos was devouring us. But Apep wasn't my primary source of fear anymore. Neither Ra's splintering barque nor the stench of Apep's insides mattered. No, my main source of terror was Khaf's face approaching mine. Not terror of a life-threatening danger but rather that of facing new uncharted territory. The shivering yet exciting type of fear.

Khaf didn't force me. I could have freed myself. I had every chance to stop this nonsense. Then why, in Hathor's name, wasn't I stopping him? Why wasn't I—

Our lips touched, and my world blurred.

Heat soared through every fiber of my being. My hands wandered to Khaf's cheek. Time itself froze. Nothing mattered at this very moment, not even our imminent death. Our world consisted only of us. The pressure of our lips. The tenderness of our trembling hands. The warmth of our breath. Our closed eyes during this moment of vulnerability. An Egyptian and a Hyksos—both sharing a moment of blind trust, of pure passion.

"Apep!" a deep masculine voice called.

Khaf and I pulled apart, and I squinted, unable to make out the man who'd spoken.

The man's laughter echoed in the serpent's dark insides. "O Apep! My first brother. My last challenger. My eternal adversary."

Golden flames ravaged the barque, illuminating Apep's revolting bowels and revealing the flames' origin. Ra, the king of the gods, stood proud on top of his cabin in all his glory.

"I am the flame which shines in the darkness," Ra declared, his deep voice booming around me, his solar flares dancing around his divine ship. "Begone, retreat, O enemy of the sun! I have consigned you to the flames, O enemy of order. Behold your punishment at the hands of your king. You shall not act as a barrier to the solar barque. Your coils will be torn apart, your head crushed. I shall always prevail over you, and order will always triumph. This I, Ra, god of the sun, promise you, Apep."

The sun god's flames spiraled around his muscular body, feeding the golden inferno inside Apep. The glow of his bronze forehead and silver eyes bounced off his tall body and broad wings, shifting their feathers from brown to gold.

"He's awake!" I said. "Atem answered Bastet's prayers! Gods, we will survive!" I glanced at our entangled hands. Oh, gods, we were going to survive!

"We have to help him," Khaf said. We helped each other stand.

"What are you doing, mortals?" Ra guided the flames, shifting and forming them to hit Apep.

"We are taking Set's and Nephthys' place," Khaf said.

Ra laughed. "Very well. Off to the front position."

We rushed to the barque's front, where Ishtar joined us. I leaned on Khaf as he steadied himself on Ishtar.

"Ready, mortals?" Ra asked.

"Ready," we said together.

Ra's flames grew stronger and brighter until they consumed the entirety of Apep's insides.

"You got this?" Khaf asked.

I nodded. "You got me?"

"Always."

I pointed the spear above my head. "Shama'at Morot!"

Set's scarlet flames rose from the spear. The ravaging infernos of the gods of the sun and destruction engulfed us and soared inside Apep, burning the serpent of chaos from the inside out.

Apep gagged and hissed until the gods' magic forced him to spit us out. The barque sailed forth on the raging waves of the divine Nile toward the Huat-gate.

"Yet again, you lose, brother." Ra pointed his fists at Apep, clacking his giant golden bracelets together. "Return to the waters of chaos. May you finally accept your defeat." He collected his golden flames and shot the blazing storm at Apep.

"Ra!" the serpent hissed, his brother's flames pushing him from the barque.

"Not today, Apep." Ra laughed as we entered Huat. "See you tomorrow, brother."

Khaf and I fell on our backs, lying with our heads next to each other.

We laughed. Gods, we laughed so loud as if the world didn't concern us anymore.

"Did we do it?" Khaf asked between his chuckles. "Did we really defeat Apep?"

"We did," I said, lost in my tears of joy. "We really did." I held his hand and raised Set's spear high. "We defeated Apep!"

Chapter 15

Egyptian Demigods

Khaf slept peacefully through eleven of the twelve gates of Huat. He seemed like a child exhausted after an eventful day. Sekhmet's healing abilities came in handy. I might've been injured, but Khaf had almost destroyed his body. His survival, however, seemed to both fascinate and disturb the goddess. She took her father and sister to the cabin for what she dubbed "an urgent divine meeting."

I was at peace at the moment. The strange hisses were gone, and my body wasn't burning hot anymore.

Khaf shifted and opened his eyes. He scanned the barque, and his tense face relaxed when he found me.

"Hey, Nef." He stretched, yawning, then sat up, leaning against the side of the ship next to me. "My fierce comrade in crime." He laid his hand on my forehead and smiled. "Your fever broke."

I hugged my legs and shrank into myself. What did he just do?

Khaf nudged me with his shoulder. "Never had someone worry about you, did you?"

"Wrong. Aunt Meriti did it all the time."

Khaf frowned. Did he seem... disappointed? As if I had ruined a master plan of his.

"I..." I pushed the lower half of my face against my knees, my cheeks burning. "I just... never had a man worry about me."

"Oh." He rubbed his arm, glancing in the other direction. "I—also never had a woman worry about me, let alone put herself in danger for my sake."

"Well... congratulations on the new experiences, I guess."

Khaf chuckled.

"Slept well?" I asked. "Sekhmet said you were very hurt when she healed you."

"Yeah. Fighting the goddess of war and the serpent of chaos sure took its toll on me."

"Yeah. And how did you survive that, exactly?"

"I was dying, but the strange maroon mist gathered over me. It pulsed in a rose color and began healing me. I thought for a moment Apep wanted to heal me so he could punish me again. That's when I saw you." He smiled at me. "You looked like a mighty goddess when you stood before the serpent of chaos as if he was a farm snake."

I covered my blushing cheeks and didn't look at him. How, in Hathor's name, did he come up with his compliments so fast? I would've needed weeks to come up with a half-decent flirtatious thing to say.

But it wasn't Apep who healed him, was it? It must've been me. When I touched the mist and tapped into Apep's magic, I wished for nothing else except to save Khaf so he could return to his family. It had been my driving force. My sole passion.

"Hey." Khaf nudged me. "Do you wish to know my secret weapon against the gods?"

I nodded.

"I feel stronger when I'm near you. I can't really explain it, but I feel unstoppable whenever I sense your faith in me." He kissed my hand.

I... I really didn't know how to react. This situation was new and unfamiliar to me, while Khaf knew how to behave and charm. Ah, curse him! Why couldn't I have had free time to spend in the Tavern of Avaris? Well, to be fair, I wouldn't have visited Avaris in my free time, let alone its tavern. I didn't think badly of the Hyksos anymore, but I wouldn't be caught dead stepping inside that scandalous establishment.

Khaf fell silent, his eyes scanning the barque.

"Everything all right?" I asked.

"Just taking a moment to admire this place," Khaf said. "It's a fine ship."

"It's Ra's solar barque. 'A fine ship' is an understatement."

Khaf chuckled.

"Do you like ships?" I asked.

He nodded. "I wanted to join the pirates and sail the seven seas with them. But, you know, I had Setu and the girls. Then you appeared in my life."

I blushed and looked the other way. Thankfully, Ishtar arrived and licked Khaf's cheek, claiming his attention. He chuckled and laid his head underneath her golden horn, murmuring something in the Canaanite language.

"I thought you hated Astarte," I said.

"I do."

"But... you like her horse?"

"I find Ishtar's warmth very comforting. Did you know she once covered me during my sleep when my blanket fell off?"

"No." Probably because I'd always fallen asleep before both of them like a spoiled child. I almost heard him pray, though, but I didn't eavesdrop. Even if I wasn't as devout as Khaf, Aunt Meriti taught me that praying was an intimate activity—a holy bond between the mortal and his deity.

Khaf's gaze drifted to the bread, water, and wine beside us. "What's all this?"

"Bastet brought it."

"Oh, praise our goddess of protection!" He grabbed a wine bottle and gulped it like water.

I laid my hand on his arm, easing the bottle away from his mouth. "Can I ask you something?"

"Sure. Anything."

"Back in Byblos, why did you go looking for a tavern instead of returning to me?"

He stared at the bottle. "I told you. Trying to destroy Ahmose was a stupid decision, and the tavern was a fine place to regroup. Also, I hadn't had a drink for a while. You can't really blame a man for missing the taste of wine."

So taverns were the place where he dealt with shame and sadness. This was good. I was finally piecing together his full story like Hatshepsut asked me to do.

"Do—you always drink when you're sad?" I asked.

"Oh, Nef." He turned his gaze to me, and his smug smile emerged. "Oh, Nefi, Nef, Nef. Khafset of Avaris never feels sad." He raised his bottle and drank.

I handed him a cup, and he gave me a confused look.

"Maybe we should watch our behavior in the presence of three gods." It would also slow his pace.

"I guess you're right." He poured the wine into the cup.

"And please eat something." I handed him a loaf of bread.

Khaf smiled and took the food.

The Hyksos finally ate and drank as a normal person should. Hatshepsut had explained that Senenmut was like Khaf. The grand architect drank for the house he couldn't build for himself and the pharaoh he loved, while the thief drank for the gem he couldn't steal—my heart.

Khaf nudged me with his shoulder.

I chuckled despite the tragic realizations. "Yes?"

"Apep would have been a glorious death for two thieves," he said.

"Indeed."

"Aren't you going to say you aren't a thief?"

"The ship has sailed on denial long ago." I waved at the barque. "Quite literally," I chuckled. "I'm a liar, a lowlife, a thief, and a traitor."

"And a damn good kisser."

"Excuse me!"

"Are you sure I was your first? You were so good I'm starting to question that whole innocent girl act."

And here he was. Khafset, the lowlife of Avaris. "What about you?"

"What about me?"

"You were quite nervous for a man who claimed his life consisted of nothing but wine and women. You were shaking so much while we kissed, I'm starting to think you were overselling yourself."

Khaf frowned. I leaned back on the side of the barque and smiled. Yep, my retorts were surely getting better.

"To be fair," Khaf said, "I kissed you while Apep was devouring us. Most men would've cried in a corner, but I guess I'm not most men."

My mouth dropped. This smug man really never surrendered. "You can't help but have the final word, can you?"

"What? I'm just telling the truth. If you don't believe me, you ask about me in the Tavern of Avaris."

"You know what? I just might."

"I should warn you, though. Most Hyksos will try to collect my debts from you if they discover we're a couple."

"C-couple?"

"Especially the women. Some might slap you, and one might try to kill you."

"Kill me!"

"Yeah, the Hostess. Avoid that one, Nef. She terrifies even me."

I sighed and looked the other way. Curse him and the Tavern of Avaris!

"Hey, Nef."

"What?" I snapped.

"I just wanted to say that... ah..." He brushed back his curly brown hair, glancing at his side. "Thank you for not abandoning me, I guess."

Now, following a long speech about being special, he showed his true feelings. Gods, I had to hold back my tears each time I peeked behind his façade.

"Yeah, well. If you died, who would drag me into a life of crime?"

Khaf chuckled. He leaned forward and kissed me. Again! And I didn't stop him. Again!

"My daughters might be right. You two are our new Set and Nephthys," Ra's deep voice said beside us.

I pushed Khaf away. "Great Ra!" I gasped for air, shifting my exhausted body to kneel before the king of the gods.

"Easy," Ra said. "Let your bodies rest. We are approaching the twelfth gate and will enter Duat soon. I hope you have enjoyed some rest and nourishment."

"We have," Khaf said.

"Yes. We are thankful for your generosity."

Ra folded his broad wings behind his back and sat, his hawk eyes scanning us.

"You carry various divine items." Ra's gaze shifted from me to Khaf. "But you, boy. You are strange. Sekhmet said those writings on your body grant you access to the gods' magic without having to word any spells. You were able to survive Apep's attacks and fight my daughter." He narrowed his eyes. "Explain."

"The queen mother, great Ra," Khaf said. "She did something to me."

"I overheard you tell the girl you feel stronger whenever she has faith in you."

Khaf smiled. "I do."

"Do you have anyone in Huat who believes in you?" Ra asked. "Do you feel mighty when you see the faith in their eyes?"

"I have my adopted family." Khaf entangled our fingers. "But I feel stronger than the serpent of chaos himself when I fight beside Nefiri."

Ra hummed, then shifted his attention to me. "I felt Set's presence on the barque. It disturbed my slumber and replenished my strength. I woke half expecting my son had returned to his senses and rejoined me. Instead, I found you holding his spear."

Oh, so it wasn't Bastet's prayers to Atem that had awoken Ra.

"I... I was chosen by the spear, great—"

"I'm aware of Horus's test. You don't have to remind me of my grandson's radical approach to mortals. I'm asking why I felt Set if he's still shackled in Abydos." His voice rose to a near shout.

Shivers ran down my spine. I extended a shaking hand, presenting Ra with the silver scarab. "I... I used this, great Ra."

Ra studied the scarab, now blackened by a burn on its silver surface.

"I found it in Set's temple." Khaf gave Ra the other burned scarab.

"Where is the third?" Ra asked.

"What..." I swallowed. "What do you mean, great Ra?"

"A god can create three scarabs. Twins and a sister. That's a fixed number. Any deviation could endanger reality itself and strengthen Apep. Set, foolish as he is, spent lifetimes fighting Apep and understands this danger." He shook the scarab. "Set's twins are silver. The sister has to be either gold or crystal."

"What are the other scarabs' functions?" I asked.

"The crystal scarab sends the human to the god, and the golden brings the god to the human."

Tuya's golden scarab could free Set right here and now! Why would she grant me that option? Not even Set's priests were stupid enough to use the golden scarab to release him.

"I ask you again," Ra said. "Where is the third?"

"My people found three scarabs and kept them in Set's temple," Khaf said. "But the third went missing."

Should I tell Khaf I had the third scarab hidden over my heart? Maybe not in Ra's presence. Yeah, I should wait until we reached the scarlet desert.

"Great Ra." I tried to divert his attention from the scarabs.

The hawk god turned his gaze from Khaf to me, his expression stern.

I paused to consider my words carefully, not wanting to reveal too much. "Do Egyptian demigods exist?"

Ra narrowed his eyes. "What an interesting question, mortal."

"Oh, you remembered!" Khaf jumped into the conversation. "Nef, you are the best!" He looked at Ra. "I'm studying in Set's temple and have always considered this question. I told Nef I would love to gain your insight into the matter if I ever had the honor of meeting you, great Ra."

I stared at Khaf. He did it again. He lied to a god, and it worked! Oh, that wonderful, deceitful lowlife.

"And you never discovered the answer to the question, Canaanite?"

Khaf shook his head. "There is no mention of Egyptian demigods."

"Because they're strictly forbidden," Ra said. "However, I know of non-Egyptian gods outside Duat who had children with mortals."

"There are gods outside Duat?!" Khaf's mouth dropped.

"Plenty. We have divided Huat among ourselves, but each group of gods has its own version of Duat. The gods can move between divine realms like you humans do in Huat. And then there is the Creator. The Awoken. The one above all. The lord of the gods. Each pantheon has a different name for him, but in Egypt we call him Atem."

"How many versions of Duat are there?" Khaf asked.

"Many. There's Duat, Olympus, the Netherworld, the Otherworld, Asgard, and Takamagahara, to name a few."

"This is amazing!" Khaf said, his body shaking. "Absolutely amazing!"

I studied him with an arched eyebrow. So he truly was obsessed with the gods. His fascination wasn't just to plan his grand heist.

"Could we return to your main question, Khafset?" I asked.

"What? Oh, yes. Of course. My question." Khaf looked up at Ra like a child awaiting a tale from his grandparent. "Could you tell us about one of the demigods?"

"One belonged to Zeus of Olympus. His son, Hercules, is half-human. Caused a lot of trouble, that one. Almost started a war between me, Zeus, and Odin of the Aesir, when he tried to claim our Book of the Dead and promised the other gods its power in exchange for helping him." He shook his head. "Our war would have destroyed our realms and Huat, had we not returned to our senses."

So it was possible. I could be Set's daughter. If foreign gods could birth demigods, then ours could as well.

"Demigods are foul creatures we do not want in our lands," Ra said, and my heart froze. "A curse to us all. Flawed humans with divine powers who are not bound to Atem's divine laws. They are not allowed in Egypt. Same as the touch of Frenzy. But apparently, the gods behaved as they pleased during my slumber." His gaze turned to Ishtar. "Isn't that right, Astarte?"

"Great Ra," Khaf said, "Ishtar is just her horse."

"No!" Ra growled. "It's an extension of her essence. An aspect of her personality. Astarte has been watching your every move through that horse."

"Why would she do that?" Khaf asked.

"An excellent question, Canaanite." Ra glared at Khaf, and the Hyksos shivered.

Oh, the contempt in Ra's voice when he spoke to Khaf. Did our gods hate the Hyksos just as we did? Were they really so petty? Ra had given a word of wisdom, however. Demigods were dangerous and delusional. *I* was dangerous and delusional. I'd believed I could defeat Set, but Apep almost destroyed me as if I was a mere bug. Gods, our entire plan was the wrong approach to fixing the Set situation.

"Everything all right?" Khaf asked.

I nodded. "Could you leave us for a moment?"

He arched his eyebrow. "Why?"

"I'm sitting before Ra. Might as well pray."

"Pray?" Khaf asked. "You, Nefiri Minu, want to pray?"

I shrugged. "Why not? I heard you pray at the end of each day since we arrived in Duat."

"Did... you overhear my prayers?"

"Oh, no. Don't worry. I respected your privacy."

"Ah." Khaf smiled. "Thanks." He stood. "Great Ra." He bowed and walked with Ishtar to join Sekhmet and Bastet.

Ra turned his head, his gaze glued to Khaf.

"Great Ra," I said, and he turned to face me. "May I ask you something?"

He studied me for a moment and nodded.

"What exactly is Frenzy?" I asked. "I hear the gods mention it whenever they talk of Set's spear."

"I truly wished no mortal would have to touch the powers of Frenzy." Ra sighed. "But I guess it is too late for that now. Horus set up his test and brought you into contact with the forbidden powers against my will. I suppose the least I could do is explain the powers you wield."

"Thank you." I leaned forward. Finally, some answers!

"The powers of the gods, or magic as you mortals call it, come from three sources. Ka, or the soul, wielded by all the gods. Creation, wielded by most. And Frenzy, wielded by a few. Those few are me, Set, Astarte, Shemzu, and Apep. There are outliers, of course. Such as Anubis and Nephthys. But they are the exception that proves the rule."

"So Frenzy isn't evil?"

Ra shook his head. "It depends on the wielder. All the gods wield their own aspects of Ka, Creation, and Frenzy. However, Frenzy is different. It is… special. If wielded by a god, it could grant them powers without relying solely on the faith of mortals. But if wielded by a mortal, it could consume their mind and turn them into a puppet of its desire. Just like Apep."

"Apep was mortal!" My mouth dropped.

"The first generation of gods were mortals once. Only Atem, the first god, was born into godhood. He didn't ascend, for he is eternal."

I sat dumbfounded before Ra. I certainly didn't expect such a straightforward answer.

"Did Frenzy taint your soul?" Ra asked. "Do you feel it the way Apep did when he was a man?"

"Feel it?"

"Do you feel warmth? Headaches? Do you hear its hisses and whispers?"

I shook my head with all the intent I could muster. If Ra knew I was anything like Apep, he might strike me down here and now. At least I was no longer hearing whispers.

"Good," Ra said. "Once you finish Horus's test, avoid the spear before it is too late. Frenzy is parasitic. If you are a good host, it *will* latch itself onto your Ka, and you saw how this turned out for Apep."

I nodded, and my eyes remained glued to Khaf as he spoke with Bastet and Sekhmet. Mostly to ignore Ra's piercing gaze. Oh, Khaf, what did we get ourselves into? We were way over our heads, weren't we?

Ra traced my line of sight to Khaf. "What secrets are you keeping from the Canaanite?"

"Not a secret. A thought. More of a fear, really."

Ra studied me. "Speak."

"Considering the divine items I carry, disregarding Set's spear, if I return to Egypt without going to Abydos, will I be strong enough to fend off Set's influence?"

"Yes. But it will be your occupation until your death. Set will not give up so long as he has a connection to Huat. If you stay away from the spear, it will not affect you. It should deactivate after your death and begin its search for a new chosen. Set should remain dormant in the meantime."

I nodded.

"Are you planning to abandon Horus's insane test?"

"Maybe. Khaf and I barely survived Apep and only by a miracle of…" I waved at Ra. "Well, a miracle of you."

Ra's tense face softened. "What would the Canaanite think?"

"He would probably understand if I convinced him his people would be safe."

"Do you fear the boy?"

"What? No! Quite the opposite! He's gentle and kind to an extent I couldn't have imagined."

Ra glanced at Khaf, who was conversing with the sisters Bastet and Sekhmet. "Then why do you fear sharing your intentions with him if he's so peaceful?"

"I have lost everything, great Ra: my family, apprenticeship, and even the right to remain in my country. If a trap awaits us in Abydos, Khaf will sacrifice himself to save me like he did against Apep. I have nothing left except Khaf, and I can't bear losing him too. He chose to trust me, but his trust remains fragile. A wrong word, and it might collapse."

"Horus took a gamble on you, mortal." Ra sighed. "A human so unbalanced even I fail to foresee how Maat's scale would judge you. But I commend your sensible thinking. You have proven yourself more insightful than my grandson. Yes, retreating from his dangerous test is the sensible thing to do." He took off one of his bracelets and placed it in my hand. "Keep this. It will grant you access to my Solar magic. If you say 'Zier,' it will launch a stream of fire. It may help you in your fight in Egypt."

I wore the wide bracelet around my right wrist. Its golden metal shrank until it was snug around my thin arm. "I'm thankful, great Ra, but don't you wield the powers of Frenzy as well? Wouldn't a divine item connected to you allow Frenzy to influence me?"

Ra smiled. "I am different. Unlike Set and Apep, my manifestation of Frenzy is more—restrained. It shouldn't affect you. As a matter of fact, the bracelet will protect you from the spear's influence. It has an overprotective nature. If it feels that you are in danger, the bracelet will protect you even if you don't actively use a spell. This paradoxically will cause it to fend off the taint of Frenzy on your Ka."

Oh! Gods, finally, some good news! I held the bracelet and stared at it as if my life depended on it.

"Father," Sekhmet called. "We are reentering Duat."

Ra glanced at the approaching black mist. "Come. Your journey is about to recommence."

I followed the god of the sun over to Khaf and the goddesses. Ishtar nudged me. I hugged her neck and smiled at Khaf. Should I tell him about the information Ra had given me? No. Khaf would only worry, and there was no need to burden him with something he couldn't control. Yes, he'd done so much for me already. Now, it was my turn to carry my weight for a change.

"Done praying?" Khaf asked, holding two dolls in his hands that resembled the goddesses.

I nodded. "What are those?"

"Nothing." Khaf walked to Ishtar's saddle and stashed the dolls inside his bag.

"For the girls?"

Khaf brushed back his hair, ignoring my amused face. "Maybe."

"No gift for Setu this time?"

"I... I took a scale from Apep's severed tail."

I laughed. "Oh, look who's a total softy after all."

"Stop laughing at me!"

I took Khaf's hand and gently guided him toward me. "Hote loved Bastet as well."

"It's not the same, all right? It's... just a little—"

I kissed him, and the Hyksos stopped talking. Oh, so kissing Khaf was an excellent method to keep him quiet! Really? Was it that easy?

Sekhmet cleared her throat. Khaf and I broke our kiss and clumsily bowed before the three gods. We glanced at each other and smiled.

"We have reached Duat," Ra said.

"Really?" I said. "When did we pass through the gate?"

"Oh!" Bastet clapped her hands together. "When you were displaying your love."

My cheeks began to burn.

"You should disembark now if you wish to reach the demon-gate." Ra grabbed Ishtar's neck with his clawed hand. "I expect to see you during the barque's next cycle, Astarte." He released Ishtar's neck and waved, commanding us to leave.

I patted Ishtar's trembling neck, then climbed on her back with Khaf.

"The demon-gate is under the barque," Ra said. "You should be able to reach it with Astarte's essence and Maat's magic."

I nodded.

"I'm thankful for the dolls, great goddesses," Khaf said. "You will hear the girls' thankful prayers when they receive your gifts."

Sekhmet nodded.

"May the dolls bring happiness to your cute little girls, Canaanite," Bastet said.

"We are thankful for everything, great Ra," I said.

"May you forever emerge victorious against Apep and keep protecting the rising of the sun," Khaf said.

Ra stared at Khaf. The god's face relaxed, and he sighed. "And may you flourish under its light. Now leave before Astarte arrives."

Khaf leaned next to my ear. "That's a good idea. I don't want to be here when that traitorous Canaanite goddess arrives."

I nodded. Khaf hated Astarte. Knowing how he behaved around those who harmed his people, he would definitely get us killed by the Canaanite war goddess if he spoke to her.

"Thihier Hawa." Wings sprang out of Ishtar's sides. I swung her red reins, and the horse's hooves rose from the barque.

Ishtar flew over the side of the barque and dove into the dark void surrounding the divine Nile's stream.

"Abis Duru!" Anubis's amulet shook around my neck, releasing its chilling Soul magic into my veins. Black mist gathered in the distance, forming the demon-gate where my greatest challenge lay before me. It wasn't whatever obstacle awaited us in the scarlet desert. No. It was convincing Khaf that, for his sake, I was going to abandon the grand heist.

Chapter 16

The Real Enemy

The raging purple clouds clashed in the scarlet heaven, mixing and reforming into horrific shapes such as snakes and skulls. The stench of rotten fish infested the desert's thick air and formed a slimy layer over my body. Wind passed through the narrow paths between the surrounding black hills, echoing a loud shriek across the scarlet desert. Even the hills were disheartening. The towering structures wore crowns of spikes decorated with a network of tiny red stones. They glowed scarlet in high intensity, then faded, mimicking the revolting shape of a spider's eyes.

Khaf and I walked beside Ishtar across Set's kingdom, our hands intertwined. Despite our panic-inducing environment, Khaf was optimistic that the journey's last stop would be the smoothest.

At least the bracelet seemed to have stopped Frenzy's symptoms. I sure wasn't hearing hisses anymore. However, I felt empty, as if a part of me was asleep. I really needed to end this fast and leave this cursed spear behind before I ended up as monstrous as Apep. Not that I had been a great person. I was a monster in my own way.

I hadn't told Khaf about my decision to abandon his grand heist. The poor man might have been the happiest I'd ever seen him. For the first time, the proud thief of Avaris was optimistic.

Oh, curse him! He had to make this more difficult, didn't he?

Purple lightning flashed above our heads, and the thunder's crushing sound shook my knees. I lost my balance, and Khaf caught me.

"Do you need a break?" he asked.

"Y-yes, please."

Khaf fetched a water bottle from my bag and handed it to me.

"Thank you." I took the clay bottle.

Khaf winked, then left to scan the ground. He whistled, picking up three black rocks with glowing red dots on their surface.

"For Setu and the girls?" I asked.

"Yes." Khaf stashed the rocks in his bag. "They're into creepy stuff. The three of them often go on their own adventures to find the most disgusting objects in Avaris."

"You miss them, don't you?"

He nodded, still holding to his smile. "They *are* my family."

I took a sip from the clay bottle to regroup in my head. It was exciting getting to know Khaf's caring side. His capacity for love was utterly unexpected. Especially toward a family that wasn't even related to him. Admirable, really. He *chose* to love and protect Setu and the girls. He *chose* to love me! The woman who harmed his people. The one whose master, whom she still adored, indirectly caused his father's death. And my people said the Hyksos were a bunch of thieves and murderers. Nonsense. Even their thieves were more loving and caring than most so-called true Egyptians.

"Hey, Nef."

I lowered the bottle and arched my brow at Khaf, whose gaze was avoiding mine as he brushed back his hair. "Yes, Khaf."

"Could you, maybe, not—mention to Setu the stuff I told you about him liking you?"

I chuckled. "How could you be so sure he doesn't like me? I sure didn't expect it from you?"

"No... how can I put this? You're not his—type."

I smirked. "What? Your brother isn't into cows?"

Khaf frowned. "You're not going to let the cow joke go, are you?"

"Absolutely not."

He approached me, laid his hand on my waist, and his incredible honey eyes stared into my soul. "You know, Hathor is often depicted as a cow, and she's known to be the most beautiful being in existence. Maybe that's what I meant by comparing you to a cow."

"Amazing how you turned an insult into a compliment. Such an admirable effort."

He grinned as he lowered his head to kiss me.

This time, I didn't dwell on the fact that I was kissing Khafset of Avaris. Was it because of exhaustion? For the most part. Did I enjoy kissing him? Maybe. But no need to make a big deal out of it. It wasn't like it reinvigorated my soul, shook my entire world, and... fine, I might've loved kissing the idiot.

He eased himself from the kiss, keeping his forehead pressed against mine. "That was lovely."

"Someone's in a good mood."

Khaf walked over to Ishtar and leaned against her. "I'm in a great mood."

"How come?" I peeled the slimy goo off my arms, fighting the urge to vomit.

Khaf stretched his arms out on either side. "We are in Set's kingdom. Here, the god of destruction tamed the demons and brought the storms under his control. We are in a holy place."

A swarm of angry flies flew over our heads, proving that Khaf's holy place was indeed disgusting.

"You're really into all this, aren't you?" I asked. "The gods and such."

He took Ishtar's reins and held my hand. "Well, I never wanted to become a priest, but I like learning about the gods. Something about them fascinates me." We continued our hike.

"Out of curiosity," I said, "what *is* Setu's type?"

Khaf shrugged.

"Is it really such a big secret?" I nudged him, hoping it was as seductive as when he did it. "Does our respectable clerk have a deviant taste?"

"*No!*" Khaf shouted, and I flinched. What was this?

Khaf took a deep breath, his face relaxing. "Not deviant. I guess... unorthodox? I don't want to talk about it anymore."

I nodded, gazing toward the black hills, my hand turning cold in his warm grip. I might've overestimated my position in the hierarchy of people Khaf loved.

"Hey." Khaf nudged me, and of course, he did it better. Curse him. "I'm sorry. I didn't mean to shout."

"No, it's fine. I understand that you still feel like you have to protect your family from me."

"It's not that. Look, I'm sure Setu will feel safe telling you about himself once he trusts you."

I chuckled, shaking my head. "Setu hates me, and I don't blame him. I badgered the poor man for the last two years."

"Setu doesn't hate. He was never the kind of man to separate the world into good and evil. He never held a grudge in his life. He would return home, complain about you, then ask about our meeting and Hote's health."

I lowered my gaze in shame, wishing the black sand would swallow me. "He sounds like a man I could've learned a thing or two from."

Khaf smiled and gave my hand a gentle press. "You'll get to know him soon. Him and Iti and Bennu. I'm sure they'll love to get to know the real you."

Yeah, right. Because the real me was fantastic; I literally was a monster with a tainted soul. But why contradict him? Khaf was happy, and I wanted to keep it that way as long as I could. If I ever wanted to repay even a fraction of what I owed Khaf's family, I would do everything in my power to return Khaf to them. They would *not* lose their brother like I did. But how was I supposed to convince him to leave with me and abandon the grand heist?

"Why so silent?" Khaf asked. "Sick of me already?"

"Not at all." I hugged his arm as we walked, tightening my grip on our entangled hands. "I like that I'm getting to know you." That was another sad realization. I didn't know the man. I knew enough to realize that I loved him. But what did Khafset of Avaris do in his free time? What were his hobbies? What kind of food did he like? There was so much I didn't know, and gods, I wanted to know *everything*! "Tell me about that dream you had. The one where you wanted to join the pirates and see the world."

"Ah, yes. I still might do it one day when Setu and the girls don't need me anymore. I want to see parts of the world that aren't on the map, like what lies beyond Syria, Libya, Greece, and Kush. Sure, the world doesn't end there. I want to know where the Nile begins and where the seas end. I want to learn about foreign gods and the mortal cultures they have forged." He smiled at me, visibly enjoying my shocked face. So much ambition, so many dreams, and we tried to contain this man in his hometown. "It would be nice if you came with me. We could become explorers together."

"Yes!" My eyes widened. This was it. My way of convincing Khaf to leave this evil place and return to Egypt. "Then let's do it!"

"Do what?"

"See the world together."

Khaf smiled. "I would love nothing more."

"Great!" Gods, I was shaking. Would it work? Could I just ask him to leave now? "We could join the pirates and sail away like you wanted."

"I didn't mean let's do it now." He chuckled. "I can't leave Egypt yet."

"Why not? I thought you hated Egypt."

"I never said that. I only ever hated your people."

I frowned. After everything I had learned about my people's brutality, I couldn't fault his contempt. "I changed, didn't I? Or at least I'm trying. Maybe my people will too."

"They will. Sooner or later. They just need some motivation."

"What do you mean?"

"I admit, I wanted to see your people suffer for their crimes. But during our journey, I learned that perhaps it isn't your fault. We aren't enemies. We're born into a world that wants us to behave as such. As my dad used to say, we were forged in the same furnace but from two different flames." He gave me a comforting smile. "I always wanted to extinguish one flame, but maybe joining the flames is the right approach."

I sighed. Why must he be so good with words? "But leaving Egypt doesn't mean you hate it."

"No, you're right."

"Great, then we can go on that trip you wanted."

"I can't, Nef."

"Why?" I asked in an exhausted tone.

"Oh, where should I even begin! The girls and Setu need me. I'm already worried about leaving them alone for so long. The girls I trust, but Setu, well, he's not really the toughest guy around. Also, I want to reopen my father's smithy to show him that his son never forgot about him. I still have to free my people, which we won't achieve simply by finishing the heist. Nefertari's royal decree is great, but changing the law doesn't necessarily change the people."

I glanced at the scarlet heaven, hoping for a moment of brilliance. I would have to say it outright, wouldn't I?

"Hey," Khaf said. "Don't worry too much." He raised my hand and kissed it. "I have a plan for the future, and if there is anyone I would love to share it with, it's you." He winked. "My comrade in crime."

I sighed. This was it. The moment of truth. "I... have something to share as well."

"You go first."

I took a deep breath. "I think we should abandon the grand heist."

Khaf froze, bringing both Ishtar and me to a halt. His gaze remained on the black sand. He didn't shout. Didn't move a muscle. He stood as steady as a palm, his warm hand freezing in my grip.

"Kh-khaf?"

"Why?"

"Just... give me a chance to explain." I stood before him and held his other hand. "Why risk going to Set? We're strong enough to fend off his influence over Egypt."

Khaf released my hands and walked away.

"We can use the gates in Huat and fight the Hittites with Ramesses and Master Paser," I said. "Trust me; I asked Ra and—"

"You asked Ra?" Khaf said. "So you've been planning this while I was left in the dark like an idiot."

"What? No! I thought of it after our battle on Ra's barque. We needed an actual miracle to defeat Apep. Set is stronger and smarter. We could be walking into a trap. If he tricked Osiris, then what chance do *we* have?"

"I... don't want you to abandon the grand heist," Khaf said, his gaze fixed on the black sand. "Please don't."

I opened my mouth, almost giving in to his demand. But I didn't. He was a passionate man. He truly believed going to Set was the right decision. I had to be the logical one. Even if it hurt him. I had to return him to his family.

"I'm sorry, Khaf. But I've already made my—"

"You took what you wanted from me," Khaf said. "Now that you're strong enough to save Paser and Ramesses, you're going to abandon me and my people."

"I have access to the magic of four gods. I'll defend both the Hyksos and the Egyptians."

"Defend the Hyksos? Would you fight your own soldiers and kill your people for us?"

"It doesn't have to come to that. I will defend—"

"After everything we have been through!" Khaf shouted. "After all I've shared, you're going to abandon me. You want to hurt me like your soldiers did years ago!"

"I don't want you to die, you idiot!"

"Liar!" His voice echoed like thunder. "You don't care about me. Never have. You tolerated me for your brother's medicine. You faked loving me for protection. But your fight against Apep showed you that you no longer need me, and now you show your true face, Egyptian."

"You'll fight Set for me, and he *will* kill you!"

"You aren't abandoning the grand heist for me. You want to avoid Set because you don't want to confront your father. That's what you are at your core, isn't it? An opportunistic woman who's afraid to confront the consequences of her actions."

"Excuse me?"

"How was I so stupid? So naive. How did I believe for a moment that there was hope for you and your people? No! I won't be fooled by you Egyptians anymore. I won't stand helpless again while you rob me of everything. Not when a single gate separates me from my goals."

This was going nowhere. Should I act as if I was leaving? Yes. It didn't matter how furious Khaf was; he would never leave me alone in a place like this.

"Despite your hurtful words, I *am* doing this for your safety." I grabbed Ishtar's reins. "I'll leave now. You can either let me wander the scarlet desert alone for its demons to kill me, or help me stop the Hittites and save *everyone* in Egypt. It's your decision, but I'll find my way home."

I pulled Ishtar's reins, but she refused to move. "Fine!" I screamed at the horse. "Have fun together, Canaanites!" I marched away, hoping Khaf would react before I wandered too far.

Of course, he wouldn't let me be alone in a place like this. Any moment now, Khaf would follow me. He was the kindest, most chivalrous—

"Oh no, you won't!" Khaf grabbed my forearm and raised it next to his face, his grip trapping the blood in my wrist, his nails digging into my flesh.

This… was unexpected hostile behavior! Was he really going to hurt me?

He tightened his grip around my arm. Ra's bracelet grew hot. Sweat leaked from underneath its golden metal.

"Khaf, let me go." He was trapping the blood in my wrist.

"I'll drag you to Abydos if I have to, Egyptian!"

Heat consumed my arm, and fire raged inside my veins. "Release me at once!"

"*I will not!*"

"I said…" A glorious burst of warmth consumed my tight fist. "Let go!" I yanked my hand, hitting his face by accident.

Khaf jumped away. He paced around, screaming into his palms. Ishtar neighed hysterically as if she was screaming. She galloped around Khaf, containing his movements.

I sighed. "Why are you both being so dramatic? Khaf, I barely touched you with…" My heart froze. Ra's bracelet was pulsating with a red glow. No! Ra had warned me it would act to protect me. What had triggered the cursed thing? I didn't want it to hurt Khaf!

Khaf's screams faded. The Hyksos collapsed on the black sand.

"Khafset!" I ran and slid beside him. My tears fell on his face. They evaporated on his right cheek's boiling skin.

"What have I done?" I shook his shoulders. "Khaf! Khafset! It was an accident. I swear. Wake up. Please! I *will* go to Abydos. I'll do anything you want. Please wake up. Please!"

Ishtar nickered and nudged Khaf's shoulder.

"Please!" My voice echoed in the empty desert. "Anyone! Help!"

Ishtar's gaze rose to the scarlet heaven. She squealed at the passing violent clouds.

"Ishtar, what are you—"

"Oh, my child." A soft voice echoed around me.

I rushed to Ishtar and grabbed Set's spear fixed to her saddle. "Who's there?"

A white bolt flashed from the heaven. It hit the ground in a massive explosion, pushing me onto my back.

"Hurt me if you want, but leave him alone!" I shouted over the buzzing in my ears. My vision remained blurry. "I warn you! Touch him, and I'll kill you!"

"Has violence become your answer for everything?" the woman said. "What happened to your wits, your resourcefulness?"

The white fog faded, revealing a silhouette that walked toward me. The closer it got, the more a crushing pressure pushed on me and pinned me to my knees.

"You can't reach your goals without the Canaanite. How are you still blind to his importance?"

"What is happening?" The spear fell from my hand. I screamed from the unbearable force crushing my bones.

My vision refocused on an approaching woman whose long hair was darker than the scarlet desert's black sand. Her silver crown carried a golden serpent holding a throne on its tail. Golden stripes decorated the edges of her white dress. Its colorful patterns glowed green, yellow, white, blue, and red. The black sand shone from her wings' white glow, and a path of flowers sprouted on her way toward me.

Flowers wouldn't bloom in the barren scarlet desert except at the bequest of one being. Isis. The mighty goddess of life.

Isis stood before me, and water sprang underneath her bare feet, forming a shallow pool.

I gazed at her, struck by the glorious being I was witnessing. Gods, her smooth brown skin, perfect nose, ageless face, and wide black eyes reflected my shocked face. Oh, such majesty. Such beauty. Such crushing presence. Even Nefertari would be tame and ugly compared to the great lady of all.

Isis smiled at me, and I gasped at the force of life that exploded in my soul from her mere attention. "I will heal the boy, for Egypt's fate is tied to both of you." She laid her finger on my forehead, and I collapsed before the goddess from the sheer weight of her divine touch.

"Sleep now, child. There is someone who wishes to speak to you."

Chapter 17

Clashing Worlds

The birds glided in Peramessu's blue sky. They danced in the heaven and sang the melodies of the Nile's rushing stream.

I stood before my home on the riverbank's Egyptian side. It wasn't much. A lonely cubical structure that overlooked Avaris across the canal. But gods, it was great to be...

Wait! Why was I back home? Did Isis send me back? Had I already failed her son's test?

I walked toward the door, past the bench where my dad sat alone with his thoughts, and entered the living room, furnished with a small red straw carpet, a short-legged table, and four cushions, two of which hadn't been used for a long time.

"Aunt Meriti," I called to our elderly neighbor. She could be fishing. That was often the reason she left her house. She always checked on us and then went fishing.

I rushed outside toward the canal, where I expected to find her.

"Good. You are still alive." A voice brought me to a halt.

I turned to Queen Mother Tuya, sitting on my dad's bench.

"You!" I said, the reality of my situation becoming clearer with each passing moment. "You're the one Isis wanted me to meet."

"Yes."

"Why am I back home?"

"This is a dream."

"I don't have time for this. Return me to Khaf right now!"

"Your tone has changed, child. Not long ago, you were crawling before me. Aren't you afraid?"

"Why? You're a mortal and an evil one at that. You could've warned me not to touch the spear."

"It's not my fault you touched the spear."

"You could've told me Set is my father."

"It's not my place to tell you about your father."

"You could've explained the golden scarab's purpose!"

"It's not my responsibility to explain the world to you."

"You could've told me why you covered for me when I stole the coins."

"It's not my obligation to justify my actions to you."

"Why are you in my dream, Tuya?" I snapped.

"To check on you." She smiled. "You ungrateful child."

"Check on me?" I threw my hands in the air. "I'm fantastic! My brother has died. Apep almost devoured me. I discovered our brutality toward the Hyksos. And worst of all, I kissed Khaf. Yes, I did it! My betrayal of Egypt is now officially complete. And you know what? I liked it! I love the lowlife. Khafset! The Hyksos thief I used to despise. Khafset—whom I hurt." I glared at Tuya, tears running down my cheeks. "So yeah, great queen mother, I'm in the best shape of my life. Thank you for asking. Now, can you *please* return me to Khaf?"

Tuya narrowed her eyes. "Do you think talking to a woman twice your mother's age in such an inappropriate manner will make you sound anything more than a little girl throwing a tantrum because life isn't going her way? Is this your way of being fierce and smart?"

"I didn't want any of this! I was happy to remain tame. I was glad to be naive. My life was bad, but at least I understood the world around me. I had to survive and care for my brother."

Tuya nodded. "Sticking our heads in the sand does indeed guarantee an uncomplicated life. It's also the reason people who lead such lives don't experience anything of value. They spend their short years in Huat and leave as if they had never come. Even their shadows have had more impact on our world than them."

"Thanks for the life lesson," I said.

"The Hyksos sure got into your head."

"And you didn't? Fierce yet weak. Smart yet naive. You knew exactly how to push me in the right direction. Why don't you check on Khaf if you're so kind? He is with me on the same journey. Maybe you could see the nightmares he lived through."

Tuya arched her gray eyebrow. "Didn't *you* burn the boy's face?"

"I... It was an accident. I wanted to save him from Set's inevitable trap."

"Oh, child. For a bad liar, you sure are incredibly talented at lying to yourself."

"I'm not lying!"

"So why are you avoiding Set?"

"It's not my obligation to explain my actions to you."

Tuya smiled. "So you are capable of learning after all." She pointed at my right hand. "Explain why the bracelet harmed the boy."

"I... I don't know. It must've misfired."

"Oh, but it didn't. You saw the boy as a threat, and the bracelet took it as a sign to activate." Tuya shook her head. "My poor child, you will never reach the truth before you stop lying to yourself. You must confront the consequences of your actions and accept what you are."

"And what am I?"

"A selfish thief."

"How dare—"

"I have heard enough. The boy is about to wake up and will need you by his side." Tuya stood, and my survival instincts overtook me, forcing me to back away. "What a sad waste of time this was." She walked away.

"Tuya!" I shouted, and she turned. I grabbed the golden scarab from underneath my dress. "Tell me about this scarab and my father. Do it, or I will throw the scarab to the first demon I encounter."

"Throw it. It doesn't matter anymore. Horus took a gamble on you, and sadly it failed. When you left, I truly believed you and the boy had a chance at reestablishing balance in Egypt, but now, seeing how unbalanced the journey has made you, I don't believe it's possible anymore. Set has already won, regardless of what you do next." She turned and walked away. "What a sad turn of events, oh daughter of Sutmheb. I don't know who is to blame for the dark days looming over the horizon. The youth who are lost or their elders who led them astray."

The sun's light faded, and darkness consumed our surroundings until Tuya disappeared, and I stood in a shallow pool inside a black void.

"Come back, Tuya!"

"Oh, daughter of Sutmheb," Tuya's voice echoed inside the void. "Still weak and even more naive."

***

I woke on the scarlet desert's black sand, my body covered in slime. Khaf lay motionless while Ishtar licked his face clean. "Khaf!" I pulled myself to my feet and made my way to him. I fell beside Khaf. His boiling right cheek had healed, leaving behind a three-clawed scar. I held his cold hand against my heart. "I'm so sorry."

Ishtar snorted and nudged my shoulder with her snout.

"You saved him, didn't you?" I asked. "*You* called Isis to heal him." I rubbed my head underneath her golden horn. "Thank you."

Khaf's hand twitched in my grip. He shifted on the black sand. His eyes opened slowly, revealing his honey-colored irises. He moaned, sitting up.

What would he do? How would he react to his scar? Gods, his face! He would never forgive me.

"Khaf." I swallowed, trying to find the right words. "I'm really, really sorry. It was an accident. I swear. Is there anything I can—"

Khaf jerked his hand away. He didn't speak. The Hyksos stared into nothingness.

He inspected his cheek with his touch, and his fingers flinched at the feel of the rough skin of his three-clawed scar. He searched for his dagger and froze at his reflection in the blade.

I crawled away in anticipation of his reaction. I awaited his screams—wished for him to unleash his pain and resentment toward me. Anything that might ease his pain.

"Khaf, I—"

"Why?" His voice was so cold it could have frozen the raging clouds, plunging them over my head. "I trusted you. I opened up to you. I fought the gods for you. Why?"

"I—"

"I'll tell you why." His gaze shifted to the glowing purple clouds violently colliding in the black sky. "It's because you can't change. Your kindness toward me was a gift, and what's gifted can be taken away. The moment I stepped out of line and refused to obey, you burned my face. The moment our goals diverged, you revealed your true face." He stared at his reflection in his father's dagger. "You, too, have given me a reminder of the Hyksos' fate when they cross an Egyptian."

"No. Please don't say that. Please! It... it was..." My voice broke.

"Your choice to activate the bracelet wasn't an accident. It was intentional." He tried to stand, his legs shaking beneath his weight. "You, like all other Egyptians, think I'm dangerous. Despite everything I did for you." He pushed his trembling legs toward Ishtar and collapsed.

"Khaf!" I jumped to his aid.

"Stay away from me!"

My knees shook, and I stumbled.

Khaf tried to stand and collapsed again. The Hyksos roared and punched the ground until Ishtar walked toward him. He fished his blankets out of his bag and laid one on the black sand.

"Khaf, I... I will go with you to Abydos. I'll do whatever you want. Give me a chance to set things right. Just... just..." I bit my lip to stop myself from crying. "Don't hate me, please."

"Hate you?" Khaf glared at me. "I don't hate you. I hate myself for being such a naive man. I almost threw it all away, and for whom?" He nodded at me in disgust. "For you." He spat the words like venom. He lay on his side and covered himself with his second blanket.

Ishtar licked the black sand stuck to my cheeks, then rubbed her snout against my face. I laid my blanket on the ground and curled up on its wet gray fabric, sticky from the thick air.

The purple lightning hit the ground in the distance, followed by thunder that echoed across the desert. I clutched the second blanket I used as a cover in a failed attempt to gain some measure of comfort.

I gazed at the dark heaven, tracing the violent dance of the glowing purple clouds. Patches of black dust swirled in the sky, resembling a swarm of angry flies.

I turned toward Khaf. He lay on his scarred side, fulfilling my fear. He was indeed self-conscious about his three-clawed scar.

Khaf had never fallen asleep before me since our arrival in Duat. In his own way, he had always looked after me the way he tended to Setu and the girls. I was the one who refused to see him for the kind man he truly was. I was too blind, too filled with hate and arrogance.

He was right. They all were. I saw him as a threat, and the bracelet protected me. Despite me being the real threat to him and those he loved, Khaf had always seen me as a person, as Nef, while he had been a pure concept I was taught as a child.

Oh, the untouchables of Avaris. A bunch of lowlifes. Beware of those Hyksos, for they are nothing but thieves and murderers.

Lies!

I had seen the truth. I saw Khafset of Avaris. A thief noble in his aspirations. The Hyksos who sheltered two little girls from the cruel life my people would've inflicted on them. The blacksmith's son who saw me like no man before him and yet never took advantage of our seclusion in Duat. Quite the opposite. He endangered himself, again and again, to keep me safe.

What did Hatshepsut say? There were always good men in our lives. How true. I had mine by my side for the last two years. Khafset, the proud thief of Avaris. My comrade in crime. The man who refused to disappoint despite how often the world had disappointed him.

I took off my cover and used it to rub the slimy layer off my hands. "Khaf, I know you're awake."

He didn't answer.

"I don't blame you for hating me. You've always met my cruelty toward you with kindness, so I understand if you've given up on me. I was selfish. I know that. There's really no excuse for what I've done." I dragged myself toward him and laid my hand on his arm. "Please tell me how to make this right. How can I even begin to show you how sorry I am?"

"You can start by getting your hand off me, Egyptian."

"Egyptian?" I laid my hand over my chest. "Won't you call me Nef again?"

"No. You were right all along. We can't be friends, let alone something more. We'll always be at odds. I'll always belong to the untouchable Hyksos, while you will always be one of my Egyptian overlords."

"Overlords? Me? Khaf, I'm on my knees begging for your forgiveness. I'm going to Abydos despite my wishes."

"How generous of you."

The thunder broke the heaven again, shaking every fiber of my being. Gods, I just wanted a moment of peace with the man.

"No matter what you do, it serves only you," Khaf said. "Sad, really. I've always pitied you for the lies in your head. I thought it was all Paser's poison. But in the end, *you* shattered my delusions. Paser had nothing to do with it. You're simply another cruel Egyptian."

He turned enough to show me his angry eyes while keeping his scar hidden. "Sleep, Egyptian. You need your energy. Tomorrow you'll find out whether my Baal is truly your father."

Chapter 18

The Heart of Darkness

Khaf led our march on a narrow path between two black mountains. Monstrous silhouettes loomed in the distance. They spawned from the shadows cast by the jagged mountains and roamed the open desert. Creatures that lurked inside Set's fallen kingdom. They emitted their chilling shrieks as they spied on us from the scarlet heaven.

I walked beside Ishtar, missing the comforting presence Khaf had denied me. He didn't utter a word that wasn't necessary. Simple phrases like "Follow me." "Stop." "Keep your eyes open." Phrases he stamped with the word "Egyptian."

"Hey, Khaf," I said, my voice shaky.

He ignored me.

"I was wondering if..." A cracking noise erupted beneath my feet. My right sandal was planted inside a cracked lion-shaped skull. I screamed and jumped frantically to free my foot from the monstrous skull.

"Oh, for Baal's sake!" Khaf threw his hands in the air.

I fell, raising a cloud of black sand, which stuck to the slimy layer on my dress. I tried to clean myself, but it was no use. That was the last straw. I began to cry.

"Why are you crying?" Khaf hissed.

"I can't take this anymore! I hate this dreadful desert."

Khaf took a deep breath and glanced at the hill behind him. Had I gotten through to him? Had my misery sparked his warmth again?

"The Abydos-gate should be at the end of this path," he said. "We are almost there."

I sniffed. "But... what about the shadows?"

"They're just demons."

"*Just* demons! How are—"

His glaring eyes widened. "Pull yourself together. Get up." He left, not even bothering to glance at me.

"Wait!" I grabbed Ishtar's reins and jogged to catch up with Khaf.

How could I convince him my apology was sincere? He had never been this mad at me. Should I compliment him? Yes. Feeding his ego had always brightened his mood.

"Hey, Khaf."

He ignored me.

"I really admire how you always find the right path for us. You also always know what to say. The way you tricked Sekhmet and Bastet into believing I was Egypt's greatest warrior." I whistled. "Gods, I admire your talents. Nefertari might have a contender for the title of Egypt's highest diplomat."

He didn't even nod. What a stupid thing to say. He was Hyksos. It didn't matter how talented he was; my people wouldn't allow him to succeed. Gods, focus, Nefiri!

Maybe teasing could work.

"Did I mention that Isis healed you? She said you're very important for saving Egypt." I hummed. "Are you secretly Hyksos royalty?"

Khaf's head twitched. He stopped and turned toward me.

Yeah, teasing him never failed.

"You need to let me focus," he said. "So if you're done distracting me with your pointless chatter, I suggest you stay quiet while *I* find our way to the Abydos-gate."

Ishtar blew the air out of her nostrils. At least she had the luxury of voicing her frustration. "Sure. I could stay quiet if you—"

"Shut up." Khaf didn't shout. It wasn't necessary. His monotone voice was more hurtful than the loudest shriek. He turned and continued his march between the mountains, their shifting shadows swallowing him.

I stood frozen in my tracks. He had never spoken to me like this. But I had always taken that tone with him. How was he able to tolerate my attitude?

Ishtar nudged me, and we followed Khaf, the thick fog swirling around him. We reached the end of the narrow path and exited into the vast desert.

Hundreds of demonic creatures lurked in the distance— black hippo-sized scorpions with broad, leathery wings and lion heads.

I grabbed the spear behind my back and planted it in the black sand. "Ga'ab Neyat!" Set's protective shield formed around the three of us.

"What are you doing now?" Khaf snapped.

"I want to protect us from these things."

"They are demons." Khaf turned to eye Set's servants through the dome's scarlet glow.

"So what's the play here? Is there a way to get past them, like with Shemzu's hyenas, or should I attack them with Set's magic?"

"What?" Khaf glanced at me over his shoulder, revealing his scar.

I swallowed. "Y-you're right. I should have used my head. Set's demons are probably immune to his magic. I should use Ra's fire."

"That's your only solution, isn't it? Burn them when they're in our way."

"I'm sorry. I didn't mean it like that. They're just ugly and don't look friendly."

"Yeah, well, I'm just as ugly now, thanks to you."

"What? No!" I gave a nervous laugh. "I never said it outright, but I've always considered you the most handsome man I've ever seen. Even that scar makes you look very man—"

Khaf's head shook, his eyes glaring at me.

"I... am sorry. I'll never mention it again."

He scoffed and walked outside the protective dome.

"Khaf, what are you doing?"

He bolted about a mile across the desert and stood beside the first row of demons.

What was that man doing?

"Come!" Khaf called.

I freed the spear from the black sand and exchanged a confused look with Ishtar. I climbed on her back and rode toward Khaf, my grip tight on the spear. We reached the Hyksos as he patted one of the demon's scorpion legs like a pet.

"What were you thinking?" I asked. "Those demons might be—"

"They're Set's servants. They won't stop us from bringing the spear to his prison."

"I—guess that makes sense."

Ishtar groaned. She was right. Since when was he this reckless? He could've gotten us both killed had he misjudged the situation. But what was I supposed to say except agree with him? At least nothing bad had happened, right?

"That's where the gate should be." Khaf pointed at the horizon where the swarms of—according to him—friendly massive, winged, lion-headed scorpions ended. "I read in the temple about a stone plate that contains the Abydos-gate. It was crafted by Ptah, the god of creation, at Horus's request."

Gods, how I'd missed his intelligent explanations.

"Very well," I said. "Hop on. Should only take us a moment at full speed."

The hieroglyphs on Khaf's chest glowed. "I won't share a horse with you. Especially one linked to the traitorous Astarte." He bolted toward the gate, leaving a trail of raging black sand behind him.

"What? Khaf, come back!" I tightened my grip on the spear, ready to fend off the demons. "Khafset!"

Everywhere I looked, a pair of demonic red eyes glared at me. The demons' lion heads growled, flashing their teeth. They flapped their torn bat wings, creating an arc of slimy black sand around them. Their scorpion legs tensed as if ready to strike. But they didn't attack. They couldn't. I was their master's chosen. The supposed breaker of his shackles. These monstrosities knew it and were visibly trying to control themselves.

I rode Ishtar across the scarlet desert at full speed, passing through a sea of demons clearing the way for their master's chosen. We emerged behind their ranks where Khaf stood.

Twenty paces away stood a giant stone plate, and a woman sat on the ground before it.

I jumped off Ishtar's back and walked toward Khaf.

"Open the gate," Khaf said. "Destroy the plate with Set's magic."

"A person is sitting there. I might harm her."

"Not a person. Can't you see her black wings? That's Nephthys."

I hesitantly pointed the spear toward the stone plate and the goddess of darkness.

Nephthys' long purple skirt was muddied and torn. Tears ran down her cheeks, smearing mascara on her paling brown skin. The loose black cloth around her chest barely held her breasts. How could a god reach such a miserable state?

Her murals in Egypt depicted her as a strong and prideful goddess, but in reality she was pathetic. What happened to her?

"What are you waiting for?" Khaf asked. "Open the gate!"

"Set's flames could harm her."

"Baal's traitorous wife deserves more than to be burned. Didn't you learn anything from Paser? This woman is vile."

Yeah, I had heard her story. Nephthys discovered Set's infertility. Instead of confronting him with the truth, she disguised herself as Isis. She visited Osiris and had Anubis with him. Legend had it that Set's roars shook Egypt when he discovered the truth, creating the mountains along the Red Sea coast. His tears flooded the Nile, turning it red and afflicting anyone who drank it with a deadly sorrowful state. No mortal was able to survive even a grain of Set's pain. Yet again, his brother had claimed something he loved. Set shunned Nephthys and banished her from his kingdom, then moved to Canaan, where he met Astarte. I used to despise Nephthys for her treason, but now I understood her actions. She just wanted to protect him. She committed an unforgivable mistake, but her love had clouded her judgment. No, I couldn't allow Khaf to follow Set's path. The gods were wrong. Khaf was *not* the new Set.

I lowered the spear. "You are many things, Khaf, but cruel isn't one of them, despite what you are trying to prove." I pulled Ishtar toward Nephthys. The horse tensed and dug her hooves into the sand. "What's wrong?"

She squealed and shook her head, freeing her reins from my grip.

"Even the horse has more brains than you, Egyptian."

"Fine!" I stormed away. One hard-minded Canaanite was manageable, but two were too much.

"Wait, you idiot, what are you doing?" Khaf rushed after me.

I walked toward Nephthys. Her sobbing got louder with each step. Khaf and I stood before the goddess of darkness. She didn't seem to have noticed our presence.

Nephthys scratched the plate's stony surface with her sharp fingernails, her black wings jittering on the sand.

"Oh, my beloved," she said. "Oh, he who commands the storms. Allow me to share your suffering. Grant me a reunion in your prison, forever bound in the beauty of your Destruction and my Darkness. Oh, he who rules over the deserts and its demons, hear the pleas of this traitorous lover who seeks your forgiveness. Oh, my beloved. Oh, he who... who..." Her voice broke, and she succumbed to her cries.

"Great Nephthys," I said.

The goddess's dark eyes darted toward us. Her head shook, her hair dancing like black flames. "That!" She pointed at me. "That's his spear!" The scarlet heaven turned black, and the glowing purple clouds vanished.

I cowered. "I... I..."

"You stole his spear and kept him away from me, mortal!" Nephthys marched toward us. Her steps turned the black sand into glowing gray glass beneath her bare feet, illuminating the otherwise dark desert. "An insignificant insect that serves Horus!"

"Just a moment, great Neph—"

Black energy spiraled around Nephthys' right hand. The goddess stretched out her arm toward me, launching a web of black threads in my direction and trapping me in her chilling magic. My skin froze in her grip, and my senses darkened. It was as if I would never experience joy again.

Nephthys raised her hand, jerking my body into the air until Set's spear fell from my hand.

I closed my fist to call Ra's flames. Nephthys lowered her gaze toward her father's bracelet. Her threads crawled on my skin and engulfed my hand, forcing me to relax my fist. The tips of her magical weavings turned into tiny, delicate spikes and pierced my skin. Chills claimed my existence. My heart stopped beating. I turned into a clouded mind trapped in a corpse. I should just stop resisting. Yes. Why did I even fight? The world was dark and cold. Joy was simply a mirage we all chased. It wasn't real. Whatever warmth was left inside me screamed that this realization wasn't true, but the darkness swallowed it.

A brilliant golden light exploded beside me. Khaf dashed toward the goddess of darkness and pointed his dagger at her neck.

"Release her," Khaf said. "Now."

My lifeless heart gave a defiant bump.

Nephthys turned her gaze to Khaf and released me from her threads. The goddess laughed the same way a cat would toy with a rat. "Should your blade scare me, mortal?" She traced her finger on Khaf's dagger, but it couldn't cut her skin.

"Harm her, and you will never see my Baal again."

"Baal?" Nephthys' face darkened. "You are one of Astarte's mortals." She snatched Khaf's neck, choking him, and lifted him into the air. "You insects and your goddess stole my..." Her eyes widened. "Oh! I can see Astarte in those eyes of yours. What a disgrace." She spat.

"You... t-traitorous women don't... get to speak of... *disgrace!*" Khaf managed to say with the little air Nephthys' grip allowed him.

"You dare, you damned freak!" Nephthys flapped her wings and rose with Khaf to the heaven. Black energy leaked down her left arm like ink, forming long sharp claws on her hand. "I will destroy you and send your ashes to Astarte!"

I grabbed Set's spear and pointed it at the goddess. "Please, great Nephthys, don't harm him!"

A loud explosion erupted in the distance. The goddess's attention shifted to the sound. Ishtar dashed toward us. She squealed, declaring her arrival and challenging the goddess.

Nephthys glared at Ishtar, her head shaking. "You!" She tossed Khaf, and he landed in front of the blue horse. "You sent your essence with your freak to witness my misery through its eyes." She pounded Ishtar's neck with her clenched hands, but the horse remained calm.

"Exactly what I should have expected from you, Astarte! What else should I await from your kind? Parasites. All parasites that came to our lands and broke our laws to rob us of everything we love. Everything *I* loved."

"Nephthys!" Khaf shouted. "Look at me!"

The goddess gritted her teeth but kept her gaze on Ishtar.

"I said..." Khaf said, his voice stern. "Look. At. Me."

Black paint spiraled around Nephthys' arms. She glared at Khaf. "I have indulged your insults for far too long, Canaanite!" She pointed her palms at the ground, shooting the energy into the sand. Her magic weaved through the ground like black vines. It spiraled around Khaf, trapping him.

Khaf's cold eyes stared at the goddess. He didn't react. Didn't even tremble.

"I will burn you from the inside out, Astarte's freak. My Darkness will consume—"

"The Egyptian over there is the only one who can free my Baal," Khaf interrupted the goddess, and she stepped back, her eyes wide with shock. "I'm the only one who can guide her to him. The horse has proven vital to our mission. Harm any of us, and you'll be the reason why my Baal will spend eternity in prison. I know betrayal is in your nature, Nephthys, but stop us, and you will betray my Baal again. Stop us, and we fail Horus's test because of you. The god-pharaoh surely would punish you for this, wouldn't he?"

Nephthys shook, her hair raging like black fire. Her chest rose and fell. She released Khaf and laid her hands on her head. The goddess mumbled to herself and took one trembling step after another until she collapsed before the stone plate.

"Oh, my beloved." Nephthys hugged the plate, sobbing. "Look what has become of me in your absence. A freak—a mere scandalous creature—threatens me, and I must accept it for your sake."

I approached the collapsed goddess, our tears pouring down our cheeks. The gods had compared Khaf and me to the fallen divine couple. Nephthys and I were the same. Two women who cried over the men we harmed. Two exiled souls away from our families and lands. I *was* Nephthys.

"We've been here for too long," Khaf said. "Get away from the gate, Nephthys."

The goddess's furious glare darted toward Khaf. A black aura raged around her. Her Darkness crawled on her skin like paint, feeding the growing claws on her hands. "You dare—"

"We could leave," Khaf said. "Or you could get out of our way. Make a damned decision."

Nephthys' head fell, and her Darkness faded. She sobbed and crawled from the stone plate, dragging her wings on the ground and losing a handful of black feathers.

"Do it, Egyptian."

I pointed the spear at the plate. "Shama'at Morot," I mumbled.

The scarlet beam launched from the spear. Set's flames consumed the plate and melted its stone. Black mist leaked from the rubble, forming the Abydos-gate.

"Finally!" Khaf walked into the gate's mist.

Nephthys stood, her breathing getting louder. This was my signal to run after Khaf. I grabbed Ishtar's reins and walked toward the gate.

"Wait," Nephthys called.

I froze.

"Just—wait a moment."

"I can't afford to have him wait alone in Abydos, great Nephthys. He might think I abandoned—"

"Shh." Nephthys waved at me. "How did he pass through the gate?"

"What?"

"Not even I can pass through the gate. So how did he do it?"

"Khaf always has a trick."

"Trick? What trick? Nobody can trick Ptah's designs."

"I don't know. It's Khaf. He tends to amaze more often than not."

"The only people who can pass through the Abydos-gate are the spear's chosen and those who have previously visited the city."

"Khaf can't be either. I'm the Chosen, and the city was moved to Duat ages before Khaf was born."

"And so I ask again. How did that disgusting creature pass through the gate?"

"Don't insult him!" My eyes widened. Had I finally lost my mind? I'd just made a demand of a goddess!

I bowed my head. "I'm so, *so* sorry, great Nephthys. Please forgive me. I'm under a lot of stress."

"You're fully under the boy's control, aren't you?" Nephthys said.

"It's—complicated. I need Khaf by my side, great Nephthys. It doesn't matter what trick he used."

"Oh, but it does matter." Nephthys approached me, scratching her arms with her long nails. "Astarte's freak found a way around Ptah's magical prison while I have spent ages crying next to a stone plate like an idiot."

"He... I really should go. Khaf will get mad."

She caught my hand. Ishtar squealed, and Nephthys released me, shooting the horse a disgusted glance. "When you free my beloved. Just... just..." She held her left arm and looked at the sky. "Just tell me how he's doing. I will be kicked out of his kingdom when he's freed. Still, I wish to witness the glorious breaking of his shackles. Even through you."

I arched my eyebrow. "How am I supposed to contact *you*?"

"Ask your queen mother. I think her name was Tuya. I struck a divine deal with her."

My mouth dropped. "Deal? What deal?"

"I can't say. It's part of the deal."

"You're a goddess. You can do whatever you want."

Nephthys shook her head. "When a god strikes a divine deal with a mortal, it binds them equally. Like the deal we have with you mortals. You worship and believe in us, granting us more strength, and in return we protect you and never harm you in your realm. We physically can't break those deals. Such was the will of the first god, Atem, when he created us." She held my hand and smiled. "Do it for me. Aren't you an Egyptian? Am I not your goddess? A supreme goddess of the Ennead. Wouldn't you wish to have the blessing of appeasing me, my dear mortal?"

I nodded. The poor goddess would probably rip me apart if she found out I was going to ensure Set stayed in his prison. But what was Tuya scheming now? Gods, that woman's influence reached even the gods in the depths of Duat.

"I will try my best, great Nephthys." I had really lied for way less. "I need to go." I bowed my head. "It was an—honor, great Nephthys." I grabbed Ishtar's reins and walked through the gate's mist.

Chapter 19

Abydos of Desolation

Giant misty skulls decorated the black heaven of Abydos, leaking a silver glow on the surface of the desolated city. There was no life in this cursed place: no wind or animals. Not even insects crawled on the buildings that were melting like clay. The only sign of life was the black vines woven through the ground's hardened gray mud.

Khaf was waiting for me and Ishtar as we passed through the Abydos-gate. "Sure took your time, Egyptian. Of course, you and Nephthys got along. You literally are one and the same."

I gritted my teeth. Enough was enough. I wouldn't be humiliated any further. If begging for forgiveness didn't work, I was going to knock some sense into this Hyksos.

"You know what, I'm done apologizing!"

"Yeah, your empty apologies sure got—"

"I've tried everything in my power to prove my sincerity. I owned up to every terrible thing I've done to you."

Khaf scoffed. "That sure makes up for—"

"No! You'll listen to me! It's about time we shared our feelings instead of resenting each other silently. We're not going to end up like Set and Nephthys." I drew a deep breath. "I truly believed Set might've planned a trap, and you would've died to save me." I took three steps to shorten the gap between us. "But you're right. I didn't want to confront my father." I took another step. "You taught me to trust, and Set did protect me against Shemzu and Apep. He cares about me, and I might find it in my heart to forgive him for abandoning Hote and me because you taught me to be better."

I gazed into his honey eyes, awaiting his response. He needed this. *We* needed it. Khaf and I were equals and rivals. That was the key to getting him to speak. Not humiliation, admiration, or teasing.

"So what now?" Khaf asked. "Does your monologue erase your betrayal?" He pointed at his three-clawed scar. "Will it heal my face? Should I feel sorry for you, even though you endanger everyone in Egypt for your own selfish reasons?"

"I would love nothing more than for you to forgive me. But I will *not* end up like Nephthys. I will *not* be humiliated like her. If you won't accept my apology, fine. Have it your way. I will help you finish the grand heist, and if that's not enough, I have nothing more to offer you."

Khaf gazed at the decaying buildings, brushing his hands through his curly brown hair. "You know, when I first spotted you in Peramessu, I planned and schemed to convince you to see me each month. I begged Setu to seek you on the Egyptian side to tip you in my direction. For the first time in my life, I begged, and it was for you. Even when you hated me, I imagined a life with you. But you have shown me what that life would be like, and I don't accept it. I deserve better. Everyone in Avaris deserves better."

"I agree."

"Good. Let's finish this to get the lives we deserve." Khaf walked away.

I grabbed Ishtar's reins and marched behind him. We followed the black vines that oozed sticky green material.

"Hey, Khaf."

"What now?"

"How did you pass through the Abydos-gate? Nephthys said only I or someone who has visited the city could do it."

"She's trying to confuse you."

"Why would she want to hinder us if she believes we want to free Set?"

"The goddess of darkness feeds off misery. It's in her nature. She can't help it."

"You're speaking nonsense. I may not know as much about the gods as you, but I have a brain."

Khaf stopped and turned. "Do you have something to say?"

"Yes."

"Say it."

"What are you hiding?"

"I was going to share it with you right before you betrayed me and burned my face. So apologies if I can't trust—"

Ishtar neighed. She jumped, freeing her reins.

Khaf's eyes darted to a row of tall houses to his right. "It's coming."

"What's coming?"

"The demon."

The tiny rocks on the ground vibrated. They shivered in a strict rhythm. Pulse. Silence. Pulse. Silence. Each pulsation returned with a higher intensity and a faster frequency until the ground shook.

I grabbed the spear from behind my back. "I hear it."

The shrieks of a hundred people echoed from behind the row of houses. An explosion shook the buildings, crumpling them to the ground in a thick cloud of dust. Boulders raced from the direction of the collapsed buildings and collided with the houses next to me.

A giant rock flew in my direction. "Sha..." I coughed from the dust, staring at the massive projectile about to crush me.

The hieroglyphs on Khaf's chest flashed. He grabbed my waist, and we bolted from the boulder, Ishtar galloping behind us. Blood leaked from Khaf's shoulders as we dashed. The boulder had scratched his skin.

It almost caught him! As with Nephthys, despite his harsh words, Khaf had risked himself to save me.

He came to a halt, and Ishtar stopped beside us. He glanced in my direction, his legs tense and his hand on my waist. "Can you word the spell now?"

I nodded.

"Conjure the protective dome."

"Ga..." I coughed and planted the spear into the ground. "Ga'ab Neyat!"

The protective dome formed around the three of us. The dust encapsulated it, obscuring our view of the outside.

Khaf turned. "I hear it." His head jittered in every direction as he scanned the area. Left, right, up, left, up. The area he was observing decreased with each movement as he narrowed in on his target.

"Found it!" Khaf pointed outside the protective dome. "It's coming from that direction."

"How did you—"

A roar erupted inside the cloud, scattering the dust and clearing a path to give us our first view of the demon.

A slimy reddish-black creature walked toward us; its flesh, the sum of decaying humans, melted together. At least fifty moving heads poked out from its body, and it was taller than Khaf and me combined.

"Khaf. J-just checking." I stepped back from the approaching monstrosity. "What about this demon? Kill it or pat it like the others?"

"Kill!" Khaf shouted. "Most definitely kill!"

I freed the spear from the ground and pointed it at the demon. "Shama'at Morot!" The beam of destruction launched from the spear's tip. The scarlet flames stopped before the demon and dissolved into nothingness.

My mouth dropped. "What the..."

"It's immune to magic. Use Ra's fire."

"That's still magic, idiot!"

"The flames themselves aren't magical, genius!"

The demon shrieked and ran toward us. Well, it was worth a try. I pointed my right fist at the demon. The bracelet glowed yellow, and Khaf retreated.

"Zier!" Ra's golden fire soared toward the demon. It consumed its body and the area surrounding it, melting the buildings around the monstrosity. The demon didn't react to the flames. It didn't cry in pain or scream. But the skulls in the heaven, oh, they shifted their focus toward me, and their shrieks covered the desolated city.

"Enough!" Khaf said from behind me.

"It's still alive!"

"I said enough!"

I relaxed my fist, and the stream of fire faded. The demon's chest lay motionless, eight heads screaming from its surface. The smoke dissipated, revealing a large melting palace hiding behind the collapsed buildings. The most horrific sight revealed itself. A sea of decaying corpses climbed on top of each other toward the center of a large square before the palace's twisted gates.

"Why are they crawling to the palace's entrance?" I asked.

"Baal!" Khaf walked toward the square. "His flesh must be what's attracting them!"

Ishtar neighed and blocked Khaf's path.

"Wait!" I caught his hand.

About fifty decaying corpses disengaged from their attempts to reach Set. They crawled toward the demon's chest, leaving a trail of black slime behind them. They lay over each other, and a repulsive, gooey hill formed over the chest. The corpses melted into each other. The demon's body reformed, and its heads poked out of its flesh. The monster stood. Its heads screamed in sync with the misty skulls in the sky, their shrieks echoing across the desolated city. And after this unnecessary display of horror, the demon launched in our direction.

"How many times do we have to burn that thing?" I asked.

Khaf jerked from my grip. "Take Ishtar and fly over the demon. On my command, shoot Ra's fire in its direction."

The golden hieroglyphs on his chest glowed, and he bolted toward the demon.

Who put him in command? I opened my mouth to protest but decided otherwise. To be fair, his plan to use Ra's fire had worked. It would be wise to trust his judgment. Not that he waited for my response anyway.

I climbed on Ishtar's back. "Thihier Hawa!" The wings sprang from Ishtar's sides. She flew toward the skulls in Abydos's black sky and hovered above the demon.

Khaf bumped against the demon at full speed, knocking it over. He disengaged. "Now!"

I pointed my fist down at the collapsed demon. "Zier!" Ra's bracelet glowed yellow, and fire raged from my fist, trapping the demon inside the golden flames.

The hieroglyphs on Khaf's chest flashed. He sprinted around the fire, collecting its flames into a fiery cyclone. Khaf retreated from the blazing storm. He trembled, smoke raging around his body. The Hyksos roared and bolted inside the flaming storm.

"Khafset!" I relaxed my fist, stopping the fire's flow. Gods, what was he doing?

Four explosions erupted inside the storm, scattering the flames. Khaf stood over the demon, blood leaking from his fists. The monster was missing its arms and legs. He'd combined his speed and strength to obliterate the demon's limbs with punches.

More corpses disengaged from the square and crawled toward the demon to reform its body.

Khaf carved a hole in the demon's chest with his dagger. He slid his hand inside the demon's body and dragged out its watermelon-sized heart that was still connected through glowing red veins to its insides. Khaf cut the veins, and the demon disintegrated into dust.

The entire sea of corpses turned its attention to Khaf. The skulls in the sky shifted their eye sockets toward the Hyksos. Shrieks from heaven and earth consumed the desolated city. The cursed population of Abydos crawled toward him, their arms stretched out in his direction.

Khaf pointed his dagger at the heart. "Stop where you are!"

I circled with Ishtar above the cursed people. They stopped, and their shrieks turned into moans.

I landed behind Khaf and jumped off Ishtar's back. "That was wild! We're getting good at this. We make a good team, don't we?" I kissed Ishtar's neck and walked toward Khaf. "Let's grab the scythe and get out of—"

Khaf raised the demon's heart to his face and bit into its flesh. I froze. Ishtar screamed. The entirety of Abydos shrieked, cries erupting from heaven and earth.

"Khafset?" I covered my mouth. "What have you done?"

Khaf ignored me and the screaming masses of decaying corpses that crawled toward him. He took one bite after the other. A new set of hieroglyphs formed on his back. Not golden. Red. Dark magic, from the heart he had eaten. The cursed object contained traces of Osiris's heart.

Khaf consumed the last chunk. He gasped for air, black blood dripping from his mouth.

"Khafset, answer me! This wasn't part of the plan."

Khaf brushed back his brown hair, smearing the demon's blood on his head. He pointed his dagger at his heart and glared at the cursed people of Abydos. "Retreat, or I will end your dreams of recreating Osiris's heart!"

The people of Abydos crawled away from the main square, freeing a path to the square's center where glowing blue shackles kept the slumbering Set on his knees. A scythe stood proud before the god's thin, naked body. His tall ears dangled beside his temples. Gods, to think Nephthys' miserable state was prideful compared to her beloved's.

"How even the mightiest fall in the end," Khaf mumbled to himself, his eyes glued to the shackled god.

"Khaf, please talk to me."

He turned but avoided my eyes. "Ra was right. There were three scarabs in Set's temple. Two silver scarabs that you used to gain Set's aid against Shemzu and Apep. The third was crystal."

My heart skipped a beat. Crystal? What was he talking about? Tuya gave me a golden scarab. If it didn't belong to Set, whose scarab was in my possession?

"Khaf?"

He nodded, his gaze glued to the ground. "The crystal scarab that allows a mortal to visit a god. The one I used to visit Set in his prison to strike a divine deal with him. Free my Baal, and he will help me with my plans."

"You didn't!" Tears slid down my cheeks.

"A deal I almost broke because of you. I almost shared it with you in the scarlet desert. But you betrayed me when I finally trusted you."

"This can't be true. You couldn't have used the scarab. You would've needed a divine item. You didn't have any."

"I did. When I visited the spear for the first time on my own. I didn't have to touch it. It only had to touch the crystal scarab. They increased security after my first visit. Little did they know I had access to the grand vizier's sole apprentice. That's how I knew the spear's location. How I knew it could only choose on a blood-moon night, and how I knew the path to Abydos. I could pass through the Abydos-gate because I *have* been to Abydos when I spoke to Set."

"But why didn't the spear choose you if you already had a deal with Set?"

"I don't know," Khaf said. "Gods, I wish I did. It neither killed nor chose me." He opened his eyes, revealing his honey-colored irises, which were... dimming? Was this the Dark magic's influence?

"It doesn't matter anymore who was chosen," Khaf said. "You honored your promise and got the spear to Set's prison, and now it's my turn to honor my promise." He walked toward me. "Your role in the grand heist is over. Hand over the spear, and I will send you home."

I retreated. "Khaf, you know you can't touch the spear."

"Same as the demon, I can now negate magic, including the spear's protective spell. Set's idea."

"How?" I held tight to the spear with both hands. "You spoke to him before I was chosen."

"I spoke to him every night in Duat after you went to sleep. Ever heard of praying?"

I scanned my environment for a viable escape route. There weren't any. I was trapped with Khaf and Set. "You don't want to do this. I know I hurt you. You have every right to hate me and every Egyptian. But you don't want to free Set. He will destroy us all. The Hyksos included. You are Astarte's people. She helped the gods defeat him. He must hate you as well."

"I will save us all. Unlike you, I have learned a great deal during our journey. Set would only play a role in my grand heist."

"You can't trick Set!"

"I will take my chances." He shrugged. "How much worse could our lives become?"

"You would die! The Hittites will slaughter every Egyptian and Hyksos. They don't care about our petty differences!"

"So be it. Should my plans fail, then let us die together. Maybe those who come after will learn from our mistakes. You said it in Maat's court. We both have committed the same crimes. We both deserve the same fate. Either we live together as equals or die together as such."

Khaf stretched out his hand toward the spear, and I tightened my hug around it, pushing its metal against my chest. Ra's bracelet glowed to defend me. The new red hieroglyphs on his back flashed. He grabbed my right wrist, and his Negation magic deactivated the bracelet's radiance.

"Please let me go," I begged, unable to find a way to fight back.

Khaf stretched out his other arm toward the spear. He hesitated for a moment, his hand hovering. We both cried, gazing into each other's eyes.

"Sorry," Khaf said. "I can't." He grabbed Set's weapon, triggering a new set of hieroglyphs on his face.

"No!"

He jerked the divine weapon out of my grip and pushed me to the ground.

"Khafset." I tried to stand. "Give me back the—"

"Stop." He pointed the spear at me, and I fell back. "Just—stop. It's over. You're not part of this anymore."

"What will you do, Khaf?" I glared at him and rose to my feet, the spear's tip tracing my movement. "Will you kill me?"

He tightened his grip. "Maybe I will."

"Then do it."

"I will."

"Don't tell me. Show me."

"I just might!"

"Coward!" I pushed the spear away. "Burn me! Kill me! End my life! Release me from my misery!" I slammed his chest with each word.

He froze, his eyes wide.

"Here, let me help you." I grabbed the spear's upper half and pointed it at my heart. "Do it! If you free Set, my Khafset has died, and I can't live without him."

The new golden hieroglyphs on his face glowed. The scarlet energy spiraled around the spear as I pushed it closer to my heart.

Khaf bit his lip. His tears returned. He lowered the spear and turned.

"Khaf?"

"I loved you!" Khaf shouted. "Gods, I loved you," he whispered. "Since the moment I saw you. I dreamed of a different life. One where you were a Hyksos or I an Egyptian. A life where we could be together. Because of you, I dreamt, and my nightmares felt like distant memories. When you kissed me and finally shared my feelings, I was—happy. I thought the life I dreamt for us together might become a reality. Because of you, I was able to dream again."

"You... we could still have this life together." I took his hands and gently rubbed his arms. "We could grab the scythe and leave. We'll cut Set's connection to our world, Ramesses will win, and your people will be free."

"It sounds like a beautiful dream, doesn't it?" He laid his forehead against mine.

I lost myself in the comfort of his warm breath. "It really does."

"I was beginning to believe in this beautiful dream as well. It made me doubt my plans. I thought maybe we should leave Set in his prison." He held my hand and guided it to his face. "Then you did this." He rubbed my palm on his three-clawed scar. "It's the reason your queen can't free my people, why we can't have this life together. It will always be a gift, and you will always have the power to take it away." He retreated, and I gasped when he robbed me of his warmth.

Khaf walked toward Set, surrounded by the cursed people of Abydos, their arms stretched out toward him.

I took my first step to follow, and froze when the monsters growled at me.

"You will always make us suffer," Khaf yelled, the distance between us growing with each step. "We have caused each other enough suffering. We will end this cycle here and now. Freedom won't be gifted. It will be earned by all."

"Khaf, come back!" I shouted, and Ishtar squealed beside me. "I love you, you idiot!"

Khaf stopped before the scythe and glanced at me over his shoulder. "And I don't love you anymore." He focused on the scythe and sighed. "What a shame."

"I'm sorry." Ra's bracelet glowed around my wrist.

He turned toward the golden light leaking from my fist.

"This is much bigger than both of us. I can't let you gamble with the lives of everyone in Egypt." I pointed my shaking fist at him. "I'm giving you one last chance."

"You're sadly right. This is much bigger than us. That's why I can't stop now."

"Idiot," I said. "Zier."

Ra's golden flames raged toward Khaf. He raised the spear, and the hieroglyphs on his face glowed. Set's protective shield spawned and sheltered him from Ra's flames. My energy ran out, and Ra's flames disappeared. I collapsed.

It was over. The thief had outsmarted me. I lost.

"Khafset, ple..." My voice broke. "I beg you."

"Don't cry." The Hyksos smiled behind his shield. "And never beg." He stretched his arm toward the scythe. "It was a beautiful dream while it lasted, Nef."

He freed the scythe from the ground. The city shook. Rubble rose toward the heaven, blasting the screaming misty skulls.

Khaf took a deep breath. "May the flames rejoin!" He connected the scythe and the spear.

A blinding scarlet glow flashed from Set's reunified weapon. Shrieks consumed Abydos. The flames of destruction swept across the city, obliterating everything in its path. Set's magic reached me. It grabbed my skin with the might of a thousand men, trying to shred my flesh. It couldn't. No matter how hard the Destruction magic tried, it couldn't harm me, unlike the desolated city falling to its doom. Explosions erupted in its streets, destroying the buildings and covering the city in dust and ash.

Then silence.

Silence that was broken by the mightiest roar I had ever heard. The roar of Set. The unshackled god of destruction. My father.

Chapter 20

Divine Deals

I pushed the debris off my back, coughing the smoke out of my lungs. Set's scarlet flames streamed through the cracked ground. Ishtar lay on her side, surrounded by a sea of ash.

I crawled toward the horse and laid her head on my knees. She looked at me, her horn's glow fading. Her golden eyes turned gray, and she dissolved into particles of radiating blue dust in my embrace.

My hands moved on their own, trying to collect Ishtar's dust as if this could save her. I couldn't help her. Gods, I was such a failure. Ishtar was yet another loss. Yet another loved one I had...

A tingling sensation irritated my foot. Set's scarlet flames danced in dizzying patterns, engulfing my leg. Could I tap into Set's magic through his flames as I did with Apep's mist?

I hovered my hand above the fire. Scarlet bolts zapped me, connecting me to the flames, which lost their color and turned from scarlet to rose. A warm wave crawled over my skin, replenishing my health and granting me that beautiful sense of might.

So, that was the reason I had survived Set's destructive wave. As his daughter, I must've been immune to his magic.

The fog faded, revealing the destroyed city. The people of Abydos had turned into scorched skeletons. Their arms pointed at the god; they stood at the square's center before the molten palace.

Set stood—twice Khaf's height—covered in gold-scarlet armor. He observed the thief, stroking the red beard below the tip of his snout.

I scrambled to my feet, searching for an escape. I gave up just as fast and fell on my knees. What was the point? No place was safe anymore. Neither in Duat nor in Huat. Gods, what had we done?

"My Baal." Khaf knelt before the god of destruction and laid the unified weapon on his palms. "As promised, I have freed you and reunified your weapon. In return, I humbly ask for nothing but your divine justice."

Set claimed his weapon and regarded its spear side. "Justice?" He flipped it and traced his long, black claw on the scythe's blade. "And how do you define justice, my promised?"

"Help me execute my plan to free my people. Destroy the pharaoh and his soldiers. Punish them for the suffering they have caused."

Set's promise to destroy the Egyptian army was Khaf's idea! Of course, Nefertari would've agreed to anything to rescue her husband and their kingdom. Such desperation would be perfect for Khaf's plans.

"And don't your people deserve their current state?" Set asked. "Doesn't their punishment fall under your definition of justice?"

"We are as guilty as the Egyptians. I... have learned this on my journey to free you. For that, I don't ask for revenge. I ask for justice. Bring down your wrath on Ramesses and his army. Let everyone in Egypt dread the Hittites as equals. Allow them to struggle and learn together. Unify them through the fear of their impending destruction. That is justice."

"And if the Hittites kill them? I still need to be worshiped."

"I will save them. I will have enough divine items to destroy the Hittites. I will lead a unified Egypt to victory and equality as their pharaoh."

What? Khafset wanted to usurp the throne! He was scheming to become the first Hyksos pharaoh since Ahmose's victory.

Set laughed. "So it's power you seek, mortal."

"No," Khaf said, stopping Set's laughter and the accusations soaring in my head. "I will return to my father's smithy after the war. I want the Egyptians and Hyksos to choose their future together. As free people. As equals." Khaf's head rose. "Those are the terms of our divine deal, my Baal. I freed you. Now you destroy the pharaoh and his army."

"You believe you will step down as pharaoh after experiencing the intoxicating taste of power." The god chuckled. "Oh, the mortals and their naivety." He waved his hand dismissively. "It doesn't matter. I am a just god, and you shall receive what you desire."

"Our deal included a gift," Khaf said. "I expect the fulfillment of this part of the deal."

"A deal you forced me to accept, considering my state when we met."

"A divine deal nonetheless, great Baal. A bond neither of us can break."

Set arched his eyebrow. "And what gift would you request?"

"I want your aid in finding the Book of the Dead."

The Book of the Dead? Wasn't that the dangerous divine item Hercules wanted to steal? So *that* was the grand heist's real goal, wasn't it? The thief wished to steal death itself!

"Oh, my promised." Set's smile turned vicious, revealing his sharp teeth. "A gift for both of us. Why desire such an item?"

Yeah, why? I wanted to scream the question but kept my mouth shut. Set hadn't noticed my presence, and I intended it to stay that way.

"I want to resurrect my dead father," Khaf said. "A god can't find the Book of the Dead on their own, but I, your humble mortal, could be of aid. Help me, and you may have the book afterward."

Set's laughter echoed through the destroyed city. The remaining scarlet flames soared from the ground's cracks. "And so shall it be!" He tapped the spear side of his weapon to the ground. "Rise, my promised. You have fulfilled your part of our divine deal, and now it's my turn to fulfill mine."

"I'm eternally grateful, my Baal." Khaf rose, his head bowed, and stepped aside.

Set's scarlet eyes wandered toward me, trapping the air in my chest. What was I thinking? Of course he was aware of me!

Scarlet energy engulfed me, forming a glowing layer over my skin. It pulled me in front of Set's feet, granting me a better view of Khaf. His eyes were both determined and... red? Was the idiot crying?

"Khaf, what did you—"

"Our guest of honor." Set walked behind Khaf. "The Chosen."

"G..." I swallowed. "Great S—"

"A worthless disappointment to both the gods and the mortals," Set said.

I nodded. "I did disappoint the man who freed you. The man I love."

"Ah, love." Set brushed Khaf's hair back as if he were a mere child. "The illusion that strikes the fancies of the gods and their mortals."

I hid my right hand behind me, obscuring Ra's bracelet from Set's vision. "What are your plans for Egypt?"

"Didn't you hear the boy?" Set asked.

"I'd love to hear it from you, great Set."

The god chuckled, walking away from Khaf. "Your pharaoh and his soldiers will die. Astarte's mortal believes he can stop the Hittites but will fail."

"I won't fail!" Khaf lowered his head. "My Baal."

Set gave Khaf a dismissive wave. "Believe your delusions, boy. I couldn't care less."

Of course, Set had his own vision for the future. Oh, Khafset, you idiot! How did I suddenly become the reasonable one?

Set rested on a boulder at the square's center and looked at me. "Egypt will fall, and its people will suffer. They will seek my help, redirecting the gods' powers to me. I will kill Horus and regain my rightful throne as god-pharaoh of Egypt."

I closed my hidden fist, and Ra's magic raged inside my veins. "Why should we seek your help when you're the one who'll cause our suffering?"

"The gods are detached, and the mortals forgetful. Drunk on power, they remain blind to the lessons of the past and the dangers of the future. They forget the approaching storm they prefer to deny. They forget the day of reckoning when reality becomes an undeniable truth. They forget—me." Set glanced at Khaf. "When lost, mortals always seek the god of destruction. A proven method. No matter the age or the people." He looked at me and narrowed his eyes. "Now tell me. Do you have any more questions, or is it time for you to attack me with my father's flames?"

My heart stopped.

Set smiled. "You can try. Maybe you will be the first mortal to kill a supreme god."

I raised my shaking fist toward Set, and the bracelet's golden glow reached its full intensity.

"No, Nef!" Khaf stepped forward, and froze when Set pointed his scythe at him.

"Let her try. It appears the girl's encounters with Shemzu and Apep have installed delusions in her head." He turned his weapon, pointing the spear at me. "Should I remind you, I was the one who defeated the gods for you? It was your link to me through my silver scarabs that empowered you. My magic

that strengthened you. My spear that delivered the final blow."
Set rose. "Word the spell if you disagree. Attack your god of
destruction, should you fancy yourself more powerful than
Horus."

More powerful than Horus? Of course not! I couldn't even
stop Khaf. Set was right. There was no stopping him now, and
Khaf was too stone-headed to see how Set was manipulating
him. My hand fell beside me, causing the air to audibly leave
Khaf's chest.

"I don't know what's more tragic." Set towered over me.
"That you assumed I wouldn't sense my father's magic or that
you believed you could defeat me."

Set tapped his spear on the ground, and a scarlet misty layer
engulfed my body, raising me to his height. Khaf's wide eyes
followed me. He swallowed, shifting the bones of his jaws. Did
he still love me after everything? No. He would've acted by
now. The Hyksos had proven how cold he'd become. The man
was a lost cause. Too fixated on one stupid goal. I knew that
state. Oh, the irony, Khaf taught me compassion while I taught
him selfishness.

"I think these divine items got into your head," Set said.

Anubis's amulet, Maat's necklace, and Ra's bracelet left
me—as if it was peeled off my flesh—and floated in a scarlet
sphere beside Set.

"Isn't this better?" Set asked. "To have that weight off your
back?"

"I beg you, great Set!" I said. "Don't destroy Egypt. Don't
harm its people. I know we did wrong. We craved justice so
much, we became the oppressors."

I looked at Khaf. "I don't blame you. It was our fault. We took
away your hope. This wouldn't have happened if our soldiers
hadn't killed your father or if I had spoken to you as an equal.
It's our fault, but you still have a chance to be better than us.
You could still change the terms of your divine deal."

Khaf opened his mouth. He swallowed, then lowered his gaze.

I turned to Set, wishing I could reclaim the spear just to hit the stupid thief on the head until he returned to his senses.

"Great Set," I said, "give us a second chance, I beg you. Grant us the opportunity to forgive."

"You will get that opportunity. But first, you have to remember the taste of despair."

"But I've learned how to forgive. I forgave you for abandoning our family. I have always hated you, but I'm willing to give you another chance, Father!"

"Father?" Set arched his eyebrow.

"Yes. I know I'm your daughter."

Set looked at Khaf. "My daughter?"

Khaf kept his gaze on the ground. "She... was asking questions about the knowledge and tools you granted me. I planted the idea in her head so that whenever she had questions, she might think her being special was the answer."

Set laughed. "You are Astarte's mortal, all right. A manipulative snake just like her."

"No," I said. "Look at me!" My scream shook the Hyksos, but he didn't obey. "You're the only one I ever told about my father, and you used it against me! You told me I was special because I was Set's daughter. You filled me with the hope that my father didn't abandon Hote and me willingly. I believed he was a good man because of you. 'Oh Nefiri,' you said, 'Set helped you against Shemzu and Apep, didn't he? His spear chose you because you are definitely his daughter.' Yet again, you used my family against me! Yet again, you took advantage of my misery to achieve your goals."

"I..." Khaf's voice broke, tears flowing down his cheeks. "I..."

"To think you two made it this far." Set chuckled. "I aided you against Shemzu and Apep because I needed you to survive." Set turned my head toward him. "You are not my daughter, and you most certainly are not special. I believed the spear would choose the boy, but it chose you instead. I assume it chose you because it would not matter if you died. The boy has always been the better alternative. It chose you because you are a nobody and evidently the easiest mortal the boy could manipulate." Set grabbed my neck, freeing me from the floating sphere, and pointed the spear at my heart. "Consider this the last lesson you will learn before my spear destroys your soul. You have lived and will die a worthless fool."

I struggled to free myself, but the god's grip didn't even tense.

Set's scarlet eyes gazed into mine. "No more miracles." His spear approached my heart, almost hitting the golden scarab Tuya had given me. "No more divine—"

"Wait!" Khaf screamed.

Set stopped.

"I beg you, my Baal. Please let me speak."

Set glanced at Khaf, growling. "Choose your next words carefully, boy."

"Nefiri... she helped free you. Yes! Even if unknowingly. She deserves a payment as well. I promised to bring her home unharmed. I beg you, great Baal. Let her go."

"You only get one gift," Set said. "Choose one."

"Khaf—"

Set covered my mouth, stopping my words. *Choose your father!*

I had no one and nothing left. Khaf still had a family. A family that, unlike mine, could still be saved.

"Well, boy, what will it be? The girl or your father?"

Khaf bit his lip. He paced back and forth, brushing his hands through his hair, his cries louder with each step.

I glared at Set, and he was smiling. That was him. The god of destruction in all his glory. The cruelest of our deities. He was the one in control here. Tuya had said it. Set had already won.

"Very well." Set pointed his spear at my heart. "Your father it is."

The scarlet glow spiraled around Set's spear.

"I choose her!" Khaf screamed. "Damn her, I still choose her." He collapsed on his knees. "Send her home. That's my gift."

My tears flooded Set's gauntlet. The proud thief of Avaris cried into his palms. Why did it have to come to this? Maat had tried to warn us. We made every wrong decision imaginable until we reached the crossroads of our journey.

Set growled at me, regaining my attention. He glared at me, his spear shaking over my heart. He had failed! Khaf's act of love ruined a critical part of Set's plans, but the god of destruction had to honor his divine deal with Khaf. That was Set's only weakness—his pride.

"When the Hittites kill you," Set said, "you will stand before Maat's scale and fail. Ammit will have her fun devouring your disgusting soul."

Set tapped his spear on the ground. Mist rose to the heaven and created a gate of black fog. The god threw me toward the gate's mist. I hurtled toward the heaven and entered the gateway back to Egypt.

Chapter 21

An Empty Home

Egypt's blazing sun scoured the sand beneath my bare feet. The consequences of my failures pressed on my aching heart. An endless ocean of nothingness surrounded me. Hisses and whispers flooded my senses as if I had walked through Peramessu's busy market. But I was alone. Stranded in Egypt's most effective death trap—its vast desert.

It was dawn when I arrived in Egypt, but I would start losing light in a few hours. I still couldn't find signs of civilization. Gods, I was doomed.

No! Focus! I had to push forward. I could survive this. Just... one... step... at...

I stopped. What was the point? Why did I fight? Where was I going anyway? There was no home without family. No journey without a destination.

My ears buzzed. Sweat covered my skin. I trembled where I stood, squeezing my head. How was I to cross the desert without water? Was I even walking in the right direction? I'd studied mathematics and politics, not navigation.

I bent and vomited on the sand. The world spun, and my vision blurred. I collapsed on my back, my right cheek buried in the sand.

This was the end of my story, wasn't it? Not in a glorious battle against the gods or judged by ancient pharaohs. No. Just me alone in the desert. An outcast's death. After everything, I had finally become an untouchable.

I turned my head toward the blue sky to admire Egypt's beauty without worries for once in my pathetic life.

A black shadow extended over my head. My vision focused on a fair-skinned woman with brown hair and honey-colored eyes. She wore a golden crown decorated with a crescent moon. A Hyksos? Had I been close to Peramessu all along?

"How far you have fallen, child." The woman sat beside me and laid her hand on my arm. "Abandoned by the mortals and their gods, and He Who Stands Between." She dug her hands under my body and lifted me. Her skin was like a raging fire. Her arms felt like spiked metal under my back.

"A god's heart couldn't help but ache for your misery." She smiled at me, her face hard and her features sharp. "Even a foreign goddess such as myself."

"Ast—"

"Shh." Astarte pressed her finger against my lips. She flapped her red wings, pushing the cool breeze against my warm body. "Don't give up on the boy, for his plan is flawed and his death imminent. I'm aware it's a selfish request, not befitting a goddess. Consider this a worried woman's plea." The Canaanite war goddess breathed into my ear, pushing the hisses in my head into a frenzy. "Fight, child. Fight for The Hidden One. For the triad is still one, and death but a distant desire."

I mumbled, unable to speak or think.

"Rest." Astarte, still holding me, took off to the sky. "For what is an end but a new beginning? What is a failure but a step toward victory? What is death but a promise of immortality?"

I succumbed to my tiredness and lost my senses in her embrace.

***

I woke in a field of golden wheat, surrounded by the most beautiful sound in Huat—flowing water. I crawled to the Nile and sunk my face in it. My head cooled, and the hisses inside my mind faded. Then I drank. Gods, I drank as if I'd just discovered water.

I rested at the riverbank, breathing in the scent of mud and sand. I was home at last, yet I'd never felt more homesick.

The air pushed the wheat against my face, but I remained frozen, unable to interact with the world. This field was familiar. The place at the edge of Avaris where Khaf and I used to meet before he began his fake apprenticeship at Set's—

Sparks of power flickered at my fingertips; more rose than scarlet. It whispered my name, guiding my gaze west of the fields where Set's temple towered. Was I still connected to the Destruction magic despite losing the spear? It made sense. The power of Frenzy took a while until I could sense its effects. It would probably take time for its effects to fade. I was the Chosen, and, according to Khaf, the gateway to Set's throne lay underneath his temple. Great! A constant reminder of my failure was all I needed.

I washed the sand off my face, then swiped my hair to clean my neck. I froze. Were those... scratches? Had Set injured me when he threw me toward the gate? How could he have harmed me despite Khaf's—

My heart sank. Oh, gods! Set broke the divine deal without noticing!

"Astarte!" I jumped to my feet. "How did Set break the divine deal? Who's The Hidden One I have to fight for?"

"My oh my," a hoarse woman's voice said. "My little girl has become so familiar with the gods that she shouts at them."

I turned, and tears poured out of my eyes at the sight of Aunt Meriti. She stood amid the golden wheat, leaning on her cane. She wore her usual white dress with a rose stitched over her heart.

"Are you going to cry for long?" Aunt Meriti pointed her long, thin finger. "Or are you going to help an old woman sit?"

I ran to Aunt Meriti and eased her to the grass.

"Good girl." Aunt Meriti straightened her dress under her legs. "So much to teach you still. So much indeed."

"Oh, my dear aunt." I laid my hand on her wrinkled face. "Words… words… c-can't begin to… to—"

"My oh my. You've unlearned how to speak. Great!"

I kissed Aunt Meriti's hand and hugged her, losing myself in her motherly comfort.

"I'm afraid sad news awaits you, my girl. Sadly, Hote—"

"I know." I pushed my face deeper against her breasts. "I just—need to hug you now."

"You need more than a hug." Aunt Meriti patted my back. "You need a good cry. There is no shame in sorrow, only in denying it."

Cry? In Huat? Why not? What was left to protect anyway?

Aunt Meriti patted my back. The pressure inside me exploded, shattering the dam that held back my tears. Finally, I cried. After all this time of being forced to pull myself together, to remain strong, I released the pain of all my miserable years. I sobbed over the poverty I couldn't end, the brother I couldn't save, the father I couldn't find, the master I disappointed, the country I betrayed, and the love I couldn't keep. The sorrow of a life filled with failure and disappointment exploded with my tears in this rare moment of vulnerability in the embrace of the woman who raised me.

"Oh, my sweet little girl. Let it out. All of it. You've finally earned yourself the beauty of tears."

"I ruined everything! Everything! I thought I was smart enough to save us all, but I'm stupid. A fool who isn't fit to achieve anything." I tightened my arms around her. "They all spoke the truth. I'm not special."

Aunt Meriti raised my gaze to her gentle smile, brushing away my stray hair. "Do you know what I admire about you?"

I shook my head.

"The fierceness of how you stand on your feet despite how often you fall." She wiped my tears. "The smartness of how you can bend the world to your will and yet never forget about those you love. Maybe the world doesn't see you like this, but to the people who love you dearly, you, Nefiri, *are* very special."

I sighed. "You're just saying that to make me feel better."

"Didn't Khafset admire you for being fierce and smart?"

"What?" I eased myself from her hug. "How do you know about Khafset?"

"This old woman knows more than you think." Aunt Meriti smiled at the Nile. "Such a beautiful place. Reminds me of the Field of Reeds in its seclusion." Her amused gaze shifted toward me. "It was smart of Astarte to bring you here."

"How do you know about Astarte? Come to think of it, how did you know I would be on the capital's Hyksos side?"

"It's easy." She laid her hand on my shaking face. "Astarte told me where to find you. Audacious move on her part, considering how much I despise her. That child-murdering monster."

I pushed her hand away. "What are you saying?"

"Her own children," Aunt Meriti continued. "Anyone that wasn't to her liking. Dead. Failed experiments, she called them."

"Aunt Meriti, are you having a stroke? Do you need some water? Come, let's get you out of the sun."

I offered her my hand, but she simply stared at me.

"For all the intelligence you possess," she said, "you truly are an idiot."

"Me? You're the one speaking nonsense!"

"Haven't you been listening?"

"Yes! You knew where to find me because Astarte told you where she left me. Then she had a casual conversation with you about her hobby of killing her children, or what did you call them? Failed experiments? Yep, I'm definitely the insane one here."

Aunt Meriti sighed. "After all my years caring for you and Hote, I still can't decide if you take after your father's hardmindedness or your mother's persistence."

"You've never met my mother. You moved next to us after her death."

"Oh, but I did meet your mother. I heard her calls when she gave birth to Hote—her dying words begging me to look after you."

"What?"

Aunt Meriti threw her cane, the grass vibrating around her. "Well, you have already met many of the other gods." She stood, and I jumped away. "No reason to hide from you any longer."

A green light flashed over Aunt Meriti's body, shrouding her entire form. Her silhouette grew taller and broader. The glow faded, revealing a tall, bipedal hippopotamus wearing a green dress underneath a blue robe. She stretched her muscular arms, clanking her golden bracelets against each other.

"Much better." She brushed back her braided black hair.

My mouth dropped at the transformed Aunt Meriti. That fragile old woman was the goddess Taweret!

Taweret grinned, her face visibly enjoying my shocked expression. "Now, if being raised by the goddess of childbirth doesn't make you special, I don't know what will." She sat on the grass, her ears pushing away the flies, and frowned at my frozen state. "Will you speak, or must I pull the words out of your throat?"

"What? How? Why?" I paced before her, mumbling to myself.

"Are you broken?"

I stopped, unable to find the proper reaction. "What?"

Taweret sighed. "As is my duty, I was by your mother's side while she gave birth to Hote. With her final breath, she prayed for me to watch over you. My heart twisted for the woman, and I visited you."

"But you stayed! Why did you stay?"

"Horus told me I needed to raise the Chosen, which was a good judgment on his part, really. Your father got obsessed when he discovered your brother's illness. He left you in my care, vowing to find a cure."

"My... my father didn't abandon us?"

Taweret tilted her head. "Well, that's a loaded question. He did leave for your sake, though."

"And you're telling me this now!"

"You're talking to a goddess, you ill-mannered girl!"

"Please!" I gave her a dismissive wave. "I've seen you fight Hote over a fish, O mighty hippo-goddess." My eyes widened. "Of course you only ate fish! Gods, I'm such an idiot."

Taweret studied me with narrowed eyes. Even if she had a hippo's head, I still knew that expression all too well.

"Should I fetch my cane, or are you done throwing a tantrum?"

I nodded.

"Use words, girl."

"I'm done throwing a tantrum, Aunt Meriti."

"And you are..." She waved her giant hand, signaling me to finish her sentence.

"I'm very sorry for raising my voice."

Taweret sighed. She stretched out her arm toward me, and I cringed. "Will you begrudge the woman who raised you a simple hug?"

I hesitated for a moment, then shook my head. I took Taweret's hand, and she pulled me to her chest. And still, despite who she was, I couldn't help but lose myself in her comforting embrace.

"Aunt Meriti."

"Yes, child."

"Can you tell me where my father is?"

"I'm afraid I can't. His path is dangerous. You must pass Horus's test before knowing the full truth."

I broke the hug and gazed into Taweret's large hippo eyes. "I'll never know then. I have already failed his test."

"So you have given up on the fight?"

"Yes." I sat next to Taweret, facing the Nile. "It's better this way."

"So you will run?"

"No. I'm tired of running. I will report my failure to Nefertari and, for the first time in my life, deal with the consequences of my actions."

"She will kill you."

"So be it. What do I have to live for, anyway? I've even lost Khaf. I harmed the only man stupid enough to love me."

"Didn't the boy betray you?"

"How did you… Oh, right, goddess."

"No." Taweret sighed. "A mother's instinct, perhaps."

"I harmed him as well. Wickedness is a competition Khaf will lose against me. If anything, I'm relieved Khaf did something stupid. He's flawed like me. Just as broken. But it doesn't matter. Like everything I held dear, Khaf is gone."

"My oh my. Set really did break your spirit." Her wide eyes studied me. "So I take it you aren't interested in the boy's letter."

"Letter?" My gaze darted to Taweret.

The goddess grinned. "The boy left you a letter before you stole Set's spear, thinking you'd return home." She grabbed a scroll from underneath her robe and handed it to me.

I unrolled Khaf's letter.

Dear Nef,

Please don't be mad at me for not delivering your brother's medicine. I swear on my parents' graves when my grand heist is over, I'll heal him once and for all.

Our world will change soon, and as I start my journey into the unknown, I thought I should share a secret I never dared tell you.

I love you, Nef. Since the moment I saw you.

I know what I am. You Egyptians never failed to remind me. Thief, orphan, untouchable, Hyksos lowlife, you name it. I never cared for those words except when they came from you because they brought me to the realization that I'm simply not good enough for you. Not because you're Egyptian or Paser's apprentice. I couldn't care less about that. I wasn't good enough for Nefiri Minu. The woman who breathed life into me the same way Isis resurrected Osiris.

I don't blame you for not sharing my feelings or even if you hate me now more than ever. We didn't choose to be born on our sides of the canal. I've come to accept that the only thing I, Khafset, the thief of Avaris, can't steal is your heart.

However, great things will happen soon, and they might seem scary. But no matter what happens, I want you to remember one simple fact, the one constant of the world. I love you, my Egyptian. Always.

Khafset, the lowlife of Avaris. Your comrade in crime.

I hugged the letter and cried. Oh, Khaf. My Hyksos. My lowlife. My love.

Taweret pulled me to her chest. "The boy sure knows how to talk."

"He's going to die!"

She brushed my hair behind my ears. "So you're going to give up without a fight?"

"I can't do anything. For all the times he saved me, I can't save him even once."

"This has been the case your entire life, and you're still here to complain about it."

"I've ruined everything!"

"Then you can only succeed." Taweret guided my gaze to her sparkling hippo eyes. She stood and pulled me to my feet. "Look at the Nile, my girl." She turned me. "You're just like that river. You flourish when you flow, and decay if you stand still. Just like the Nile, in all the years I've known you, there wasn't an obstacle you couldn't overcome." She placed her thick finger under my chin and guided my head toward her. "What will it be? Will you flourish or decay? Do you wish to surrender, or fight against this new obstacle?"

She... had a point. If I was good at anything, it was getting back on my feet no matter how painful the fall was. I had clashed with the gods, but I was still here. Khaf and Set had won, but I lived. My dear master always... sometimes spoke the truth. I was a survivor, and I sure was wiser now.

"I—will fight?" I said, almost asking myself. "Yeah. Of course I won't surrender. I never have. Why start now?"

"Great!" Taweret clapped her massive hands.

"Yeah, Aunt Meriti." I paused. "Taweret? Aunt Taweret?"

The goddess smiled. "Aunt Taweret sounds nice."

"Yes, Aunt Taweret. I will save Egypt and rescue the pharaoh and my master."

"My oh my. I sure love the enthusiasm."

"I will save Khaf and free the Hyksos."

"Love the ambition."

"I *will* defeat Set."

"There she is. My Nefiri."

I spun around in the tall, golden wheat, ideas and plans rushing into my head. I wasn't a priest like Khaf; I was a mathematician and a politician. I must approach this problem my way. Same as with Master Paser's quizzes, I had to rearrange the variables of the equation to pass Horus's test, then I would get the answer to the most important question of my life. What happened to my father? I wouldn't die just yet.

"I will succeed," I said. "It doesn't matter how long it takes me; I will pass the test."

"Well, actually..." Aunt Taweret said. "You have a week to save Ramesses from the Hittites."

"What?" My mouth dropped.

"Ramesses did capture Kadesh, but Set has possessed two merchants who fed him false information. His army has suffered a massive defeat." She sighed. "The poor man is trapped in Kadesh, and the Hittites will storm the city within the week."

"I was with Set a moment ago. When did he do all this?"

"Time goes a lot faster in Duat."

"Why didn't you tell me that from the start?" I shouted.

"A moment ago, you were daydreaming about the sweet release of death! I had to fix that mess first, you stupid little girl!"

Harsh but fair. She sure was my temperamental aunt.

"Fine!" I said. "I'll fix it all today."

Taweret arched her eyebrow. "Today?"

"Yes." I hugged her. "Out of all the gods, you are my favorite, Aunt Taweret."

She hugged me back. "Should I tell your mother and Hote anything when I return to Duat?"

"That I love them both. Tell them that, like the Nile, their Nefiri will never stop flowing."

Taweret eased me out of our hug. "Are you sure you can defeat Set and save Ramesses today? Even I can't see this happening."

"Of course, I will succeed." I chuckled at the absurdity of her question.

"Yeah, right." Aunt Taweret rolled her eyes. "Forgot who I was talking to. Nefiri Minu, the grand vizier's sole apprentice." She gave me a dismissive wave.

"Wrong." I gave Aunt Taweret a challenging smile. "I'm Nefiri Minu, the thief of Peramessu. And I am going to outsmart Egypt's highest diplomat."

Chapter 22

Thieves & Monarchs

The waiting area before the royal palace's throne chamber was busier than anticipated. Scribes, priests, and statesmen passed by the chamber's gates, unsuccessfully demanding an audience with the queen.

Every person I'd seen during my wait would be slaughtered in the case of a Hittite victory. The queen's life might be spared, yet her fate would be the grimmest. Grieving for her dead husband and fallen kingdom, she would be shipped to the Hittite capital and presented to the king as a spoil of war. That was Khaf's justice. He wanted the lady of grace reduced to an untouchable.

Gods, the thief's heart held no compassion for my people. Could I blame him? No, not really. Would I do everything in my power to stop him? Absolutely, and it all depended on the outcome of my meeting with Egypt's highest diplomat.

My eyes had remained glued to the floor since the last official gave up on meeting the queen, while my hand kept fumbling with my master's ring around my thumb. I rubbed my arms, trying to cool my burning skin. Something terribly wrong had been happening to me since my arrival in Huat. My skin was irritated as if insects crawled on its surface. My body was burning. The hissing noise visited my hearing each time someone so much as breathed near me.

I must cut the connection I had to Set. Whatever Frenzy was doing to me would drive me insane soon.

The gates to the throne chamber opened, their loud squeak echoing against the ceramic walls of the waiting room. A guard stepped outside. A tall, balding man holding a bronze spear. His yellow kilt declared him a member of the Thunderbolts. Ramesses' newly formed royal guard. The army's deadliest and most vicious troops.

"Traitor," the guard said.

"That's me." I stood, holding to my smile so I wouldn't antagonize him.

The guard tapped his spear on the floor, signaling me to approach. I obeyed.

"The Lady of The Two Lands has granted you the honor of her presence," the guard said.

"Great." I stepped around him but froze as he extended his spear.

He gritted his teeth, his body tense. Gods, like Set's demons, he was visibly fighting the urge to rip me apart.

The guard narrowed his eyes, tensing his stone-like features. "Do anything, traitor. Make a sudden move or utter the wrong word, and my men will have the honor of sending your traitorous soul to Ammit." His nose touched mine. "Am I understood?"

"E-extremely."

"We'll see." He stepped back, taking the stench of sweat with him.

I followed the guard—who'd just become my least favorite person in the world—into the throne chamber.

Nefertari sat on Ramesses' silver throne. Tuya sat on a golden throne to her left, and Slayer, the lion, lay on the ground to her right. Four guards stood beside the thrones, and six were spread along the room's edges, their spears pointed at me, all Thunderbolts.

I followed the guard to the chamber's center and hid behind him.

"Your Majesty," he said. "Nefiri Minu, the thief of Peramessu."

"I'm aware," Nefertari said. "Take your men and leave."

"But the traitor might be—"

Nefertari raised her hand. "I'm more than capable of dealing with the traitor myself." She tapped her finger on the throne's arm, and Slayer rose.

Was that lion always so small? Wasn't he a lot bigger? He was a kitten compared to Shemzu and Sekhmet.

"As Her Majesty commands." The guard bowed and evacuated the chamber with his men. The gates closed, leaving me alone with the queens and Slayer.

"Your Majesties, I—"

Nefertari pointed at me. "Kneel, traitor." She lowered her finger toward the floor, and I collapsed. Yep, she was as intense as I remembered.

"Now, there are two possible outcomes for our unpleasant encounter," Nefertari said. "Either you have saved my husband and his kingdom, in which case I expect you to leave Peramessu by tomorrow and Egypt and its territories by the end of the month." She leaned forward. "Or you have failed, and Slayer will devour you here and now."

"Daughter." Tuya smiled. "Let the girl speak before you instill the gods' fear into her heart."

"No!" Nefertari's voice rang across the throne chamber, and Slayer shifted away from her. "I shall indulge her no further. This traitorous snake has slithered her way around the consequences of her actions for far too long." Her chin rose. "Last chance, traitor. Report the fate of my pharaoh and his kingdom."

She cared about his fate more than hers, didn't she? The great Nefertari Merytmut was a mortal, after all. A woman torn between the husband she wanted to rescue and the people she wanted to protect. It had always come down to this, hadn't it? Regardless of our ranks, we all tried to navigate the fine line between love and duty.

"My queen, we did reach Set's prison—"

"Then it's done. Ramesses and Egypt are safe."

I fought the urge to smile when she spoke his name. "I'm afraid not, Your Majesty. It was a trap. Set has successfully reclaimed his spear. He's free now and has caused our pharaoh a great defeat. The Lord of The Two Lands is trapped in Kadesh with what's left of his army. I'm afraid Set's prophecy regarding the pharaoh's death will be fulfilled within the week."

"You!" Nefertari jumped from her throne. "You caused all this. The lowest of traitors!"

"The girl has more to say," Tuya said.

"I have heard enough! Slayer!"

The lion flashed his teeth at me.

Nefertari's eyes met mine. "Make her suffer."

Slayer roared. He walked toward me with steady steps, his body tense, his claws ready to shred me. To be fair, Nefertari was still more frightening.

I stretched out my arm toward Slayer. The lion slowed down. He studied me as if bewildered by my reaction.

"Great Shemzu," I said. "O great protector of the virtuous." The lion sat on his haunches. "Does it satisfy the god of blood for his beast to slaughter a soul who fought Apep and was judged innocent by Maat?"

The lion sniffed my outstretched arm, his face relaxing. He lay on his side, rubbing his snout against my palm.

"See." Tuya laughed. "Even Slayer wants to hear the girl."

"What is the meaning of this?" Nefertari retreated and bumped her legs against the throne. "What magic do you wield, traitor?"

"I wield no magic. Not anymore." I smiled at the queen, brushing Slayer's mane. "I fought Shemzu and Sekhmet, Your Majesty. To me, Slayer is a little cat."

I approached Nefertari, tempting fate to disrupt the system and maximize the gain—Khaf's strategy. I stood before her, an arm's length separating us. "You can call the Thunderbolts, of course. But what would your husband's elite soldiers think when you call for help because a mere thief tamed the pharaoh's lion in your presence?"

Nefertari's face twitched. It was a numbers game. She could undermine her authority either before ten guards or before me. Given how much time had passed, she chose me.

"Now." I raised my chin, mimicking the queen's prideful stance. "I propose—"

The queen stretched out her arm with a serpent's speed and precision and caught my neck in her clutches, digging her sharp nails into my flesh.

"Nefertari!" Tuya jumped to her feet.

I struggled against the queen's grip, but she was surprisingly strong. I struggled for air, my vision flickering. The power of Frenzy crawled on my skin, screaming in my ears to let it explode.

Yes, I could just let go. I could have my way. I only had to release the Destruction magic building inside me. I wouldn't die here! Not before saving Egypt and knowing the truth about my father. Not before rescuing Khaf.

I opened my eyes, ready to give in to the hisses in my head, unable to think or defy them any longer. I met the queen's gaze. Her face was harsh, but her eyes betrayed her. They released a sparkling drop over her love and the country she was struggling to save.

The queen mother shifted beside us, her hand covering her mouth. She stared at me, shaking her head, unfocused on her daughter-in-law, who was squeezing the life out of me. Did she know that I... Gods, what was I thinking? I almost gave in and killed them all!

I summoned every ounce of strength I had left and denied the cursed power of Frenzy. It abandoned me, almost tearing my soul apart as it left.

My arms fell beside me, and my struggle stopped. "Y-your Maj..."

"Did you think I needed Slayer or the guards to make you pay for your crimes?" Nefertari said. "Girl, I sent you to Duat before, and I can do it again with my own hands."

"I... I... can... save—"

"Oh, you can save Ramesses, can you now?" The queen pulled me closer to her red face. "No. Your schemes end—"

Tuya laid her hand on Nefertari's arm.

"Mother?" Nefertari asked.

"Hear her out," Tuya said. "Grant me this wish."

Nefertari glanced at Tuya and, following a long pause, took a deep breath. She pushed me to the floor and sat on her throne. "In honor of the queen mother, you may speak your final words, traitor."

Tuya sat, sighing. Gods, for the first time, her presence worked in my favor. Or had she always helped me? It was impossible to tell with Tuya.

"I can stop Set," I said, rubbing my neck. "I know how to save our pharaoh and his men."

"Don't you value your life?" Nefertari asked. "If so, give me something more tangible than empty words."

"We have to fight on two fronts," I said. "The Hittites and Set. I need your help to defeat the Hittites, but I'll take care of Set myself." Nefertari's glaring eyes widened, and I crawled back. "Y-your Majesty."

"And how will you—*take care* of Set?" Nefertari asked.

"I'm working on it." I smiled at Tuya and laid my hand on the golden scarab. "But I know the last piece is close to my heart."

Tuya gave me a slight nod, smiling.

"Speaking of hearts." Nefertari narrowed her eyes. "Where is the untouchable you betrayed us for?"

The power of Frenzy flashed up my spine. "His name is Khafset!" I covered my mouth and cowered from the queen's glare. No! I had lost control again!

I could still fix this. I must fix this! "He's executing our plan to stop Set and save us all."

The queen's face relaxed, and she gave me a dismissive wave with her hand. Well, that was the best possible reaction after the catastrophe I had just uttered. Wasn't my mission difficult enough? Why must Frenzy make my life harder?

"The Hittites," Nefertari said. "How do we stop them?"

"We fight."

Nefertari sighed, rubbing her temples. "Didn't you say the Egyptian army got decimated?"

"True, but we can send reinforcements."

"What a brilliant idea! How did I not think of it?" She glanced at her mother-in-law and rolled her eyes. Gods, I was cutting so deep into the queen I might've dug out her sarcastic side. "The pharaoh took every man in Peramessu who can fight."

"I'm not talking about those men."

Nefertari scoffed. "What? Do you want me to send the women to Kadesh?"

"No," I said. "I was thinking of something more radical."

Nefertari arched her eyebrow.

"We have men in Peramessu who happen to be Egypt's best blacksmiths and riders."

"You want me to arm the Hyksos?" Nefertari's eyes widened. "Girl, have you gone mad?"

"They can fight, Your Majesty. Maybe it's time we admit that, after five hundred years of living in Egypt, the Hyksos of Avaris are Egyptians."

"Do you have any idea what you are suggesting?" Nefertari asked. "Those untouchables will be a greater danger than the Hittites if we allow them to arm themselves. Who is to say they won't help us defeat the Hittites only to kill Ramesses themselves?"

I clutched my left arm and lowered my head. Memories of Khaf's love, compassion, tenderness, kindness, devotion, betrayal, and cruelty soared through every fiber of my being as if I had experienced him with all his contradictions in the blink of an eye. He freed Set, unleashing destruction on the world, and yet sacrificed his reunion with his father to save me. That was Khafset the Hyksos at his core—a creature capable of both wickedness and love—an Egyptian.

"Are they to blame for their betrayal?" I asked. "What reasons did we give them to love us? We've always met their hope with tyranny. We've granted them enough reasons to give up on us. Despite their misery, poverty, and despair, they remained in Avaris. Despite how cruel Egypt has been to them, they never abandoned it. Isn't this the core of what it means to be an Egyptian? Regardless of our ancestry, we are all bound to the land, and despite today's hardship, we remain hopeful of a better tomorrow."

Nefertari stared at Slayer, who slept behind me. I knew what she was doing. This was Master Paser's regroup tactic. She wanted me to feel unimportant in order to grant herself a moment to recollect her thoughts. She was almost there. She only needed a little nudge.

"If they betray us," Nefertari said, her voice hesitant, "I'll be the queen who undid everything Ahmose secured for us. I'll be the Egyptian who gave her country to the Hyksos. Our descendants will curse my name for ages to come."

"Maybe. But they would also question why you stood by when your kingdom needed you." I stood. "When you sent us to Duat, you promised me the seeds of my brother's medicine. I wondered why you cared despite your hatred toward me. Now I understand. You cared about the ill little boy whose only hope of survival was a traitorous sister. Khafset of Avaris taught me caring is a trait that separates the kind from the wicked, and you, Your Majesty, care about your subjects. Isn't it time to give the Hyksos a chance to prove they are your people?"

Nefertari leaned back on her throne and looked at Tuya. "What is the queen mother's advice?"

Tuya smiled and laid her hand on Nefertari's arm. "Sometimes, in decisive moments like these, history is kinder to a ruler who gambles and fails than one who does nothing."

Nefertari nodded and returned her gaze to me. She opened her mouth and closed it. Following a long pause, she spoke. "Let's say I accept your plan. How do you intend to convince the Hyksos to fight in Kadesh?"

"I'll speak to the high priest of Set. He's the mayor of Avaris, and if I give him a showing of goodwill, he might agree to help save the pharaoh."

"Goodwill?" Nefertari asked.

"Yes. I need a royal decree granting the Hyksos their freedom if they rescue the pharaoh. It's the same deal you struck with Khafset. But wouldn't you rather have this agreement with the high priest of Set instead of a lowly thief?"

"And you think the high priest will accept this offer?" Nefertari asked.

"Why wouldn't he? He's a Hyksos as well."

"You really are a naive little girl," Nefertari scoffed, glancing at Tuya. "She thinks Sethos cares about the Hyksos. That gluttonous man who sells us his people's orphans."

"I'm aware," I said. "I used to..." My heart twisted at the memories. "I used to collect those children. I led the Medjay into Avaris to crush any rebellious thoughts the Hyksos might have had. I... I..."

"Are you all right, child?" Tuya asked.

I raised my gaze, my tears raining on the ground.

"And she's the one who's supposed to convince Sethos and stop Set." Nefertari gave me a dismissive wave. "Poor Ramesses. His father got Paser, while *he* was going to get this broken teenager. Gods, what—"

"Don't underestimate her tears, daughter," Tuya said, silencing Nefertari and capturing my attention with her glowing smile. "For some tears are mighty. Don't forget that our very souls are but the tears of our first god, Atem."

"I—have experience with the Hyksos," I said, Tuya's excitement feeding my confidence and Frenzy tickling the sides of my neck. "I'm not proud of it anymore, but I can beat them into submission. Sethos, high priest or not, is still a Hyksos, and I will get him in line."

Frenzy hissed its approval in my head. Gods, no wonder Set was so unhinged with this type of foul magic influencing him the entire time. If anything, it was remarkable he didn't go mad and destroy the world. But again, he was a god, and I a mortal.

Nefertari raised her head and gave a slight nod. Really? Was cruelty the only means of gaining her respect? Khafset would have said something like, *Yeah, right, Egyptian. Khafset of Avaris never falls in line.* Gods, I missed him.

However, my last words about getting Sethos in line weren't entirely mine. Frenzy had twisted my thoughts before I spoke. Was it trying to pave the way for my return to Set, or was it on my side? Regardless, it did get better results with Nefertari. Maybe I should listen to—

"Don't stay in your head for too long, child." Tuya pulled me out of my head. "Beware of the easy path and its whispers."

She was right. I had tried the easy path before my trip to Duat and now hated the person it had made me. This time, I would fight the temptation of destruction.

I nodded at the queen mother.

Tuya looked at Nefertari. "Daughter?"

Nefertari sighed. "Even if I agree and she manages to convince Sethos, how will the Hyksos reach Kadesh in time?"

"Khafset and I discovered there are gates in Huat. The Hyksos are Canaanites, and according to Khafset, they've mapped all the gates in Egypt and Canaan. Kadesh is a border city between Canaan and Syria. If anyone knows how to move the Hyksos to Kadesh in time to save the pharaoh, it has to be the Hyksos high priest."

Nefertari rose from her throne. She paced around the chamber, shaking her head. "This plan of yours will doom us all if it fails."

"That... is kind of the Hyksos way of doing things."

The queen fell silent. I couldn't blame her. A matter this big needed months or even years to settle, but she had to make a decision here and now. She glanced at Tuya's stoic face. The woman was good. Did she even care about the war? Did she have a secret plan? What was her connection to my father? How would her golden scarab defeat Set? How did she sense Set's magic inside me? Was she a goddess? Nobody knew—and that made her terrifying.

"Fine," Nefertari said.

"I want something added to the royal decree," I said.

Nefertari crossed her arms and glared at me.

"My exile. I want it annulled if my plan succeeds."

"You are pushing your luck, traitor."

"Your Majesty, I'm not leaving Egypt anyway, and you will kill me for it. But don't I deserve a peaceful life in my land with the man I love if I save Egypt and defeat the god of destruction?"

"The god of destruction that you and your Hyksos freed?"

"Set tricked Osiris, a supreme god of the Ennead. What chance did two mortals have against him and his schemes?"

"And those two mortals are going to defeat Set, who, may I remind you, is also a supreme god of the Ennead?"

"Of course not." I smiled. "I'm actually counting on losing to Set. That's how I will win."

Nefertari arched her eyebrow. "What?"

"I'm still working out the exact details. First, I need the royal decree."

Nefertari gave a very understandable sigh of frustration. "I will call a scribe and get you the decree." She waved me away, walking to her throne. "A scribe will meet you at the palace entrance." She sat, and her chin rose. "Now get out of my sight."

I made my way to the chamber's gate. Who could ever envy the queen for her job? Well, at least she wasn't alone like Hatshepsut and Ahhotep were. Gods, those women who had sat on Egypt's throne were simply a force of nature.

"Child," Tuya called, stopping me before the closed gates.

I turned. "Yes, Your Majesty."

A wide victorious smile overtook the old queen's face. "Show Set how fierce and smart you have become."

I bowed before the queens, smiling. "Your Majesties." I retreated from the chamber.

One last stop before facing Set. One final step before saving Khaf and my master. I had to confront my past sins. It was time for my return to Avaris.

Chapter 23

The Tavern of Avaris

The full moon shone over Avaris, revealing broken homes hiding behind garbage mounds. The homeless occupied the roads. They raised their hands toward me, begging.

"Please, mistress," one called.

"Show mercy," said another.

"My child is starving."

Their pleas shredded my soul.

Those people used to be my responsibility. I should've helped them. Gods, each face was a reminder of my sins. I'd been so proud when Master Paser entrusted Avaris to me. He was finally showing faith in me, I thought.

No. Avaris was inconsequential to him — the perfect playground. No matter how grim my mistakes, they wouldn't have mattered because the Hyksos didn't matter.

How much of the misery of these people could be traced back to my orders? How many people died, lived on the streets, or lost their Hote because of me?

So many sins and not enough time to make amends. Not even a lifetime would suffice. Set spoke the truth. I was destined to fail Maat's scale and be devoured by Ammit.

I abandoned the main road that connected the port to Set's temple. Here, deep inside Avaris, there were no Egyptian soldiers to protect me, and yet, I remained unharmed. Why had I ever feared those Hyksos? If anything, *they* avoided me. The Egyptian who might cause their death. Gods, how was I supposed to convince them to rescue the pharaoh who ruled over the system that caused their misery?

I reached the Tavern of Avaris, where I would find Khaf's adopted brother—Setu, the clerk—my only connection to High Priest Sethos.

The tavern's multileveled wooden structure vibrated from the upbeat music. Sounds of laughter, singing, and fighting escaped the tavern's common room and flowed into the surrounding roads. A man bent over and emptied his stomach, while several couples showed too much skin as they... declared their love.

Yep, everything here screamed Khaf.

I pulled on the straps of my leather bag—where I had stashed the royal decree—trying to gather my courage. I pushed the tavern's wooden door and entered the infamous Tavern of Avaris.

The music guided me through a narrow corridor toward the common room. Bewildered, Hyksos eyes traced me on my way.

A large man moved away from the wall and blocked me in the corridor. He crossed his arms and looked down at me, grinning.

"Looks like someone wandered to the wrong side of the canal," he said.

"Oh, look at this pretty little thing." A black-haired woman emerged from behind the man, holding a cup of beer. "Join me tonight. I'll give you an exclusive Hyksos experience."

"Maybe she wants to join *me*," a man said behind me.

My heart pounded in my chest. I couldn't run past the big man, and the man behind me might be hiding a weapon. I was trapped, wasn't I?

Frenzy crawled over my skin. It reached my neck, and I lost myself in its warmth.

"Are you all right, sweetie?" the woman asked.

"She doesn't look well," the big man said.

"Come," the man behind me said. "Let's take you inside."

He laid his hand on my shoulder.

"No!" I shouted.

A wave pulsed from me, pushing the woman and the man behind me to the ground. The big man managed to stay on his feet. He did the sensible thing and retreated from me.

The Hyksos on the floor looked up at me, trembling. I walked to the big man and held his terrified gaze.

"Out of my way," I said.

He stumbled to the side, and I ran through the corridor until I reached the door at its end. I pushed it and entered the common room. I stood alone, dumbfounded, taking in the place and what had just happened. People sat together, singing and drinking. Couples touched each other as if they were in their own private rooms.

I laid my hands on my head, trying to catch my breath. All these people had received the same invitation I received in the corridor, hadn't they? It wasn't considered hostile behavior in the Tavern of Avaris. I could've just said no and acted accordingly if they refused to...

Inside? The man behind me had wanted to take me inside to rest, and I attacked them! They were trying to help me. Gods, it was as if I hadn't learned anything from my time in Duat.

I straightened my white dress and took a deep breath, trying to get over my relapse. Starting now, I wouldn't allow Frenzy to influence me. I was going to ignore my prejudice and assume that every Hyksos was a good person unless proven otherwise.

My only consolation was that Khaf had spoken the truth for a change. Judging by the affection the tavern's residents showed me despite being an Egyptian, and what the woman called me, I, Nefiri Minu, was indeed pretty.

Finally, I spotted Setu in the common room. He sat alone at a table next to a huge open window. He wore a blue kilt, its edges decorated with golden patterns, and a white-and-scarlet Hyksos shawl over his shoulders. Unlike Khaf, Setu was short and relatively thin. He hunched his back forward as he drank, revealing the spikes of his spine. Like any self-respecting future priest, the clerk was bald.

Yeah, Khaf was by far the more attractive brother. While Setu wished to be left alone, Khaf had this entertaining fight-me-and-find-out energy surrounding him. Gods, so much complexity and variety to these people, and they had simply been the Hyksos of Avaris to me all this time.

I reached Setu and stood behind the opposing chair of his two-seat table. I smiled, my body swinging to the melodies of the harps and flutes.

"Look who it is. Khafset's Egyptian friend." Setu took a sip from his bronze cup. "Egyptian soldiers aren't allowed in the Tavern of Avaris, so they can't beat me up, I'm afraid."

"I'm not here to harm you." I pulled out the chair and sat.

I scanned the area for escape routes. Not that I believed that the Hyksos were evil, of course. But... I was a thief. Yes! A good thief always planned an exit; the window beside me was the perfect height from the street. Not that I would ever need to escape from these lovely people. Khaf was a great man, and he was Hyksos. But he had also doomed the world. High Priest Sethos was also a horrible man. And all the Hyksos criminals I had caught during my apprenticeship and... fine, they might not have been model citizens, but neither was I.

"Egyptian?" Setu called.

I blinked, my vision refocusing on the clerk, who regarded me with an arched eyebrow.

"Are you still with us?" Setu asked.

I nodded. "Have a lot on my mind, that's all." I signaled the waitress to bring me a cup of beer. Wait, how would I pay for my drink? Oh well, I was a thief now, wasn't I? "I really don't understand what Khaf likes about this place."

"Khaf?"

"You said it. I'm his Egyptian friend."

"Well, sorry to disappoint, but you'll have to wait until tomorrow to punish me for the false scrolls. You know, on account of your Medjay not being allowed to enter the Tavern of Avaris." Setu tried—and failed—to mimic Khaf's smug expression. "But I'm sure Khaf won't be happy to know you harmed me."

"We both know Khaf isn't around," I said. "And he won't return for a while."

"You're the reason he disappeared!" Setu's smile vanished. "You finally did it! You threw him in the dungeons, didn't you?"

"What? N—"

"I'm so, so sorry for the scrolls!" He sipped his beer, his hands trembling. "I... I wanted to give you the corrected scrolls, but you didn't visit for weeks."

"I don't care about the scrolls anymore."

Setu nodded, his eyes turning red. "Could you give me until tomorrow? I must—take care of something before you throw me in the dungeons."

"Setu, I—"

"Could you send me to the same place as Khaf? I... I wish to die with my brother."

I shook my head, unable to think of any response.

"You've already killed him!" Setu gasped and covered his mouth. "You killed him and came to kill me as well!"

I stretched out my arm to calm him, and he flinched.

"I didn't kill Khaf," I said. "And I'm not going to kill you. That's not why I'm here."

Did I sound sincere, or was the conversation coming across like an interrogation? *Yeah, Setu, I don't wish to harm you, but only if you give me an extensive list of your orphans so I can sell them into*

slavery. Remember, your brother isn't here to protect you anymore.
Gods, it was difficult to filter out Master Paser's teachings. I
had to win Setu's affection before I asked for his help. But how
could I make up for the last two years in a single conversation?

"I want to be your friend," I said.

"Friend?" Setu arched his eyebrow.

I nodded. "Do you know, you and Khaf are the only people I
know who are my age? I guess, in my way, I always liked being
around you."

"Right." The clerk narrowed his eyes. "Why is the grand
vizier's apprentice in the Tavern of Avaris?"

"I don't work for him anymore." Maybe this revelation
would ease the tension a little.

"What? Got married and became a housewife?"

"Actually, I got promoted."

"Set's mercy! Paser died in Kadesh, didn't he?" Setu's eyes
widened, his breathing becoming ragged. He bowed his head,
holding tight to the table's edges. "Grand Vizier Nefiri, my
condolences for your master's heroic death. May the gods aid
you as they have aided him."

Grand Vizier Nefiri? Curses, that sounded amazing. No! That
life was behind me now. I was going to follow Tuya's advice. No
more shortcuts. Neither my apprenticeship, nor the cruelty it
forced me to practice, nor Frenzy and the destruction it could
cause.

I chuckled, and Setu raised his head, his eyebrow arched.

"I'm not grand vizier, Setu."

"But you got promoted."

I nodded. "I'm a thief now."

"What?"

"Quite the promotion, really. Worked very hard for it." I
leaned back in my wooden seat when my drink arrived. "You
know how life is. I was friends with a thief for so long that I

became one myself." I raised my cup. "So here's to my new life. A future full of crime."

"Did it finally happen?" Setu asked while I drank my beer. "Have you gone mad?"

I tilted my head. He wasn't entirely wrong.

A woman appeared beside us as if Hathor had conjured her out of thin air. She leaned on the table, and the strong scent of her lotus perfume assaulted my nose. Her naturally cherry-colored lips pressed together to send Setu the most charming smile I'd ever seen. She turned her gorgeous face toward me, shaking her silky brown hair.

"C-can I help you?" I asked, unable to fully comprehend the divine beauty before me. Was she another deity? Hathor, the goddess of love, incarnate? I didn't know. I simply lost myself in her wide brown eyes.

She smiled, revealing a perfect set of white teeth. "Did I hear you say you are Khafi's friend?"

I snorted. "Khafi?"

"Yes," she said in a voice that matched the harps' soft melody. "My Khafi. The thief. Do you know him?"

I nodded. "Are you his friend?"

She giggled. "Yes. I'm his—friend. Do you know where he is, by any chance?"

I hesitated. No! I shouldn't assume the worst from her. She was even pleasant. Nobody who looked like her could be anything but good. She even knew Khaf... or Khafi! Oh, curse him and this place!

"I'll see him soon," I said.

"How marvelous. I, too, am dying to see him again." She laid her soft hand on my warm cheek. "Could you give him something from me?"

I swallowed. "Of... of course."

"Great."

She slapped me so hard that I almost fell off my chair. My vision flickered. My ears rang. Frenzy screamed in my mind. I shook my head while I waited for my senses to return.

"Tell him this is from Naunet." She stormed away.

Oh, she had a nerve, didn't she? It wasn't humiliating enough to be forced to enter this scandalous place because of Khaf, no! I was beaten here because of him. Oh, Khaf was going to receive this slap. I swore by the Holy Ennead. I was done being beaten by Khaf and those linked to him, and expected to accept it. This time I was going to hit back. Holding my bronze cup, I stood, ready to hunt down that woman.

Setu caught my hand. "Don't do anything stupid, Egyptian. She works for the Hostess."

I glared at Naunet as she spoke to a woman who sat alone. A bald, muscular woman who was even taller than Khaf. That was her, wasn't it? The woman who terrified the proud thief of Avaris. The Hostess.

"Please leave before the Hostess gets involved," Setu said, shifting my focus away from the women.

I sat and caught Setu's hands despite his initial struggle. I was done trying to get him to trust me. Time was running short. Egypt's future hinged on me, and I was done playing games.

"Listen very carefully." I tightened my grip on Setu's hands. "Khaf's in danger. We all are, and you're the only one who can help me."

"Help an Egyptian?" Setu laughed. "I'd rather die."

I tossed his hands on the table and rubbed my surprisingly burning temples. That was the reason I needed to win his trust first. Of course, he didn't believe me. Why was I so impatient all of a sudden? Why was Setu in the tavern anyway? As a clerk, he should avoid such places and remain in the temple, where people could converse in a civilized manner.

I took a deep breath to calm my nerves. I shouldn't take this out on him. It was my fault I had been so impatient. I'd tormented this man for two years and shouldn't blame him for distrusting me. A week ago, I would have had the Medjay force him to do whatever I wanted. Or was it a month ago? I still couldn't figure out the time difference between Huat and Duat.

"Setu, please, I—"

The tavern's music stopped, and the people fell silent. The wooden floor squealed to my right. The Hostess walked toward us, holding a knife. Each step that lioness of a woman took vibrated the beer in my cup. She stood next to our table and towered over us.

"I heard a rumor," the Hostess said, her voice mimicking the squealing wood, and her haunting gaze glued to me. "That Khafset has adopted a new stray."

"Khafset?" I cringed, holding tight to the strap of my bag. "Who's Khafset? I don't know anyone by that name." I looked at the shaking clerk. "Are you friends with this Khafset?"

Setu gave a nervous laugh. "He's more of an acquaintance, really."

"So, he does the crime," the Hostess said. "Disappears and simply sends his friends to mock me."

"Mock you?" I gasped. "Us?"

"We would never!" Setu said, his voice trembling.

The Hostess eyed us. "Naunet said you know where Khafset is."

"I have more of a general idea, really," I said. "He isn't in Egypt. I know that much."

She hummed, nodding. "I want you to give him something."

Both my hands flinched to my cheeks. The Hostess grabbed Setu's right arm and pinned it to the table.

"You'll give him this young man's hand." The Hostess hovered her knife over Setu's wrist. "Tell Khafset I will cut his lying brother limb from limb until he returns."

"No, please!" Setu struggled to escape the Hostess's grip.

She punched his face. The force of her assault launched Setu's head back as if it was about to detach from his body. His head fell forward, and blood poured from his nose.

I jumped to my feet, my chair falling behind me. "Harm him, and you'll regret it."

The tavern's attendants gasped. The Hostess released Setu and stood before me. I craned my head and held her gaze. Gods, the woman was at least twice my size.

"Repeat that, girl."

"Setu is my friend. I'll protect him with my life."

Setu's mouth dropped.

The Hostess narrowed her eyes. "Your Medjay won't save you here, Egyptian. Their authority ends at the doorstep of my establishment."

"I don't need the soldiers. I have defeated beings bigger and scarier than you."

The Hostess grinned. "You will die here, Egyptian."

I smiled. "I don't think so."

Frenzy hissed in my ear, urging me to submit to its destructive powers. I denied it, and its foul easy path. I grabbed my cup, splashed the beer in the Hostess's eyes, and smashed my wooden chair on her head. The Hostess stumbled back, holding her head, her body bent. But she was standing! How was this woman still standing?

"What have you done?" Setu yelled.

I rushed around the table and grabbed his hand. "Run!"

We jumped from the open window onto the street.

"Catch them!" the Hostess shouted.

We sprinted across the roads of Avaris, the cursing Hyksos chasing us. They were drunk and slow, but their fear of the Hostess would be enough motivation for them to chase us until dawn, and I had neither the time nor the energy.

Frenzy crawled on my skin, pulling my gaze toward the yelling Hyksos. Maybe just this once, for the sake of our country, I could... no!

We passed by some beggars on the street. I stopped and pointed at them. Their faces lit up with anticipation.

"Stop them in the name of the grand vizier, and you will be rewarded!" I said.

The beggars ran off to intercept the Hostess's men. Well, technically, freedom *was* a reward.

We escaped into the abandoned slums. Set's temple towered in the distance, leaking its red candlelight. I gasped at the sight as Frenzy raged inside me. It was eager for my reunion with Set. It craved a... battle? Why did it want me to fight him? Apep's Chaos magic was also connected to Frenzy and pushed him to fight Set. Gods, I was becoming more like Apep by the second!

Setu grabbed my hand and dragged me into a dark alley. We ran between the deserted homes until we reached a dead end.

"What now?" I asked.

I was in the slums of Avaris. Alone with a man I'd tormented for two years. Hyksos men were chasing me with the intent to kill me, and my Medjay were far away. Frenzy surrounded me. It tickled my skin, inviting me to touch it. My master's teachings screamed in my head. He warned me the Hyksos would kill me given a chance, and here they were, trying to kill me.

I shouldn't have come here. I shouldn't be in the slums of—

"Egyptian." Setu knelt beside the wall to our right. He sat and laid his back against a metallic box on the ground. "Help me push it."

I pushed until the box slid from its place, revealing a wide hole in the wall behind it.

Setu looked at me. "Can you trust a Hyksos?"

The angry Hyksos mob cursed in the distance. Frenzy crawled over my skin. Everything I'd learned, everything I knew, urged me to... no! I didn't trust the Hyksos. In the same way, I didn't trust every Egyptian. It depended on the individual.

I knelt beside Setu. "I trust *you*."

I followed him through the hole into an abandoned shop. We crawled across the room and sat with our backs underneath the windows overlooking the street.

The shop was shaped like a hollow rectangle with rooms lining its edges. It contained two levels connected by spiraling fenced stairs. Rooms were visible on the upper floor, the bottom half of their doors obscured by a brick wall. Children lived here. Whoever built that wall feared a kid would fall from the hallway on the upper floor.

"Will they search the building?" I whispered.

Setu shook his head. "Not even the Hyksos like to remain in the slums for too long on account of the rumors about the demons and evil spirits living here."

They had their own hierarchy and superstitions! Who could've known? Me. The warden of Avaris should've known.

"Are you," Setu said, "going to comment about the scary rumors?"

"Why? Demons aren't that scary, really." I shrugged and Setu's eyes widened. He must've thought I was some pampered Egyptian noble girl who would scare easily. He really didn't know me, did he? Why should he? I'd never spoken to him like an equal. But no more! "The Hostess... did scare me, though. Khaf is sure popular with the tavern's women."

"It's a matter of perspective."

"Gods, to think I used to punish innocent people in Avaris while I left the Hostess alone."

Setu raised his eyebrow, his face not impressed by my words.

"What?" I asked.

"The Hostess is a great woman," he said.

"She literally tried to cut your hand off!"

"She wouldn't have done it."

"Oh!" I laid my hand on my chest, my heartbeats increasing.

Setu nodded. "The Hostess feeds the poor people in Avaris. She cares for us all. She's just mad at Khaf on account of him disrespecting her. The same way you disrespected her with your assault."

"I... I'm sorry." I lowered my gaze and shook my head. I'd done it again. I'd given in to Frenzy's influence. No. It wasn't Frenzy. *I* chose to impress Setu by being violent. I didn't even know the woman. Gods, I never learned, did I? "Why's the Hostess so mad at Khaf?"

"She's his fiancée," Setu said.

"What?" My mouth dropped. That lowlife was engaged the entire time!

"Their wedding was last month, and Khaf was broke. So, the Hostess broke tradition and gave him a wedding gift. She treated him like royalty. Even gave him a silver bracelet to prove it."

"So, he's married?!" I shouted.

Setu shushed me and glanced outside the window. "Khaf never showed up for the wedding. He gave me the bracelet, and nobody has seen him since."

Oh, it was all fake. Thank the gods!

"That man," I said. "You've got to admire his dedication."

"Still a matter of perspective."

"He did it for you and the girls."

Setu's eyes widened. "You know about the girls."

"Iti and Bennu." I nodded. "How are they doing?"

"Fine." Setu's eyes avoided mine.

"Where are they?"

"Safe."

I didn't push him. Of course, he would keep them hidden from me. Were they in this shop? Both floors were empty except for a blanket, a mattress, and some empty bottles of wine scattered on the bottom floor.

There was one object, though, that revealed the shop's tragic history. A furnace. This was a smithy. One that was abandoned long ago.

"Hey, Egy..." Setu swallowed. "Nefiri."

I smiled at him. "You can call me Nef."

"I—think I'd rather stick with Nefiri."

I nodded, blushing. Oh, how the tables had turned. Now I was urging them to use my short name, and *they* refused.

"Thank you. For saving me, though," Setu said. "Even if it wasn't necessary, the thought counts. Never expected *you* to jump to my defense."

I nodded, wishing the ground could swallow me so I could hide my shame. "Nobody in Avaris should ever thank me. No matter how much good I try to do. I could never make up for all the harm I've caused to your people."

Part of me wished Setu would contradict me. He didn't.

My focus returned to the old furnace. The cold device that had once contained the fire that forged Khaf's dagger. The weapon that killed his father transferred the furnace's raging flames to Khaf's soul.

"This was his father's smithy," I said.

Setu nodded.

"For what it's worth," I said, "sorry I've been so cruel to you in the past. I promise I'll be better."

Setu smiled. "That would be nice."

"Can I ask you something?"

"Yes."

"Why do you wish to be a priest of Set? There are better, gentler gods."

Setu opened his mouth and closed it. "What do you think the cult of Set does?"

"Master Paser taught me it's evil, corrupted by the Hyksos. He said the Hyksos love Set because they both tried to usurp Egypt's throne and failed."

"Set's cult," Setu said, clearly calming himself after what I'd said, "studies the mistakes of our Baal. Set was a hero once. He fought Apep, pushed away the deadly storms, and contained the demons' danger so we could flourish in peace. But his story warns against greed and tyranny and how the best of us could fall. Yes, our story is similar to Set's, but unlike him, the Hyksos alive today are paying for a crime they didn't commit. That's the lesson. Evil begets wickedness. Destruction begets chaos."

"That's... beautiful."

My master didn't always speak the truth, did he? Everything he had taught me about the Hyksos was false. But again, everything he'd learned about them was a lie. He would've protected them had he been taught they were his people. That was what Khaf failed to see. There were no heroes and villains. Our nation had been wounded, and we ignored the infection for far too long.

I took off Master Paser's golden ring. "The grand vizier gave me this to pay for my brother's healer. Khaf won't be here for a while. Sell my ring and feed the girls until he returns."

"What? No. I can't take this from you."

"Ah, stop being so proud." I pushed the ring into Setu's hand. "I don't need it anymore."

"But what about your brother? Didn't Khaf's medicine—"

I shook my head.

"Oh." Setu hesitated, then touched my hand. "I'm sorry."

I smiled. Bless him; he had truly believed the medicine was real.

"Where is Khaf?" Setu asked. "You said he's in danger."

Finally!

"Something terrible is about to happen. Khaf might die. We all might die. But together, we can save everyone."

"And... how can I help you with something like that? I'm just a clerk."

"Exactly. You have access to the high priest of Set. I must speak with him."

"Even if I agree to wake up the high priest at night, there's no way he'll talk to you."

"Tell him the grand vizier's apprentice requires his audience."

"I thought Paser fired you."

"Sethos doesn't need to know that."

Setu shook his head. "There is no guarantee he would meet with you. Not even the pharaoh could force Sethos to do anything, on account of him being a high priest. Even if he's Hyksos like us."

"He will come."

"You want him to come here!"

I smiled. "He will."

"Are you mad? I'm grateful for this ring, but there is no way I'll tell him some Egyptian is ordering him to leave his home at night and meet her in an abandoned shop in the slums."

"Not some Egyptian." I caught Setu's hands. "Set's chosen."

Chapter 24

The Gift of Freedom

Khaf's smithy was dark and sad. Its cold furnace, empty rooms, and cracked walls told the story of a place that could've been a lovely home, yet the world decided otherwise. No, *we* decided otherwise.

I sat on Khaf's mattress and hugged his blanket, pressing out his smell. For the first time since my return to Egypt, Frenzy left me in peace. At last, even if for a brief moment, there was no voice urging me to return to my old ways. Gods, I was trying so hard to be better, but it was difficult. Every false lesson I had learned about the Hyksos' wickedness clouded my judgment.

Was I misjudging Sethos? I knew he stole most of the Hyksos taxes and sold us his people's orphans. For that, I deemed him evil. But I had also misjudged the Hostess based on one action she did in a moment of anger. Perhaps there was a hidden side to Sethos. Maybe he was simply trying to do his best in a dreadful situation. He could've appeased the Egyptians to shelter his people from our wrath. Was it prejudice to assume Sethos's wickedness, or naivety to believe in his goodness?

Oh, Khaf. The world wasn't as black and white as we both wished to believe, was it?

Nevertheless, Hyksos or not, Sethos was a high priest. A position that rivaled the pharaoh's. While Ramesses had a divine mandate from Horus to rule over mortals, the high priests also claimed their authority from divine sources. But Sethos was mortal, the same as Ramesses. Both could experience fear, which should be my target—his human emotions.

That was the reason I'd chosen Khaf's smithy for our meeting. The emotions it provoked, and the symbolism it portrayed. Sethos rarely left his luxurious temple, and now he was forced to visit the slums. In this smithy, where Egyptians had murdered Khaf's father, an Egyptian would fight for his people's freedom.

Footsteps echoed on the top floor. Frenzy flashed through my bones, pulling me to my feet. I grabbed a shard from one of Khaf's broken clay bottles and hid in the corner.

The stairs connecting the smithy's floors vibrated with the intruder's steps. The footsteps descending the spiraling walled stairs grew louder, but nobody appeared. A stray animal, perhaps?

"Setu." A brown-haired girl emerged, rubbing her sleepy eyes. "Are you..." She froze, standing barely taller than my knees. Her wide eyes stared at the shard I pointed in her direction.

"Bennu!" the girl screamed. "Bennu!"

"Please don't..."

Another person ran down the stairs. The top of the sister's head poked over the stair wall as she rushed to the aid of her crying sister.

"Iti!" Bennu shouted. She reached Iti and hugged her. "What happened?"

Iti pointed toward me.

Bennu turned. She flinched. Her breathing grew ragged, and her eyes widened. The little girl held tight to her younger sister. "Egyptian!"

"Setu!" the girls screamed. "Help!"

"No, no! Please. I'm not here to harm..." I tossed the shard to the side, and Frenzy left me. Gods, I was an idiot. "I'm Khaf's friend. He sent me to check on you."

"You're Egyptian," Bennu said. "Khaf told us to stay away from you."

"Yeah." Iti pushed her face deeper into her sister's chest.

"Don't you remember me?" I asked. "You saw me with Khaf. You played with my little brother."

"Hote!" Bennu's face brightened.

I smiled at the older sister. "Yes. Hote."

"Where is he?" Bennu asked.

I knelt before the girls and dragged Khaf's blanket from behind me. "He's in the Field of Reeds."

"What's that?" Iti asked.

"The most beautiful place in the world." I tightened my hug on Khaf's blanket, remembering his comforting embrace. "A blue Nile glows in its sky, and tiny scarabs crawl between the reeds, leaving a shiny trail on the grass." I smiled at the sisters. "And, girls, do you know what the reeds do when you touch them?"

Bennu and Iti leaned forward, their eyes wide.

"What do the reeds do?" Bennu asked.

"Yeah, what do they do?" Iti broke free from her sister.

"They release the smell of blue lotus accompanied by the most charming melodies. Khaf used to play with them to cheer me up."

"Is Khaf there?" Bennu asked.

"Yeah, can you take us to him?" Iti asked.

"We have to wait for Setu," Bennu whispered in her sister's ear.

"But I want to see the glowing scarabs!" Iti stamped the floor and cried.

"Please don't cry," I said. "You'll visit the Field of Reeds one day, I promise."

"R-really?" Iti asked.

I nodded. Hopefully, not for a long, long time, though. "Khaf isn't there anymore."

"Where is he then?" Bennu asked.

"He..." I kept telling Khaf he had no idea what caring for a helpless younger sibling was like. But he didn't just know *my* misery. His burden was double my own. Worse, his was voluntary. "He... is... bringing gifts!"

"Really?" The sisters' faces brightened.

"Yes! Oh, girls, wait until you see his incredible gifts for you."

The girls' eyes sparkled. Tears fell on their chubby cheeks, and their cries filled the smithy.

"Why... why are you crying?"

"I miss Khaf!" Iti screamed.

"Why isn't he with you?" Bennu cried.

"Because... I... he still has to get you one last gift. Yes! The best of them all!"

The girls' cries vanished. I might've been starting to get the hang of this.

"What gift?" Bennu asked.

"Yeah, what gift?"

A free future for both of you.

I shot the girls a teasing glance. "Wouldn't be a surprise if I told you, now, would it?"

They nodded. Yep, I definitely had the situation under control. They were cute. Their tiny white dresses were clean, and they seemed well-fed. At least the golden coins I had been stealing made these two happy and healthy.

"What's your name?" Iti asked.

"I'm Nefiri."

The girls' eyes widened, and their mouths dropped.

"She's Khaf's Nefiri," Bennu whispered in her sister's ear.

"Khaf is in love with an evil Egyptian," Iti said.

I frowned. "I heard that."

The girls giggled.

"Khafset always talked about you," Bennu said.

"All the time!" Iti said in an exhausted tone. "Nefiri this. Nefiri that."

I chuckled, my cheeks turning warm.

"He acted like when he returned late from the tavern," Bennu said.

"Yeah," Iti said. "But he didn't smell funny when he talked about you."

The girls giggled, glancing at each other. I tried to chuckle to humor them, but I knew what those two little girls didn't understand. Khaf really had a drinking problem! Despite how cheerful he acted, despite how hard he tried to make everyone feel good, the poor man was depressed with no one to help him. His monthly meetings with me, where I kept insulting and belittling him, were the only time he felt happy. Gods, my heart twisted at this grim realization.

"When will Khaf be back?" Bennu asked.

"Soon," I said. "I'm leaving tonight, and we'll return together with your gifts."

"Promise?" Iti asked.

I nodded.

The girls hugged me. I froze in their embrace, fighting to hold back my tears.

I would've enslaved those girls if Khaf hadn't stopped me. Gods, how many children were suffering because of me? How many Hyksos wished for death to escape the lives I had forced upon them? I was a pile of pure evil. Why did Khaf love me? What did he see in me despite all my evil deeds?

I hugged the girls. Now it was my turn. I wouldn't give up on Khaf. Those girls wouldn't lose their brother like I had.

The smithy's door opened, and Setu entered the shop, holding a clay bottle. He cringed at the sight of me and the girls. We broke the hug, and the girls squealed.

Setu signaled to the sisters to stay quiet before they could shout his name. I turned to the girls and pressed a finger to my lips. The girls mimicked my gesture and nodded, smiling.

"J-just a moment, Your Holiness!" Setu shouted in the door's direction. "I ask a moment to make this disgusting place adequate for your presence."

"Fine!" a man barked outside the smithy. "But make haste, boy."

"Of... of course, Your Holiness."

Setu beckoned the girls toward their rooms on the upper floor. He was right. Under no circumstances should Sethos find those girls.

"Girls," I whispered, "I need your help if you want Khaf to return quickly with your gift. Can you help me?"

The girls nodded.

"I need you to hide in your rooms. No matter what you hear, wait until Setu picks you up. This is important for Khaf's very secret plan that only we girls and Setu know. Do you understand?"

The girls nodded and, to make me hate myself even more, wiped my tears with their little hands before they left.

"Boy!" Sethos shouted. "What's taking so long?"

Setu's gaze followed the girls as they ascended the stairs.

I stood and straightened my white dress. I took a deep breath and signaled Setu to bring in the high priest.

"Be blessed by his presence!" Setu announced. "His Holiness, Sethos, the high priest of Set."

"Finally!" A short, widely built man barged through the door. He stood beside the furnace and scanned the smithy. "Set's mercy, how did this filthy place look before you prepared it for..."

Sethos's eyes caught mine. He tried—and failed—to wrap his expensive leopard skin around his imposing belly, clanking his expensive jewelry with each movement.

"Girl." Sethos pointed at me. "Setu said you are Set's chosen. Did my clerk speak the truth?"

"Yes," I said, not entirely focused on the high priest's words.

How many children was each of his ten rings worth? How many Hyksos starved for Sethos's belly to grow? How many innocent people died in the dungeons for that Hyksos to afford his expensive necklace and earrings? That was the reason Master Paser refused to grant Sethos an audience with me. Despite everything, my master didn't want me to become like Sethos. He wanted me to be ruthless in the name of duty, not greed.

"Where is the spear?" Sethos asked.

"With Set. The god of destruction is free."

Setu gasped. He retreated until his back hit the wall.

"Liar," Sethos said.

"Excuse me?" I said.

"Set would have never allowed you to leave if you were the spear's chosen. He must destroy your soul to regain full control over his weapon."

"I can prove it to you." I stepped away from the high priest and Setu. I took a deep breath and worded the spell. "Shama'at Morot!"

We scanned the area for any signs of magic, but our surroundings were defiantly ordinary. Great! *Now* Frenzy had decided to leave me alone!

Sethos scoffed. "Is this a joke?" He caught Setu by the neck and growled at him. "You brought me to the slums to see this imposter! Boy, even the dead Hyksos in the depths of Duat will hear your pleas for mercy when I'm done with you."

"No, I beg you, Your Holiness," Setu cried, caught in Sethos's clutches. "She said... I trusted—"

"You trusted an Egyptian, you fool of a clerk!" Sethos said.

My heart pounded in my chest. A tingling sensation crawled on my skin. Then they returned — the hisses.

"Let him go!" My voice shook the smithy. A wave pulsed around me and pushed Sethos away from Setu. Thunder erupted in the clear heaven, and a crack slithered along the smithy wall.

Frenzy demanded more destruction. It yearned for more. It wished for nothing more than for me to rip Sethos apart. I didn't obey. I denied it. The high priest had his demonstration, and that was enough. I wouldn't indulge the foul magic any longer.

Sethos snapped his fingers, breathing loudly, sweat leaking down his temples.

Setu's eyes remained glued to me, his head trembling.

"Boy!" Sethos snapped.

Setu shook his head. He ran to the high priest and presented him with the clay bottle. Sethos drank, leaking red liquid onto his chest.

"Do you believe me now?" I asked.

"What do you want, Egyptian?" Sethos asked, wiping the wine off his chin.

"I want to defeat Set and save our pharaoh."

"Not interested." Sethos handed Setu the bottle and walked toward the door. "Let's leave, boy."

"Not interested? Did you hear me? Set is free! Egypt and its pharaoh are in danger!"

Sethos turned. "I couldn't care less about Ramesses, and a mortal can't defeat a god."

"Maybe. But what about the invading Hittites? You must care about their danger." I grabbed the royal decree from my bag and presented it to the high priest. "This might motivate you to care about the pharaoh."

Sethos snapped his fingers, and Setu rushed to fetch the royal decree. The high priest unrolled the scroll and read its content, Setu standing beside him, trying to steal a glance.

"That is a royal decree from Queen Nefertari," I said. "It grants the Hyksos of Avaris equal rights if they rescue the pharaoh in Kadesh. You will be Egyptian citizens if you achieve this goal."

"Gods!" The bottle fell from Setu's hand and splintered on the floor. He stepped back, his hands over his bald head. "How did you get the queen to sign something like this?"

"Khaf did. He risked his life to secure this deal. I only finalized it." Well, he also might get us all killed, himself included, but Setu didn't need to know that. I never wished for Hote to know of my cruelty, and Khaf's family shouldn't know of his stupidity either. Khaf had to remain a symbol of hope for Setu and the girls.

"It's going to be over!" Setu trembled. "All our misery in Avaris will end. We just have to rescue the pharaoh."

Tears poured from Setu's eyes. That was a good sign. If this was a clerk's reaction, most Hyksos wouldn't refuse to fight for the pharaoh to gain their freedom.

But the high priest was a different story. He regarded Setu and grunted. Why would a Hyksos fight against his people's interests?

Sethos rolled the scroll and looked at me. "Do you think this piece of paper has any meaning?"

"What?" Setu shouted. "Of course it does! It's a royal decree!" He recoiled from the high priest's glare. "I a-apologize, Your Holiness."

"No, it doesn't change anything," I said.

Setu's shocked gaze darted toward me. "It doesn't?"

I shook my head. "Not on its own."

Sethos shook the scroll at Setu. "This royal decree you're so worked up about is just ink on papyrus. Not even signed by the pharaoh. The Hyksos could fight and die in Kadesh, only for Ramesses to return home victorious and burn everything in Avaris, including this decree. May I remind you that Nefertari isn't the pharaoh? There is absolutely no guarantee Ramesses will honor his wife's word."

"You're right," I said, "but if the Hittites conquer Egypt, they will kill us all. So if Hyksos blood will be spilled anyway, let it happen in Kadesh. Allow Egyptian and Hyksos blood to mix on the battlefield while they fight for their home. Show the Egyptians you have changed since Ahmose's days. Save the pharaoh, and he will be in your debt."

"No," Sethos said. "Those are ridiculous fantasies, and I won't indulge them. You children are too young to understand how the real world operates. I'm not sending Hyksos men to die for the pharaoh, only for the rest to die when he returns. You are tyrants, and you will never change. It's in your blood, Egyptians."

"High Priest Sethos, please see reason," I said.

"Couldn't we ask the people what they want, Your Holiness?" Setu asked.

"That is an excellent suggestion," I said.

"No, boy. Don't live the girl's fantasies. Even if I accepted her nonsensical proposition, there is no way we could reach Kadesh in time to rescue Ramesses."

"He's right." Setu gritted his teeth. "It's too far."

My body shook. Sethos refused to let his people decide their fate and now hid his knowledge about the gates. Nefertari was right. I'd been a naive little girl for believing in that man. He didn't care about Hyksos life. He wanted to maintain the system that made him rich.

This wasn't going to be easy. I knew it wouldn't. I shouldn't give up—no more easy paths for me. The road to redemption was supposed to be steep. I failed to save my brother and pursue my interests as the grand vizier's apprentice. I couldn't change the past, but I could still save the people of Avaris and the girls hiding upstairs.

No more temptation. No more whispers. No more destruction.

I could still win this. My master had taught me better. A politician always remained calm to assess the situation. But I wasn't calm. I was livid. Not because Sethos was Hyksos. No, they were like us, just as Khaf tried to teach me; they were capable of both good and evil. Sethos wasn't an evil Hyksos. He was an evil man.

"Oh, you lying bastard!" I shouted.

The high priest's eyes widened, and Setu's mouth dropped.

"Excuse me!" Sethos demanded.

"Nefiri, did… did you just insult a high priest?" Setu covered his mouth.

"Your high priest is lying to you," I said. "He could get the Hyksos to Kadesh in time."

"How?" Setu asked. "It would take at least a month."

"The gates." I returned my gaze to Sethos. "You know about the gates. You can move the entire Hyksos force from here to Kadesh in a moment, and I know that for a fact."

"Is she speaking the truth?" Setu asked.

"She's lying to you, my boy. Don't trust those Egyptians. They want nothing more than to see us all dead."

So my master fueled our contempt for the Hyksos, while Sethos did the same in Avaris.

No. I would never compare that man to my teacher. The grand vizier, though flawed, was still an honorable man who cared for his people. His definition of 'his people' just needed some work.

Setu looked at me, his wide eyes sparkling. Bless him; he truly wanted to believe me.

"Setu," I said, "I'm leaving this place to confront Set, and, to be frank, I will probably die. According to your high priest, Set must destroy my soul to regain sole control over his weapon. What do I have to gain from lying to you?"

"This was a waste of time." Sethos turned. "Come, boy, let's get you away from her poison."

Setu's gaze shifted between the high priest, walking toward the smithy door, and me. He laid his hands on his bald head and stared at Sethos.

"Now, boy!" Sethos shouted, stepping over to the doorstep.

"Your Holiness," I begged. "Please, wait. I have more to say."

"I have heard enough."

"High priest, please!"

He gave me a dismissive wave.

"Sethos!" I screamed. Frenzy engulfed me, tempting me to force Sethos into submission. I shouldn't have been so lenient. Some people had to be punished! I should force that wicked man into—

"Nef," Setu said, his voice almost a whisper, trapping me in his gaze. Did... did he, oh gods, he finally called me Nef!

My heart skipped a beat, the warmth of Frenzy turning into a cold abyss in my chest. My trembling hands fell on my head, and I retreated until I hit the wall. *Gods, help me.* I had been about to unleash the cursed magic, hadn't I? I was becoming more dangerous and unstable with every passing moment. I had almost forced Sethos into submission through sheer force. I didn't want to be this person anymore. I tried to be better, wished for it, and yearned for it. But I was an evil person, rotten to my core, no matter how hard I tried.

Setu sent me a comforting smile and followed Sethos. Bless him; he really tried his best. If only Khaf were here. Despite his admirable effort, Setu wasn't Kha—

Setu picked up a shard from Sethos's broken wine bottle. Then the most unfathomable yet glorious thing happened. Khaf's allegedly weak brother yanked the royal decree out of his high priest's hand.

Sethos turned. He lunged toward Setu and tried to grab the scroll.

"Stay away from me!" Setu threatened the high priest with the shard.

Sethos froze before the defiant clerk. Where did this come from? Gods, I had completely misjudged him, hadn't I? Setu wasn't weak. He'd grown up in the slums of Avaris. He was like Khaf and the girls. Setu was a survivor!

"What..." Sethos retreated, glaring at Setu. "What's the meaning of this?"

"I won't allow you to ruin this for us!"

"Allow? Can you even comprehend the consequences of your actions? You're a temple clerk, boy. I can whip you in front of the temple and leave you to die under the desert sun."

"I... I don't care! Evil begets wickedness. Destruction begets chaos. It's people like you who caused our suffering. All the way back to the Hyksos who usurped the... the..." Setu bit his lip, shaking the shard in his hand.

Come on, Setu! You can do it!

"Who usurped the throne on account of their greed! People who would do anything to keep their power. People... who want to keep everything the way it is until we grow old and repeat all your mistakes. I will *not* allow it. I will be damned if I stand by and watch you ruin our people's chance at freedom."

My heart almost broke out of my chest. I might've just discovered another wonderful lowlife! Setu didn't have magic, authority, or strength, yet he was the bravest person in this room. Oh, what a remarkable family lived inside this great smithy.

"Do you think the Hyksos would want to fight even if I agreed to this nonsense?" Sethos asked.

I opened my mouth to tell him they definitely would, but it was Setu's turn now. A Hyksos had to take the leap of faith.

"We'll see about that," Setu said. "I'll leave this place and run to the tavern. I'll show everyone the royal decree. Let's see what the Hyksos think about their high priest's rejection of their freedom. Let's see which institution holds more power. Set's temple or the Tavern of Avaris. You or the Hostess."

"Boy, come back to your senses." Sethos stretched out his hand toward Setu. "Give back the scroll, and we'll discuss this at the temple. All will be forgiven. I understand the passion of youth."

"No." Setu stepped back. He shook the shard at Sethos. Blood dripped down his white-knuckled hand as he gripped it. "If Khafset can stand up to the likes of you, then so can I!"

I smiled. There it was. Khaf's influence. The proud thief of Avaris who inspired both Setu and me to take a stand. There was no stopping it now.

"Who is this Khafset who brainwashed you all?"

"The thief who came to you asking for redemption," Setu said. "He begged you to take him in as a student for the priesthood, and you agreed."

"Really? He begged?" I asked, bewildered at how Khaf had secured a free apprenticeship with Sethos, who didn't seem to remember him. Gods, he was a great thief.

"Yeah, he begged." Setu glanced at me. "I almost believed he was sincere."

"A bunch of thieves and liars!" Sethos shouted.

"Last chance, Your Holiness," Setu said. "What's your decision?"

"Boy, the Thunderbolts will kill us all the moment we arm ourselves!"

"No," I said. "I have the queen's word. As long as the Hyksos stick to the plan, the Thunderbolts won't intervene."

Sethos tightened his fist and looked at the smithy's cracked ceiling.

"I also need access to the gateway beneath Set's temple," I said. "Khafset told me it's the shortest way to Set's throne. The spear's calls come from the temple, so he must be right."

"We'd need someone with access to Anubis's Soul magic," Sethos said.

"Then get a magician from Heka's temple if you don't have anyone who wields that magic," I said.

Sethos scoffed. "And they would simply open the gates for the armed Hyksos? They are part of the clergy. They couldn't care less about your deal with Nefertari."

I walked toward him. This was taking too long. I stood before the high priest, a finger's width separating our noses. "If they don't agree, I'll ask the queen mother for help."

He laughed. "And Tuya will come with you."

I smiled. "We could try if you don't believe me. But the queen mother wouldn't come alone, of course. She would enter Avaris with the Thunderbolts, and you would lose authority in her presence. High priest or not, this is a time of war, and normal rules no longer apply." I narrowed my eyes. "And trust me, Your Holiness, even the gods can't comprehend what our queen mother is capable of."

Sethos walked off through the smithy, shaking his head, and gave us his back.

"Very well," I said. "Setu, let's go."

"Wait," Sethos said.

We turned.

"I—might have access to Anubis's magic," Sethos said.

That snake of a man. Like a fish on land, he jumped about until he ran out of air.

"Do you accept Nefiri's plan?" Setu asked. "Will we fight the Hittites in Kadesh with the Egyptians?"

Sethos sighed. "Yes."

I turned to Setu. "Setu, go—"

He hugged me and cried. "Thank you, friend! Thank you! Thank you!"

I bit my lip to stop myself from crying and hugged him. "It was all you and Khaf. I only brought a piece of paper to Avaris." I eased him away and wiped his tears.

Setu studied me, tracing his hands on my arms. "Nefiri, you're burning!" He laid his hand on my forehead. "Are you all right?"

"There's no time, and I'm not important." I caught his hand, which was soaked in my sweat. "Go now. Hide the scroll and tell someone you trust about its location. I'll wait for you at the gateway below Set's temple. I won't leave until I know you're safe."

Setu hesitated for a moment. He nodded and ran out of the smithy.

I waited until Setu was out of sight and collapsed to my knees. I hugged myself. My body trembled, my skin burned, the world spun around me, and the hisses returned stronger than ever.

"Did you get what you wanted, Egyptian?" Sethos scoffed.

Punish him! The hissing voice screamed at me.

No!

"Typical, isn't it?" Sethos said.

Nobody cares about Sethos! The voice hissed. *He deserves to suffer!*

Nobody deserves to suffer!

"Your pharaoh rushes into a nonsensical battle," Sethos said, "and we Hyksos have to die."

Punish him! Punish him! Punish him! Embrace me and punish him!

N—

"Girl!" Sethos snapped his fingers. "Are you listening to me?"

I looked up at Sethos and stretched out my hand toward him. Rose energy sparked around my fingers, granting me an indescribable sense of might.

Sethos stumbled back, his eyes wide, sweat pouring down his temples. "Set's mercy!"

You are not good! the voice hissed, and my head flinched.

I'd tried to be better.

You're rotten to the core!

But I could seek redemption.

You are Passion!

I... I...

What do you desire, Passion?

I... I desire to save the girls' brother.

Very well.

Energy leaked from my skin like ribbons of glowing rose mist. It felt similar to Set's scarlet magic and Apep's Chaos magic. However, it was more powerful, more driven, and more—passionate.

"Set, protect me!" Sethos fell to his knees. He stared at me as a glowing rose hue engulfed me and illuminated the dark smithy. A stinking liquid leaked from the crying high priest and fed the yellow pool forming around him. "You... you're a child of Frenzy!"

"Sethos..." I wanted to scream: *Please, help me! Something is wrong with me. Send for the queen mother!* Instead, I smiled at him, and the hisses consumed my thoughts. "Be a good high priest and take me to the gateway."

Chapter 25

He Who Stands Between

I stood in an empty room beneath Set's temple. Black mist leaked from the gaps between the red bricks, forming my gateway to the Land-Between-Realms.

Sethos cowered in a corner. He hugged himself and mumbled a prayer to Set for protection. The high priest was... cooperative now. This had been my goal. However, the means by which I achieved this goal were... unsettling.

I had regained control over myself after Sethos opened the gateway, as if the strange rose magic left me once it had fulfilled my desire. A child of Frenzy. That was what Sethos had called me. An emerging monster, just like Apep once was. The magic I was wielding since my arrival in Huat wasn't Set's. It was mine. Passion magic. I was just like Apep, except I was already in Huat.

But why did it take effect in Huat? Why did the hisses speak to me when I needed them? How was I wielding magic without divine items? I didn't know, and it didn't matter. The gods, including Set himself, fought Apep to keep him away from Huat, and here I was, another child of Frenzy, yet I roamed free in the mortal realm. The right decision to make while I was still sane was to protect everyone in Huat from the monster I would become. I was dangerous and should never return to Huat. For everyone's sake, I must die during my fight against Set.

I would *not* revert to my old ways. If I couldn't be better, I would rather die than continue living as a heartless monster.

My plan was now in full motion. The Hyksos would gain their freedom by rescuing Ramesses in Kadesh, ruining Khaf's radical plan of unifying Egypt through fear. Now, I had to stop Set.

I laid my hand over my heart, feeling the bulge made by Tuya's golden scarab. That would be my weapon against Set. A divine item that could summon a god. I just had to reclaim the spear to activate it. But which god would the scarab call? Horus perhaps? Probably. Besides Ra and Atem—who swore neutrality—Horus was the only god strong enough to fight Set. The scarab must've been his key to enter Set's kingdom.

First, I had to wait for Setu's return. Fighting Set would consume every ounce of my brain, and I couldn't fight while worrying whether Sethos had sent someone to harm Setu.

I turned to Sethos. The man was still lost in his prayers. He knew what I was, so perhaps he could give me more information. If I was going to die anyway, then there was no harm in using my new magic against Set.

"High priest," I said.

Sethos raised his head, revealing his pale face.

"How did you know I was a child of Frenzy?"

Sethos returned to his prayers.

I gritted my teeth, and the hisses returned. "Answer me!"

Sethos shook. The hisses left me, and I lost my balance. Curses!

"R-rose magic," Sethos said. "Frenzy."

"But I refused Apep's offer. He wished for me to join him, and I said no."

"Frenzy is a primordial force that transcends the gods. It is parasitic. You're a perfect host, grand vizier's apprentice."

He hissed those last words. Gods, I was so twisted that even Sethos looked down on who I used to be.

"But," I said in a low tone, trying not to trigger the Passion magic and its hisses, "I don't have any divine items to connect me to any god. How am I drawing magic without a divine link?"

"You don't need a divine item. Your Ka is already connected to Frenzy. Same as the gods themselves."

I crossed my arms, almost hugging myself. My soul was engulfed in Frenzy. Was I that far gone? My Ka was only tainted when Anubis inspected my soul. Yep, I definitely had to die.

"Sethos." I eyed him, and the high priest cowered deeper against the wall. "If a word about me gets out or if you do anything to harm Setu, I swear—"

"I would never!" Sethos knelt before me, his face stuck to the floor.

I regarded the high priest kneeling before me. It wasn't long ago that I would have loved this scene. Me, Lady Nefiri Minu, standing tall over the kneeling High Priest Sethos, the strongest and most influential Hyksos. Now, I only felt disgusted, mostly at myself for ever enjoying this but also at the world that turned such an unnatural state into an ordinary reality.

I walked to Sethos and knelt before him. I held the old man's hands and eased them away from his face, sending him a comforting smile. He was a despicable person, the worst of the worst. But so was I.

It only took a good man's faith in the goodness buried deep within me to unveil the grim reality of my behavior. I had to be reminded that my duty was to help the people of Avaris, not harm them. I had learned my lesson too late, but Sethos still had time to act.

"High Priest Sethos." I flattened my palms around his hands and bowed my head, taking a praying position. "I ask you to keep the Hyksos of Avaris and our men in Kadesh in your prayers. I hope you will pray for me to pass Horus's test. I have sinned, my high priest. I have misused my power, hurt the innocent, and…" I bit my lip, my tears dropping on our hands. "And I failed my brother. I ask you to pray for my success. May it be the one good deed I can show Osiris before I fail Maat's scale. May it be the one bright spot in my heart when Ammit devours my soul. This I humbly ask of you, High Priest Sethos."

I raised my gaze toward the old man's trembling face.

"You can leave now if you wish," I said.

Sethos scrambled across the floor toward the door. He managed to get on his feet and ran out of the room as if he'd been trapped in a cage with a wild beast.

I sighed and wiped my tears, hoping that I might have awakened something in that man. Probably not.

Setu entered the room, pointing in Sethos's direction. "What's wrong with the high priest?"

I stood and dusted off my dress. "Oh, where do I start?"

Setu chuckled. He laid his hand on my forehead and smiled. "Your fever broke."

I nodded, smiling. "Is the scroll hidden?"

"Yes. The Hostess has it."

"The Hostess! Setu, have you lost your mind?"

"She's a harsh woman but has looked after the Hyksos more than Sethos ever did. You should trust her. She allowed me to leave the Tavern of Avaris unharmed despite our personal issues. She's already rallying the men. According to her, preparations should take a day."

I nodded. "I trust your judgment."

"Will Sethos open the gates to Kadesh?" Setu asked. "Or will he change his mind once you're gone? You know, on account of him being a traitor."

"He will cooperate." If I understood anything, it was politics. "He'll be too scared of the Hostess's growing influence and the decree she holds." He was also terrified of me.

Setu turned to the gateway's black mist. "So, this is it."

I nodded.

"We'll be waiting for you and Khaf," Setu said.

"I will bring him back to you. I promise."

"You too."

"Me too?"

"I mean. Just—don't die."

I chuckled. "Those are some impressive words of encouragement."

He smiled and stretched out his hand. "Thank you."

"Get that thing away from me." I pushed his hand aside and hugged him.

Gods, I had tormented this man for two years, and he had been nothing but loving and caring from the moment I showed him the bare minimum of the respect he deserved. No wonder Frenzy deemed me the perfect host.

I had to pull myself away from the hug and turned to the gateway's black mist. I took a deep breath, then stepped into the blackness.

The rose energy engulfed me, accompanied by the now familiar hisses, and pulled me through the Land-Between-Realms toward the destruction-gate.

So it wasn't Set's magic that urged me to fight him. It had been Passion magic all along. It made sense. Passion had driven me my entire life, whether to save my brother, prove myself to Master Paser, or save Egypt and the man I loved. Set was an obstacle in my way, and my Passion magic knew it.

The black mist vanished. I reached for the ground but found none. No! I plunged toward the sand, screaming. The air screeched in my ears and pushed violently against my body, burning my skin.

Such a stupid mistake. The rose magic pulled me toward the gate, but it couldn't tell my position relative to it. It transported me into the sky above the destruction-gate. Now that Khaf wasn't with me, it became painfully clear how I was out of my element in Duat.

I closed my eyes and retracted my body into a ball, anticipating an inevitable crash.

Suddenly, the air thickened. The wind swirled beneath me, forming a cushion that decreased my velocity. I descended gently to the ground before a giant collection of black mist. That was it. The destruction-gate. The way to Set's throne in the scarlet desert. And before it stood the man who had saved my life again. Khafset of Avaris.

My divine items decorated Khaf's body—Anubis's amulet, Ra's bracelet, and Maat's glowing necklace. The items covered his arms and neck in unique sets of writing. The glow around his neck faded with that of Maat's necklace. He had saved me by wielding her Air magic. He tapped into the goddess's power more than I ever could, bringing the wind of the Land-Between-Realms under his control to stop my fall.

The hisses in my ears vanished at the sight of him. It was as if Passion magic was scared of Khaf. Terrified even. That was… unexpected. Why? He was just a man. But he was also my passion. He occupied a place in my soul, same as Frenzy.

"Khafset." I either chuckled or cried. I couldn't tell. It might have been a squeal. I couldn't quite place my current emotion.

"What are you doing here?" Khaf hissed.

"I'm so happy to—"

"I gave up my only chance to resurrect my father to save you!" Khaf said. "And you come back to Set willingly. Don't you have any limits? Can't you even respect my sacrifice?"

I didn't answer. Didn't even give him the courtesy of a polite frown. I stood and began dusting off my dress and picking the sand out of my hair.

Khaf crossed his arms. "I'm waiting for an—"

"No." I raised my finger. "We're not having this conversation while I look like this. Give me a moment."

Khaf took a deep breath, but to his credit, he waited. And wait he damned should! After everything he'd done, he should count himself lucky I still loved him, the infuriating lowlife.

"Why are you waiting by the gate, Khaf?" I asked, adjusting my golden shawl around my neck. "Don't you have a grand heist to finish? Oh, right, you wanted to usurp Egypt's throne first. So much to do, and yet you're still here."

Khaf swallowed.

"You don't have to answer. I already know." I grinned and pointed at him. "You missed me, didn't you? You sat here, waiting for me to arrive."

"I couldn't care less about—"

"Ah, stop it already! You say you hate me, then save my life!" I breathed in to calm my nerves. Gods, I wanted to hug and kiss him but also punch him in his stupid face.

"I'm here because I won't allow you to stop Set!" Khaf said.

I walked toward him. "You truly believe I can stop him, don't you?" I gazed into his beautiful honey eyes and smiled. "You're sweet, but I can't stop Set without you. We are at our strongest when we work together. It's just a fact."

"You'll find a way to stop him. You always find a way." Khaf narrowed his eyes and pushed his face closer to mine. "You will not pass through the gate, Egyptian. I won't allow you to ruin my people's only chance to gain their freedom."

"Speaking of your people..." I narrowed my eyes as well, enjoying the presence of my comrade in crime. "I have something for you."

Khaf arched his eyebrow. "What could you possibly—"

I slapped the idiot. Gods, I slapped him with all the might I could muster from every muscle in my body.

Khaf retreated, his hand covering his scarred red cheek. "Did... did you just slap me? Who do you think—"

"That was from Naunet. I promised to forward this slap to her... Khafi."

Khaf's eyes widened.

"Oh yeah. I almost forgot. The Hostess, you know, your fiancée, she almost chopped off Setu's hand and sent it to you. But don't worry. I saved him." I planted my fists on my hips. "You were right. The woman was terrifying. But to be fair, I caught a glimpse of her heroic side before leaving."

"Leaving from where? How... how do you know all this?"

He looked cute in this new, overwhelmed state.

"Did you really think I would simply go home and cry over my bad luck? Oh, no. I kept busy in Peramessu. I had a pleasant time in Avaris with Setu. I even visited your home and met Bennu and Iti. Your sisters really love you, Khaf. They kept asking when you'd return."

"You met the girls? They agreed to speak to you? Alone!"

"The gods have blessed you with a wonderful family, Khaf," I said. "My plans would've failed if it wasn't for Setu's help. We really don't give him enough credit. I pray to Bastet Sethos won't harm him."

"Setu!" Khaf's face turned red. He gritted his teeth and caught my wrist. "What did you do, Egyptian?"

"The Hyksos of Avaris are on their way to Kadesh as we speak. Your deal with Nefertari has changed. Now the Hyksos must rescue Ramesses to gain their freedom."

"You sent my people to die?"

"They chose to defend their land. As you said, freedom can't be gifted. Your people are on their way to claim it."

"You ruined everything!" Khaf released me and paced to and fro before the destruction-gate. "Gods, Nefiri! There isn't a thing you can't destroy! You endangered my people to save Ramesses and Paser. The lives of those two men are worth more to you than those of everyone in Avaris."

"Listen to me for one cursed second!" I caught his arm, bringing him to a halt. "Your goal was noble, but your means were wrong. You don't inflict pain or fear. That's not who you are. You grant hope. You inspire. I didn't give up because I believed in your dream. Setu stood up to your corrupt high priest because *you* inspired him."

"But why?" Khaf asked in a voice mixed with both anger and exhaustion. "I have Set under my control. My divine deal with him is flawless." He pulled his hand out of my grip and gave me a dismissive wave.

Was he mad at me? Oh, the nerve! He forced me to steal, compared me to a cow, scammed me with my brother's fake medicine, lied about my father, freed Set, endangered the destruction of... nope, I had to calm myself and remain pleasant to pull the idiot back. But once we arrived home, oh, I would tie him to the cow he loved to kiss and have her drag him across Avaris for all its... nope, not now.

"Set wants to punish us all." I tried hard to keep a reasonable tone. "He will kill you. You'll die before you can save Egypt from the Hittites, and the country won't have a ruler or an army to protect it."

"Set can't kill me. Even if he finds a way to break our deal, which he can't, a god can't attack mortals inside Huat. He physically can't break Atem's divine laws."

His words made a lot of sense. But there had to be a reason why Astarte was certain Khaf would fail. Why couldn't the gods explain their reasons in clear words?

"So what now?" Khaf stood between me and the destruction-gate. "Do you plan to stare at me until the Hittites arrive in Egypt?"

"Astarte warned me your plan would fail, and Set would kill you."

"You couldn't have spoken to Astarte without Ishtar."

"She found me in the desert and saved me."

Khaf scoffed. "Of course Astarte would save you, Egyptian."

I studied his eyes. Were they glowing more than usual? Yes, I knew those eyes like the back of my hand. I lost myself in them each time I gazed into their honey-colored irises. They had a different glow to them today. But their glow had faded in Abydos. It also faded right before I burned his face. Both times I feared him. Both times I lost my faith in him. Why did Ra ask if Khaf had people in Huat who believed in him when discussing his strength? Could the glow of his eyes be connected to people's faith in him? But how?

I traced the unreadable hieroglyphs on his chest. His body reacted this way to every divine item he touched, so it wasn't connected to Tuya's enchantment.

"Astarte told me not to give up on you," I said.

"What?"

"She said I had to fight for The Hidden One. He Who Stands Between. She said Set would kill you when he discovers the truth."

"For Baal's sake! How often must I say this? A god can't kill a mortal in Huat!"

My eyes widened. My heart froze. The world spun. Gods, how was I so blind! Set couldn't kill a mortal in Huat, but he could kill Khaf.

My knees shook, and Khaf caught me to keep me on my feet.

I stared at the truth. I gazed into his honey eyes, which had captivated me since I first saw them. Those pearls for eyes the Canaanite possessed. They had been the answer to all my questions, and I was too blind to see them for what they meant.

I walked away from him and paced before the destruction-gate. He caught my hand and let go, cursing. He rubbed his palms as if he'd held a piece of burning metal.

"Nef?"

The hisses in my head subsided, freeing my mind for the information flow soaring inside my skull. Every anomaly related to Khaf. The strange behavior of the gods in our presence. Their words, anger, and nervousness. How they always turned on Astarte when they saw us. How Ishtar remained by his side when I hurt him. Isis's and Tuya's investment in him. I had always thought their reactions were connected to me. But it wasn't me, was it? It never was. It was Khaf. Always had been. Astarte said it. He was the one who stood between.

"That's it. I'm taking you home," Khaf said. "You look—"

I raised my gaze, and Khaf jumped back, his eyes wide.

"What's happening to you?" he asked.

"I see Astarte in those eyes of yours!" I repeated Maat's and Nephthys' words. "Canaanite. Why did the gods always call you 'Canaanite'?"

"What?"

"You know what I love the most about you? You're funny, smart, and caring."

"That won't work on me anymore."

"You're strong enough to survive a punch from Shemzu or a lashing from Apep or even Ra's flames."

Khaf released me and stepped back. "Leave."

I caught him and laid my hand on the hieroglyphs on his chest. "You can tap into the magic of the gods without needing to word any spells. Every item of the gods reacts strangely to your touch."

"What..." He swallowed. "Tuya's enchantment."

"Not quite." I repeated Maat's answer. "You've always been the better choice for the spear, but it chose me." I laid my hand on his three-clawed scar. "The irony. You tried so hard to convince me I was Set's daughter, knowing very well it was a lie. But the magic has turned on its caster wheel. The gods can touch the spear while unchosen mortals die at its touch. But you confused it. It couldn't tell what you were; and it pushed you away. It couldn't choose you because you are neither a mortal nor a god. You're Astarte's hidden one. Her son. A demigod."

"My mother is dead!" Khaf pushed me away. "Are you really using my own tricks against me? Are you going to disrespect a dead woman? Have you fallen that low?"

Aunt Taweret had tried to tell me the truth. Astarte killed her children. She tried to hide her crimes. She didn't wish to be caught over failed experiments. She was trying to create an Egyptian demigod. That was the reason Aunt Taweret liked Khaf. He was the child Astarte didn't kill. He had survived his mother.

"That's why your plan will fail," I said. "Astarte broke a crucial divine law, so she hid you. She birthed a demigod whom Set or any god could kill, even in Huat. You can't have a divine deal with Set because it only works between a mortal and a god. You are neither."

"Have you lost your mind?" Khaf walked away, shaking his head.

"That's why Tuya secretly enchanted your father's dagger to grant you access to your mother's war magic. The queen mother wasn't ashamed she helped a Hyksos. She knew you had to remain hidden; otherwise, the gods would hunt you for what you are. But you weren't the monster they expected. You charmed them. The same way you charmed me."

"No," Khaf mumbled, pacing. "My mother is dead." He turned, and tears sparkled at the corner of his eyes. "No!"

I pushed away my hair, revealing the scratches on my neck. "What's this?"

"Set scratched my neck when he threw me toward the gate in Abydos. He broke your deal without realizing it. I'm sorry. You have no deal with Set, and it's only a matter of time until he realizes it."

Khaf fell to his knees and stared at the ground. His tears dropped from his cheeks, soaking into the sand beneath him.

I sat before him. "I'm sorry. If only I had figured it out earlier."

"What have I done? I've doomed everyone in Egypt. The girls and Setu will die because of me."

"You couldn't have known."

"I should have known. Everything in my life screamed the truth, and I ignored it. My strange eyes. My strength which increased whenever people believed in me. I ignored all those signs until I doomed us all."

"I've made many mistakes as well. But together, we have a chance to defeat Set. You're a demigod. Set won't even know what hit him. We *can* do this."

"My mother is Astarte," Khaf mumbled to himself.

"Yes." I laid a finger under his chin and raised his gaze to my smile. "You're the son of the Canaanite war goddess herself."

"My father was murdered, and my mother, the goddess, didn't protect him. I grew up an orphan. My childhood was filled with cruelty, cold, and hunger while my mother, the goddess, just watched and did nothing!"

I held his shaking hands and pressed them against my chest. "I'm sorry."

"Why should I fight at all? If even the gods are flawed, what's the point? What meaning is there to our lives if there is no higher standard we can strive toward?"

"We've both spent each day of our lives answering that question. Despite our mistakes, weaknesses, and arrogance, we fought for those we love."

"I doomed them all. Bennu, Iti, Setu, and the Hyksos of Avaris will be slaughtered by the Hittites because I freed Set." Khaf's head fell, and his tears returned. "Because of me, Set... oh gods, he will destroy you!"

"No, Khaf, you—"

"Ra was right. Demigods are dangerous. They shouldn't exist. I shouldn't exist."

I hugged his motionless body. "Don't say that. I love you. We all do. We can fix this."

"You tried to warn me, and I didn't listen." Khaf's tears continued to drip down my shoulder. "I doomed us all. I shouldn't exist."

"Khaf." I guided his head toward me. "Khafset!"

He repeated those last two phrases in an endless loop. The man wasn't reacting to the world anymore.

I'd broken him, hadn't I? As he said, I destroyed everything— even the hopes and dreams of the proud thief of Avaris.

"You don't have to fight anymore." I rubbed his scarred cheek and gazed into his divine honey eyes. "My Khaf. My Hyksos. My comrade in crime." I kissed his stiff lips. "My love."

I rose and walked to the destruction-gate. I stood before its black mist and glanced at the collapsed Hyksos.

He kept repeating the exact two phrases.

"I doomed us all. I shouldn't exist."

Chapter 26

The Flames of Destruction

The destruction-gate's mist faded, blasting the scarlet desert's rotten stench in my face. I walked on the black sand, rubbing off the sticky layer that formed on my arms.

Set's empty throne stood in solitude. Scarlet lines slithered across its black metal and pulsed whenever thunder shook the desert.

The demonic kingdom felt alive, as if celebrating the return of its monarch. Set, the mighty god of destruction. The Baal of storms and tamer of demons. A supreme god of the Ennead. Yeah, so I was supposed to defeat *that*!

"I sense your fear," Set's voice echoed, pushing the purple clouds into a frenzy. "I sense your pain, your frustration, your— despair."

The wind pushed against my back. A long monstrous shadow extended before me. The god of destruction stood behind me, and despite my courage, my conviction, my passion, I couldn't help but feel like an autumn leaf vowing to defeat a raging storm.

Set's golden-scarlet gauntlet stretched beside my head, and his long, black claws clutched my shoulders. He lowered his snout beside my left ear, drilling his heavy, growling breath into my flesh. "So you chose for your destruction to be by my hands instead of Ammit's."

"I don't seek destruction. My goal is to defeat you."

Set hummed. He circled me until we faced each other and stretched out his right hand beside him, calling a scarlet bolt from the heaven. The lightning's glow faded, revealing the god's reunified weapon—the spear faced the ground while the scythe curved beside his head.

"And how are you supposed to defeat the god of destruction?" Set asked, following his unnecessary display of power. "Anubis, Apep, Osiris, Isis, Nephthys, Astarte, Sobek, and Thoth."

I arched my eyebrow. "Why are you naming gods?"

"They each opposed me and lost. Why would a mere mortal believe she can defeat me while those mighty gods fell before me like flies?"

Despite my struggle to remain confident, my knees trembled. Was he right? How was I to succeed where those gods had failed? I was breathing because *he* allowed it. I hugged myself and retreated, my brain urging me with each step to return to my senses and escape, while my heart encouraged me to stand my ground and fight for those I loved. But the god was smiling. He didn't seem the least bit worried about my return. Of course, he wasn't concerned. Why should he be? I couldn't defeat him. I was too weak, too naive, too...

No!

I steadied my feet.

I'd survived Duat and clashed with its gods. I'd sent the Hyksos to fight for their freedom. I'd opened my heart to those I used to despise. Everyone in Egypt was doing their part, and I *had* to pull my weight. I was fierce and not weak. Smart and not naive. I was Nefiri Minu, the thief of Peramessu, and I was going to pass Horus's test.

"I have already defeated you," I said.

"Defeated me?" The god smiled. "Fine. I will humor you." He tapped the spear side of his weapon on the ground. Scarlet mist spiraled upwards, forming a floating disk between Set and me. "Have a look."

Images of a battle flashed in the floating misty circle. Egyptian soldiers pushed back against the flooding Hittite army. The blood of our men rushed on the streets, painting a city red. The enemy carved through their ranks. The poor men were both outnumbered and out-armed, failing to hold formation.

"Is this the battle of Kadesh?" I asked.

"Yes."

"Another prophecy?"

"No."

Was I too late, or had a week passed in Huat already?

"Ramesses and his men are doomed," Set said. "They are scared—weakened by hunger and thirst. Despair has already claimed their hearts. They seek death, their only escape from their misery."

Set tapped his spear on the ground. The image blurred and refocused on a blood-soaked man fighting alone with a broken blade. His iconic red hair raged like wildfire under the glaring sun in the heat of the battle. That was him—the Lord of The Two Lands. Pharaoh Ramesses the Great.

A magnificent falcon floated around the pharaoh, warning him of approaching enemies. Its eyes shone golden, like Ishtar's. This wasn't a normal falcon. It must've been an extension of a divine essence. Horus!

"Here it comes," Set said. "The moment I promised you. The demise of your pharaoh."

An arrow pierced Ramesses' shoulder. He screamed. His cracked sword fell. Despite his pain, his fear, his despair, the pharaoh remained on his feet. A soldier jumped behind Ramesses and struck his head, knocking him off balance. The man pointed his sword at the pharaoh's chest. The falcon attacked the soldier's face, cutting his flesh with its claws and forcing the enemy to fall back. Ramesses plucked the arrow from his shoulder, stabbed the soldier's eye, and claimed his dagger.

"See." I waved at the floating disk. "He's doing great. Magnificently, even."

"Horus is pushing Atem's laws to their limit to empower his vessel," Set said. "But Isis's good son will not break the divine laws, even if it means his defeat. He's flawed that way. Another reason he should not be the god-pharaoh."

"And yet they are winning." I grinned. "Our pharaoh is still on his feet under the protection of our mighty god of the heaven."

"Don't celebrate too early. For here he comes. The executioner."

A soldier emerged on horseback from between the Hittite ranks. The man we had seen in the vision back in Peramessu who decapitated Ramesses. He galloped toward the distracted pharaoh.

"Ramesses, watch out!" I screamed.

The falcon screeched, pulling the pharaoh's attention toward Set's charging executioner. It was too late. The pharaoh had neither the time nor the right weapon to counter the attack.

"It's done," Set said.

The soldier raised his ax, ready to strike the pharaoh's neck. He shouted at him, seated on his black stallion. Ramesses' attention shifted to the soldier, and his eyes met those of his prophesied executioner. The ax fell toward Ramesses' head as the Hittite horse almost intercepted his body.

A spear hurtled from behind the pharaoh, scratching his cheek, and hit the Hittite soldier in the chest, pushing him off his horse.

"What?" Set approached the disk, glaring at the images that defied his prophecy.

Countless horses charged on both sides of Ramesses toward the Hittites, their riders shouting one name that shook the battlefield. Egypt.

"The Hyksos!" I raised my fist and smiled at the god's twitching face. "Told you, great Set. I have already defeated you."

"You truly believe this, don't you?" Set waved the disk out of existence and walked to his throne. "What strange little creatures you mortals always prove to be. Love divides you, while hatred brings you together. If anything, this proves the flaws of your design." He sat on his throne and tapped the spear side of his weapon on the ground. "So what now, mortal? You think you won because your pharaoh survived a battle?" He scoffed. "So be it. There are many more battles to come." He pointed the spear at me. "I have an eternity to reclaim my throne, and I still intend to destroy you to regain sole control over my spear. I—could let you go, of course. You will die eventually, and Ammit will destroy you for me. What are thirty-six more years to a god? A blink of an eye. All you have to do is kneel before your Baal."

I drew a deep breath, dreading the stupid words I was about to... Thirty-six? Really? That was all the time... no, focus!

"I'm thankful for the offer, great Set. But I came here to die. I'd like for us to fight."

"Fight?" Set chuckled.

"Yes, and before we fight, I would like to strike a divine deal."

Please, take the bait!

Set narrowed his eyes. "What deal do you propose before we—fight?"

"If I imprison you—"

"Imprison me? You? A mere mortal? A naive little thief who doesn't know her place. A scared little girl who thinks she's a hero."

"I'm not a hero. I know I'm not. But I'll be damned if I don't try."

Set studied me from his high throne. "And you think your words will send me back to Abydos?"

"Not Abydos. Ra's barque. Apep is getting stronger, and Ra needs your help. I pass Horus's test not by keeping you in Abydos but by bringing balance back to Egypt. I have to send you back to the barque where you belong. You against Apep. An eternal struggle between destruction and chaos. Both keeping each other in check. So that's the divine deal I propose, great Set. If I send you to Ra's barque, you will remain there to fight Apep until Ra allows you to leave."

"And you believe you can defeat me?" Set asked. "Do you think an ant has any chance of defeating *you*?"

"A very persistent ant might."

The god smiled. Were our deities aware of how human they behaved sometimes? It made sense. All of our gods, except Atem, were mortals at some point or, in Set's case, were descendants of former mortals.

"I will grant you this, mortal. You are becoming more entertaining by the second." Set rose from his throne. "I accept the divine deal." He pointed his spear at me. "Now perish, insect."

The scarlet beam exploded from Set's spear and soared toward me. I smiled at the flames of destruction that consumed the desert between Set and me.

My Passion magic crawled under my skin, hissing its desire to fight. It leaked from my pores like ribbons of glowing vapor. I gritted my teeth, challenging the approaching wave of destruction.

Then I finally did it. In a split second of calmness, I gave in. I touched Frenzy.

A glorious burst of radiant rose energy exploded around me. It engulfed me in a glowing sphere where I radiated with the passion of a thousand Egyptian suns. Set's Destruction magic clashed with my Passion magic. They fought, challenging each other for supremacy. Finally, Set's magic caved in and destroyed the area around me like a child throwing a tantrum.

I stood unharmed amid the fading scarlet flames of destruction. I gasped for air and breathed in the scarlet desert's cold, thick air, only to breathe out a flaming breath. Gods, this was exhausting. It felt like I'd been running uphill for hours.

Set eyed me, his snout wide open and his head twitching.

"Is Frenzy hissing in your ears as well?" I grinned. The god's eyes widened, and his leg twitched as if he was fighting the urge to step back. "Told you, great Set. I'm a very persistent ant."

"That is why the spear could only choose you," Set said, his stance returning to its imposing state. "It could only be touched by a child of Frenzy. That is how the Chosen is determined."

"Of course," I said. "I knew this all along." I didn't. But he didn't need to know that.

"Horus allowed Frenzy to walk the mortal realm to spite me," Set growled. "Such a pathetic child."

I couldn't tell whether he meant Horus or me. Probably both.

"Last time I went easy on a child of Frenzy, we ended up with Apep." His body tensed. "I shan't repeat my mistake." Set struck the ground with his right foot, bolted across the burning desert, capturing the flames with the winds of his sprint, and snatched my neck.

He looked down at me. I tried to tap into my Passion magic to call his spear into my hand, but... but... oh gods. I couldn't feel my magic! I searched, but I felt normal again.

The god smiled.

"What did you do to me?" I asked.

"So much you don't know, mortal," Set said. "But you shan't have time to learn. You were right. You must die. Another Apep shall not emerge."

Well, at least we agreed on something.

Set planted his spear in the ground. Now was my chance. I tried for the weapon's golden shaft but couldn't reach it. My arms were too short. Great!

I didn't have to hold the spear. I simply needed it to hit the scarab. Maybe if I urged Set to attack me, I could grab the spear and guide his attack toward my... oh, gods! That was the reason I had to keep the scarab close to my heart. Oh, Tuya, you wonderful queen mother!

"Do it!" I screamed at the god. "Destroy me!"

Set didn't reach for his weapon. Instead, he stretched his black claws toward my eye.

"Why are you using your claws?" I jerked to free myself. "I thought you needed the spear to destroy my soul."

"True." Set's smile overtook his long snout, revealing his sharp teeth. "We will get to that eventually. First, you will suffer for challenging me."

Oh, such an evil, cruel, sadistic...

"Please, just kill me with the spear," I begged.

"Oh, no. I shall savor this moment."

Set's claw descended toward my eye. I closed my eyelids as if that would protect me!

The violent wind raged beside me, and Set's claw stopped, its tip touching my flesh.

"And what do you think you're doing?" Set snapped.

"I... I'm not doing anything!"

"You promised you wouldn't harm her!" Khaf's voice erupted. "That was my gift for freeing you."

I opened my eyes. Khaf stood beside me, pushing back Set's claw with both hands. He had come back! Oh, that beautiful lowlife!

I struggled to reach Set's spear. Khaf's eyes caught my movement. He tapped into his Dark magic, and the red hieroglyphs on his back glowed.

Khaf freed the spear from the ground, triggering new hieroglyphs on his face. Set tossed me and hit Khaf's head with his gauntlet in a smooth, uninterrupted movement. He grabbed the scythe side of his weapon. The Hyksos screamed, blood leaking down his face from underneath his brown hair, but he didn't release the spear.

Passion magic soared through my veins like raging fire when Set's attention shifted to Khaf.

God and demigod fought over the divine weapon. Set kicked Khaf in his stomach. My Hyksos took the hit like a beast. He spat blood and roared at the god of destruction.

Set's face twitched. "How are you still standing?"

Khaf smiled, introducing Set to his most beautiful yet infuriating expression. His smug smile. The hieroglyphs on his face glowed, triggering Set's destruction flames. The scarlet flames reached Set's body but didn't harm the god.

"Did you think that would work?" Set shouted.

"No," Khaf said behind the blazing wall of destruction separating them. "It's a good distraction, though."

Khaf tightened his right fist, and Ra's bracelet glowed yellow in unison with the hieroglyphs on his right arm. Fire erupted from Khaf's wrist and spiraled around the weapon toward Set. The flames of sun and destruction caught Set and ravaged his body.

The god roared; the breastplate of his armor broke, revealing his upper body. He kicked Khaf in the chest, thrusting him in my direction. I caught the Hyksos, and we fell to the ground.

"Khaf!" I pushed him off me and helped him sit.

"I... I'm fine." He coughed.

Set glared at Khaf, his claws tapping his weapon. On his now naked body, a long scar appeared, slithering from his chest to his stomach.

"What are you?" Set asked.

Khaf slung his arm around my shoulder, pulling me closer; then the Hyksos smiled at his Baal. "I'm your worst nightmare."

The god of destruction roared. He turned his weapon, pointing its scythe side toward us. Its blade glowed scarlet. Set kicked the ground and bolted.

"Oh no, you don't!" The hieroglyphs on Khaf's left arm pulsed. Anubis's amulet vibrated, and his skin chilled.

Black mist rose between Set and us. The god reached us and swung his scythe. I closed my eyes, screaming, and hugged Khaf, digging my face into his chest.

The wind swooshed against us, but Set's blade never hit me. I opened my eyes, and Set wasn't there. Just Khaf, sitting beside me on the sand.

"What the... Where is he?" I asked.

"I sent him through a gate," Khaf said.

"To where?"

"Dunno." Khaf shrugged. "Just opened whatever gate could be summoned in this spot."

My mouth dropped. Gods, what a brilliant idea! Why didn't I ever think of it?

"It's not over!" Khaf took off Ra's bracelet and presented it to me. "He'll find his way back any moment."

I donned the bracelet, but Frenzy remained this time. Ra's bracelet couldn't remove it from my Ka anymore. I was too far gone.

Khaf inspected his wounds. Blood covered his face. His chest and stomach were bruised, and his breathing overpowered the surrounding thunder. He had been hurt before, but never like this. Gods, he'd almost died, hadn't he? Why did I let him take the lead? I had the situation under control. Well, for the most part. Nevertheless, I was supposed to be the one to die—Khaf needed to return to his family. I had promised to save their brother, and I would *not* break my promise again!

"Hey, Nef."

I raised my gaze to his smile. "Y-yes, Khaf."

He took my hand and kissed it. "Are you hurt?"

"Me? Khaf, *you* are hurt. You... you must leave!"

"Ah, it's nothing." Khaf stood and pulled me up. "See? We thieves always get back on our feet."

I clutched my chest while Khaf's glowing honey eyes stared at me. Despite his smile, tears ran down his cheeks.

"You came for me," I said.

"Of course I did. I just needed a moment to—cope." He laid his forehead against mine. "And you came back for me as well."

I lost myself in the comfort of his warm breath. "Of course I came back."

"I'm sorry. For everything. Hote's medicine, your father, just—everything. Please forgive me."

"Don't cry." I rubbed his tears. "And never beg."

He chuckled. "What a couple of idiots we have proven ourselves to be."

"*Very*—persistent idiots."

Khaf gently laid his hand on my cheek. He kissed me, creating a small realm of comfort for the two of us inside Set's demonic kingdom.

Thunder raged across the scarlet heaven, shifting my attention to the sky. Set's scarlet bolts rained on the desert, and the black sand waved like an ocean. The surrounding hills cracked. Their collapsed chunks rose to the heaven and twirled above our heads.

"Damned mortals!" Set's voice shook the scarlet desert. The rotating debris trapped us in a ravaging cyclone. Set's scarlet lightning flashed between the colliding rocks as if binding them together. "You shall witness true horror."

"He's pissed," Khaf said.

"Can you blame him?"

He sighed. "Not really. Just hoped for more time to rest."

"Khaf." I held his arm. "We have faith in you. Me, the girls, and Setu." The glow in his divine honey eyes grew brighter. "With every fiber of our being, with all our hearts, we believe in you."

Khaf smiled. "I believe in you, too, my Egyptian." His gaze shifted to the darkening heaven. "What's your plan?"

"Tuya gave me a golden scarab to call for a god's aid. I assume it belongs to Horus. Set's spear is our only divine item that could pierce objects. If I could get my hands on it, I could call Horus, and he might stop Set."

"What?" Khaf shouted. He glanced at the gathering storm, his breathing raging with the winds. "Assume, if, and might? Is this your plan to defeat a supreme god of the Ennead, Egyptian?"

"Do you have a better plan, Hyksos?" I asked, shouting at the idiot.

"I could've come up with a better plan!"

"Well, you weren't there, you infuriating, backstabbing—"

Chunks of the collapsed hills clashed with each other. They raced in our direction like mountains raining on ants.

The glow on Khaf's chest flashed. He rushed in circles around me, cursing. He raised his wide eyes at the approaching doom. The glow on his chest faded, and his hands fell. "There is no escaping this." He hugged me and kissed my head, his tears raining on my shoulders.

The falling chunks caught fire, illuminating the scarlet heaven that appeared to be collapsing on our heads.

"Sorry," Khaf said. "I... couldn't protect you."

Protect me? No! He'd protected me enough! Now it was my turn!

The hisses returned. Fire raged in my veins. The world slowed around me.

"On your knees," I said.

Khaf looked at me. "What?"

"Trust me." I caught his shoulder and pushed him down.

I closed my eyes and took a deep breath. The world faded around me as the air filled my lungs until, for a brief moment, a fraction of a heartbeat, I stood alone in a realm of my own creation, basking in the indescribable warmth of my magic. For a mere flash of time, I could decipher the speech of the hisses. I understood what I truly was.

I was Passion.

I opened my eyes. The world raced. My powers exploded in a glorious burst of passionate rose light. The raging pulse pushed against the raining molten inferno.

Set's screams filled the heavens. I roared back. Our powers clashed. His Destruction magic vowed to eradicate us, while my Passion magic empowered me to protect the man I loved.

The energies of destruction and passion eliminated each other. They exploded, consuming Set's inferno. Glowing red fog covered the sky as if the two powers had returned to their primordial state.

I fell to my knees beside Khaf. I was panting, unable to hold air in my scorching lungs. My skin burned under my touch no matter how much I rubbed my arms.

"Nef!" Khaf touched me. He drew back his hand and cursed. "You're burning!"

"I... know."

"What was that?"

"Passion..." I smiled at him. "Of a thousand Egyptian suns."

Khaf's mouth dropped. "You stopped Set's attack without divine items!"

I shrugged, my breathing returning to normal and my skin cooling. "Passion magic."

"There is no such thing."

I chuckled. True, I could feel Set rushing through his kingdom toward us. We were connected through our shared access to Frenzy. But I still had a moment to enjoy what might be the most significant moment of my life.

"Oh, Khaf." I held his hands. "Oh, Khafi, Khaf, Khaf. Of course, there is Passion magic. You've just witnessed it."

He arched his eyebrow. "Are you having a stroke?"

I opened my mouth, but goosebumps crawled on my skin. A brush of wind guided my gaze to my left.

"He's coming," I said.

"What?" Khaf asked, his voice shaking. He did sound cute whenever he lost control of the situation. "Even I can't feel him."

"No time to explain." I stood and pulled Khaf to his feet.

"Nef, what's—" His gaze darted in Set's direction. "I hear him." A raging storm approached us. Its winds carried the chunks of the collapsed hills.

"Die!" Set roared, and boulders shot from the upcoming storm in our direction.

I tried to recall my Passion magic, but it didn't respond. My body must still be regaining its energy. I clenched my fist and pointed Ra's bracelet toward Set. "Zier!" Flames raged from my fist toward the projectiles and evaporated them.

Set roared, and all the debris inside the rotating storm hurtled toward us.

"On second thoughts..." The hieroglyphs on Khaf's chest flashed. "Your plan sounds good enough." He grabbed my waist, and we bolted between the molten rocks as they rained down.

We evaded the falling doom with Ra's flames, Khaf's speed, and Anubis's gates in the most delicate dance only Khaf and I could execute with our well-coordinated casting of the different spells. We were in perfect sync, communicating without a word or even a glance. We were in total control of the situation until reality showed its ugly face, and Set emerged from the chaos.

The god caught Khaf's neck and bolted with us, matching Khaf's insane speed until he assumed command over our motion. Set kicked my stomach, thrusting me away. Our movement's high velocity, mixed with the enormous power of

Set's kick, smashed me into the ground in a collision so powerful it drained the air out of my lungs.

I should have died from this collision, but I didn't. Same as during my fights against Shemzu, Apep, and Nephthys. But now I understood the secret to my survival. It was the heat under my skin. My Passion magic that kept me alive.

Set and Khaf came to a halt. I tried to stand, shooting a flash of pain up my spine. My legs crumpled, and I couldn't move. I needed more time to heal, but I had none. Khaf had to survive. I had to save him. Unlike me, he had loved ones who awaited his return.

"Khaf!" I crawled toward him.

He struggled against Set's grip around his neck. "Burn him!"

I tightened my fist and pointed Ra's glowing bracelet at Set.

"Do it, and you will only kill the boy." Set glanced at me. "His Negation magic is useless against Frenzy."

My hand fell. Set was right. This was a stupid idea. "Let him go! Please! I'm the one you want to kill!"

"True," Set said. "I don't have to kill him. I desire it."

Khaf and Set stared at each other in silence.

"I have beautiful eyes, don't I?" Khaf chuckled.

"The eyes of a mortal who survived my attacks and broke our divine deal." Set tapped his spear on the ground, forming a protective dome around him and Khaf. "No mortal should be able to achieve this. But you aren't a mortal, are you? Oh, I know those eyes all too well. I used to admire the hatred they contained. The foolish search for purpose they revealed. Astarte's eyes. She has committed the greatest sin, hasn't she? The Canaanite has birthed a demigod in our lands."

"My Baal." Khaf's hands fell beside him. "Astarte may have birthed a demigod, but my father birthed something much greater."

"And what did your mortal father birth?"

Khaf grinned. "A damned good thief."

I lowered my gaze toward Khaf's feet. Bare feet! He had taken off his sandal while distracting the god.

Khaf touched the spear with his toe. Hieroglyphs glowed on his face, triggering the destruction of flames around Set's spear and startling the god. The hieroglyphs on Khaf's chest flashed. He grabbed his dagger and stabbed Set in the stomach. Khaf kicked Set's knees, thrusting himself into the air and cutting Set from the stomach to his chest.

Set growled and swiped his scythe above his head. The hieroglyphs on Khaf's back glowed red. He grabbed Set's weapon, deactivating its protective dome. He raised himself over the vertical weapon and jumped off it, thrusting himself away from Set.

The Hyksos landed, and both the god and demigod stared at each other, gasping for air.

Despite the scarlet blood leaking from Set, the god was... smiling? Why was the god enjoying our defiance?

"Astarte's son!" Set said.

What did he mean? Khaf had cut Set exactly where his old scar... oh, Astarte gave him the original scar. Who could have known? Set was of a poetic persuasion. He was a monster with an inclination toward twisted beauty. Perfect!

"Now!" Khaf shouted.

I pointed my fist at Set. "Zier!"

Ra's golden flames soared toward Set. Khaf tightened his grip on his dagger and ran for the distracted god, aiming for his heart.

Set spun his weapon over his head, rotating Ra's flames around him and Khaf, and forming a blazing cyclone around them.

Oh, the idiot! I broke the spell.

A scream erupted from inside the fiery prison. Scarlet beams soared from the raging flames and consumed the fire. The scarlet light faded, revealing the most terrifying scene. Khaf's dagger was an inch away from Set's heart, and the spear was planted in Khaf's chest.

"Khafset!" I screamed.

The Hyksos held tight to the spear, steadying his shaking knees, and stared into the god's eyes.

Set glanced at Khaf's dagger. "Not bad, Canaanite. You almost did it." He laid his hand on Khaf's cheek, digging his claws into his skull. "Your mortal father named you Khafset, didn't he? 'He who appears like Set.'" He pushed his snout toward Khaf's face. "You are *nothing* like me."

Khaf spat blood onto Set's face. "You... d-damn... r-right."

Set growled, Khaf's blood dripping on his snout. "You betrayed your people." Set emitted his scarlet energy like rays of the sun.

"No, great Set! Please forgive him!"

"You betrayed your ancestors." The Destruction magic spiraled around Set's weapon.

"Please!" I screamed.

"And most importantly..." Set's gaze met Khaf's defiant eyes. "You betrayed your Baal."

Set thrust his spear deeper into Khaf's chest, and it emerged from his back.

"Khafset!"

He gasped for air, blood pouring out of his mouth, but he didn't scream. His knees trembled, but he refused to fall. The brave Hyksos remained determined. Remained defiant.

Khaf's paling face turned toward me. "I..." he mumbled, his voice muffled by the blood. "Am... s-sorry." The glow in his eyes faded, and his honey eyes turned black. The proud thief of Avaris collapsed on Set's weapon and dropped his father's dagger.

Set kicked Khaf's motionless body and freed his weapon from his corpse.

"No!" I planted my fingers into my skull, my body burning. The rose Passion magic sparked around me in my moment of pure rage, replenishing my strength.

"No!" Glowing rose mist evaporated from my skin. It spiraled around my arm, feeding the luminosity of Ra's bracelet as his fire raged through my veins. "No!" I pointed my fist at the cursed god of destruction. "Zier!" Flames exploded from my hand toward Set.

The god flipped his weapon and conjured a protective shield.

I panted, my body shaking, fading rose mist evaporating from my cooling body. "Z-zier!" A weaker stream rushed toward the god.

Set walked toward me as if nothing was happening.

"Zier!" Nothing happened. "Zier! Zier! Zier!" The bracelet didn't react—neither a glow nor a spark. The hisses went silent, and the Passion magic left me. "Please! Zier."

My head fell, and my arm dropped. I didn't have the energy. I couldn't save Khaf, even if just this once, and now I couldn't even avenge him. After everything, I was still weak.

Set's shadow extended on the sand. "It's over." He tapped his spear on the ground, stripping me of Ra's bracelet. "Your story ends here."

"Khaf." I shook my head, unable to fully comprehend what had happened. "You killed my Hyksos," I said the words, yet I still couldn't wrap my head around them.

"He was loyal to you. The boy didn't take after his mother in that regard." He placed a claw under my chin and raised my head. "You might think of me as a cruel god, but Astarte is the one to blame. She cursed the boy by creating him as a tool for her schemes."

"You're the one who killed him! Why? You could've just killed me." I wiped my tears and glared at the god. "I know why. You're lonely—burdened by a fake sense of importance and glory. That's why you killed Khaf. You were jealous of him. Unlike you, he was loved."

Set growled. He kicked me, and I fell on my back.

"The abomination Astarte birthed in our land shall receive no salvation. Death has released his divine essence from its mortal vessel. He will wander Duat alone, to be hunted and destroyed. Even his mother won't be able to protect him. Not that Astarte would risk herself for anybody."

He stood on my arms, pinning me to the ground. I should've screamed—should've been in agony. I understood my body was dying, but I felt disconnected from the world. I could only watch what was happening to me.

"I will make certain Astarte and her freak languish in Duat for eternity," Set said. "They will suffer for attempting to trick me, Set, the Baal of Huat and Duat. The rightful god-pharaoh of Egypt." He pointed his spear at my heart. "And you, well, you will not exist to witness the boy's grim fate. I shall answer your prayers, mortal. You will die. Consider it my divine mercy."

I wanted to scream at him. To tell him he was nothing. I couldn't. There was something more important. Set needed to do something for a... plan? I had one of those, didn't I? I couldn't think, only watch. I feared the pain if I regained control over my body. Pain from Set's feet on my arms, the hole he left in my beloved's heart, and the grim fate that awaited my people, whom I had failed.

Set raised his weapon, aiming at my heart. I regarded my reflections in his eyes. I looked scared. I seemed like a frightened little girl waiting to be hurt. The reasons changed, but it had always been the same outcome. I'd always tried to win, only to be forced to accept my defeat. Was this how I wished for my story to end? Was I still weak and naive?

But I was still breathing. I was defeated, but I survived. I was like the Nile. My soul flourished whenever I flowed, and would decay if I ever stood still.

I was fierce and not weak. Smart and not naive.

I was a survivor.

Pain soared from my arms beneath Set's feet. My heart ached from my love's death. My head shook from the thousand ideas fighting in my skull.

I was Passion.

I was alive.

I was in pain!

Set thrust his weapon toward my heart. The spear slashed through the air. It pierced the white fabric of my dress and hit me. I gasped from the force that squeezed the air out of my lungs. Yet my dress remained pure and unsullied by blood. The spear didn't touch my flesh. Instead, it struck Tuya's golden scarab.

A chilling wave pulsed from the scarab. The scarlet sky dimmed. The thunder faded, and the lightning froze in the sky.

Set scanned his fading kingdom. He tried to free his weapon, but my skin and the spear were joined to the golden scarab.

"What did you do?" Set shouted.

"You were right, great Set. I can't defeat you. I'm just a mortal." I smiled at the trembling god, flashing my teeth at him. "I summoned a being that can send you to Ra's barque. I called for Horus. Our mighty god of the heaven. The one true god-pharaoh of Egypt."

"No, you fool, this isn't Horus." Set stepped back, freeing my hands. "This is much worse!"

"Wh-what?"

Black energy crawled from the scarab like endless paint. It leaked on the sand and spread across the desert, swallowing all of existence.

"No!" Set stared at the now black sky.

It was now or never. I grabbed the spear. The black paint that had claimed heaven and earth climbed on Set's spear.

Set's gaze darted toward me. "What are you doing?"

He tugged his weapon, pulled me off the ground, and smashed me against it.

The black paint reached the scythe. The divine weapon bent and shook.

Set banged me against the ground. I grabbed the spear and pulled. A sliver of red light pierced through the center of the weapon's shaft. It was breaking. Just a little more force!

"No!" Set screamed. "Wait!"

"You shouldn't have killed my Hyksos!"

I landed my fist on Set's weapon, increasing the crack at its center. Set kicked my stomach, pushing me on my back. He growled at me, his gaze drifting between me and his dimming kingdom.

I pulled the spear. A blinding red glow exploded from its crack. The divine weapon broke into a spear and a scythe.

I turned the spear and, following my version of Khaf's viper stance, thrust it into Set's chest. The god gasped. His scythe fell from his hand and disintegrated into scarlet mist. Set reached for me, but the poor god's arms were too short.

The black paint crawled inside Set's chest through his wound. It consumed him, dwindling his body and devouring his muscles. His hair turned gray, and his glorious armor crumbled into dust.

"What have you done!" Set whispered in a hoarse voice.

"It's over." I pushed the spear until it emerged out of Set's back. "This is for Khaf." The scarlet and black energies spiraled around the spear. "Shama'at Morot!"

The scarlet beam erupted from the spear, thrusting Set toward Khaf's corpse. The god lay on his back, clutching his chest.

I fell to my side, surrounded by darkness, and hugged the spear.

"Oh, my beloved." Nephthys' voice echoed in the dark void. "Look what has become of us." She emerged behind Set and walked toward him, dragging her black wings on the ground behind her. "Mortals. Mere mortals insult us." The goddess smiled as she walked past Khaf's corpse, and her chin rose. "The queen mother kept her end of our divine deal. That was worth the scarab I gave her."

Khaf's death had been the price for the golden scarab! He was essential to Tuya and Isis because he had to die. Oh, curse them. Curse them all!

"I broke the rules for you, my beloved," Nephthys continued. "I created a sole scarab just to reunite with you."

"You... strengthened Apep," Set said, his voice fading. "You foolish woman."

"Let the world burn, my beloved, as long as we are together. I shall do anything to remain by your side." Nephthys sat beside Set, who was gray and thin like a skeleton. "Do you wish for me to kill the mortal?" She kissed Set's forehead. "Ask, my beloved. Anything for your forgiveness."

I reached for the spear but couldn't find the energy to move.

"K..." Set coughed. "K-kill!"

"Will you forgive me if I do?"

Set nodded, growling.

Nephthys smiled at me, and her Darkness spiraled around her arms.

How, by all the gods, did Tuya believe Nephthys was a good weapon against Set? The queen mother was heartless, but had she also been stupid? Nephthys was unstable. She was a broken goddess with only one goal. She couldn't even see through Set's lie. He wouldn't forgive her no matter what she did for him. He wasn't like Khaf. But... Nephthys was like me!

"I have a divine deal with Set," I said. "If he returns to the barque, he can't leave until Ra allows it. Kill me, and the deal ends. I know you don't believe his lies, great Nephthys. I know because I used to see through my beloved's lies and chose to believe that he was sincere. Set will never forgive you. He'll use you to kill me and push you away the moment he regains his strength. His promise isn't real, but my divine deal with him *is*. Take your beloved to his new prison where he can't escape you. Return home, great Nephthys. To Ra's solar barque where you and Set belong."

Nephthys' arms fell beside her, and her Darkness magic vanished. She looked at Set, who regarded her with shaking, wide eyes. A vicious smile overtook Nephthys' face. The goddess lay on top of Set and hugged him, cracking his fragile bones.

"What are you doing?" Set jerked but was too weak to free himself. "Kill the mortal!"

"Oh, my beloved." Nephthys flapped her black wings and rose to the heaven with Set. She tightened her embrace, and her Darkness magic spiraled around their conjoined bodies.

"Let us return home."

"Kill the girl!"

"Let us fly to the solar barque."

"Release me at once!"

"Let us spend eternity together."

"No!"

"A life surrounded by the beauty of your Destruction and my Darkness!"

"I will kill you, Nephthys!"

"OH, MY BELOVED!"

Scarlet light flashed from the floating gods. I closed my eyes and cowered under my arms as Set's screams and Nephthys' manic laughter shook the surrounding dark void.

Chapter 27

Love & Death

The heaven regained its scarlet color, yet Set's kingdom was dull, its signs of life lost, its vibrant lightning and vulgar thunder hidden, just like my Hyksos, whose head lay motionless on my lap. The proud thief of Avaris had fulfilled the wishes of gods and monarchs. He died to defeat Set.

I laid Set's spear on the black sand and caressed Khaf's brown hair. "Oh, Khaf. My Hyksos. My comrade in... in..." I closed his lifeless honey eyes. "Oh, my love." I kissed his forehead and hugged his cold body.

I had failed his family. I couldn't save their brother like I couldn't save mine.

A stray beam of light reflected into my eyes. Khaf's dagger lay on the black sand. I grabbed the tragic weapon. This blade had one more life to take. I'd failed. It was over. Nothing left except to accept my defeat and end my life. I couldn't return to Huat. I was too dangerous. I would end up a monster like Apep.

Even if Frenzy didn't infect me, I didn't wish to live. What joy could I ever find in a world without Hote and Khaf? A world without purpose. What was the value of passion if I couldn't share it with someone I loved?

I kissed Khaf's cold hand and pointed his dagger at my heart. I closed my eyes and took a deep breath.

This wasn't too bad. I'd die in the company of the man I loved, knowing those he loved were now safe. My brother had joined our mother in the Field of Reeds, both enjoying an eternal life filled with joy.

I wouldn't be reunited with them, of course. Someone like me couldn't possibly dream of passing Maat's scale. Set spoke the truth. The demon Ammit would feast on my soul.

But all were happy, whether they were in Huat or Duat. There was a calmness in knowing this before I sent my tainted soul to Ammit.

I tensed my muscles and pressed the dagger's blade against my chest.

"That would be a waste, child," said a woman's soft voice.

My hand froze, the dagger's tip a nail's length inside my flesh. I turned to the voice's origin. Isis stood proudly before a gate of black mist. Her vibrant white wings gave the illusion that even Set's demonic kingdom could become the liveliest place in the realms.

"Is this how you wish for your story to end?" Isis asked, standing before the gate.

"I have nothing left. No reason to live. What's a life without family or love? Please tell me, O great goddess of life."

"You still have love in your life. Didn't you open your heart to the people you once hated? Aren't they worth living for?"

"They don't need me. They probably tolerated me because I promised to return Khaf to them. I failed. Of course. They are better off without me. Everybody is better off without me. Everyone I love dies. Khaf spoke the truth. I'm a mortal inflicted by Frenzy. I'm a monster. There is no future for my soul."

I hugged Khaf's head and brushed his hair away from his closed eyes.

Why must he die? We used him—all of us. I wanted him for comfort, Tuya as a weapon, and Astarte as a tool. But what about his wishes? He only ever wished for a happy life with the people he loved, and now that his dream of freedom had come true, he wasn't here to enjoy that new life.

My heart pumped in my chest. My face steamed. I gritted my teeth and raised my head, glaring at Isis. "I don't accept this outcome."

"And how would you change it?"

"Apep. He wanted me to become his agent of chaos. He can resurrect Khaf."

"You are speaking nonsense, child. I will strike you down here and now before you take your first step toward Apep."

"Then… then you! Yes, *you* can resurrect the dead. I beg you, great Isis, don't we deserve a happy ending?"

"I can resurrect him. But it's not allowed."

"So it's fine to resurrect Osiris, but Khaf is where you draw the line?"

"Atem's divine laws forbid me from resurrecting a mortal. Think about that before comparing the boy to my husband, the supreme god."

"But Khaf is only half mortal!"

"That is the half that concerns me."

"Cruel. All of you. Every single god. The rules are always in your favor. You use us until you don't need us anymore. We're just a source of your powers. You're no different from Set. Why are you even here?"

"I came to take you home."

"I can't go home. I'd be dangerous to everyone."

"No." Isis stretched out her hand. She opened her palm, revealing a pair of golden earrings. Isis's white Life magic engulfed the earrings. They floated and landed in my hands.

"What are those?" I asked.

"I can still offer you a life, child. Wear the earrings, and they will keep Frenzy dormant in your soul. Enjoy your life before the inevitable happens after your death. I can't save you from Ammit. A mortal soul afflicted by Frenzy must be destroyed. I can't offer a peaceful death, but I can grant you a safe life."

"You can take me to Ammit right now, then!" I threw the earrings aside. "I can't go home. Nobody is waiting for me. I failed everyone. I don't want a safe life or a peaceful death." I dug my face into Khaf's cold chest and cried. "I... I want Khaf!"

What could I do? Where should I go? With whom could I speak? I wasn't Isis. I couldn't travel to the ends of the land to resurrect my love. That was the frustrating truth, wasn't it? Khaf's chest would remain cold. His comforting presence would never shine on my world again.

Isis sat beside Khaf. She laid her hand on my cheek and guided my gaze toward her. "Do you love the boy so much?"

"More than anything. More than life itself. But the god of destruction destroyed our happiness. Set took away the man I love."

Isis stared at me, holding tight to my cheek. Then the most bizarre thing happened. A sparkling drop fell from her eye and wandered down her divine face.

Isis released me and wiped her tear. "Set... took my love from me once."

I nodded.

"You know," Isis said, staring at the scarlet heaven. "Right now, since his divine essence is free, the boy is a minor god. Technically, I wouldn't be breaking any divine laws if I repaired that empty body you hold and forcefully bound the boy's essence to it. Shackle him in a mortal form, to be precise. I wouldn't be resurrecting a mortal but rather cursing a god."

My eyes widened. "Do you mean —"

"I'm suggesting a divine deal, child."

"Yes! Please! Anything!"

"It's not a deal a goddess of life should strike. However, I must maintain the delicate balance between life and death. If you want him back, there is a steep price to pay."

I nodded eagerly. I didn't care what my part of the deal was as long as I would have Khaf back so he could return to his family.

Isis stood, straightening her white dress. "Half your life for the rest of his."

I opened my mouth to agree, but Isis raised her hand. "Think, child, before you agree to an unbreakable bond."

Set said I was supposed to live until I was fifty-two. Half of that, minus the sixteen years I had lived, would leave me with... oh.

I lowered my gaze toward Khaf. I would have ten years with him. After everything I had done, all the suffering I had caused, ten years of happiness with the man I loved was too good for me. Ten years before Ammit could devour my soul and end my existence.

"I accept. Take half my life. Take it all. I don't care. Just bring him back to his family. Please!"

"Are you sure?"

I nodded.

"And the earrings," Isis said. "A crucial part of our divine deals is for you to wear the earrings for the remainder of your life. You will not be able to take them off. You will fight anyone who tries to take them, god or mortal, until they stop or die trying. Do you accept?"

"I accept." I wiped my tears.

"Then wear the earrings, child."

I picked up the golden earrings from the black sand and cleaned the slimy layer that had formed over them with my dress. I put them in my ears, and passion left me. I felt normal again. A mere mortal. Boring and dull.

No! I still had passion. I had my thief and the look on his family's face when their brother returned home.

"I'm ready." I smiled at Isis. "I'm forever grateful, O great lady of all."

Isis expanded her white wings. She flapped them, scattering dozens of glowing white particles over Khaf and me. The white glow engulfed us, linking our hearts with a white string.

Khaf's wounds healed, and a faint pump vibrated his chest, followed by another, then another. Each stronger than its predecessor. Each returning the heat to his body and the color to his face.

I gasped, laughed, and cried, unable to comprehend which emotion I was experiencing.

Khaf's eyes opened. Their black irises glowed, returning to their honey color. The Hyksos had jewels for eyes, befitting a great thief.

"Nefiri," Khaf said. His voice was deep yet soothing. A very useful attribute for a smooth-talking thief. "Gods, Nef!"

He jumped to his knees and hugged me. "Oh, Nef. Thank the gods! I thought Set was going to kill you." He released me and inspected me for wounds. "Are you hurt? Where is Set? How did we survive? Try for a single moment to get over your obsession with my handsome face and—"

I jumped on the idiot, pinning him to the ground, and kissed him with the passion of a thousand Egyptian suns.

After what felt like a lifetime, we eased from the kiss, keeping our foreheads joined.

"That—was nice," Khaf said, gasping for air.

"Gods, I love you so damn much!"

"I love you too." He chuckled. "How did we survive? I thought I died. Osiris shouted my name. He called me... Astarte's Amun? That means Astarte's 'hidden one' in High Egyptian, right?"

I nodded, smiling. A flash of annoyance tugged at me. Why had Osiris given Khaf such a cool and unique nickname? Amun, The Hidden One.

"Oh, Nef, Osiris did *not* sound happy to see me."

"It's his loss," I said, glancing at Isis, whose otherwise serene face twitched at the mention of her husband.

I arched my eyebrow at what was a complete mental breakdown by the goddess's standards.

Isis crossed her arms, and her chin rose, returning to her stoic state. "The girl made a deal to prolong your time in Huat."

Khaf's eyes darted toward Isis. He slid from underneath me. "Great Isis?" He sat, laying his hands on his head. "Gods, I really did die! Nef, what did you do?"

"She struck a divine deal with me," Isis said.

"Deal? What deal?"

"Its terms don't concern you."

"Oh, I feel very concerned."

Isis sighed. "Half her life for the rest of yours."

She kept the earrings part of our deal secret. Smart. Of course, she was brilliant. She was Isis. A simple fact that I still struggled to comprehend.

"No. No. No!" He grabbed my hands. "Why did you do this?"

"It's fine, Khaf."

"It most definitely is not!" He looked at Isis. "Reverse it. Give Nef her life back."

"It's impossible to break a divine deal. As you are aware, Canaanite."

"Why, Nef? I don't want this. I can't live with this."

I laid my hand on his cheek and smiled. "I would rather live a short life with you than a long life without."

Khaf opened his mouth and closed it, his eyes wandering across the desert. He knew the truth. We both did. Divine deals were unbreakable.

"Then I promise you this." Khaf took my hands, tears rushing down his cheeks. "I will dedicate the life you granted me to *you*. Forever yours. Forever by your side. I will always love you. Throughout my life and what awaits beyond my death."

"I will always love you too."

Khaf raised my hands and kissed them.

"Did you ask about your father?" he asked.

I shook my head.

"Are you ready?"

I nodded. I needed to know. I had to close this chapter of my life.

"Great Isis," I said, tightening my grip on Khaf's hand. "I would like to know about my father."

Isis nodded. "Unlike what he had you believe, Sutmheb didn't work for Seti as his messenger. Your father was the late pharaoh's treasure hunter."

My eyes widened. Hatshepsut had spoken of the treasure hunters—the secret royal thieves who stole divine items for the pharaohs.

"He was the greatest treasure hunter Egypt had ever seen," Isis said. "A man who knew Huat and Duat like the back of his hand. Never did he return to Seti empty-handed. Even the gods required his services on occasion. However, when Sutmheb's wife died, and he couldn't find a cure for his son, the proud treasure hunter pursued a radical method. He decided to let his son die of his incurable illness and resurrect him and his beloved wife. A method that required the most difficult object to obtain. The Book of the Dead."

"Your father is doing the grand heist!" Khaf said. "*My* grand heist!"

"He was searching for the Book of the Dead all along!" I said.

"Sutmheb never gave up," Isis said. "He continued his research and awaited Seti's death. Once free from the late pharaoh's command, Sutmheb began his journey into the unknown, leaving you and Hote in Taweret's care."

"Taweret?" Khaf gave me a baffled look.

"I'll explain later," I said.

Isis waved her hand, and a silver metallic slab appeared before me. It was as long as an arm and as wide as a hand, with a finger's thickness. Its metal was strange—a dark silver element decorated with weird black lines waving beneath its surface like ink in water.

"What's this?" I asked.

"Not even the god of knowledge and wisdom knows," Isis said. "Sutmheb found it and stashed it in Duat. He never returned."

"Do you know where he is?" I asked.

"The Olympians informed us he was last seen in Greece," Isis said. "He wished to seek an audience with Hercules, who also sought the Book of the Dead. We don't know what happened. Unfortunately, Hercules is as much of a wild card as your father."

"Oh," I said. "So he could be alive or dead."

Isis nodded. "Keep the slab. Sutmheb might return to you if he's alive, and if he died, then may you find comfort knowing that your father touched what the gods can't comprehend to save your family."

I nodded. There was comfort in that. Even if he failed, at least he tried his best to save our family. Yes, I could live with that.

"Nef." Khaf laid his hand on top of mine. "Are you all right?"

I smiled and wiped my tears. "Let's go home."

I picked up the metallic slab and pulled myself to my feet with the spear's help. My motion shifted the black lines underneath the slab's dark silver surface. I offered Khaf my hand and pulled him up.

"Your master," Isis said. "Paser."

My heart went silent. My grip relaxed, and Khaf fell on his back. I shook my head. No. No. Please! I couldn't survive this. Not my dear master.

"He survived the battle of Kadesh," Isis said. "It will take him months before he returns to Egypt. Horus informed him and Ramesses of your victory. Paser wished for you to know he's proud of you."

My heart shook my chest as if making up for the beats it had missed. I ran to Isis, crying, and hugged her. "Thank you, great Isis!"

The goddess stood stiff in my embrace. She patted my head. "You are—welcome."

"I understand you're happy, but maybe... don't touch the goddess." Khaf held my arm and eased me away from Isis. "Now, that's something you don't get to say every day."

I chuckled and bowed my head, Khaf mimicking my stance beside me.

"We are forever thankful, great Isis," I said.

Isis smiled. "You have done well, children. Both of you. You have passed my son's test, and for that, I congratulate you." She stepped away from the gate, clearing our path toward its mist. "Return home, travelers. Enjoy the lives you desire, for you deserve each other's love, and your goddess is most pleased with you."

Khaf and I shared a smile and entered the gate's black mist, holding hands.

Chapter 28

An Untouchable Family

The Egyptian sun shone over Avaris, embracing its inhabitants for the first time since their arrival in The Two Lands. The Hyksos who didn't join the battle of Kadesh celebrated on the streets after Nefertari's messenger declared the pharaoh's victory and the integration of the Hyksos into Egyptian society, granting them their long-awaited freedom.

Beer, wine, and food flowed from the Tavern of Avaris. The Hostess even extended her invitation to the residents on the Egyptian side of Peramessu. Most Egyptians declined the invitation, of course, but to my people's credit, some did cross the canal and were cheered by the celebrating Hyksos.

Despite the festivities, today would be the most stressful day of my life—my journey through Duat and meeting with Nefertari after our return included. Today Khaf and his family had invited me to visit them at their home. Not as the grand vizier's apprentice, thief, or Khaf's comrade in crime. They invited me simply as Nef.

It had been a week since our return to Peramessu. Isis's earrings had been working perfectly. No hisses or weird phenomena since my return. I tried to remove the earrings once to satisfy my academic curiosity, but the divine deal took control over my body, stopping my hands from moving.

Last I heard of Khaf, he wished to settle his debt with the Hostess so he would be allowed into the Tavern of Avaris—as if Khaf, the broke thief, could ever repay the silver bracelet. I tried to convince him that the Hostess hated him more than any man in the world, but he insisted she was a reasonable woman. So yeah, Khaf was probably dead now, and I'd lost half my life for nothing.

I went into the slums, where the sounds of celebration grew quiet and distant, and stood before the wooden door of Khaf's smithy. Pain weakened my feet—I struggled to fit into my small sandals. I clutched the white fabric of my old dress and took a deep breath. I didn't wish to visit Khaf's family empty-handed, so I'd exchanged the clothes Aunt Taweret had given me for a ridiculously priced apple cake with honey and dates—my sweet Hote's favorite food. The last meal I shared with him.

I knocked and waited. How would they react to me? Was this a one-time invitation? Were Setu and the girls nice to me only because I promised to return Khaf to them?

Gods, I hadn't even considered that! Of course, they didn't really like me. Why should they? I stood before their home after everything I had done to them and their people, and what was I offering? A cake? As if cake could make up for my past actions. If anything, this cake was insulting. It was a symbol of the injustice that divided us. Here in Avaris, people starved while we stuffed our mouths with overpriced desserts on the Egyptian side.

I threw the cake into the gap between Khaf's smithy and the neighboring abandoned building. It smashed into the wall, releasing expensive juice and fruits onto the dirty ground. I stood empty-handed before the closed door, my hands folded over my stomach. I was shaking, my knees trembling, my stomach turning, and my feet, gods, my feet were killing me.

I was such an idiot. Of course they would never forgive me. Khaf must've been the one who invited me. That was the reason no one had opened the door. Khaf was probably convincing them to be nice to me just this once.

Should I leave? Yes. Khaf could visit me at my place. There was no reason to force myself on them. Setu and the girls were probably celebrating Khaf's return, and they wished to spend time together as a family. There was no place for me here.

I retreated toward the canal.

"Hey, Nef!" Khaf called, and I froze after having walked past two empty houses. Gods, I only had one building left before I could turn left and escape this situation.

I took a deep breath—no need to panic. Khaf didn't know what I was thinking and didn't see the cake.

I collected my composure again and turned, my back straight, my hands folded over my stomach, my chin raised high, and my feet begging for mercy in my small sandals. "Yes, Khaf?"

Khaf stood before the half-opened wooden door. He climbed the two steps that connected his sunken smithy to the street and stood before me. "Where are you going? Why didn't you come inside?"

"I knocked."

"Oh! Sorry about that. We were discussing something."

Discussing? I was right! He was convincing them to tolerate me!

Khaf laid his hand on my waist and kissed me. "I missed you."

"It's only been a week. You used to see me once a month."

"I fought five gods, one of which to my death, for the privilege of seeing you more often."

"Privilege?" I chuckled.

"Of course." He laid his forehead against mine. "To think we're finally home and together. I still can't believe it."

His honey eyes gazed into mine, his smile shining on his handsome face. Two years. I had had the past two years to be with this man, and I had chosen to hate him because he was Hyksos. Now that we were together, we only had ten years before Ammit would devour my soul. Was it cruel? Sure. Was it unfair? Absolutely not. To spend ten years with him was more than I deserved.

"You know…" Khaf released me. "You didn't have to knock. You could have just come in…" He sniffed and walked toward the gap between his smithy and the neighboring abandoned home where… where… oh gods! Where I threw the cake. Oh, curse him! Why did he have to be a demigod?

Khaf stared at the cake, which had turned into a battlefield between flies and ants. The persistent ants were winning.

"Oh, Nef. That's why you're wearing your old clothes. Why did you throw the cake away? Why did you buy it in the first place? We really weren't expecting—"

"What did you do with the Hostess?" I tried to divert his attention.

"What? That's not important right—"

"It's *very* important! I haven't heard from you for a week. I was worried sick!"

"Oh! I'm sorry. I was just busy reopening the smithy and wanted to give you some time to rest. I thought you'd come when you had the time."

I glared at him, tapping my foot on the ground. Each tap sent a wave of pain from my swollen feet to my spine. This was the best strategy against Khaf. Make him feel like he'd done something wrong.

"Fine." He sighed. "In a last-ditch effort to get into our Hostess's good graces, I told her what we did to free the Hyksos. She promised to keep it secret and won't come after us, but she insisted on partnering with the smithy until I repay her for the silver bracelet." He crossed his arms and scanned my face. "Now tell me about—"

"I spoke with Nefertari as well!"

"Nef, we can talk about this later. Right now, I'm more interested in—"

"No, no, this is *very* important."

Khaf sighed.

"Nefertari said we're free so long as we don't make her aware of our existence. If she as much as hears a whisper of our names, 'the gods in Duat will cover their ears from our screams.'"

"That's... actually fair. To think Nefertari of all people would... oh no, no. You're not getting off that easily. Now tell me about the cake. Why did you—"

"I want to go home."

"What?"

"I'm not feeling well."

"You can rest in the smithy."

"No!" I shouted, and Khaf flinched.

"Nef." He walked away from the cake and approached me in slow, steady steps as if I was a crazy person. I wasn't crazy. He was crazy. They all were for inviting me here.

"What's wrong?" Khaf asked.

I paced back and forth in front of the smithy. "This was a mistake. I'm sorry about the cake. I thought it was a nice gesture but realized it was a dumb idea. I... I..."

Khaf caught my arms and steadied me. "Take a deep breath."

I tried to take a deep breath. I failed. Miserably.

"Now, let's go inside," he said.

"I don't belong here, Khaf."

"In Avaris?"

"No, with your family. They hate me."

"Where did this come from? They don't hate you."

"You don't have to lie to me. It's fine if they do. I understand. I just want to leave you alone. I can't be with you."

"Do… you mean me? Don't you want to be with me?"

"What? Of course, I want to be with you for the rest of my…" I shook my head and sat, granting my feet the rest they craved.

I wouldn't have him to myself for my remaining ten years, would I? He had another family that needed him. He couldn't ignore them for my sake. Even if he could, I wouldn't let him. Their survival depended on Khaf, just like Hote's had depended on me. No, Khaf was better. He kept his family alive.

I couldn't even wait for the girls to grow up. By the time they were old enough to be independent, my soul would be sliding down Ammit's throat.

"It's about your deal with Isis, isn't it?" Khaf asked.

My eyes widened. How did he know?

He sat beside me. "I know you, Nef."

Could he read my mind?

He smiled. "No, I can't read your mind."

I crawled away from him. Khaf chuckled. He caught my hand, stopped me, and gently guided me closer to him.

"A good thief can always read his target's reactions."

I arched my eyebrow. "How am I your target?"

"Well, I stole your heart, didn't I?" He winked.

"You did." I smiled and laid my head on his chest. "You really did."

"How much time do we have?"

"Forty years."

"You're lying."

"You can't possibly know that."

Khaf frowned. "Forty remaining years, added to the sixteen years you have already lived and then doubled, would mean you would've lived past one hundred. Nobody lives that long."

"Oh." Gods, such a stupid mistake. And I was the one good at math.

Khaf took my hand. "Tell me the truth."

"T-ten."

"No!" Khaf's face turned pale. He patted my hand, but his gaze remained glued to the ground. What was he thinking about? Gods, what I would give to get a glimpse—

"Ten years should be enough time," Khaf said, his gaze absent.

I shook my head. "I wanted a lot more time with you."

"No, I meant enough time to break your deal with Isis."

"Divine deals are impossible to break."

"Oh, Nef." Khaf grinned, color returning to his face. "Oh, Nefi, Nef, Nef."

"What?"

"If anyone could achieve the impossible, it's us."

"Do you really want to waste the little time we have on an impossible task?"

"We should at least try. Even if we fail, we know for a fact the Field of Reeds is real. What are ten or even forty years compared to eternal life together?"

"I won't..." I threw myself into Khaf's arms and cried in his embrace. "I won't enter the Field of Reeds!"

"What makes you say that?"

"Ammit will eat my soul."

Khaf kissed my head. "You're exaggerating. Ammit won't—"

"It's fine. I deserve it. It's a good punishment. I was cruel to the Hyksos. I betrayed my country. I stole from my master. I failed my brother. I don't deserve to enter the Field of Reeds. Just... go back to your family. Don't let me take you from them. You don't have to choose between us. They need you. Enjoy a long, happy life with the family you love for both of us."

"You're right. I don't have to choose between you and my family." Khaf raised my gaze to his smile. "You freed the Hyksos. You saved our country. You made your master proud." He laid his hand on my cheeks and wiped my tears. "And you have been the greatest older sister anyone could ask for. If you don't pass Maat's scale, then none of us stands a chance. We're not judged by our mistakes but by how we deal with them."

"I've made so many mistakes."

"Congratulations, you're like everyone who has ever lived."

"Look who's speaking like a god now."

Khaf raised his finger. "A demigod. *And* my wisdom is unrelated to my divine side."

"Wisdom?"

"Yeah. For some reason, people overlook how wise I can be." He sighed. "The curse of having my looks, I suppose."

And just like that, as he always did in my darkest moments, the Hyksos made me smile. The poor man had missed a crucial piece of information. I could be the greatest woman in the world, and I would still be fed to Ammit because of Frenzy's taint. The same way I'd fed all those Hyksos to the lions. Yep, my fate was definitely fair.

But Khaf didn't need to know this. He couldn't change my fate anyway. He deserved to be happy.

"Fine." I smiled. "Oh, great Amun."

Khaf chuckled. "You know, if I'm The Hidden One, then so are you?"

"How come?"

"I was secretly a demigod while you were the Chosen. Astarte hid me while Horus hid you. We're both The Hidden Ones. Amun and Amunet."

"I like that." My eyes sparkled. "Amun and Amunet. Lovers and comrades in crime."

"Yes!" Khaf stood and pulled me to my aching feet. "Now, come on. I'll show you how much everyone in the smithy hates you."

"What?"

"Just come."

Khaf led me toward the smithy. I didn't want to be here. I wanted to run home. Why couldn't he leave me—

Khaf opened the door, and I froze at the sight of the renovated smithy. It was clean, every spot shining, and the cracks in its walls were repaired. A new dining table stood before the clean furnace on the ground floor. All sorts of delicacies decorated its surface: goose, chicken, milk, cheese, apples, dates, and wine.

"The smithy looks beautiful," I said.

"Thanks. It's just the main hall, though."

"But that's an incredible achievement for a week's work."

"Told you we've been keeping busy." He raised my hand and kissed it. "We wanted it to look perfect for your arrival."

My heart pounded, and an alien sensation crawled inside me. Was this angst or excitement? It could've been hunger. The food did smell amazing.

"Nobody ever did all this work for me," I said.

"Well, get used to it."

"How... how did you afford all of this?"

"It's a gift from the Hostess to the evil Egyptian that everybody *definitely* hates."

I turned to him. "Khaf, I—"

He laid his finger on my lips. "I'm not done yet." He looked up at the top floor. "Setu!"

Setu exited his room and walked down the stairs, smiling. He reached me, holding a piece of fabric.

"I see you took my advice," Setu said. "You didn't die."

I chuckled.

"I knitted you this." Setu presented the fabric.

I unfolded the gift, which expanded into a white Hyksos shawl decorated with black dots and scarlet patterns.

"I—don't understand," I said.

"Thanks to you, we're officially Egyptians," Setu said. "I thought it was only fair we return the favor by welcoming you as a new Hyksos." He laid the shawl around my shoulders. "The black dots on the white background symbolize that despite your mistakes, your heart remains pure. I've added the scarlet patterns on account of you being Set's chosen. Just like the god of destruction, you eliminate the old and weary and make space for the new and strong."

"Setu, I… I don't know what to say."

"You don't have to say anything. I know all of this because your coins paid for my education. Consider it a small thank-you for everything you did for me."

My eyes widened. Gods, his education. "Setu, how will you pay for your education now?"

"Don't worry about it," Setu said.

"Of course I worry."

"Sethos fired him, Nef," Khaf said.

"Oh, no." I clutched my chest. "Setu, I'm so sorry."

"Ah, don't worry about it." Setu tried—and failed—to give me a reassuring smile. Yeah, he wasn't as good a liar as Khaf. I kind of respected him for that.

"I'll figure it out," Setu said.

"*We* will figure it out. I promise." I hugged him, and for the first time Setu didn't flinch or look at Khaf for protection.

I eased Setu from the hug and smiled at the clerk and the thief. "It's the most beautiful gift I've ever—"

"Nope." Khaf laid his finger on my lips again. A gesture that was getting increasingly annoying. "We still have more gifts to show how much we hate you."

Setu glanced at Khaf. "Hate her?"

"Don't get me started." Khaf sighed.

I rolled my eyes but kept quiet. Oh, sorry for being anxious about meeting the people I hurt for the past two years.

Khaf shifted his gaze toward the top floor. "Girls!"

Iti and Bennu barged out of their room. "Nef!" They ran down the stairs.

I knelt to greet the girls. They caught me in their embrace, almost pushing me over.

"I'm so happy to see you," I said.

"We are too!" Bennu said.

"Yeah!" Iti said.

"Don't you have something for Nef?" Khaf asked.

The girls handed me a gift wrapped in a white cloth.

I smiled at them and unwrapped the present, revealing a stuffed doll of a woman with black hair and white wings.

"Is this Isis?" I asked.

"It's like the dolls Khaf brought us." Iti raised her Bastet doll.

"He said, 'Remember that sisters love each other no matter how different they are,'" Bennu said in a deep voice while raising her Sekhmet doll.

"They wanted to give you an Isis doll so you would become their sister," Khaf said. "You would be Isis. The oldest and wisest sister who always protects her family."

I stared at the doll, my tears falling on its cotton fabric.

"Please, don't cry." Bennu wiped my tears.

"Did we make you sad?" Iti asked.

"Oh, not at all." I hugged the girls and kissed their foreheads. "I have never been this happy in my life." I poked their noses, smiling. "Thank you—sisters."

I turned to Khaf. "I don't know what to say. It's all just—"

Khaf launched his finger toward my lips. I caught his hand and glared at him. "Khafset, I swear."

The Hyksos grinned. "We have one more gift."

Khafset and his family assembled before me, all smiling.

"We have a proposition for you." Khaf drew out a key from underneath his brown belt. "This key is the first thing forged in my father's smithy since he died. We'd like you to live with us as part of our untouchable family. If you wish."

"You don't really mean this," I said.

"Of course we do," Setu said.

"But why?" I asked.

"Because we love you," Iti said.

"Why would you love someone like me?"

"Because you're our sister," Bennu said, and I couldn't help but suppress a chuckle when Khaf tilted his head.

"So, what do you think?" Khaf asked.

"Do you really want me to be part of your family?"

"Of course we do," Bennu said.

"You fought a god for us," Setu said.

"You're amazing," Iti said.

I scanned their faces, hugging myself. They all awaited my answer, their eyes filled with anticipation. Gods, they meant it, didn't they? They loved me!

"So what will it be, Egyptian?" Khaf asked.

"Your proposition intrigues me, Hyksos." I stood, opening my arms to them. "I'd be honored to be part of your family."

They rushed toward me, and I lost myself in their embrace. Isis was right. This was worth living for. Despite my loss, my life was filled with new things to love and protect.

Khaf pulled me from the group hug and kissed me. He took my hand, and we sat at the dining table with the rest of our family.

Khaf and I sat at opposing ends of the table, Setu and the girls between us, the clean furnace standing behind them.

"Let's raise our cups to our new lives," Khaf said, and we all lifted our cups. "May we remain safe in this home we share, knowing none of us will ever be alone."

"May we find strength in our differences," I said. "And may the furnace always remain aflame."

We cheered, and Khaf's honey eyes caught mine. We smiled at each other. The two flames that had tried to extinguish one another. The thieves who schemed and betrayed. The Egyptian and the Hyksos who led each other to the light even when the black mist was at its darkest. Khafset and Nefiri, Amun and Amunet, thieves of Avaris and Peramessu, comrades in crime.

Note to the Reader

Hi there. I hope you have enjoyed the story and, same as Nefiri and Khafset — or should I say Amunet and Amun — were able to learn something new from this crazy adventure.

You know, after everything you have learned about the Egyptians and their gods, you could even call yourself an Egyptologist now. If any of the "real Egyptologists" tell you you're not an Egyptologist, tell them that Amr said so. Now if they ask you, who is this Amr you speak of? First, shame on them for not knowing who I am. I mean, it makes sense but still. Ouch. Second, tell them the following:

Amr Saleh is an Egyptian-German author from Munich, Germany (yes, the one with the Oktoberfest and Lederhosen). He was born and raised in Cairo, Egypt (the country Nef and Khaf have just saved). He loves stories in all their forms, which includes video games (yes, they're art! Even Apep agrees!). He also loves traveling and learning about geography and history.

If you are still reading, well, thank you. Maybe consider visiting my website (www.amrsalehduat.com) to get more information about this story and the real history behind it, find out where to find me in Duat (or social media), and track the progress I've been making in *Treasures of Egypt 2* and other stories.

Oh, yes. Nefiri and Khafset asked me to send you their thanks as well. Setu plans to offer a tribute of gratitude at Set's temple in your name. You know... once he sorts out his "argument" with High Priest Sethos. But more about Setu in volume 2.

Acknowledgments

To...

my parents, who made me the man I am today

my brother, who is my wish come true

my grandmother, who is my real-world partner in crime

my grandfather, who taught me to be myself

my aunts, who have acted as both my moms and my sisters whenever I needed them

my uncles, who I am grateful to have in my life

my cousins, who make me feel old

my friends, who put up with me and allow me into their lives

my incredible critique partners, who taught me how to become a writer

my history, music, and social studies teachers, who ignited the passion within me that led to this story.

To every amazing person I've met or will meet, thank you.

OUR STREET
BOOKS

JUVENILE FICTION, NON-FICTION, PARENTING

Our Street Books are for children of all ages, delivering a potent
mix of fantastic, rip-roaring adventure and fantasy stories to
excite the imagination; spiritual fiction to help the mind and the
heart; humorous stories to make the funny bone grow;
historical tales to evolve interest; and all manner of subjects that
stretch imagination, grab attention, inform, inspire and keep
the pages turning. Our subjects include Non-fiction and Fiction,
Fantasy and Science Fiction, Religious, Spiritual, Historical,
Adventure, Social Issues, Humour, Folk Tales and more.
If you have enjoyed this book, why not tell other readers by
posting a review on your preferred book site.

Magnificent Me, Magnificent You – The Grand Canyon
Dawattie Basdeo, Angela Cutler
A treasure-filled story of discovery with a range of
inspiring fun exercises, activities, songs and games
for children aged 6 to 11.
Paperback: 978-1-78279-819-4

Q is for Question
An ABC of Philosophy
Tiffany Poirier
An illustrated non-fiction philosophy book to help
children aged 8 to 11 discover, debate and articulate
thought-provoking, open-ended questions about
existence, free will and happiness.
Hardcover: 978-1-84694-183-2

Relax Kids: How to be Happy
52 positive activities for children
Marneta Viegas
Fun activities to bring the family together.
Paperback: 978-1-78279-162-1

Rise of the Shadow Stealers
The Firebird Chronicles
Daniel Ingram-Brown
Memories are going missing. Can Fletcher and
Scoop unearth their own lost history and save the
Storyteller's treasure from the shadows?
Paperback: 978-1-78099-694-3 ebook: 978-1-78099-693-6

Readers of ebooks can buy or view any of these bestsellers by clicking on the live link in the title. Most titles are published in paperback and as an ebook. Paperbacks are available in traditional bookshops. Both print and ebook formats are available online.

Find more titles and sign up to our readers' newsletter at www.collectiveinkbooks.com/children-and-young-adult